THE
BODYGUARD
SITUATION

THE BILLIONAIRE SITUATION SERIES

LYRA PARISH

CONTENT WARNING

This book features a romantic suspense plot with rom-com vibes. It includes adult content and situations that are not suitable for minors.

For a complete content warning list, please visit: https://lyraparish. com/pages/the-bodyguard-situation-content-warning

OFFICIAL PLAYLIST

Anxiety - Doechii

Bad Moon Rising - Creedence Clearwater Revival

Love Me Not - Rayvn Lenae

run for the hills - Tate McRae

Breakaway - Kelly Clarkson

Funeral - Teddy Swims

back to friends - sombr

Don't Put It All On Me - Noah Cyrus, Fleet Foxes

Miss Americana & The Heartbreak Prince - Taylor Swift

Silver Lining - Laufey

Dive - Ed Sheeran

Oscar Winning Tears - RAYE

The Boys Are Back In Town - Thin Lizzy

Bluest Flame - Selena Gomez, benny blanco

Stay - Rihanna, Mikky Ekko

Karma - Taylor Swift

Here Comes The Sun - The Beatles

LISTEN TO THIS PLAYLIST:
https://bit.ly/bodyguard-playlist

To the ones who are waiting for sunshine after the storm. It's coming.

**Brody Calloway is always watching,
Little Miss Trouble.**

We're so sad, we paint the town blue
Voted most likely to run away with you

-Taylor Swift,
Miss Americana & the Heartbreak Prince

1

BRODY

The room is dark, except for the flickering blue light from the television mounted above the fireplace. It casts eerie shadows across the walls of my penthouse, which feels emptier with each passing day. I sink deeper into the plush cushions of my couch, twisting off the cap of the beer I just grabbed from the fridge.

Today has been a complete mindfuck, hours wasted, staring at my laptop screen and chasing digital ghosts. My brain feels bruised from overthinking.

As the cold bottle meets my lips, a loud pounding shatters my solitude. It's hard, aggressive, like someone is using their entire damn fist.

I glance toward the door and let out a long sigh, wondering if it will stop if I ignore it. I'm willing to try.

Pound. Pound. Pound.

Only assholes knock like that, and unfortunately, I know more than my fair share. My mind ticks off possibilities. It could be my identical twin cousins, Easton and Weston Calloway—the biggest pains in my ass, who are also my employers. They're like my brothers, though, and I've risked my life for them on more than one occasion, but they're not exactly who I want to see right now.

The condensation from my beer bottle drips onto my knuckles as I decide whoever it is can fuck straight off. My feet hit the coffee table as I crank up the TV's volume and let the crisp, bitter liquid slide down my throat.

"Brody! I know you're in there! I can hear *The Golden Girls* in the background!" Billie shouts from behind the door.

I roll my eyes.

Billie is my younger cousin by eight years, and she's a constant but lovable thorn in my side. But there's something in her voice that I can't ignore. It's a tightness, edged with panic, that makes me pause mid-sip.

She pounds again.

"Brody! *Please*! Damn it! It's about Harper!" Her voice is more strained and urgent.

The mention of Harper's name sends a jolt through my chest, slicing straight through my irritation. My heartbeat increases—a reaction that surprises even me. I lower my feet from the table and set my beer down against the wood with a clank.

Harper and Billie have been inseparable since childhood, cofounders of Bellamore—the billion-dollar fashion empire, born from their teenage sketches. If Billie is coming to me about Harper, it's serious.

Dread twists in my gut as I cross the room and open the door.

Billie stands there with red-rimmed eyes and cheeks stained with tears. Beside her is her *secret* fiancé, Asher Banks. They haven't exactly told everyone yet and are currently in the process of making the announcement to close friends and family.

Asher's tense, and his jaw is locked tight. It's a tell of his when he's upset. Right now, his anger is simmering beneath a controlled surface. Asher's presence is protective, and he shadows Billie closely. I know as long as he's around, my cousin is safe. Asher won't let anything happen to her. But it doesn't stop the alarm bells from ringing loudly in my head.

"*Not* the assholes I expected to see," I say dryly, stepping aside to let them in. "What a fucking delight. Now, what's going on?"

Billie brushes past me and immediately turns to face me. Her gaze locks on to mine, and it's fierce but fragile. Something's very wrong.

I soften my voice instinctively and push all jokes aside. "Tell me what happened."

"We invited Harper and Micah to dinner at Asher's," Billie says, her voice trembling. "I went to grab a bottle of champagne, and Micah followed me into the kitchen and ..."

Instantly, my muscles tense, and my fist tightens with anger because I know Micah is skeezy. The guy gives me the fucking creeps.

She draws in a deep, shaky breath, fighting to steady herself. Billie is resilient, a force of nature, a survivor. The ice queen doesn't melt easily, but the fear shining in her crystal-blue eyes as she searches for her words makes my blood boil.

She isn't easily shaken, which makes this situation worse.

"Take your time." My jaw hardens. I don't like seeing her like this.

"Brody," she whispers, "Micah's my stalker. He whispered in my ear in Asher's kitchen. The same way he did the night of my twenty-first birthday. I'll never forget the sound of his voice in my ear." She physically shudders.

The memory from over a decade ago will be forever burned into my mind. I remember a young Billie Calloway, vulnerable and terrified, after an older man invaded her space, her safety. For years, Billie was tormented by an unknown predator who broke into her vacation homes several times and even went as far as to assault her in public. My little cousin is my honorary sister, and anyone who messes with her fucking messes with me.

Suddenly, Asher's murderous expression makes sense. Micah

3

Rhodes isn't just dangerous. It's clear that he's a fucking psychopath.

"Harper isn't safe with him," Billie continues, her eyes pleading.

"Where are they now?" I demand, trying to keep my voice calm.

"Not sure. She left with him," Billie struggles to say.

I see more than worry on her face. I see guilt—a guilt that she doesn't deserve to carry. She's already blaming herself for her best friend being with that fucking loser.

"I don't know if anyone can get through to her other than you," Asher says grimly. "Micah's gotten into her head. She wasn't herself tonight, almost like she was under his spell."

"*Fuck*," I whisper under my breath, recalling how Harper acted around Micah a few nights ago when I was following her. It wasn't in a stalker sort of way, but more like I was watching out for her. Seeing her with another man is torture; to make it worse, I don't trust him.

Watching them together made me physically fucking ill, but I noticed how her smile never fully reached her eyes. I also picked up on the subtle tension in her shoulders as she sat next to him. She laughed when she was supposed to, but I recognized the doubt in her gaze.

My instincts were right. They usually are.

"They're engaged," Billie blurts out, tears spilling down her cheeks. "She's going to marry him."

"*Engaged?*" I repeat, disbelief and anger squeezing around my heart. Maybe some jealousy too.

He has Harper. *My Little Miss Disaster.*

Adrenaline surges through me, and my fists clench tight until my nails dig into my palms. The realization of what this really means nearly knocks the damn breath out of me. Micah fucking Rhodes has fully manipulated Harper, and he's the same predator who's traumatized them both for over a decade.

"Do you still have that friendship app installed? The one you used to track each other when you went on dates?" My voice is dangerously calm, despite the anger bubbling inside me.

Billie pulls out her phone, hope flashing across her face. "I forgot about that."

Her fingers tremble as she opens the app. The small blue dot moves steadily northeast, away from New York City. I take the device, zooming out to figure out their route. They're heading to Newport.

Before I return her phone, I text Harper from it.

BILLIE

YOU'RE IN DANGER! WAKE THE FUCK UP!

Billie shakes her head. "She doesn't care, Brody. She didn't listen when I begged her to stay. Harper always chooses me. *Always.* This time, she didn't, and I'm really worried."

I see the same fear in her eyes that I saw the night of her twenty-first birthday. I remember the threat he made—that he'd eventually take away everything she ever loved.

For Billie, that's Harper.

She's her ride or die.

Her best friend in the entire world.

Billie would sacrifice herself for Harper in a single heartbeat. I would too.

"Sick fuck," I mutter.

Asher wraps a protective arm around Billie, holding her tight. He plants a comforting kiss in her hair. I feel a pang in my chest at the raw, pure connection between them. It stirs memories of Eden Banks—the woman I loved and lost—memories I've kept buried beneath layers of grief and guilt. Seeing the look on Billie's face pulls at my own wounds. Eden's death haunts me—a ghost that reminds me I wasn't there for her.

No way will I allow Harper to suffer the same fate.

Pulling my phone from my pocket, I text Weston.

BRODY

I need a car now.

WESTON

Hmm. Wonder what car that'd be...

BRODY

STFU. Open the garage for me with your dumb-as-fuck thumb.

WESTON

Someone is craaaaankyyyyyy.

BRODY

WESTON

😏 I'll send an SUV your way. Meet you in the lobby in 15.

"Where are you going?" Billie asks, anxiety filling her voice.

"Park Towers," I reply, heading upstairs to pack.

I stuff weapons, clothes, and essentials into a couple of duffel bags, like I'm preparing to leave for war—because that's exactly what this feels like.

Billie follows behind me with anxiety etched on her pretty face. "What if she won't leave him?"

"She doesn't have a choice," I say as I take inventory of everything I've packed.

"She's stubborn," Billie reminds me.

"And? Harper will come with me, kicking and screaming if necessary," I say matter-of-factly, glancing over my shoulder at her.

Billie cracks a smile, and it's the first time I've seen that since she and Asher arrived tonight and messed up my *The Golden Girls* wind-down time.

"You know, I never understood why you never gave Harp a chance. You two could be gr—"

"Stop," I say, grabbing the duffels in each hand. "You know why."

6

"You can't let the guilt eat away at you. That's not your fault," she whispers.

"I could never give her what she deserves," I mutter.

"What the fuck? Brody, are you kidding me right now?"

I ignore her and walk past her.

She grabs my arm and pulls me back to look at her.

"Enough," I say, not wanting to have this discussion.

Billie lets me go, and I walk down the stairs to the first level with her trailing behind me. It's like we're kids again.

Asher watches me closely and sees I'm unnerved. I recently learned that he knew about me and his older sister's secret relationship. Still not sure how. He said she told him, but I know that's a lie. Eden never claimed me. I shake my head. We were just a fling.

"Okay, kids," I say, holding the door open for them. "Let's fucking go."

"You can at least say please," Billie tells me as we move into the elevator together. "You get the best education and formal training in the whole damn country, and you still have zero manners."

I roll my eyes at her.

"Do you really need all that?" Asher questions skeptically as he sees the handles of the guns, along with some of my tactical gear.

"You must be new here." My voice drips with irritation.

He falls silent, choosing not to challenge me further. Wise choice. I have as much patience as Easton right now, which is zero.

When we walk outside, I see the blacked-out SUV that Weston sent for me.

Billie hugs me tight, her arms trembling with emotion. "Please be safe," she whispers. "Please save Harper."

"I will," I assure her before meeting Asher's eyes firmly. "Take care of her."

He nods.

He will. Asher already walked through the fire for Billie. Now that she's with him, I breathe a little easier.

I climb into the back and close the door, sealing my fate.

Ten minutes later, I enter Park Towers—the high-rise building on Billionaires' Row, where the top stories are nothing but penthouses. Weston meets me in the foyer, wearing jeans, a T-shirt, and some flip-flops. My cousin and I are the same height, and people often confuse us for brothers. In a way, we are. Sometimes, when I look at him, I know my life could've been the same, but I chose a different route from them. My own path.

Weston senses trouble when he notices my duffel bags in my grasp.

"What the fuck is going on?" he asks, running his fingers through his dark hair, keeping pace with me. His brows are furrowed, and his Calloway blues shine with concern.

"Micah is Billie's stalker. He's manipulated Harper, and he took her," I say bluntly.

Weston's expression darkens instantly. "What do you need?"

"A getaway car that can get me to Newport fast," I explain.

"And then what?" he asks as we step into the elevator and go to the ground floor, where his and Easton's private parking garage is. They have handfuls of cars, trucks, and motorcycles stored below one of the most expensive high-rises in New York City.

"I'm taking her to the cabin. That's where I'll be. Tell no one," I confirm.

Weston nods slowly, then tilts his head. "You haven't been there in five years."

"I know," I reply, my heart aching when I think about Eden.

Weston knew about our relationship but never told a soul.

"It's the safest option. Off-grid. Secret. It's a fortress on top of the mountain. Small-town life. Not many people talk. She'll be safe there until I figure this out."

"Stay in touch. Flip Easton off on the cameras for me," Weston says, squeezing my shoulder firmly. "Return home whole."

"I will."

He pulls me into a brotherly hug, then lets me go. He presses his thumb against the door reader, and it snaps open for me.

"See you," Weston says.

"See you."

I walk into the garage and go directly to the vintage, blacked-out 1969 Dodge Charger. My hand slides over the freshly waxed paint, which gleams like a challenge. This car is coaxing me forward as adrenaline pumps through me. Without hesitation, I snatch the keys out of the case, feeling the cool metal against my palm, and climb inside.

I wave at the camera in the corner of the room, then shoot it a middle finger. "That one was from Weston."

I open the door to the car, running my hand across the smooth leather of the dash, then sink back into the seat. I hold the cool steering wheel tightly and feel rebellion buried deep in my grip. I push in the clutch, crank the engine, and it roars to life. I let out a laugh because this car is pure fucking joy. The rumble vibrates through my bones, and a smirk touches my lips because it's music to my damn ears as I buckle in.

Easton swooped in and bought this car minutes before me. And it's pissed me the fuck off *ever* since. "Motherfucker. You should've been mine," I whisper, revving the engine a few times to let her warm up.

Raw energy settles beneath my fingertips, and one thing Easton is right about when it comes to this car is, it's a "fuck around and find out" kind of ride. It's always called to me—*steal me*—like a whisper in the night. I guess the time has arrived.

I adjust the rearview mirror, glancing at my eyes, and see a flicker of something behind them. Something I don't recognize. This moment is the chaos I've craved deep in my bones, the kind that wakes a sleeping dragon. I'll have to give Harper a thank-you when I find her. Oh, and I will fucking find her because for the first time in a long damn time, I have a real purpose.

With a swift push of the clutch, I slide it into first gear, barely rolling through the concrete tunnel. At the end, the automatic garage door rises, and the street opens up. The tires scream as I peel out of the parking garage, hanging my hand out the window, throwing another middle finger. Now, that one was from me.

I leave rubber on the road and smoke in my wake. My only regret is not getting to see my dear cousin's reaction when he watches the replay of that video. Because he will the moment he realizes his car is missing.

I steal a glance in the rearview mirror and scan for anyone following me. In the back seat are my two duffel bags. One's crammed with clothes; the other is filled with weapons and ammo. I can never be too careful in this game.

This car's a beast, ready for the hunt, ready for the fucking challenge, just like me. The engine echoes through the streets, between the tall buildings.

As I speed away from the city, darkness blankets me, but my clarity has never been sharper.

Harper's tangled herself in a dangerous web, but I'm determined —more than fucking ever—to free her, even if she hates me for it.

I can already picture her smile, that cocky little grin that says she knows more than I do.

But she doesn't. Not this time. Not when it comes to Micah. Or what she desperately needs.

Right now, I'm searching for trouble, and it's spelled H-A-R-P-E-R.

I can't fail again—not after Eden, not after experiencing this haunting guilt that never goes away. If something happened to Harper and I didn't try my damnedest to save her, I'd never forgive myself. With every mile, my determination grows stronger. My pulse beats to a rhythm of sheer protectiveness.

Harper Alexander may have run away with him, but I'll find her. I always do.

For his sake, she had better be safe and well taken care of or else.

"WHERE THE FUCK ARE YOU, BRODY?" EASTON'S VOICE ROARS through the phone as I answer, jolting me from a shallow sleep.

I squint against the harsh morning sun slicing through the motel's musty cream curtains. When I glance at the bedside clock, the red numbers tell me it's barely past seven. Easton's anger is obvious, even hundreds of miles away.

"Your car is safe," I respond calmly, despite the annoyance crackling through my cousin's voice.

"If my car was safe, it would still fucking be in my goddamn garage," he snaps, irritation lacing every word.

I smile, but I hold back my laughter.

"You could've taken anything else. *Anything.* But that one—"

"Should've been mine to begin with," I snap, sitting up on the edge of the bed, needing to wake up. I have a long day ahead of me, and I need to get my mind right.

"Please tell me you're not still butthurt," he says.

"Yes, I fucking am. And I will be for eternity."

"I should report it as stolen. Teach you a fucking lesson."

I know he's grinning. *Asshole.*

"If something happens to your precious Charger"—I rub my temple—"I'll replace it with two of my vehicles."

Silence settles on the line between us, and I know he's considering it.

Finally, he speaks, and when he does, his voice is calmer even if it still carries the impatient edge that he's known for. "Which two?"

"Dealer's choice. Have your pick," I say, my throat feeling like sandpaper.

I imagine Easton mentally browsing through my collection, inevitably landing on my mint-condition '67 Corvette and the '69 Roadrunner. Both treasures, both worth the sacrifice to keep his peace and my sanity, both vehicles he wanted, but I bought first. Things don't make me happy. Money doesn't make me happy. At this rate, I'm not sure anything could.

"Are motorcycles included?" He's pushing his luck.

"Anything with wheels," I say, picturing him already eyeing my '51 Vincent Black Lightning. He knows my collection almost as well as I do because he wanted many of them. "And to sweeten the pot, I'll even have them delivered from my warehouse straight to your garage."

A reluctant sigh of agreement follows. "Fine. That's a deal I'll take any day of the week. But be careful. That car only chooses you when it's time to fuck around and find out. Guess you're about to have the ride of your fucking life."

"Noted," I reply dryly, already feeling the thrill of the hunt creeping back into my veins. "I've gotta go."

"Brody," he says abruptly, pulling me back. "Be careful. And if shit hits the fan, call me. I can send resources."

"Will do, but it won't be needed." I disconnect before he can drag the conversation somewhere else.

I drop the phone onto the bedside table and move to my laptop to review the intel I managed to scrape together late last night after I arrived. Addresses, properties, holdings—all tied to Micah Rhodes or his shell corporations.

I stand and stretch, adrenaline pumping beneath my skin. My duffel bags sit ready, and clothes are stuffed alongside my gear. Being prepared is key, even if it looks more like a kidnapping than a rescue. This is a war against Micah Rhodes, and I'm determined to win. It's personal. Very fucking personal. He's a predator, and he will harm her. I can't let that happen.

Harper's in this town somewhere. I can feel her.

A single daisy sits in a vase by the window, and I pick it up and twirl it between my fingers. Thoughts of Eden drift in and out of my mind. Grief is now a permanent resident in my soul, intertwined with regret. She broke it off. Eden ended us, and afterward, I decided to hide from the world.

Had I been in the city the weekend she was killed, things could've turned out differently. Instead, I'd isolated myself in Tennessee, at one of the only places that'd ever felt like home to me. My cabin in Sugar Pine Springs was a place where I always went to escape from the world when it felt too fucking heavy. I went there to heal. Had I known we didn't have more time, I'd have never left the city.

I imagine how different things would be now if I had met her for that drink and we had the conversation she wanted to have. Maybe we'd be together, married, with a family. Or maybe we wouldn't. It's the what-if that haunts me and the final message she left on my voicemail.

I wasn't available though. I'd given up on her, on us, and the little time we had left slipped through my fingers. Now, she's not here.

I can't let anything happen to Harper.

Scanning through my notes again, I zero in on a particularly secluded estate one of his shell companies owns near the water— high walls, gated entrance, but also grand in nature. My gut instinct says it's the type of place he'd take Harper to impress her.

I sling my bags over my shoulder, slipping on my baseball cap and dark sunglasses.

Easton's Charger sits in the motel parking lot, sleek and defiant. I place my shit in the trunk and snap it closed.

As I settle behind the wheel, the engine roars to life, like a beast eager for battle. I rev it once, twice, then pull out onto the open road, leaving rubber on the pavement. The power beneath me is intoxicating.

"Ready or not," I mutter, eyes narrowing as the highway and sunlight stretch endlessly before me, "here I fucking come, Harper."

2
HARPER

"Are you okay?" I ask, my throat tightening with worry. His lip is swollen and busted from the chaos earlier, and there's a dark bruise forming under his left eye. Every time I look at him, my heart sinks, and guilt curls inside me like a strand of wire with razor-sharp barbs. I thought tonight would play out differently than it did.

"Yeah, baby girl. I'm so much better now." His soothing tone usually calms me, but tonight, it feels off.

As Micah drives us away from New York City, like he's running from his demons, he interlocks our fingers, then presses a gentle kiss to my knuckles. My mind is a jumbled mess, and there is a thick fog that just won't clear. I feel nothing but confused, so I try to replay the events to figure out where it all went wrong.

The evening had started out perfectly. The garden behind Asher's place was full of spring flowers. Their scent mixed with laughter and the soft glow of the city at night. I was buzzing with excitement as Micah and I shared our engagement news. But Billie's reaction wasn't what I'd expected. Her crystal-blue eyes—which are usually so bright for me—dimmed, replaced by something unreadable and almost dark.

14

"She's just jealous," Micah says now, squeezing my hand, as if he can read my thoughts. His voice is soft and patient, but he grips the steering wheel with his other hand very tightly. It's the micro-anger I start to notice. "I'm really sorry. I wanted tonight to go differently for you, Harper. I know how much it meant to you to tell her."

The scene plays back in my mind—Billie's shocked face and Asher's bloodied knuckles from hitting Micah. Everything feels ... *wrong*.

It hurts, knowing Billie wasn't happy for me, wasn't happy for us, but I can't pinpoint why.

We've been inseparable since we were five years old. Our lives are intertwined in every way that matters, both personally and professionally. Losing her support feels like losing a part of myself, and the ache gets worse with each mile marker we pass.

"I'm so sorry, Harper," Micah says again, glancing at me with those reassuring green eyes.

"It's okay," I whisper, even though it isn't. "It's not your fault. I'm sorry too. I should've listened to you."

"Don't apologize," he insists, his thumb tracing little circles on the back of my hand. "You can't control how she reacts. That's on her, not you."

Billie and I have always navigated life's ups and downs together, understanding each other in ways no one else could. No one else *can*. Until tonight, she'd always been my ride or die.

"Please tell me what happened," I say, feeling my stomach twist as I picture Asher unleashing on Micah while Billie stood frozen and watched. "I can't put the pieces together."

Because I don't have all the information.

Micah's jaw tightens, and I see something dark flicker across his face. "Only if you promise you won't be upset."

"I promise," I say quickly, desperate for answers.

He hesitates. "Are you sure you want to talk about this now? We can discuss it tomorrow, when emotions aren't so high."

I'm growing more frustrated.

"I won't be able to sleep until I know the truth," I say.

He seems to enjoy making me wait, and the silence drags on for an eternity. I really hate the uncertainty that grips me so tightly that I can barely breathe. My anxiety is at an all-time high, and I try to take deep breaths in and out before I spiral.

He inhales sharply. "I wanted her blessing for our marriage. I asked if she'd be your maid of honor when we eloped. I told her I wanted to marry you soon, and she flipped out, got angry, and grabbed my cock. Then Asher barged in, saw her hand on me, us standing close, and lost it, like a jealous boyfriend. He wouldn't listen and attacked me because of *her*. You saw the rest."

"Billie touched you?" My voice sounds far away, even to me.

My heart drops, disbelief hitting me hard. This isn't something my best friend would do, especially after what she's been through.

Nothing about tonight feels safe. Not even now.

His eyes flicker, like he's remembering something painful. "She came onto me, Harper. She touched me inappropriately and said she wanted me for herself, that she couldn't stand us being together. I can't be around her," he says, looking at me earnestly. "Do you believe me?"

Doubt creeps in. I want to trust Micah. He's been nothing but kind and a steady part of my life for the past eight weeks. His jaw tightens, so I quickly answer.

"Of course I believe you," I whisper.

"Then why did you hesitate?" he directly asks, and I don't like his tone.

"I just ... I find it difficult to comprehend." I shake my head slowly, confusion still clouding my thoughts.

She's always crushed on Asher, even when she said she wasn't, even when she gave him hell. We all saw it—everyone did but her. Billie making a move on Micah doesn't make any sense, and it's hard for me to believe. I don't question much of what he says, but when it comes to my best and most loyal friend, alarm bells sound.

One time, Billie dropped everything just to comfort me after a shitty breakup with a mediocre man. She skipped vacations and important plans to be there for me when I was upset. I feel uncomfortably wedged between being loyal to her and this guy I've fallen head over heels for, the one I'm supposed to marry.

I glance down at the engagement ring that still feels foreign on my finger. It's big and gaudy, and I just always imagined having my mother's ring.

"I wish I knew why she acted that way," Micah says. "I should've let you talk to her first, but I know how much this wedding means to you—means to us. You're the missing piece of my puzzle, Harper. I can't imagine life without you."

His words wrap around me, and I search for comfort in them.

I lean into his hand as he cups my cheek. "I want you two to get along. She's been my best friend for twenty-seven years."

"I can't," he says.

We drive down the dark streets, and the silence makes my anxiety worse. Billie's frantic face pops into my mind. Micah's thumb strokes my palm, but it doesn't do much to calm me.

"What if I tried for you?" Micah asks.

"That would be amazing," I reply.

"I love you. Anything for you," he whispers.

A mix of hope and uncertainty fills my heart.

"I want the absolute best for our future."

"I love you too," I say, but I ask myself if that's true.

Do I love Micah Rhodes? Or do I love the thought of not dying alone in my penthouse with fifteen cats?

As we settle into the quiet, Micah reaches over and turns on the radio. Soft music fills the car, and I take a deep breath, trying to untangle the knotted thoughts in my mind.

My phone vibrates, breaking my fragile calm. I hesitate, my hands shaking as I check my messages.

BILLIE

YOU'RE IN DANGER! WAKE THE FUCK UP!

My heart races as a chill runs down my spine. Panic washes over me. Billie's blunt warning is so sharp that it cuts deep. I quickly delete the message, anxiety flooding through me as I switch off my phone. My chest tightens, and I struggle to breathe as I give Micah a weak smile.

"Everything okay?" he asks, watching me closely.

"Just a spam message," I lie smoothly. A lie. Why do I even have to lie right now?

His gaze lingers on me for a moment too long before he turns back to the road.

"Are you absolutely sure you're okay?" Micah's voice is more stern this time.

"Of course, babe." I smile, but it feels forced. "Just tired after everything. Happy to be spending some alone time with you."

Right now, I don't feel like I know the man sitting next to me. After seeing Billie's expression, followed by her text, I've been jolted awake.

"You're such a good girl, Harper." His voice softens, almost easing the panic in my heart. "The best girl. Just close your eyes and relax."

Micah's grip on my hand tightens, and the possessiveness feels unsettling. My mind fills with confusion and dread as I do what he said. I lean back and see Billie's message burned behind my eyelids.

"Micah," I say, needing to know more, "when you said you wanted to marry me soon, how soon are we talking?"

His eyes light up with real happiness. "This upcoming week."

Shock hits me like a wave. "This week?"

He nods calmly, his gaze both gentle and serious. "I'm forty-four, Harper. I'm not getting any younger. Unless you're having second thoughts ..."

"No," I reply quickly, seeing a glimpse of a monster behind his eyes.

YOU'RE IN DANGER! lingers in my mind like a ghost.

"Good. We're on the same page then," he says, relief softening his tone. "Now, get some rest, baby girl. We'll be home in a few hours."

Home.

The word feels as foreign as the ring on my finger.

I close my eyes like he instructed, but sleep feels miles away.

Billie thinks I'm in danger. Her warning echoes in my mind as I sink deeper into darkness. *WAKE THE FUCK UP!*

THE SOFT THUD OF THE CAR DOOR CLOSING WAKES ME FROM A restless sleep. My eyelids flutter open, heavy with fatigue. Through the windshield, the headlights shine on a grand two-story mansion that looks impressive but also eerie under the pale moonlight.

My door swings open, and Micah stands there, smiling.

"We're here," he says, reaching his hand out to me. The other one is effortlessly holding our duffel bags.

I packed a few things quickly, mainly just the essentials, since he promised we wouldn't be going out.

"This place is amazing," I say, totally taken in by the architecture. Then I freak out when I realize I don't have my phone. I quickly swing the car door open wider and bend down to check the floorboard.

"Looking for something?" Micah asks.

"My phone," I reply, my voice tense.

"I've got it," he says casually. "This week, we're focusing on our wedding with no distractions. I turned mine off too."

An uncomfortable feeling washes over me, tightening my chest. "May I please have it back?"

"No," he replies, still smiling, but now there's a hint of control in his tone.

The moonlight casts shadows on his face, highlighting the

unsettling determination in his jaw. "You'll get it when we head back to the city. You'll thank me later."

A tense silence hangs between us, and I don't know what to say. My phone is my only contact with the outside world.

"Okay," I finally say. He won't budge.

I follow him toward the mansion. With every step up the grand staircase leading to the entrance, I feel more and more disconnected from the real world—my *safe* world.

He unlocks the heavy front door and pushes it open effortlessly. We enter, and as beautiful as it is, the mansion feels like an isolated fortress. It's only then that I realize I have no clue where I am. The entryway lights flicker on, revealing a gorgeous staircase that spirals upward toward the second floor.

"Wow," I whisper, my voice echoing in the spacious foyer as I take in the elegant archways and high ceilings.

Every step forward only highlights the mansion's cold emptiness.

"I designed this place myself," he says proudly, watching me closely. "Pretty cool, right? Just like I imagined it."

"It's incredible," I agree, feeling oddly small, standing inside his creation.

"And to think, you're marrying someone so fucking talented," Micah adds playfully, giving me a flirtatious wink.

I manage a soft laugh, though it doesn't quite reach my heart.

He leads me up the stairs, guiding me by the small of my back down the hallway.

He opens the door to the bedroom and sets our bags down as he turns on the recessed lighting. A huge balcony outside the glass sliding doors overlooks the sea that sparkles in the moonlight, but it feels strangely distant.

Am I in the Hamptons?

A huge four-poster bed takes center stage in the room. It's decked out with soft linens and surrounded by shiny oak furniture. Hanging above the bed is an abstract painting with strokes of bright blues, yellows, and reds, which feels too vibrant for my mood.

"Do you like it here so far?" Micah asks, stepping closer, his voice hopeful. "I think it'll be perfect for our little getaway. After we're married, maybe we can take full residence here."

I nod, and he takes a step toward me. I notice how he holds my waist and the way his fingers grip me roughly.

"It's beautiful," I whisper, though my voice wavers. My eyes catch the bruise under his eye—a reminder of what happened earlier. "I hate seeing you like this."

"I know," he says as he breaks away from me and opens a drawer. He drops our phones inside, locking it with purpose, and then he tucks the key into his pocket. "No distractions," he says smoothly, staring at me. "No outside world."

I somehow manage to speak. "Of course."

A reassuring smile spreads across his face as he pulls me into his arms. His hug is warm, but there's something boiling underneath that I can't shake off.

His mouth crashes against mine, and it's unsettling.

"After all this time, my dreams are coming true," he whispers against my lips, his breath mingling with mine.

His words hit me harder than I expected, and so does the nagging feeling.

Micah's lips move to my neck, and his hands tangle in my hair. I know where this is headed, and I'm not feeling it.

"I'd prefer not," I say.

"Oh, come on. It'll make you feel better," he suggests. "An orgasm always does."

"No." I shoot him a glare. It's a complete sentence.

"Fine," he says, getting snippy.

I refuse to feel pressured into having sex with anyone. No means no.

"Thanks for understanding. I'm just exhausted."

The truth is, I'm still upset about what happened earlier.

He steps closer and kisses my forehead. "I'm sorry. Just get some rest, baby girl. We've got a big week ahead of us, spending every minute together."

I crawl under the blankets and pretend to fall asleep right away, but I stay wide awake in my head for what feels like hours. This is starting to feel like a weird nightmare that I woke up in the middle of, and nothing adds up. It takes all my willpower not to freak out.

THE NEXT MORNING, I WAKE UP TO AN EMPTY BED, EXHAUSTED. FOR a second, I'm totally disoriented, staring at the unfamiliar ceiling. Panic flutters in my chest until reality kicks back in. The memories of last night's tension linger at the edges of my mind, softened by the gentle morning light coming through the sheer curtains.

I sit up, let out a slow breath, and look toward the balcony. Beyond it, the calm sea stretches out, with boats lazily drifting on the water. It's beautiful, but I have no idea where I am.

I stretch, shaking off the lingering discomfort, and head into the bathroom. The white marble feels nice under my bare feet, and the golden fixtures are cold against my fingers. The room is fancy, definitely my style, but it feels too sterile and fabricated. There's an emptiness in this house that I can't shake as I go through my morning routine.

Everything is impersonal, like a set that was put together just for me.

Once I'm dressed, I head downstairs, searching for Micah. My eyes scan over the paintings on the wall, and I don't like them. I spot Micah on the back porch, his dark hair a mess, and he looks relaxed. Muscles ripple down his back, and I never realized how clean-cut he is. He's not normally the type I would date.

I usually go for the rough-around-the-edges, tattooed-bad-boy type. The ones my mom always warned me about when I was a little girl.

A faint smile creeps onto my face as I watch him through the window, admiring his confident stance. As if he senses me, Micah turns around, and his green eyes light up when he sees me. He waves me over, and I notice he's on his phone, like the rules don't apply to him. I instantly grow frustrated.

I step onto the porch, joining him.

Micah pulls me close with one arm as he continues his conversation. "We can talk about this later. My fiancée just showed up. Absolutely. Bye."

As he hangs up, the screen of his phone lights up for a second with a text, and I can't help but glance at it. I thought I saw a woman's name, and curiosity eats at me. He puts it away before I can see anything more.

"Good morning, baby girl. How'd you sleep?" he asks, kissing my forehead.

"Great, actually," I reply with a lie, taking in the fresh morning air and trying to shake off my worries. "I'm starving."

"Perfect. I made a brunch reservation in town. We'll leave as soon as you're ready."

"I don't know if I have clothes that are public-worthy. I packed fast. Can we have it delivered instead?"

"It's just brunch, Harp. My God. I'm sure no one here will even recognize you," he encourages, but he lied to me, leaving me unprepared to be seen.

I run a fashion company; I have to be camera-ready at all times. I have an image that I must uphold for Bellamore, for Billie, and myself.

"Okay," I say as I turn to go inside, trying to remember what I stuffed into my bag.

His hand reaches out, grabbing me playfully yet firmly as he pulls me back to him. Our lips crash together, and the intimacy of it surprises me.

I cover my brief discomfort with a teasing tone. "Also, I thought you said no cell phones."

"It was an emergency," he says smoothly, pulling it from his pocket and holding it out. "You can have mine since I have yours."

I hesitate, looking at the phone in his hand. A text reminder from Blaire Bowers flashes on the screen, and I look back up into his eyes.

"Go on," he says, but something about his offer feels like a threat, like he's testing me. I choose the safe answer, protecting myself however I can.

"I trust you, my love," I say, giving him a smile, knowing I need to change the subject. "Now, back to brunch talk. Is this place casual or fancy? Trying to figure out what I should wear today."

"Nothing." His eyebrows rise as he steals another kiss. "But it's a somewhat busy spot in town. Don't want the locals seeing too much of you."

"Give me ten minutes," I tell him. "Can't wait."

He gives me another kiss, and this time, I successfully pull away from him.

I climb the stairs and head into the bedroom, setting my weekend bag on the bed. I pull out a sundress from our spring line and slip it on, smoothing out the wrinkled fabric. I pause for a second and glance over at the nightstand drawer. My curiosity gets the best of me, so I tug on it. Locked.

I want to text Billie. I want to ask her what happened. The fact that Micah took my phone has me panicked. He's isolated me, and I have no idea where I am.

Downstairs, Micah's waiting for me, looking relaxed and totally unaware of my racing heart. He takes my hand and leads me outside to the car. The mid-morning sunshine feels amazing, wrapping everything in a warm glow. We drive along the coast, and the little town is buzzing with beachy blues and yellows as tourists stroll by. The next street is lined with cute boutiques, antique shops, and charming cafés. Even though I'm feeling off, the scene is super cute, and it helps distract me for a moment.

Micah smoothly parks in front of the restaurant and hops out to open my door. His sweet gesture makes me smile, easing some of my worries. To anyone watching, he's the perfect man.

But is he?

Once we're inside the restaurant, we move to the front counter, and he gives his name. Right away, the host's eyes slide up and down Micah like he's a snack. A pang of jealousy hits me when he shoots her a charming smile.

"I have a reservation for two. Would you and your daughter like a table or a booth?" she asks casually, her words stinging.

"Daughter?" I mutter, shocked and then annoyed.

I shoot Micah a look, expecting him to correct her.

"Doesn't matter," he says simply, not saying anything more.

He didn't claim me. No man ever does.

She leads us to a booth by the window with a white linen tablecloth, and I watch Micah openly stare at her ass. I swallow hard, not wanting anyone I'm with to even look at another woman. I slide into the side where sunlight pours in. I glance outside, trying to figure out where we are while pretending to admire the view. This isn't the Hamptons. I've never visited this town before.

As I glance down at the menu, I notice the address in the top corner.

I'm in Newport, Rhode Island, hours away from the city. I tense, realizing he's taken away my phone and isolated me from everyone who cares about me. If I wanted help, I couldn't get it.

How did I let this happen?

3

BRODY

My hat is pulled low and sunglasses on as I chill in a booth by the window of this fancy restaurant Weston insisted I check out. The menu looks straight out of a 1950s diner, but they're serving smoked salmon and avocado toast. Go figure.

I lift my steaming coffee to my lips, enjoying the bitter warmth, and skim the menu again. I'm starving after skipping dinner to chase ghosts out of state, and my frustration keeps piling up with every dead end.

After I eat, I'll visit the big house by the bay that Micah owns on this side of town.

"Whatcha havin', doll?" the server—a woman with jet-black hair and a Jersey accent thicker than syrup—asks.

"Surprise me," I mumble without looking up, still scanning the restaurant through the side of my sunglasses. I'm never relaxed in public settings, no matter how hard I try.

"How hungry are ya?" she presses, her gaze lingering appreciatively over my broad shoulders.

I ignore her flirty looks. "Starving."

She bites her lower lip, scribbling on her pad. "I gotchu. The superhero breakfast."

The irony almost makes me laugh. If only she knew I wasn't feeling very heroic right now—more like a guy chasing shadows, haunted by past failures. She walks away, and I notice the local newspaper lying on the edge of the table. The bold headline says: **JANE DOE IDENTIFIED.**

I barely register the server topping off my coffee when my heart starts racing. Harper and Micah walk in, and a sick feeling twists in my stomach at the sight of him touching her. My fingers tighten around the ceramic mug, knuckles going white. I didn't expect him to bring her out in public, but, hey, it's a nice surprise. My luck couldn't have timed this better.

Harper's scowl tells me everything isn't as perfect as she wants people to think. I quickly unfold the newspaper, hiding behind it to watch their reflection in the tall windows as they sit behind me. Harper's scent—a mix of coconut and vanilla—fills the air, and it's sweet torture. I close my eyes, knowing I could pick her out in a crowd.

The server greets them, and Harper immediately orders. Micah follows her lead. The tension stretches between them as their coffee is delivered.

Micah finally clears his throat. "Everything okay?"

Harper's voice shakes, irritation and vulnerability creeping in. "That woman thought I was your daughter, and you said nothing."

My jaw tightens, teeth grinding. He's way too old for her— honestly, there are moments when I feel like I am too. Harper's only thirty-two, and I'll be forty in six months. Eight years. It's one thing that has held me back. Truthfully, there's a list of reasons we could never be together. But age was why I rejected her when she made a move on me at eighteen. Harper needed to grow up and experience the world. Dating a teenager at the age of twenty-six isn't okay in my book. She was barely legal.

"Why does it matter?" Micah's words are like nails on a chalkboard.

His dismissiveness sends a fresh wave of anger rushing through me. My fingers twitch, and I seriously want to smash his smug face in with this coffee mug. It takes everything in me to stay put and not make a scene. Getting arrested would do no one any good, especially not Harper.

"If you don't understand why it matters, then I can't explain it to you," Harper shoots back, surprising me with the strength in her voice. I haven't heard that in weeks. "Maybe I should've ordered from the kids' menu, *Daddy*."

Oh, she's very pissed.

I almost choke on my coffee, trying not to laugh. I watch as the server brings over a plate, piled high with pancakes, bacon, eggs, and hash browns, her earlier flirtation forgotten in the tension between Harper and Micah.

Micah tries to save face. "Does it bother you that I'm twelve years older than you?"

"No," Harper snaps back. "What bothers me is when the man I'm supposed to marry doesn't claim me publicly."

The thought of Harper marrying him hits me so fucking hard that it nearly takes my breath away. Time is precious, and life is fragile.

"I'm sorry, baby girl. I'll address it moving forward if it upsets you so much." Micah's apology breaks me out of my thoughts. His words sound empty but wrapped with a thin layer of care to cover his shitty facade.

"You know," Micah goes on, changing his tone to sound kind, "I was thinking about this marriage discussion we had. What if we just went to the courthouse this week and got secretly married?"

My stomach drops. He's trying to rush things, to trap her faster than even I thought.

Harper hesitates. "I need to think about it. This is too big of a decision to make on a whim."

Good girl.

"You're marrying me before the weekend, or I'm calling it all off," Micah demands, and it's too aggressive.

The silence that follows is intense. I want to turn around, to step in, to pull Harper away from him, but if I do that now, I might lose her for good. I swallow my anger, tasting the edge of defeat.

Harper pushes back. "Are you serious right now?"

Before Micah can respond, their food arrives. I quickly pay my bill, leaving a nice tip as a silent apology for having to deal with them.

Another minute passes, and neither of them says anything. I know when Harper is really pissed, she says nothing at all.

"You're not eating," Micah snaps, his voice loaded with anger.

Harper fires back defiantly, "Are you going to force me? Ground me?"

A small, proud smile tugs at my lips. Whatever Billie said to her last night must've sparked something in her. That fire within her has been missing.

"Starve then," Micah retorts, and I hear his fork scrape harshly against the plate.

"Excuse me. I need to go to the ladies' room," Harper says, and I hear her move across the booth.

"Don't take too long," Micah warns, and it feels like a threat.

I don't waste any time, and I move toward the hallway that leads to the restrooms. I cross my arms and wait, my heart racing as the door finally swings open.

She looks so damn pretty with her brown hair in bouncy curls. Her blue-gray eyes shine when they meet mine, but they're full of surprise, irritation, and something softer underneath. She freezes.

"What the hell are you doing here, Brody?" she snaps, glancing around nervously.

"Saving your ass," I reply, grabbing her wrist and pulling her back into the restroom.

I lock the door and glance around for any escape windows, but there aren't any.

"I don't need to be saved." She hesitates but doesn't fight me.

Her breath quickens as I take off my sunglasses and lock eyes with her. "You need to leave," she says, her voice shaky.

"Not a fucking chance. You're coming with me, Harp."

"No, I'm not," she insists, trying to pull away, but I don't let her.

"Yes, you are," I whisper harshly, desperation thick in my voice. "Where's your phone?"

"He took it from me," she admits.

I shake my head in disbelief. "And you think that's okay? *Wake up, Harper!*"

Her eyes blaze with intensity, fierce yet vulnerable. "You're acting like a jealous boyfriend."

I almost laugh, frustration and heartache mixing inside me. "You wish."

"What do you plan to accomplish?" she asks, her voice breaking, tears shimmering.

"Micah is Billie's stalker," I blurt, needing her to understand how serious this is. "The guy from her twenty-first birthday. The one who broke into her house and jacked off in her bed. The guy who terrorized you both for years. That's who you've been fucking. What a nightmare."

"You're *lying*," she whispers, eyes wide, searching mine desperately for the reassurance I can't give.

"I wish I were. Now, come with me willingly, or I'm taking you later by force."

"I can't," she says.

"Why?"

A loud knock startles us both.

"Harper?" Micah's voice is full of fake concern.

"Sorry, my stomach hurts really bad," she quickly replies, clearly shaken.

Micah's response is smooth, way too calm. "Just a few more minutes. Okay?"

"I'll try," she says.

Those minutes pass by.

I lean in closer to her, keeping my voice low and urgent. "I will find you, and I will come for you. That's a promise. You're my responsibility, Harper."

She stiffens. "No, I'm not. Let me handle this."

"No can do, *baby girl*," I say, throwing Micah's words back at her. Anger radiates from her. "He'll never let me leave with you."

"You're right. Only problem is, I don't give a fuck. Oh, before you go, where are you staying?" I step closer until we're almost touching. "At his prison by the bay? The one with the balcony and tall fucking walls?"

I study her, and her silence says it all.

"The confirmation I needed. I'm coming for you, Harper," I promise, leaning down so my words brush against her ear. "We'll do this your way, but just know that I live for this shit. I love a good game of cat and mouse." I back up, and a smirk spreads across my lips as I see the fury ignite even brighter in her eyes. "And you must love it too."

"I'm so used to you *not* saying much, and now you won't shut the fuck up. Lucky me," she snaps, each word dripping with venom.

Her agitation is intoxicating, captivating, and so fucking hot.

I know her anger isn't really aimed at me, but at the nightmare she's stuck in.

Harper is ridiculously independent, and I knew she wouldn't walk out of this diner with me today, but I don't need her to.

"I know you're pissed."

"Yes, I am," she says.

"At yourself," I add.

There's something thrilling about seeing her emotions finally break free from the polished surface she's tried to maintain since getting with him.

"Can't handle the truth?" I ask calmly. "Looks like no one else has managed to get through to that pretty little head of yours. Not your best friend. Not your brother. So, they sent me. How many red flags will you ignore, Harp? Have some fucking self-respect.

Are you going to marry that psycho, knowing who he really is? Tell me."

"Fuck you," she snaps, narrowing her eyes. Her voice drips with disdain, and I can tell I struck a nerve.

But this is a truth only I can share because, deep down, she knows I won't lie to her. Her jaw tightens, nostrils flaring like she's about to scream—or maybe slap me. Honestly, I almost wish she would. At least then I'd know I made an impact.

I promised her honesty years ago, and I've stuck to it, whether she's liked it or not. No one else is as straightforward with her as me.

"I have this under control," she adds.

I chuckle. "No, you don't."

"I need to go. So, please fuck off."

"Is that an invitation?" I tease, pushing her buttons, daring her to lose it.

For a second, she looks like she's about to blow up, but then she holds back, and it says more than any words could. For a few tense moments, we just stare at each other. Harper opens her mouth once, then shuts it, deciding not to waste her breath on a comeback. Her silence always hits harder than any insult.

She turns and storms away, her heels clicking against the tiles as the door slams behind her. The sound echoes in my chest, and her leaving feels heavier than I thought it would.

Standing alone in the empty restroom, I let out a frustrated sigh. I didn't want to catch her off guard, but what choice did I have? Every word I said was true, every threat a promise. Tonight, I'm coming for her. She might hate me, she might fight me, but at least she'll be safe. I don't trust Micah Rhodes.

When I finally leave, I cross the street to a little café and sit at a table where I can see Harper and Micah clearly. I grab a black coffee and focus on them. Harper's body language says it all—she's tense, her shoulders are tight, and she looks away every time Micah gets too close. She seems sick, and I hope the weight of what I told her has finally hit her.

A week ago, I tried to warn her that Micah was trouble. She brushed me off like it was nothing. Classic Harper. Stubborn and proud.

I'm determined to dig up every dirty secret and twisted thing he's done. I hired some dark-web data miners, but I haven't heard back yet—hopefully, I will soon. I'm going to take him down personally. For Billie and for Harper.

He kisses her, and I roll my eyes when she gives him a fake smile. She's so easy to read, or maybe I've just memorized her like a book.

The thought of her being stuck with Micah, even for another day, makes me fucking sick. But I know Harper too well—if I push too hard, she'll just run further into his arms to prove a point.

This isn't the first time she's ignored my concerns. His charm and polished look blinded her. And I've watched them together on more than one occasion, noticing their weird dynamic. Nothing about the relationship has ever seemed normal. They've never spent more than two days together, and now he's pushing for marriage *this week*—in Rhode Island, of all places, where annulments don't exist, only messy divorces.

I grit my teeth, simmering as I watch them. Part of me wants to let her live that painful *I told you so* moment. Her stubbornness will be her downfall. Harper has always had to touch the stove to see if it's hot instead of just taking everyone's word for it. But I can't let her suffer, no matter how much she drives me wild and infuriates me.

Micah points aggressively at her, and rage floods through me, nearly making me jump out of my seat. I tell myself to stay calm, silently promising that the second he lays a finger on her, I'll unleash years of pent-up anger I've had for the faceless terror that hurt my cousin.

Harper should've seen through his fake, over-the-top charm.

But she wants to believe in love so bad that she'll overlook the shortcomings, the weird vibes and tension, and settle for less when she can do so much better. She deserves the absolute fucking best, and he ain't it. Then again, I'm not sure anyone will ever be good enough for her.

I focus on Harper and Micah through the big glass window. Harper looks sick, her eyes going from confused to horrified, like she's realizing who Micah Rhodes really is.

Frustration bubbles up in me—at Micah, at Harper's stubbornness, and especially at how helpless I feel. I take a deep breath and try to calm myself down.

I won't let Harper be another regret. Not this time. Not ever again.

I take a sip of my coffee, and its darkness matches my mood perfectly.

Tonight, this ends.

Harper's either leaving on her own, or I'm dragging her out myself. I glance at her pretty face again, my heart aching under my anger. She looks lost and confused as she silently pieces it together.

I know she's upset with me right now, but she'll be grateful later. She'll be alive to feel that anger because, right now, I'm not sure what Micah is capable of, but I have an idea.

No matter what it takes or how much she fights it, Harper Alexander is coming with me tonight.

4

HARPER

I return to the table, cracking my neck to release the tension knotted there. I can't afford to let Micah charm his way back into my head, not after what Brody revealed. I would've gone with him, but I knew there was no way I could, not with how Micah would make a scene.

Brody has never been a liar. In fact, his blunt honesty is something I've relied on since I was eighteen. He promised me then that he'd never skirt around the truth, even if it was harsh. The rare times Brody has spoken to me, I've learned to brace myself, knowing he's about to deliver a reality check. And it's probably one I'd rather avoid. His words aren't always nice, but at least they're honest. I prefer it.

My pulse pounds so hard that it feels like my heart might rip from my chest. Regret crashes into me, so overpowering that it nearly steals my breath. I steady myself, drawing a shaky inhale as I sit across from Micah. My mask slips into place—the familiar shield I've worn since I was eight years old, after losing my mom.

I lift my coffee cup, letting the warmth seep through the ceramic and into my trembling fingers. As I take a careful sip, my gaze lifts to meet Micah's green eyes—eyes that, only days ago, filled me with excitement and hope. Now, a shadow of darkness lingers there, something that makes my stomach twist with dread.

Am I only noticing it now because Brody forced me to see it, or has this always been visible to everyone?

Billie must have sensed the evil but couldn't find the words to explain it. She tried to warn me away from him, and I ignored her. I ignored everyone. I'm so fucking stupid!

My throat tightens painfully as the entire evening replays vividly in my mind like a movie, forcing me to face the truth.

I walk into the kitchen and find Asher on top of Micah, punching him over and over again. I freak out, not knowing what's going on.

"What are you doing?" I shriek, seeing blood, watching Micah nearly lifeless as Asher does his worst. I push Asher off of him.

"She came onto me!" Micah points up at Billie.

My brows furrow as I glance between them.

"No! I did not!" Billie says, grabbing me and trying to pull me closer to her.

"Let me go, Billie!" I say, moving away from her.

The room is in chaos. Micah's bleeding, and I bend down, brushing my fingers across his already-bruised face.

"I'm so sorry," I whisper. "Let's leave, baby."

He looks up at me, and I can tell he is in pain.

"Harp, don't go with him. Please!" Billie's voice rises as she reaches for me again.

"Don't touch me, Billie," I say as Micah grabs my hand, pulling me away.

I meet his eyes, knowing this is one of his concerns. He didn't believe Billie or Asher would be happy for us.

He squeezes my hand hard, pulling me into him, then whispers, only loud enough for me to hear, "I told you so."

I turn back to look at Billie. He did warn me, and we had a two-hour discussion on it.

"He predicted you'd ruin this for us. You can never be happy for me, can you?"

"Harper, please." Tears stream down her face. "You can't be serious!"

Micah pulls me away with him.

ASHER LOSING HIS TEMPER MAKES MORE SENSE. HE'D RISK everything to protect Billie; he already did when he stepped in to help us save our fashion company. And how did I repay him? By bringing a predator into his home and into their safe space. I put my best friend in danger. Shit, I've done the same to myself.

I recall Billie's frantic expression as she tried to pull me away from Micah. Her voice was raw with panic. She pleaded with me, practically begging. Micah must've known exactly what he was doing—he'd probably planned to push Billie into a corner that night, counting on me to blindly defend him. And like a fool, I walked straight into his trap.

He must think I'm a goddamn idiot.

I stare at Micah's handsome face now—those magnetic eyes and smile once felt like a gift meant just for me. I wonder how I let myself be manipulated so easily. I know better, but I turned a blind eye for him, for what I thought was love.

Disgust burns inside me, but it's aimed more at myself.

I've always craved affection. I've wanted to be enough for someone—*anyone*. I'm the poster child for daddy issues, and look where it's landed me. Right back in the same place—used, betrayed, and humiliated.

Micah chuckles, interrupting my spiraling thoughts. "Are you okay? You look like you saw a ghost in the bathroom."

What I saw was much worse than a ghost. It was my damn reality. He's already haunting me.

"I don't feel well," I whisper, my voice unsteady.

This situation hits me with a sickening force: I've been sleeping with Billie's stalker, the man who terrorized her—*both of us*—for over a decade. Nausea surges violently, burning the back of my throat, and I struggle to swallow it down.

Micah single-handedly destroyed Billie's twenty-first birthday, the party I had meticulously planned. It was supposed to be perfect —memorable. Instead, that night shattered Billie's sense of safety forever. Since then, she's lived life glancing over her shoulder, wary of every shadow and dark hallway. He stole something priceless from her, and she's never gotten it back.

"I might throw up," I mutter as the horror of Micah's deception washes over me.

He targeted me—I was nothing but a stepping stone to get to Billie. She's the real prize; the ice queen; untouchable, elite royalty, and I'm the pawn who led him straight to her.

Micah's expression shifts to fake concern, but his voice is tender. "We can leave. I'm so sorry," he says, reaching across the table to touch my hand.

I force myself not to flinch or pull away. I want to break each finger at the knuckle, but I swallow that rage, masking my emotions with practiced ease.

"Can we get some to-go containers?" Micah snaps impatiently at the server, and irritation flickers across his face. His tone is rude and dismissive.

How he treats others, those he believes he's better than, isn't okay. It only adds to my growing disgust with him.

"Sure. And would you also like the check?" she asks politely, clearly sensing the tension at our table.

"What do you think?" Micah says sarcastically with an eye roll as he slides beside me on my side of the booth.

His arm wraps around me, and my body stiffens, though I force myself to remain outwardly calm. One thing I learned while growing up under constant scrutiny: never ever let your enemy predict your next move, and keep your cards close to your chest.

Micah has no idea Brody is here. And he will come for me. Brody never breaks his promises.

My gaze drifts down to the engagement ring glittering mockingly on my finger. The diamond feels like it's burning straight through my skin.

"I need some fresh air before I embarrass myself," I whisper, wanting to put distance between us before completely losing my composure.

The humiliation feels like it'll cling to me forever. I just hope Billie will forgive me for what I've done.

"Okay, I'll meet you at the car," Micah says, standing to let me out.

As I walk away, I glance back to find him watching me, like he's trying to decipher my thoughts. I plaster a smile, hiding the shiver crawling up my spine. I'll never be able to look at Micah the same way again.

When I step outside, the sunshine hits my skin, and I close my eyes, drawing in a deep, steadying breath. The warmth does little to ease the chill settling within me. My eyes sweep up and down the sidewalk, searching for Brody—my unwanted shadow—because I know he's nearby. I can feel him.

I scan the street and storefronts, playing my own private game of Where's Waldo, the Brody Calloway edition. His presence is as familiar as it is irritating. I don't always appreciate his blunt honesty, but today, his words were a bitter pill I needed to swallow.

"Have some fucking self-respect."

A wave of hot, angry tears threatens to spill over, but I clench my jaw, refusing to let them fall.

"Hey," Micah says from behind me, startling me, and I jump. "Are you good?"

"Mm-hmm. Thank you." I smile casually as I turn to face him, hoping the rage inside me isn't written on my face. "My stomach's uneasy. I think the smell of the food got to me." It's the best excuse I have.

His fingertip traces a path down my cheek, but it's invasive. "Do you think you're pregnant?"

I laugh lightly, shaking my head. "No. I'm on birth control."

We've talked about this several times.

Before we got serious, we discussed having children and agreed we wanted to wait at least a few years. We were on the same page—at least, I thought we were. The man standing before me isn't the man I thought I knew. The mask has slipped and revealed someone I don't know.

He looks at me, his eyes serious. "I'd prefer if you took a test. *Today*," he stresses in a tone that leaves no room for argument.

"You're serious." A laugh escapes me, but it's strained.

"I am." His voice holds no warmth, and he reaches past me and opens the car door.

I slide inside as my chest tightens.

Micah leans in, reaching across me, and buckles the seat belt, pulling it tighter than necessary. Before, I found this protective, even sweet, but now it feels like he's making sure I don't bolt the second he closes the door.

Micah walks around the car, climbing into the driver's seat. Without hesitation, he leans over, brushing his lips against mine. I force myself to react normally, returning the kiss mechanically.

"I love you," he says, pulling away to meet my eyes.

"Love you," I whisper back, words that now taste bitter on my tongue.

A wide grin spreads across his face. "How about we get married tomorrow?"

"*Tomorrow?*" I repeat. Panic bubbles inside me again.

"Baby girl, aren't you ready to make me the happiest man on the planet?"

"Of course," I lie with a smile, trying to understand why he's pushing this so hard and so fast.

It's clear Micah's after something, but we've not signed a prenup. My inheritance won't be available until I've been married for at least one year, and my father won't sign off on releasing it early. On paper, nothing is accessible; my penthouses, apartments, vacation homes—they're all protected. Micah's assets aren't. If he forces this marriage, I'll take everything he has.

He reverses out of the parking space abruptly, and I check the side-view mirror, scanning for vehicles following us. Nothing seems out of place, but I know Brody is out there somewhere—close, waiting, ready to intervene if Micah crosses a line. At least, I hope.

We drive a few short blocks, stopping at a grocery store on the corner. After parking, Micah's hand finds my thigh, as if he's staking a claim, reminding me who I belong to.

"Dreams are coming true," he says, a smile playing at the corners of his mouth. But it's not kind. It's not gentle. It's cold.

This isn't a dream at all. It's a living fucking nightmare, and I'm wide awake.

As Micah unbuckles, my mind frantically replays the conversations we've had over the past few weeks—at dinners, during pillow talk—and I see every question he asked about Billie in a new, horrifying light. He wasn't interested in our friendship dynamic or casual details. He was systematically gathering private, personal information about her.

Nausea rises again. How did I miss so many glaring red flags?

I remain frozen in my seat.

"You're joining me," he says firmly, leaving no room for debate.

"I'd prefer not," I reply. My voice is steady, but my pulse quickens.

I want to open this door and scream for someone to help me. But every instinct begs me to wait for Brody to intervene. This isn't fun anymore.

"Harper," he snaps, my name coming out like a warning shot. His eyes narrow dangerously as he gives me a sideways glance. His tone and body language have shifted into something I can't ignore.

I'm not the naive girl he thinks I am, not anymore. But I can't let him see I've finally woken up, that I'm onto him.

"Okay, sure." I give him a compliant smile, and my gaze doesn't falter. "I'd *love* to join you."

"My baby girl." His words make me cringe as he gets out of the car.

I watch Micah as he circles the front quickly, opening my door. Without hesitation or gentleness, he grabs my hand, pulling me toward the store entrance.

My pulse spikes, and I glance around, hoping and praying Brody is nearby. I know he is.

5

HARPER

I nside the brightly lit store, Micah wastes no time, guiding me directly to the aisle with the pregnancy tests. Without hesitation, he picks one off the shelf with a practiced ease, as if he's done this countless times before. Maybe he has. I grow uneasy at the thought. How many other women has he manipulated and forced to take a pregnancy test?

He hands it to me, and I hesitate briefly before taking it. I'm not pregnant. The cardboard feels cold and heavy in my trembling fingers, mocking me. Micah guides me to the register, his grip tight and unyielding.

As we wait at the back of the line, he leans in close, his breath brushing my ear as he whispers, "I can't wait to see you carrying my baby."

Rage washes over me, but I mask it by nodding slightly. My anger flares white hot. The only thing that keeps me calm is the image of him paying for hurting Billie and me.

"I can almost imagine it," I say, thinking about my revenge with a smile.

He seems pleased with my answer, but he has no idea what Brody Calloway is capable of. I do.

A few eyes shift toward us, and anxiety claws at me. Before I can shield my hands, a teenage girl nearby snaps a photo of me holding the pregnancy test. I quickly hide the box behind my back, knowing exactly how damaging a pregnancy rumor could be.

"Not good," I whisper urgently to Micah, turning toward him.

But he's absorbed in his cell, ignoring me, fueling my frustration further. I impulsively grab the phone from his hand, wanting his full attention, and he roughly yanks it back. People stare at us.

"You said this trip was a detox for both of us," I whisper, narrowing my eyes. "If that is no longer the case, return my phone."

"*This* is important," he replies dismissively.

He finally registers how upset I am. To keep up appearances, he leans forward, pressing his lips against my forehead. The gesture is performative, and it makes my skin crawl. I want to rub his saliva off my skin.

When he pulls away, he meets my eyes. "Don't embarrass me."

Although it comes out like a whisper, it's a warning I hear loud and clear.

"Please offer that girl a thousand dollars to delete that photo," I nearly beg.

"You're making a scene," he hisses, shaking his head. "I cannot deal with this paranoia again."

I grit my teeth, heat flooding my cheeks. I've never felt so helpless.

"Micah, please," I insist, frustration bleeding into desperation.

I've lived under scrutiny my entire life, thanks to my family owning high-end ski resorts and hotels. My brother and I had to use aliases growing up, just to maintain some semblance of normalcy. One careless snapshot can spiral into a media frenzy within minutes. It's one that I can't afford right now, and his gaslighting won't change that fact.

"I want our private moments to stay private," I stress again, but my words fall on deaf ears. When he doesn't move an inch, I decide to take things into my own hands. "Fine. I'll ask her myself."

I step away, but he lunges quickly, grabbing the back of my dress roughly, jerking me backward. I stumble slightly, my heart racing at the unexpected aggression. Quickly, I smooth my features, conscious of eyes and cameras potentially fixed on us.

"Stay here," he commands harshly, slapping the test on the conveyor belt at the checkout.

The cashier scans the barcode, her eyes flickering to mine, as if sensing something isn't right.

My cheeks flush with shame, and I instinctively whisper, "I'm not pregnant," hoping to reassure her somehow.

Her gaze darts toward Micah, clearly uneasy, before she discreetly slides a folded piece of paper toward me. Without hesitation, I snatch it and shove it into my dress pocket, my fingers closing around it.

Micah returns seconds later, swiping his card with a smug smile.

"We don't need a bag," he says, ripping the receipt from the cashier's hand before pushing the box firmly into mine.

He leads me toward the exit, his grip like iron around my wrist.

I manage to keep my voice calm, though my anxiety is spiraling. "Did she delete the photo?"

"Yes," he answers bluntly, not meeting my eyes.

My pulse spikes again. "Are you sure? Did you see her delete it?" I press, needing confirmation. I've been burned too many times, and trusting his word feels impossible.

"Fucking yes! Jesus, Billie." He raises his voice as a younger couple strolls by, giving us curious looks.

I freeze in place, my blood running cold.

Micah pauses, blinking rapidly, his expression carefully neutral. "Harper," he corrects.

I shake my head slowly, suspicion hardening inside me. I clench the pregnancy test in my hand, trying to keep it hidden. Being out in the public view makes me feel vulnerable and exposed. This is my version of walking a tightrope, fully naked, for the whole world to see.

"It was an honest mistake, Harper. I'm really sorry," he says calmly, his tone reassuring but his eyes guarded. "I just keep thinking about the other night and how she came onto me."

"I forgive you," I reply smoothly. I play along, acting like we're on the same page, but hearing him lie so effortlessly about Billie pushes me to the edge of what I can handle. One more word about her, and I don't know if I'll be able to hold my tongue. My patience is ready to snap.

I glance nervously around the parking lot, searching for something familiar, anything comforting. Relief floods my chest when I spot the unmistakable gleam of Easton's blacked-out Dodge Charger. It's parked discreetly toward the back—the car he jokingly calls his "fuck around and find out" ride. And Brody chose that one —how convenient. At least, in some messed-up way, there is humor in it.

I let out a breath of relief. I'm still safe. The tension in my shoulders loosens just a fraction because I know Brody is here.

Micah catches my eye and grins, unaware he's being watched by a man who can destroy him in less than five seconds. I return the gesture, hiding my true emotions. It's the first time I've relaxed since we left the restaurant.

"There's my baby girl," he says affectionately as he opens the car door for me.

He noticed my slight change in demeanor. How long has he been watching me closely?

I slide in, allowing him to buckle me in, as usual, though this time, his touch makes my skin crawl. These past two months, I was blinded by loneliness, and I settled for *this*. I *chose* this. I can't trust myself or my own judgment anymore.

On the short drive back to his beach mansion, Micah makes light conversation. He's carefree and animated, as if nothing's wrong. I react appropriately, silently questioning everything.

Was anything we experienced together real?

Or had it all been meticulously planned to make me fall for him?

Over the years, I've learned to recognize people who wanted to use me to get closer to Billie, to exploit our friendship or success. I was always cautious and guarded—until now. I was too easy for him. He played on my weaknesses, on my need to be loved.

How fucking pathetic am I?

"I thought we could go sailing after we visit the courthouse tomorrow," Micah says casually, breaking into my thoughts. "I contacted the county judge—a friend of my father's—and can get our marriage license in the morning. We can be hitched by lunch."

Surprise flickers across my face, and I don't know what to say.

"You have a boat?" I question.

This is more proof that I barely know him. I convinced myself we were perfectly aligned, ignoring the gaps in my knowledge about who he was.

"I have several sailboats and a few yachts," he says smoothly, pride evident in his voice. "Next year, I'd love to sail around the world with you."

"Hmm. Only one problem with that—I don't like large bodies of water," I admit, hoping to mask the rising anxiety in my voice. The thought of being trapped at sea with him or anyone sends panic racing through me. "I thought you knew that about me."

"You enjoyed sailing in the past, didn't you?" he presses, glancing over at me with his eyebrows knitted in confusion.

I shake my head firmly, unease prickling at the back of my neck. "No. Billie enjoys sailing. Not me."

A momentary flash of irritation crosses his face before he smooths it away, giving me a neutral expression. "I'll make an appointment with my doctor to get you some motion sickness medicine."

I nod enthusiastically, forcing my voice into a cheerful pitch. "That would be incredible. I'd love that. Maybe I'll finally be able to enjoy the ocean."

But internally, my guard shoots up higher. There's no way in hell I'll allow any doctor he knows near me, much less allow them to prescribe me anything. I don't like large bodies of water because of my anxiety, not because of the motion. He's too fucking narrow-minded to realize that or even ask.

"Almost time to see if we're expecting a little one," he announces, pulling the car toward the towering gates of his oceanside mansion.

My heart pounds as we slow to a stop, waiting for the heavy gates to open. Walls at least ten feet high surround us, obscuring everything outside. Last night, this property felt secluded, peaceful even, but today, in the sunlight, it's more like a prison, just as Brody said.

As Micah drives down the long driveway, I glance toward the backyard and notice a small group of people leisurely strolling along a pathway.

"What's back there?" I ask curiously, wanting any information to help me escape him.

Micah follows my gaze. "A very famous trail that follows the oceanside. It's just over three miles long. It passes lots of historic homes."

I commit this detail to memory, just in case I have to run.

We exit the car, and Micah snatches the pregnancy test from my hand, studying the instructions intently as we enter the house. I'm ninety-nine point nine percent certain I'm not pregnant, considering the implant in my arm, but I'll do this to appease him.

He leads me toward the bathroom, pulling the test from its box and holding it out like a silent command.

"Take it," he finally says, so I do.

His gaze never leaves me as I pee on the stick. My face burns hot with discomfort, and I don't like how he's staring at me. However, I need to maintain this fragile peace we have, even if the tension is thick and suffocating me.

"How long until we know?" I ask. My voice is much quieter than I intended as he rips it from my hand.

"Three minutes," he says flatly, eyes glued to the test.

He leaves the bathroom, and I hear his footsteps echoing down the hallway. When I know I'm alone, my trembling fingers reach into my pocket, unfolding the crumpled note the cashier handed me at the store.

The scratchy handwriting screams at me.

That man almost murdered my daughter. Leave him now!

My heart rate increases, and panic nearly chokes me. Instinctively, I throw the paper into the toilet, flushing away the evidence. I watch it swirl around the porcelain bowl, vanishing from sight, though the words are seared into my memory. This is more evidence.

"He almost murdered her daughter?" My whispered voice almost echoes in the small space, filling me with a new wave of dread.

I rush to the sink and scrub my hands under hot water until they're nearly raw, trying to calm my racing pulse. I suck in deep, shaky breaths, then join Micah in the kitchen.

He calmly places the to-go boxes in the refrigerator as he whistles. The pregnancy test rests innocently on the counter. The casualness of this feels sinister, and I try not to get in my head about hypotheticals. As I pass him, I slide my hand lightly across his lower back. While it's a familiar gesture, I do it so he thinks I'm still caught in his web of deceit.

I quickly reach into a cabinet, pull out a glass, and fill it with water. My throat is suddenly dry. As the cool liquid hits my tongue and slides down my throat, my mind races. That woman's frantic handwriting flashes in my mind.

Micah moves beside me, washing his hands in the sink. "Are you feeling any better?"

I nod quickly, downing another gulp of water. "Yes, thank you."

LYRA PARISH

The alarm on his phone sounds. It's a cheerful tune that only aggravates me. He picks up the pregnancy test, his eyes lighting up with anticipation. His smile widens dramatically, but mine vanishes when he turns it around, revealing the result.

Pregnant.

"No. That can't be correct," I whisper, my voice quivering. "I refuse to believe this."

Micah holds the test firmly. "Refuse it all you want. It says pregnant."

"I don't care. It's wrong," I say firmly, panic tightening my throat. I frantically try to remember the timing of my last period—it was last month.

This isn't possible. This can't be happening.

He has me questioning everything.

His brows pinch together, confusion clouding his face. "You're supposed to be happy. Ecstatic."

"Micah," I say, softening my voice despite the storm raging inside me. "We've talked about this ad nauseam. Do you have another test? It could be a false positive," I suggest, rushing back into the bathroom and grabbing the empty box. There was only one test inside.

His jaw clenches as he steps into the doorway, blocking me inside. "This isn't the reaction I expected from my soon-to-be wife."

I inhale, my eyes squeezed shut as I seek control. Could I be pregnant with his baby? *No.*

"I need a few minutes to process this, please. This is a very big step, and I'm in shock."

"It's a miracle," he offers, roughly slamming the test on the counter. The harsh noise echoes between us. Without looking at me again, he leaves me to myself.

I pick up the stick, praying it'll somehow read differently, but the word *Pregnant* glares back at me, mocking me.

"This is wrong," I mutter. "Right? *Right!*"

50

The next few minutes stretch out painfully, and I'm trapped inside my own head. I'm completely isolated, and I need Billie or my big brother, Zane—someone who knows me and someone I trust. I force myself to leave the bathroom and find Micah waiting in the hallway, his head lowered—a perfect picture of vulnerability. Wet tracks of tears glisten on his cheeks, and I feel a chill ripple through me, knowing it's an act, a manipulation tactic.

"I will always be by your side," he says, sincerity coating his words, yet my instincts scream danger.

"I know," I say, appearing calm even though the hairs on my neck stand straight up. "May I please have my phone now?"

"No," he replies, voice gentle but firm.

"I'd like to ask Billie if she can attend our wedding tomorrow. She might change her mind and take a helicopter here now that I'm pregnant. Easton can—"

"She already said no. Look, I can tell you're getting upset. Maybe you need some rest after the morning you've had. Maybe some tea to help calm your nerves. Earl Grey with a splash of milk?"

"Okay," I say, feeling nauseated by this revelation.

He's manipulating me, right? I'm growing more confused by my reality with each passing second.

"Let's go upstairs," he offers, stepping toward me, pressing his mouth roughly against mine.

I want to resist as he fists the back of my dress, but I play along. His fingertips brush my hair behind my ear when he finally pulls away.

"I'll never let you go, Harper," he whispers intensely.

"I know. That's why I'll spend the rest of my life making sure you get exactly what you've always deserved," I reply carefully, smiling sweetly at him, knowing my words hold a darker meaning. "That's a promise, my love."

"Thank you. I love you," he says, his eyes sparkling triumphantly.

"I love you," I mutter.

"Forever." He wraps his arm firmly around my shoulders, guiding me upstairs.

Each step feels heavier, like chains tightening around me, sealing me further into this nightmare I need to escape.

Brody, please come for me. Please.

6

BRODY

Night falls. Moonlight spills across the ocean, illuminating the dark landscape just enough for me to see. As I park near the Cliff Walk trailhead entrance, my mind replays the unsettling conversation I overheard at breakfast between Micah and Harper.

He wants to marry Harper this week, which can't happen. It won't fucking happen as long as my heart beats and I have breath left in my lungs. She will be out of his reach within the next hour. The thought of that makes me smirk.

As I continue down the paved trail, I picture Harper with him, touching him, kissing him. It makes anger boil under my skin, and it twists deep in my gut like a knife. I shouldn't give a single fuck who she chooses to be with, but I do. I just want the best for her because that's what she deserves—even if she refuses to see it.

Harper's charm is undeniable. She's a beautiful woman, wrapped up in a fiery-spirit package. Her sassiness and stubbornness drive at my nerves, but underneath that is pure sunshine. When she smiles, it lights up an entire room. When she laughs, it's contagious. Harper spreads happiness effortlessly and can find the silver lining in any situation, even a shitty one. It's both endearing and annoying. I just selfishly hope she can still find something good in this mess she's gotten herself tangled in. The one I'm rescuing her from.

Right now, I personally find it hard to be positive. There's no bright side to Micah Rhodes or to Harper being with him.

Fuck.

I should've forced her to come with me when I confronted her at the restaurant, consequences be damned. Yet I know Harper or Micah would've made a scene, drawing more attention than either of us needed. Micah's father has influence in this town that can ruin lives. Had he seen me today, he might have tightened his grip on her even more, put me in jail, and then my rescue mission would've been severely delayed.

I grit my teeth, remembering the possessive way he secured her seat belt earlier. It took every ounce of self-control I had not to rip him from the car right then and bash his face into the pavement in broad daylight. I imagined taking her and leaving him to bleed out on the concrete.

My phone buzzes, pulling me from the spiral of my thoughts. Billie texted me a picture.

I click on it, lowering the brightness of my screen so I don't draw any unnecessary attention.

It's Harper at the grocery store, Micah behind her, whispering something sinister in her ear while she clutches a pregnancy test in her hand. My chest tightens painfully as I recall seeing her carrying it when they left the grocery store. I hoped no one recognized her.

BILLIE

WTAF IS THIS? Did you know about this?

She immediately sends several links to articles about Harper and Micah expecting a child. My jaw clenches so tightly that it aches. I'd have said it was an AI-generated hoax if I hadn't witnessed it with my own eyes. Unfortunately, it's real. The thought of Harper carrying that man's baby brings me to a level of disgust I've never experienced.

BILLIE

This is an actual nightmare! How can it get any worse than this?

I didn't tell her earlier when I watched it through binoculars because I wanted to discuss it with Harper first. This doesn't involve me. It's not my business.

BILLIE

Well? You have nothing to say?

BRODY

No.

BILLIE

I'm freaking out.

BRODY

She'll be with me tonight.

When the phone vibrates again, Billie's name flashes on the screen, and I silence the call. I'm not ready to talk. Right now, I need my full attention on what's to come. My mind needs to be right because I have no idea what situation I'll be walking into when I enter that house. I have to expect the unexpected.

BRODY

I'll text you later.

I exhale, forcing out the distractions. I close my eyes, mentally reviewing every detail of Micah's house from the virtual tour I studied earlier today. Every hallway, room, and entrance are imprinted in my memory, along with the expensive art he proudly flaunted for the cameras.

The crisp night air surrounds me as I continue forward.

BILLIE

You're SO rude!

It's not the first time I've been told that, and I'm sure it won't be the damn last.

BRODY

That emoji is enough to set her off—I know it.

BILLIE

I HATE THAT REPLY!

BILLIE

👇👇👇👇👇👇👇👇👇

I can't suppress the faint smirk that forms on my lips. I know my cousin better than she knows herself.

The trail winds and curves. Shadows dance through the branches before the path straightens out, revealing the obnoxious fountain in Micah's perfectly manicured backyard. Earlier today, when confirming Harper's location, I scoped out this exact spot. Now, cloaked by darkness, I move with quiet determination, heart pounding in anticipation, ready to rescue Harper and end our nightmare once and for all.

I just hope she's learned her lesson.

When I passed his house earlier, the ten-foot brick walls and iron gate guarding his property in front stood out. It was designed to keep out unwanted visitors—or perhaps more accurately, to keep them trapped inside.

I continue along the trail, the cool ocean breeze grazing my skin and mingling with the faintly bitter scent of saltwater. On any other night, I'd pause, soaking in the moonlight, shimmering like diamonds across the inky waves. But right now, urgency hums in my blood. Each heartbeat echoes with a need to save her.

If Harper still had her phone, this rescue would be simpler. But knowing Micah, I'd guess he's either destroyed it or hidden it from her. My jaw clenches, frustration mixing with protective fury as I move even closer to the property's edge.

From my position in the shadows, I study the large house. A muted glow from the TV flashes from the downstairs living room. Upstairs, the primary bedroom's light spills onto the balcony. Harper sits on the edge of the bed, her head hanging slightly forward, shoulders slumped, as if she's struggling to stay upright. My pulse spikes as unease knots my stomach. She looks unsteady and vulnerable.

"Fuck," I breathe out, urgency tightening its grip on me.

With silent precision, I scale the chain-link fence, boots landing with a thump on the soft grass. I hug the perimeter, and my gaze remains locked on her silhouette as I reach the ivy-covered lattice work that stretches upward to the balcony.

The lattice groans but holds firm beneath my grip as I test it. I don't have time to find an alternate route and go for it. My muscles are tight as I climb upward, and my heart pounds hard.

"Hold on, Harper," I whisper, determination driving me forward.

Once on the balcony, I pause, my breathing steady as I listen for any sounds inside. The night around me is eerily quiet, filled only with distant waves and wind. I ease the balcony door open and step into the room, immediately seeing Harper more clearly. Her face is pale, her eyes glassy and unfocused. She turns toward me slowly, confusion and relief warring openly in her expression.

"Brody?" Her voice trembles, barely audible. "You promis—"

"Later," I interrupt, moving to her side.

Up close, she looks dazed, her pupils dilated, and the faint tremors in her hands ignites a fury deep within me.

"Harper, what did he do?"

"I don't ..." she mumbles, voice trailing off weakly. Her eyes flutter, lids heavy as she struggles to keep them open.

On the bedside table is a mug with a tea bag hanging from it.

I grasp her shoulders carefully, forcing her to focus on me. "Did he give you something?" My words are edged with a control that scares me.

I'm fucking feral. I will fucking kill him tonight.

She nods—a slow, uncertain movement—and points. "Tea."

My jaw locks tight, anger flaring hot beneath my skin.

"Fuck," I mutter harshly, quickly gathering her limp form into my arms. "We need to get out of here now."

Harper doesn't resist, melting into my hold, her breathing shallow and uneven. As I carefully move toward the balcony, my heart races, as I'm hyperaware of every subtle sound beneath my feet.

"Close your eyes," I whisper, voice gentle despite the turmoil raging inside me. "I won't let you go. I won't let anything happen to you."

With Harper secured against my chest, I descend the lattice carefully, each movement precise. It creaks under our combined weight, tension knotting my shoulders, but the wood holds.

When my boots finally hit solid ground, adrenaline surges in a wave of relief.

"You're safe now," I assure her, moving toward the fence, holding her protectively close. "I've got you."

I carry her the half mile back to the car, and as we approach, Harper stirs faintly, murmuring, "Brody." Her fingers weakly grab my shirt, her fragile body trembling against mine.

The white-hot anger nearly takes me over, but it's extinguished by my desire to shield her from harm.

I carefully place her in the passenger seat and buckle her in. She reaches out blindly, grabbing my hand, and her eyes flicker open, cloudy but pleading.

I'm going back, and I'm going to fucking kill him.

"Don't leave me," she whispers, the words heavy with fear and vulnerability. It's like she can read my thoughts.

My breath huffs out roughly. The need for vengeance outweighs my responsibility to protect her, but her quiet plea pierces me directly in the goddamn heart, forcing clarity through my intense anger.

"*Please,*" she begs, her voice breaking.

"Fine. But this isn't over. He will fucking pay," I promise her firmly, gripping her hand briefly before shutting the door, the sound echoing across the empty parking lot, mixing with the rushing waves.

Every muscle in my body screams to turn back, to make Micah suffer for fucking drugging her, but Harper's safety comes first. This time, that bastard gets a free pass. Next time, he won't.

We leave this godforsaken town, and the night is endless. Headlights carve through the darkness as I push the Charger harder, every mile creating more distance between her and the nightmare she's leaving behind. Harper sits curled in the passenger seat, head resting against the window, eyes closed. She's pale, breathing shallow, forehead damp from whatever Micah gave her.

My knuckles whiten against the steering wheel every time I glance at her. I'm careful to watch for signs of distress, but the steady rise and fall of her chest reassures me she's stable—at least for now.

After nine gruesome hours of driving, my eyelids grow heavy, the adrenaline finally slipping away. I spot a neon vacancy sign flickering weakly in the distance, and when I'm closer, I pull into the parking lot of a small roadside motel.

The gravel crunches beneath the tires, the noise barely stirring Harper. Her head wobbles slightly, eyes cracking open.

"Where … are we?" she mumbles, then clears her throat as she struggles to focus.

"Somewhere safe," I promise, my voice gentle. "Stay here. I'll be right back."

I watch her from the window inside the tiny lobby as I secure a room. The manager slides me the keys, and I quickly return to the car. As I drive over to the room across the parking lot, I see the tobacco-stained mini blinds dip down, knowing we're being watched. I offered her two thousand dollars to pretend like she never saw us. Just in case anyone is searching. She haggled me for double.

When I open Harper's door, she tries to move on her own but nearly falls. I catch her easily, lifting her into my arms. Her head nestles against my shoulder, and I ignore the unsettling longing that fills my chest.

The motel room is small and simple, decorated in shades of beige and pale blue, faintly smelling of tobacco and disinfectant. It's the type of place people rent for a few hours to rest because it's in the middle of nowhere.

I set Harper on the bed, and the mattress barely flexes. She opens her eyes and coughs.

"Oh God," she whispers, panicked, and I know she's about to puke.

I scoop her back into my arms and rush her to the bathroom. I set her down, allowing her to grip the edge of the porcelain sink just in time. She trembles violently as her stomach empties itself.

I rub slow circles against her back, whispering, "It's okay. Get it out of your system, Harp. Just breathe."

"Don't leave me."

"I won't."

After several long moments, she sinks against me, exhausted. Without thinking, I reach for a washcloth, wetting it under the cool water. I carefully wipe her face, cleaning away tears and lingering sweat. She looks up at me, eyes glassy, embarrassed.

"I'm sorry," she says weakly. "Looks like I'm still Little Miss Disaster."

I don't say anything—because it's not the time. Instead, I help her back to the bed. She sits, eyes half closed, swaying.

"My body is on fire," she says, tugging weakly at her clothes, clearly uncomfortable.

My heart constricts because I know she can't manage alone. I swallow, carefully removing her clothes, fingers light and respectful. Her skin is damp, and I notice how her hair sticks to her forehead. Her eyes droop heavily as exhaustion threatens to claim her.

"My hero." She breathes, barely audible.

I keep my eyes averted, fighting to control my breathing. This isn't the way I ever imagined touching her for the first time—with her vulnerable, scared, trusting me to take care of her.

My anger pulses again, fierce and protective.

I guide her under the blankets, covering her with just the sheet.

"I want to go back tonight and fuck him up."

"Stay," she whispers, reaching out weakly.

"I'm not going anywhere," I promise, sitting on the edge of the bed.

I brush gentle fingers over her forehead until her breathing evens and she drifts away. We're seven hours away from my cabin in the Smoky Mountains, and then we'll be safe. There's only one way up the mountain and one way down it. If Micah comes, I have a bullet with his name on it.

As I watch her rest, every protective instinct I have blazes to life. Her face softens in sleep, and it's the first time I've seen her so vulnerable.

How the hell did we end up here?

I've kept Harper at arm's length for so long, knowing I had no right to complicate her life or mine. Eden's memory always served as a reminder that loving someone puts them in danger. But Harper ... Harper makes me forget all the reasons I should stay away.

She's been hurt, betrayed by someone she trusted, and somehow, I've become her only safe haven. My chest tightens painfully, as I'm caught between the fear of something terrible happening to her and the need to fuck up Micah Rhodes.

I lean back in the chair near the bed, unwilling to sleep, too vigilant to relax.

Tomorrow will come with its own complications, but for tonight, she's safe. And for the first time in years, I feel a sense of clarity.

Whatever comes next, I'll handle it. Because protecting Harper Alexander isn't just my job; it's something deeper, something I'm finally ready to admit, even if only to myself.

7

HARPER

My eyes flutter open. The harsh sunlight streams through unfamiliar thin curtains and stabs painfully into my temples. A sharp ache pulses behind my eyes, making me groan as I turn my head. I glance over and see Brody asleep in the chair, his body cramped, his lips slightly parted. He looks peaceful, like we did when we were kids.

My mouth is dry, and my limbs are heavy with fatigue, like I barely have control. For a second, panic tightens in my chest as I glance around the motel room. My memory is fractured, and I try to piece together how I ended up here.

Then it all floods back—Micah, the pregnancy test, Brody climbing onto the balcony, his arms wrapped protectively around me, whispering reassurances into my ear as he carried me away. I press my palms into my eyes, battling nausea that's as emotional as it is physical.

How did I let it come to this? How did I fail to see the truth that was right in front of me?

I sit up, swallowing hard against the bile rising in my throat. My stomach turns, and I barely make it to the cramped bathroom before I collapse over the toilet to empty my stomach. The cold porcelain grounds me, even as shame washes over me in dizzying waves.

"Harper?" Brody's deep voice filters in from the doorway. "You okay?"

"Having the time of my life," I croak out sarcastically, my voice hoarse and strained. But another violent wave of nausea hits, and I lean forward again, my body trembling uncontrollably.

"At least you have your humor."

He enters, and while I don't want him to see me at my worst, I don't have a choice. Brody kneels beside me, gathering my tangled hair away from my face, holding it back. His touch is tender, and his warm hands steady me more than I'd like to admit.

"I'm fine," I whisper, puking again.

"You're not," he says. His voice calms me, and I turn to glance at him, only to see the tension in his jaw. "Let me help you."

I sit back against the cold wall in the tiny bathroom with my eyes squeezed shut in humiliation. Brody doesn't say another word as he wets a washcloth and presses it against my forehead. He swipes over my cheeks and my lips. His gentleness contrasts so starkly with the harsh reality of my situation that tears well in my eyes.

"I'm sorry," I whisper. The weight of everything—Micah, the pregnancy, the betrayal—feels suffocating. "I should've listened to you, to Billie, to Zane, everyone. I—"

"Stop. You owe no one an apology." He kneels lower, his gaze meeting mine, unwavering and intense. "This isn't your fault. You're not responsible for Micah's lies."

His words cut through my fog of self-blame, and for a quick, fragile moment, I actually believe him. I let out a shaky breath as he stands up and turns on the tub faucet, checking the temperature before glancing back at me.

"Would you like a bath? You'll feel better," he says.

I nod, suddenly realizing how weak I am. He helps me stand, his strong arms steadying me as my legs wobble. When I stumble,

Brody wraps his arm securely around my waist. His touch sends a confusing warmth through me that I can't deal with right now.

He helps me out of my clothes, keeping his gaze averted as he guides me toward the steaming tub. I don't have the strength to be shy.

The water is hot, but I sink into it gratefully, wanting to feel anything other than guilt and disgust. I lean my head against the wall and close my eyes.

"Just call if you need me," Brody says. He slips out of the bathroom, leaving the door cracked.

I scrub my skin raw, wanting to wash away every trace of Micah —his touch, his scent, his possessive grip. The water swooshes around me, and steam rises in the small space. My hands tremble as I wash my hair, memories of Micah's smile and his manipulative whispers creeping back into my thoughts. He's haunting me, and it's too much.

"Brody," I say, my voice sounding distant and fragile, even to me. I feel drained and disoriented.

He appears at the doorway, eyes closed. "You okay?"

"Can you help me get out?"

He nods without hesitation, stepping closer and extending a steady hand, eyes still shut. I cling to him as he helps me rise from the water. Quickly, he snatches a towel from the counter and wraps me in it.

"I laid out some of my clothes for you," he says, leading me out of the bathroom to where a neatly folded shirt and sweats with a drawstring are on the bed. "Figured you'd be more comfortable in those."

"Thanks," I whisper, slipping them on as he turns away.

I breathe in his familiar scent on the soft fabric, and it calms my racing heart.

I sit on the edge of the mattress, my legs shaky. Brody sits beside me, close enough for comfort but still keeping some space between us. A lump forms in my throat.

"I'm scared," I admit, feeling too exposed.

He immediately takes my hand, holding it securely. His thumb strokes across my knuckles. "I won't let anything happen to you. Ever. Micah messed with the wrong fucking one."

Tears fill my eyes again, spilling down my cheeks despite my best efforts to stop them. I look away, unable to face his intense gaze, but he doesn't pull back. Instead, silence hangs in the air, heavy but somehow safe, like a protective cocoon.

"Harp, you need to rest," he finally says, helping me lie down. "I'm right here."

I curl onto my side, facing away, my heart still racing. As my eyes drift shut, Brody brushes wet strands of hair from my face—the simple gesture speaking louder than words.

Sleep comes quickly, but I'm thrown into restless nightmares. I jolt awake, gasping, my pulse hammering as fragments of memories crash through my mind. It's relentless, like Micah poisoned my subconscious.

The door creaks open, and Brody steps inside, instantly calming the frantic rhythm of my heart. He holds two bottles of water and a packet of crackers. His phone is pressed to his ear, and when he sees I'm awake, he ends the call without a word.

"Sleeping Beauty finally awake?" he asks, concern softening his eyes.

"Barely," I whisper, attempting a smile.

Brody keeps his distance. "You feeling any better?"

Tears blur my vision again. "A little."

He exhales, tension tightening his jaw. "Harper, I'm sorry—"

"Don't," I interrupt. "Don't you dare apologize. I should've listened. You tried to warn me."

His eyes soften further, guilt mixing with anger. "I shouldn't have let you get that close to danger. It was reckless."

My voice trembles as the truth cuts deeper. "I had to figure it out myself."

Brody instinctively moves closer but pauses. "None of this is your fault. He targeted you, Harper. He knew exactly what to say to draw you in."

I meet his eyes. "Did Billie know?"

"She figured it out at dinner," he explains. "He fooled everyone."

"But not you," I whisper.

He shakes his head slightly. "No, never me."

"Thank you," I say, my voice breaking. "For saving me."

His expression grows fierce. "Always, Harp."

The simple promise unravels something deep within me, comforting yet unsettling. I inhale, trying to ground myself. "What happens now?"

"We leave," he replies firmly. "You'll stay with me until it's safe to return to the city."

I nod, accepting his words, clinging to the solid certainty he offers in this uncertain world.

"Eat and drink," he instructs. "We have to hit the road soon."

"Do you have a plan?" I ask, sipping water and feeling my strength somewhat trickle back.

He smirks slightly. "When do I not have a plan?"

"True." I manage a small smile. "Does Billie hate me?"

He shakes his head immediately. "Never. Do you want to talk to her?"

"Eventually," I admit. "Not yet. I'm not ready. Right now, I don't know what was real and what wasn't real."

"I get it," he says, handing me the crackers.

When I struggle to open them, he helps. I nibble one, and even though it's stale, it's good.

"Micah drugged me. He could've killed me. I want him to pay," I whisper, determination in my chest.

Brody's expression darkens with fury. "He will."

8

BRODY

An hour later, we're finally on the road. Harper still isn't herself, and it might take another day for the drugs to fully work themselves through her system. That motherfucker could've killed her.

I grip the wheel tighter, battling the fatigue from the little sleep I managed to get in that uncomfortable chair. Thoughts of Harper and what Micah did to her keep racing through my mind. Each mile we drive puts more distance between her and him, but it doesn't ease my tension at all because I want revenge.

Harper shifts restlessly, her breathing still uneven. Quiet mutters slip from her lips, but I can't make out a single word. Every time she stirs, I glance at her, and my heart squeezes a little tighter.

She looks fragile, broken in ways I've never seen. It didn't have to be like this.

A chill shakes her body, and without thinking, I reach for the jacket I tossed in the back seat earlier and carefully drape it over her. My fingers linger, brushing over her shoulder. She sighs at my touch. This tenderness is dangerous territory, a place I promised I'd never go again.

The clock on the dashboard ticks forward relentlessly, minutes slipping away in silence. After another hour of driving, I dial Billie's number, and she answers right away.

"Is she okay? Tell me she's okay, Brody." Her frantic energy is hard to ignore. It makes me wonder how many paces she took around her office today.

"Yes," I assure her, keeping my voice low so I don't disturb Harper. "We're headed somewhere secure."

"Where?"

"The less you know, the safer everyone is," I explain firmly, glancing back at Harper to make sure she's still sleeping. "Just trust me, little cousin."

Billie sighs. "Keep her safe, Brody."

"Always." My voice comes out more intense than I mean to. "I'll call again soon."

Before she can say anything else, I hang up. The silence in the car feels heavy again, and it's usually something I can handle. I prefer it. I crave it. But right now, it's smothering me.

Harper shifts once more, but she settles back, snuggling my jacket tighter.

Guilt roars bitterly in my stomach because I know this could've been avoided. I should've gotten to her sooner. I should've protected her better. I should've taken her when she was alone outside the restaurant, but I hesitated. There were too many people around.

My thoughts spiral as I get stuck in the should've loop.

I glance at Harper, noticing the soft lines of her face, how peaceful yet troubled she looks, even in sleep. I promised myself I wouldn't let anyone else in. Yet here I am, driving Harper Alexander to the one place I've avoided for five long years.

As the sun rises higher in the sky, brightening the highway ahead, I tighten my grip on the wheel. This isn't just about keeping Harper safe from Micah anymore; it's about protecting her from everything, including me. But deep down, I know I'm fighting a losing battle.

I keep my eyes on the road, grip tight around the wheel. Memories of Eden flood my mind—the laughter, stolen moments, the loss that still stings. The fact that Harper doesn't know this secret history feels like a blessing and a curse. She's already suffering enough without carrying the weight of my hidden grief.

"Are you going to tell me where we're going?" Harper eventually asks, breaking the silence. Her voice is soft, hesitant, as if she's scared of interrupting my thoughts.

I glance at her briefly, noticing how the sunlight highlights the tired circles under her eyes. I think about not telling her, but I know the truth is the best policy with Harper. It's what she responds to most, and it's what I promised I'd always give her.

"Sugar Pine Springs. It's off the radar."

It's not linked to me in any way—by design.

She nods, processing my words. "And Micah won't find us?"

"He can try," I reply, my voice hardening with anger, "but he won't succeed. And if he does—well, he'd better not."

"You sound sure of that," she whispers, leaning her head against the window, eyes heavy with uncertainty.

"I am." My confidence is unwavering.

Micah doesn't know what he's unleashed in me. My jaw clenches.

Harper shifts, turning slightly to face me. "Why do you care?"

The question catches me off guard. My heart pounds as memories of Harper and me over the years mingle with current emotions.

I keep my expression neutral. "You're Billie's best friend. Protecting you is part of the job."

"I'm a job to you?" She exhales a soft laugh, bitter and disbelieving. "It's more than that, isn't it?"

My pulse quickens, and I stare straight ahead. Harper is close enough to see the truth written on my face, but I can't let her.

"I've seen the way you look at me sometimes," she whispers. "There's more. I can feel it."

"You need to rest." I deflect, avoiding her gaze. "It's been a rough couple of days."

"That's not an answer," she challenges, but her voice is softer now, tinged with disappointment or exhaustion—maybe both.

I exhale heavily, considering what I could possibly tell her without shattering the careful boundary I've kept around my heart for years. "Everyone has a past. Sometimes, that past shapes how we handle the present. You don't need to know all the details to trust that I'm here for you and you're not *just* a job."

"Fair enough."

Silence fills the car again, heavier this time. Harper eventually sighs, settling deeper into the seat.

As more miles pass us by, I glance at her from the corner of my eye, noting the slow rise and fall of her breathing as she drifts off again. I allow myself to look at her peaceful expression, and I think about Eden. The similarities between them tug painfully at my chest, but the differences—Harper's stubborn defiance, her spirited resilience—are very clear.

Maybe history repeats itself, or maybe it's giving me a chance at redemption. Either way, Harper Alexander has become my responsibility, my purpose, and I'll do whatever it takes to protect her.

When the tires finally crunch along the gravel driveway, I let out a slow exhale. I've avoided this place for five years. Memories of my past live here in the rustling leaves, the creak of the porch swing, and in every shadow that flickers past the windows. I told myself I'd never come back. Yet here I am, with Harper beside me, and there's nowhere else on the planet I'd rather be.

Her presence eases the ache of my memories. She doesn't know my history with this cabin or how deeply it's woven into my past or my pain. It's not the time. But someday soon, I'll tell her everything, if she wants to know.

"We're here," I say, touching her arm to wake her.

Harper blinks a few times, her blue-gray eyes slowly finding focus as she gazes through the windshield.

"It's beautiful," she whispers, taking in the secluded cabin, surrounded by towering pines with dappled sunlight breaking through the branches. "You've always owned this?"

"Yeah," I answer, my throat tight. It was my secret escape for years.

She yawns, pushing her hair away from her face. "It's peaceful."

"It used to be," I say, mostly to myself. But she hears it and turns toward me, curiosity in her eyes. I quickly change the subject before she can ask any more questions. "Come on. Let me show you inside."

Stepping out of the car, I take a deep breath, absorbing the scent of pine and moss that once felt like freedom. Today, it feels like a reckoning. I grab my bags from the trunk and lead Harper up the porch steps. My heart rate increases with every creak of wood beneath my boots.

When I push open the door, the familiar mustiness hits me instantly—a bittersweet reminder of happier days long gone. Harper steps inside behind me, looking around the cozy space—the stone fireplace, the worn couch and chair, both draped with old knitted blankets; the kitchen table I built one lazy summer afternoon from wood I'd chopped myself.

"It's like stepping back in time," she mutters, trailing her fingers over the back of the couch.

"In some ways, it is," I admit, setting the bags down. "Are you hungry? Tired?"

"Mostly tired," she says, turning to face me. Her gaze softens. "Are you okay? You're tense."

I force a smile. "It's been a while since I've been here. Memories, you know?"

She nods slowly, her eyes searching mine. "Good memories or bad?"

"Both." My voice comes out rough, and I clear my throat,

turning away. "I'll get a fire going. It gets cold up here really fast. Even in the spring."

I busy myself, stacking logs into the fireplace, my hands shaking slightly. Harper watches me, her silence heavier than any words she could say. She knows something's off, but she's giving me space to find my footing, which I appreciate.

"Brody," she finally says, stepping closer, "whatever it is, you don't have to tell me right now. But I hope you know you can."

I meet her gaze, swallowing hard, emotions threatening to spill over. "I know. And someday, I will. I promise."

She nods, her gentle acceptance nearly undoing me. "Okay. Until then, I'm here."

This woman in front of me deserves to know every truth, every hidden scar. Yet Eden's memory—my hidden grief—isn't ready to surface, not yet.

"You should take it easy," I say, guiding her toward the small bedroom down the hall. "We can figure everything else out tomorrow."

She leans into me as we walk, her warmth easing some of the tension in my chest. For tonight, Harper is here with me and safe, and maybe that's enough. But as darkness settles over the cabin, and the old, familiar stillness wraps around us, I know the hardest truths still wait ahead, buried just beneath the surface, waiting to be freed. I don't know if I'll ever be ready.

9

HARPER

I blink awake slowly, disoriented at first as I stare at the unfamiliar wooden ceiling. Then I remember Brody rescuing me, and my chest floods with relief. He saved me.

Stretching beneath thick, cozy blankets, I listen to faint sounds coming from elsewhere in the cabin—the sizzle of a skillet, light footsteps moving around, and the low hum of oldies playing on a radio. It feels like I've been transported to another time period—when life was easy and slow, where the weight of the world didn't exist.

A smile tugs at my lips as I slide out of bed, shivering slightly at the chill lingering in the early morning air. I slip my feet into oversized slippers that Brody thoughtfully placed by the bed and wrap a warm plaid robe around my shoulders that I found draped over a chair. For the first time in days, I feel safe and guarded.

I look down at my finger, noticing the gaudy engagement ring is still on it. I take it off, placing it in the drawer next to the bed. Removing it feels like freedom.

When I step into the living room, the scent of coffee and savory food greets me instantly. Brody stands at the stove, his broad shoulders filling out a snug black T-shirt. Tattoos line up and down his arms as he casually flips bacon, looking oddly domestic and completely relaxed. It's a side of him I've never seen.

I watch him for a few more seconds before I make myself known.

"Morning," I say, my voice still raw from sleep.

His lips twitch in a teasing smile. "Well, good morning, Sleeping Beauty. Nice of you to finally join the living."

I make a face at him, moving to the kitchen counter and leaning against it. "You're *hilarious*."

"I know." He grins, eyes warm. The tension I saw last night has vanished. "Sleep okay?"

"Better than okay," I admit, pulling the robe tighter around myself. "Honestly, I haven't slept that well in weeks. Maybe years."

He nods knowingly, his gaze growing softer and more serious. "You deserve solid rest."

Something in the way he says it makes warmth spread in my chest. I know he means it.

I bite my lip as butterflies stir in my stomach. "What about you?"

"Sure." He shrugs lightly, turning back to the bacon. "The couch isn't exactly a king-size bed, but it's better than the floor. I can't complain."

I hesitate, a tiny pang of guilt nudging at me. "Sorry."

He flashes me a look of mild amusement. "No apologies, Harp. You looked comfortable. But I did notice you drooled all over my pillow."

My mouth drops open. "No, I did not."

He chuckles, reaching out to teasingly tap beneath my chin. "Whatever helps you sleep at night."

I swat his hand away, laughing despite myself. "You're the worst."

"You say that, but here I am, cooking you breakfast like a saint." He points at the coffeepot with the spatula. "Fresh coffee too. Only the best for the best. Empty mug waiting for you."

I shake my head and smile while filling my cup. As I hold the warm mug, savoring the rich aroma, I glance around the cabin, taking in the rustic charm of the exposed wood beams, the stone fireplace, and the books stacked haphazardly on the shelves against the wall. It's so different from the chaos of our world and far away from Micah's sterile, perfect mansion. This one-bedroom home with an open floor plan feels like a true escape—one I've needed for a long damn time.

"You're staring again," he says lightly, loading up two plates, piled with scrambled eggs and crispy bacon.

"Just thinking," I admit, meeting his gaze. "This place suits you. Quiet, cozy, hidden."

"Sounds like a polite way of calling me a loner." His lips curve slightly as he sets our plates on the small wooden table that's only large enough for two.

"Maybe," I tease, taking a sip of coffee and smiling over the rim of my mug. "Or maybe you seem happy here. Like it's home."

"Right now, I am."

The sincerity in his voice tugs at my heart.

I glance down shyly, my cheeks warming again. "Me too."

He pauses, suddenly serious. "Good."

He studies me for a moment, his eyes gentle as he glances at my bare ring finger, but he doesn't say a word about it.

We eat in comfortable silence, exchanging occasional glances. The sun brightens the cabin, chasing away lingering shadows of fear and uncertainty. For the first time in days, my shoulders actually relax. I sneak another look at Brody, catching his small smile before he quickly looks away. It makes me wonder if maybe, just maybe, waking up to mornings like this—safe, warm, and with someone who makes me feel genuinely seen—is exactly what I've always needed.

After breakfast, I curl up on the overstuffed chair by the window, wrapping a thick quilt around myself as I watch Brody step off the back porch. The morning fog still hangs over the trees, creating a sense of solitude. For the first time in days, my mind isn't racing; it's simply quiet.

I close my eyes and drift off because I'm so relaxed.

When I wake hours later, Brody is nowhere to be found. I get up and step out onto the porch, letting the midday breeze brush across my cheeks. The forest is silent, bathed in the muted sunlight that filters through the trees. I breathe in fresh air, letting it fill my lungs, and take it all in.

The only thing that pulls me away is the rhythmic sound of an axe splitting wood.

I glance to my left and see Brody standing near a woodpile, muscles flexing with each powerful swing of the blade. His tattoos are on full display, and he's a work of art. I freeze, momentarily mesmerized by his movements—the precision, the control. The wood splits effortlessly beneath his hands, pieces scattering neatly around him like confetti.

He pauses, rolling his shoulders and stretching slightly. His dark hair clings damply to his forehead, and even from here, I can see the focused intensity in his deep blue eyes. I'm captivated by his strength. It's not flashy or arrogant, but solid and dependable.

My stomach knots as my thoughts drift to Micah. I recognize him for what he really is—a monster cleverly hidden behind smiles and whispered promises. The shame of believing in that illusion claws at my throat. How could I have been so blind?

Yet, watching Brody, I clearly see the stark contrast between the two men.

Brody doesn't wear masks. He doesn't hide behind carefully constructed lies. He's authentic and fiercely honest. He never pretends to be someone he isn't, just himself. I trust him more than I've trusted anyone, but still, questions about him linger beneath my skin.

He swings again, powerful and precise, sending pieces of wood tumbling to the ground. The force behind his motions hints at something personal and unresolved. It's raw and almost painful.

I bite my lip, curiosity mixing with cautious hesitation.

Why is Brody so protective of me? His loyalty to Billie explains some of it, but not all—not this burning intensity I feel from him. There's an unseen layer beneath his steady surface, and he guards it as if his life depends on it.

He sets down the axe, wiping sweat from his forehead with the back of his arm. His breathing is heavy but even. His gaze lifts, meeting mine across the distance. A slow, soft smile warms his features, as if he felt me watching the whole time.

"Enjoying the view?" he calls lightly, the teasing tone breaking through my thoughts.

Heat rises to my cheeks, but I manage to smile back. "Impressive technique."

He chuckles, shaking his head. "Plenty of practice."

He takes a drink of water, then continues with his mission.

My thoughts still swirl; I know he's had decades of practice hiding his secrets, but I hope one day he'll trust me enough to share them.

I find myself watching him, noting how the muscles of his back shift beneath his T-shirt with each careful movement. I notice a gentleness that makes him even more intriguing.

His expression is distant, almost haunted, and I realize how little I actually know about him—this man who's risked everything to keep me safe.

He must sense me watching again because he turns his head slightly, his blue eyes locking on to mine.

"You okay over there?" he asks, his voice soft.

"Just thinking," I reply.

"Dangerous habit." He smirks, but his eyes hold mine, gentle and attentive. "Care to share?"

I pause, biting my lip, as he sets the axe down and moves closer to me.

"I was just thinking about how little I actually know about you. I mean, you were always around, growing up, but we're not kids anymore. So much has happened."

He raises an eyebrow, his expression becoming cautiously playful. "I'm an open book, Harp."

"Oh, come on. No, you're not." I laugh. "You're more like a tightly sealed diary—locked twice and hidden under a mattress."

A deep chuckle rumbles from his chest, and I like the sound of it. "Maybe. Or maybe you're just too afraid to ask. I've never lied to you."

I study him, tracing the shadows beneath his eyes and the careful guard behind his smile. "Maybe a little," I admit honestly. "You never talk about yourself, and I don't want to bombard you."

His gaze drops, thoughtful. "I'm not trying to be secretive. It's just … some things, like my past, are hard to discuss, so I don't."

The hint of vulnerability in his voice tugs at my heart. It's strange to see him like this—strong yet guarded, gentle but distant. Brody is a man who has scars that I can't begin to understand, but I want to.

"That's okay," I whisper. "I don't want to pry."

His eyes lift again, meeting mine. "You aren't prying. I've just gotten good at avoiding conversations."

"Why?" I ask.

He exhales slowly, fingers threading together as he stares down at his hands. "Because, sometimes, it's easier not to talk about things, especially things I can't change."

I sense an untouched pain beneath his carefully chosen words. The urge to comfort him, to understand him, overtakes me.

"You're not alone in that feeling," I say. "I get it. Trust me."

His lips curve into a slight, vulnerable smile. "I know you do."

We stand quietly for a moment, but his eyes still carry that faint flicker of something unresolved.

"Tell me one thing then," I say. "Anything."

He considers this for a long moment, and when I think he won't answer, his voice comes. "My parents used to bring me here when I was little. Before they passed. That's why I love it here—it's the last place that ever felt truly safe for me."

My chest tightens at his confession. Such a small detail, but it feels enormous, coming from Brody—like a treasured secret he rarely shares. His parents and sister died in a plane crash when he was fourteen, and he moved in with Easton and Weston. He's been around them for as long as I have.

"Thank you," I whisper.

His eyes hold mine. "You're welcome."

As we lapse back into silence, something shifts subtly between us. I've glimpsed a side of Brody that he's protected, and the mystery of him only makes him more compelling.

Maybe we're both learning that there's courage in letting someone else in, even just a little bit.

We linger on the porch for another moment, the intensity of the earlier conversation still stretching between us. Finally, Brody nods, offering me a gentle but reserved glance before returning to the pile of wood he was chopping before I interrupted him.

I step back into the cabin, feeling oddly restless. Needing something to distract myself, I decide food would be a good start.

The kitchen is tiny, rustic, but well-kept. I open the cabinets, hoping for inspiration, but find rows of canned goods and very little else. I frown slightly, picking up a can of ravioli and some sliced carrots. Cooking has never been my thing, but even I can manage canned goods—at least, I hope so.

I pop open the ravioli, grimacing at the tomato slop, and carefully dump it into a ceramic bowl. The carrots are next, and I scoop them into another smaller bowl. Pausing, I stare at the microwave like it's a foreign object, fingers hovering over the buttons. This thing looks ancient.

After a minute of frustration, I settle on three minutes, hoping that's enough for both.

The microwave hums, and I lean against the counter, my mind wandering back to Brody.

When the microwave finally beeps, I pull the bowls out carefully, the ceramic hot against my fingertips. The ravioli looks questionable, but at least it's steaming. I stir it and take a small bite. It's not as bad as I expected.

I glance out the kitchen window, watching Brody swing the axe again, muscles rippling under his shirt. Deciding I shouldn't disturb him too abruptly, I take a few moments to collect my thoughts before stepping outside again.

"Brody," I call from the porch steps, my voice breaking the silence.

He pauses mid-swing, the axe hanging loosely in his grip. Sweat glistens on his forehead. His eyes are warm but still carefully guarded as he shifts his attention toward me.

"Hungry?"

He hesitates, then gives a small nod, placing the axe against the woodpile and wiping his hands on his jeans as he walks toward me. We step back inside, and I lead him toward the table.

"It's not exactly gourmet," I admit sheepishly, gesturing at the food. "But ravioli and carrots were pretty much all I could find. Well, and eggs."

His lips turn up into an amused half-smile as he takes a seat. "Works for me. I should've stocked up before bringing you out here. I stopped at a small gas station and grabbed what I could for breakfast."

"It's okay." I slide his bowl across to him, taking the seat opposite. "We'll definitely need groceries soon, though, unless you have a deep love for canned Italian."

"I don't," he says simply, and we share a laugh, easing some of the lingering tension.

A comfortable silence settles between us, but beneath the easy moment, I feel something deeper still simmering. I glance at Brody, his gaze distant and thoughtful as he eats.

"You know," I start, pushing around a ravioli in my bowl, "being here, out in the quiet, it reminds me a little of my childhood. Before my mom died, we used to spend summers and early fall in Colorado in Cozy Creek. I remember running barefoot through the grass, feeling completely safe and at ease, away from the city. It felt like home too. Now Zane is there living his best life."

Brody watches me, setting his fork down and giving me his full attention. Encouraged, I continue.

"I lost her when I was eight," I say, a familiar ache tightening my chest.

"I know," he says. Because he was there. He's always been there.

"Ever since, I've carried this emptiness inside me. Like there's a piece of me missing. I've spent years trying to fill it, always with the wrong things or the wrong people. My dad was never around much because he was too busy running the company. So, it was just me and my brother and Billie." I lift my gaze to his, vulnerability pooling behind my eyes. "It's exhausting, always chasing something you know you'll never get back. For me, I lost my sense of family. It was never the same after Mom was gone."

Something flickers in his eyes, as though my words resonated deeply within him. A shadow crosses his features, and his jaw tightens as he shifts in his seat.

Brody visibly stiffens, his body instantly guarded again. I know he lost his parents and sister. I know he understands grief more than even I do.

"Thank you," he says, but I see tension return to his shoulders. He's rebuilding those invisible walls to keep me out.

The openness I glimpsed is replaced by a neutral expression. He clears his throat, turning his gaze toward the window.

"We all have our scars, Harp," he says, his voice low. "Some of us are just better at hiding them."

I nod slowly, feeling the careful evasion in his answer, but not wanting to push too far. The heaviness in the air is undeniable.

"Fair enough," I reply, easing the tension with a gentle smile.

Brody's expression softens again, an apology in his eyes. I give him a reassuring smile. Opening up to him wasn't easy, but it was a start.

We finish eating without saying much else. My curiosity still lingers. Whatever secrets Brody guards are deeply rooted and painful. Despite his careful deflection, I feel closer than ever to understanding him and unraveling the mystery behind his strength. I thought maybe it was the loss of his parents or something he experienced when he was in the Marines. Now, I'm not so sure what happened or why he's so guarded, but I hope, one day, he really does tell me. And when that time comes, I will be there to listen.

10

BRODY

After dinner, the lingering tension between us evaporates.

It's surprising how quickly Harper has settled into the rhythm of the cabin. The soft sound of her moving through the space, creating a peaceful background noise, is something I didn't realize I'd been missing.

I gather an armful of firewood from the neatly stacked pile on the porch, then step back inside, shutting the door behind me. Harper is curled comfortably on the sofa, a fluffy blanket wrapped around her shoulders. She's flipping through a magazine that has to be from the early 2000s.

Harper looks up at me, her bright blue eyes following my every movement.

"What are you smiling about?" I ask, suspicion edging my voice as I place the logs carefully in the fireplace.

I strike a match, and the dry wood crackles to life instantly. Flames flicker and cast long shadows around the room. It was in the upper fifties today, but it will dip into the lower forties tonight.

"Just enjoying the view." She shrugs, pulling the blanket a little higher, clearly hiding a grin behind its soft folds.

I lift an eyebrow, feeling heat creep up my neck. Her teasing always seems to catch me off guard.

"Should I be concerned?"

"*Definitely,*" she replies playfully, her eyes twinkling mischievously as she reaches for the remote and flips through channels. "Now, what kind of entertainment do we have in this secret hideout of yours?"

I settle onto the couch beside her, intentionally leaving just enough space between us to maintain some semblance of control. Her warmth radiates toward me, tempting me closer. I swallow, focusing instead on the TV.

"It's not a hideout. It's a dainty cabin." I smile, remembering my mom saying that once.

Harper hums thoughtfully, a smile tugging at the corners of her mouth. "Hmm. Cozy, rustic, secluded, only one bedroom—sounds like a hideout to me."

I shoot her a playful scowl, but her teasing feels comfortable, normal—something we haven't had in a long time. Without thinking, I tug the remote from her hand, flipping to *The Golden Girls* and turning up the volume slightly. I smirk when Sophia says some smart-ass comment. I think she's my spirit animal.

"Oh my God," she says. "You actually like *The Golden Girls.*"

"Shut up."

Harper scoffs, laughing. "You're a softy."

"You'd better keep my secret," I tell her, lifting a brow.

"It's one of my faves too."

Harper moves closer to me and rests her head against my shoulder. I don't move, nearly frozen in place as I zero in on Blanche, acting like a scandalous Southern belle again.

Laughter falls out of Harper's mouth, and then the show cuts to the next commercial break. "If I were a Golden Girl, I think I'd be Blanche."

I chew on my lip, and she sits upright, glaring at me.

"Oh my God, you agree!"

I tilt my head. "Come on. It's obvious."

"Yeah, well, you'd be Sophia! Crotchety, always mouthing off before leaving the room."

I shrug. "No lies detected."

"And who would Billie be?"

We meet each other's eyes and say, "Dorothy," at the same time, and laughter escapes us.

It feels good. It feels right.

Our shoulders brush, and my breath catches. Suddenly, the air feels charged with something different, warmer. Neither of us moves away.

The episode comes back on, pulling our attention back, and the ladies are arguing in the living room about property taxes. Dorothy's wearing a puffy-sleeved shirt, and it does kind of remind me of Billie.

I lean back on the couch, kicking off my boots to get more comfortable. I can still feel the heat of Harper's body close to me. She returns to my shoulder, and I wrap my arm around her, keeping my hand relaxed. We sit in silence, my heart racing, watching my favorite fucking show in the world.

She breathes me in, and I try to ignore it. We laugh at the same jokes the girlies make and scoff at the same time too. Harper keeps her hands to herself, which I'm happy for. At least we still have some boundaries. But I know with every passing second, our guards are falling.

One of us has to stay strong, and every time, it is me.

Harper has tried her damnedest to crack me and has never succeeded. I don't know what her result will be this time.

Her presence beside me feels natural, easy, and yet I feel the undercurrent sweeping below us.

"What other shows do you like?" she finally says, breaking the silence.

I glance at her. "*Frasier.*"

"No way! I love *Frasier*. They kinda remind me of Easton and Weston."

"So, I guess that makes me their dad?"

Laughter howls from her. "You are absolutely Martin. The reality-check character who understands the real world, outside of wine tastings and opera houses. Hilarious."

She's smiling so wide, and I love to see it.

"This feels right," I confess, watching her carefully.

Her eyes meet mine, the playful glint replaced by something softer, deeper. "It does."

She swallows hard, and I look away from her. Her vulnerability is so rare and precious, and I feel so goddamn lucky that she shares this part of herself with me.

I force myself to swallow past the sudden dryness. "It's really good to see."

"What is?" she asks.

"Your real smile."

Her gaze softens further, and she nudges my shoulder with hers. "What am I going to do with you, Brody Calloway? I think I might keep you all to myself, just like this."

I try to hold back a smile but fail. The admission settles heavily between us. I don't move away as she snuggles into me. The firelight flickers over us, and for once, I don't question the closeness. For once, I allow myself to enjoy it.

An hour later, we're fully invested in an episode of *The X Files*. The eerie music during a dramatic scene bounces off the cabin walls. The scene grows suspenseful.

"Ah!" I say, jump-scaring her.

"Fuck!" she screams, then playfully smacks me. "I used to hate it when you did that."

Harper scowls at me, and I'm unable to suppress my grin.

"You and Billie would scream so loud that my fucking ears would ring."

"You deserved it," she says. Her head rests back on my shoulder. "One time, I peed myself because you'd scared me so bad."

"Aw. I'm sorry," I say, but I'm sincere. "I didn't mean to go that far."

"It's okay. I got you back."

I tilt my head. "How?"

"I stole a pair of your military jogging pants."

I shake my head. "The gray ones with the super-soft inside that say *USMC* on the thigh?"

She nods. "One time, when you were home, Billie and I snuck into your room and dug through your shit."

"How dare you! I always wondered where those had gone," I say teasingly, but it warms my heart that she took them.

She smiles. "I still have them. They're tucked in one of my drawers at my place. More comfortable than they were back then."

"After all this time?" I ask, realizing the fifteen-year-old mystery of what happened to those has been solved. "Guess that will no longer keep me up at night."

I glance back at the TV, but Harper pulls my attention back to her.

"Years ago, I had a boyfriend break up with me because I refused to get rid of them. Was also accused of fucking around with a Marine over it. Was really good times. It was kinda how I determined if someone was a red flag or not."

My brow lifts. "My stolen clothes ended one of your relationships?"

"Actually … it was kinda how I determined all of my relationships. If the guy I was with became insecure over old joggers, I couldn't be with them. *Major red flag.*"

"How many relationships are we talking about?" I ask.

"Five," she mutters.

I don't know what to say. "You're welcome?"

"Saved me a lot of trouble, to be honest. So, a thank-you is totally in order. Thanks."

I smirk, knowing I need to get a grip as I sink deeper into the worn cushions of the couch. We fall into silence, watching TV together. It's slow and easygoing, and my eyes grow heavy because I'm so fucking comfortable with her. I try to keep them open, but sleep takes me under, and I drift away.

I don't know how long I'm out; I only wake when I feel Harper's arm slung over my stomach as we hold each other tightly, like the other might disappear. I try to steady my breathing, realizing only two hours have passed. She stirs and sits up, pulling away as she realizes how close we are. I immediately feel the loss of her touch.

"I fell asleep," she says. Her hair is pushed up on the side. With a barely awake sleepy face, she looks adorable.

"Sleeping Beauty is awake," I say, knowing she's always loved her naps.

Harper rolls her pretty eyes, grabbing a throw pillow and hitting me lightly on the arm. "Hush. You're comfortable. I can't help it."

I reach for the remote, flipping through channels, not landing on anything interesting.

"Have you ever celebrated a holiday here?" Harper asks. "I can almost imagine a Christmas tree in the corner."

I smile, remembering the one Christmas we spent here. My mom, dad, sister, and I were all huddled in this small space. It felt a million miles away from the city.

"A few times," I tell her, reminiscing. "One of my favorites is Fourth of July. The town throws a huge celebration with a parade, a festival, and an incredible fireworks show. Everyone watches from blankets in the town square. It's an experience. A must."

"Really?" she asks. "Wow. I'd love to go."

"It's a date," I tell her.

Her cheeks heat. "A *date* date?"

I see how her heart rate increases in her neck and notice her grin. She wants it to be. Maybe I do too.

"I didn't stutter," I confirm.

"Okay then." She shyly glances away from me, then meets my eyes.

I can't stop the amused grin that pulls at my lips as I watch her struggle with that revelation, until she suddenly blurts out, "Like a *date*, date?"

"Harp, you know that thing you do where you overanalyze things for no reason?"

She nods. "I'm doing it, aren't I?"

"Yeah. You're being a Frasier right now," I explain, referring to something she might understand a little more clearly.

"Yeah? Well, you're being a Martin."

She chuckles, then growls as she picks up a pillow from behind her and playfully smacks me with it. I grab another one and pop her upside the head.

Harper leaps off the couch, ready to go to battle with me. "Did you seriously forget who my brother was?"

I grab another pillow. "How could I? You both won't let anyone forget. Don't go to war with me, Harp."

"Then concede and make me breakfast in the morning, Calloway!" she declares proudly, her grin infectious.

"And if I don't?" I tease, shaking my head, unable to hide how damn happy she makes me feel with her competitive nature. It's ingrained in all the Alexanders.

"Then prepare to lose," she retorts, snatching a big cushion off the chair by the window.

With all her strength, she steps forward and whacks me with it, and it actually hurts.

I drop the pillow and hold my hands up. "Breakfast is yours. You win. I'll drive to the small store at the bottom of the mountain tomorrow morning, and I'll grab food. We can go grocery shopping next week."

"Music to my ears. I don't want to be in public yet," she says with a firm head nod and a smile.

She returns the cushion to the chair, and a comfortable silence settles between us. It's only punctuated by the crackling of the fire. I note the curve of her smile and the ease in her posture. For the first time since I brought her here, she looks genuinely relaxed.

"You really are something—you know that?" I say, my voice deeper than I intended.

Her cheeks faintly flush, her eyes brightening with warmth. "Could say the same about you."

I surrender and sit on the couch. Harper rejoins me, and we return to where we were.

The evening slips away, and it's filled with gentle teasing and effortless conversation while we watch TV. Though it's late, it's almost like neither of us wants the night to end because, tomorrow morning, the magic that surrounds us might be gone.

Harper's breathing shifts against my shoulder, and I realize she's fallen asleep. I'm not paying attention to anything but her. My entire focus narrows down to the woman beside me—her body warm and relaxed, pressed into the curve of my side. It's easy.

My heart jolts in my chest, a sharp reminder that this—this casual intimacy—is far from simple.

I glance down carefully, trying not to disturb her. Harper's dark brown hair cascades loosely over my arm, and her lips are parted slightly in peaceful rest. Something about her right now squeezes my heart, pulling at feelings I've tried desperately to bury.

"Brody," she murmurs, shifting even closer, her cheek pressed firmly against my chest.

I freeze, every muscle in my body tensing for a heartbeat before slowly, cautiously relaxing as she holds me tighter. I'm not going anywhere. She's still asleep.

I click off the TV, and the cabin plunges into a comfortable silence, filled only with the faint crackle of the fireplace. Memories I've fought to keep locked away start to surface—Eden's laugh, Eden's strength, Eden curled up next to me, just like this.

Tonight, Harper's warmth against me is a balm, not salt in a wound.

She stirs again, a faint sigh escaping her lips. Gently, I twist my body, slipping one arm beneath her knees and the other around her shoulders, lifting her easily. Her eyelids flutter open, her sleepy gaze confused at first, then softening when she realizes it's me.

"I'm floating," she says.

"It's magic," I whisper. *Just like tonight*, I think as I walk slowly toward her room.

She curls instinctively closer, her head tucking beneath my chin. The scent of her shampoo—coconut and vanilla—wraps around me.

"You're carrying me," she whispers, sounding surprised and something else—grateful maybe.

Her trust—even now, even after the betrayal she's experienced —hits me harder than I would have expected.

"Yeah," I reply, my voice barely audible.

Carefully, I lower her onto the bed, making sure the pillow supports her head just right. Pulling the blankets around her shoulders, my hand lingers a second too long.

Her eyes briefly meet mine again, heavy yet filled with warmth. "Night, Brody."

"Night, Harp," I reply.

"Will you stay?" she asks.

"I can't, but I'm just a holler away, okay?" I say, forcing myself to step away.

Closing the door, I stand alone in the dimly lit hallway. I exhale deeply, tension knotting between my shoulder blades. This— whatever's unfolding between Harper and me—is dangerous. It's complicated. It's fucking terrifying. And as much as I want to bust through that door and hold her until she falls asleep, I can't. But as I return to the living room, the spot on my shoulder where her head rested still feels warm, like a part of her remains.

Maybe I'm losing this fight against my own emotions, but

tonight, for the first time in forever, I don't want to keep running from them.

A lingering smile touches my lips, and I realize I don't feel weighed down by my past. Instead, there's a flicker of hope, a feeling that maybe, just maybe, something good can come from all this chaos. Maybe, in some universe, Harper and I can be something more.

I chuckle to myself, shaking my head—because she's the one who's supposed to see the silver lining in shitty situations, not me.

Maybe it's because she is one, and damn, did she shine bright tonight.

I WAKE EARLY, MUSCLES TIGHT AND ACHING FROM THE COUCH AND the restless night spent wrestling with memories and emotions I'd buried. Harper being in the next room didn't help matters. It only reminded me of how easily she'd slipped beneath my carefully maintained armor. I'm teetering on a dangerous line between protecting her and falling for her.

Pushing those thoughts aside, I step outside into the brisk morning air and lock the cabin. The property is wrapped in a hazy dawn, the sky streaked in hues of muted oranges and pale pinks. Wisps of clouds stream across the sky, and for some reason, it feels lighter, like it's a new beginning to something exciting. My breath smokes in front of me as I move to the car that's covered in a layer of frost.

I take the short five-minute drive down the mountain to the small store that carries a few groceries for those who don't want to drive all the way to town. I grab more groceries than I intended, enough to last us at least five or six more days. I double up on bacon, sausage, eggs, bread, milk, and peanut butter cups. They're Harper's favorite.

I pay and quickly rush back to the cabin. After I park, I get out of the car and grab the bags, knowing I've been gone for less than fifteen minutes. Through the kitchen window, movement catches my eye.

Harper's awake, her slender frame illuminated by the soft morning light. She rummages through the cupboards, and I watch her carefully. She looks softer like this, absolutely fucking gorgeous in the muted glow of morning.

I move onto the porch and press my code into the door lock, and it clicks open.

"There you are!" she says, smiling, happy as fuck to see me. It's undeniable.

"I always keep my promises to you," I say, placing the groceries and keys on the counter.

She looks at me with wide eyes, her hair a mess from sleep. Her pouty lips turn up into a smile. "I was just going to make us some coffee, so—"

"Harp," I interrupt as I add wood to the fireplace and start the fire to take the chill out of the room. "I conceded. I owe you."

Her eyes sparkle with amusement as she considers it. "How about we do it together since you *let* me win? I promise not to burn the place down."

I hesitate before nodding, trying not to let the easy warmth of her smile slip past my defenses any further. "Deal."

Side by side, we navigate the tiny kitchen. Harper pulls the items from the bags while I make coffee.

"Peanut butter cups?" she asks as the rich aroma quickly fills the cabin.

"Your favorite," I say, glancing over at her as she smiles.

Then I see her emotions break, and she almost starts crying.

"Harp," I say, "what's up?"

She shakes her head. "Nothing. I know you think I'm losing it because I'm crying over candy. But … it's just a sweet gesture and something only Billie has done for me. Thank you. I wouldn't have thought you'd remember."

"Ah, well, you're welcome. I only have one request though. When you do eat them, you'd better dig the middle out and stick your tongue through the hole, like old times."

Laughter spills out of her.

"Deal," she says as she awkwardly cracks an egg into a bowl, tiny shards of shell dropping inside.

I chuckle, dipping my finger into the bowl to remove them. "Maybe you should stick to making coffee."

"You already did that." She nudges me playfully with her elbow. "Give me something easier."

Grinning, I shake my head. "Or let me teach you."

I take a step closer to her and swipe an egg out of the carton. "When you crack it, you never do it on the side of the bowl because of the edge. Instead, try a flat surface." I smack it down on the counter to show her. "Then you lightly dig your thumbs where the crack is. See? No shell."

She stands back and watches me, impressed. "Where did you learn to cook?"

"My mom," I admit, smiling at the old memories. "Breakfast was always her favorite. One day, I'll have to make you her famous sausage bread."

"You'd better," Harper says, following my instructions. "And I'll make you my mom's roasted pumpkin seeds."

"You'd better," I repeat back to her.

She's genuinely excited when she cracks them and no shells are in the bowl. "You're a great teacher."

"Maybe it's the student," I offer. "Three more, please."

"Yes, Chef," she offers with a wink.

There's an easy silence as we work, our arms occasionally brushing, each contact sending tiny jolts of electricity through me. It's frustratingly pleasant.

"Brody?" Harper speaks, pausing her task to look up at me. Her expression is sincere, vulnerable.

My pulse quickens involuntarily. "Yeah?"

She hesitates, her gaze dropping momentarily. "Thank you for everything. I know I've been a lot to handle."

Gratitude and sadness mingle in her voice.

"Hey," I say, turning fully toward her. "I know you're Little Miss Disaster, but you're not a lot to handle. It's been fun. I think I needed this."

A faint blush colors her cheeks, and she ducks her head shyly. "That's some high praise, coming from Mr. Grumpy."

"Don't let it go to your head," I say, unable to hide the smile pulling at my lips.

I put cheesy scrambled eggs, sausage, and toast on plates for us. Harper grabs forks and napkins, and we sit at the small table together.

"More coffee?" she asks, and I nod.

Harper grabs the pot and fills both of our mugs.

The tension of the past few days has quickly been replaced by comfortable companionship. I watch her discreetly as she eats, noting the ease in her movements, the genuine smile she shares freely.

When we finish eating, she reaches to clear the dishes, but I stop her, my fingers wrapping lightly around her wrist.

"Let me take care of it."

Our eyes lock, and the air thickens instantly. We're actually closer than I realized, and her breath hitches. Harper's gaze drops briefly to my mouth before meeting my gaze. My heart warns me to pull away, to maintain our distance, but I find myself frozen, completely under her spell.

Just as the air between us grows impossibly charged, Harper draws back, offering a shy, teasing smile that nearly undoes me completely.

"Careful, Calloway," she warns, her voice teasing yet uncertain. "I don't want to embarrass myself again."

I clear my throat, forcing a smirk, remembering the time when she was eighteen and tried to kiss me, but I stopped her. Harper was embarrassed, and I told her not to be, but I could not cross that line with her.

This time, she steps away, leaving me staring after her, the space between us feeling emptier than before. I take a deep breath, steadying myself against the unfamiliar surge that rushes through me. It's a spark, a flicker in the dark, and I can almost feel its heat.

No matter how much I fight it, she's quickly slipping past my defenses, and I'm not sure I can stop it. Or if I want to.

As we finish cleaning up our breakfast mess, Harper stands by the sink, staring out the kitchen window, her eyes bright as she scans over the backyard. I brace myself, knowing that look like the back of my hand. It always means trouble, though I have to admit, it's an expression of hers I've missed.

"Hey," she says, spinning to face me. "Can we go outside and play?"

I burst into laughter, recognizing the restless energy radiating off of her. She crosses her arms in playful defiance.

"Come on. Fresh air, a little adventure—it's exactly what we need," she practically begs, and I can't deny her.

On the way here, I stopped and got her a few plain T-shirts and leggings, along with a pair of off-brand tennis shoes. It's nothing nice, considering it was a small general store, but at least she has something to wear that fits her.

"Fine. But if we see a bear, I'm tripping you first." I exhale, giving in, but I was going to anyway.

Her eyes widen in mock outrage, but her laughter breaks through anyway. "Wow, thanks for having my back."

"Always," I tease lightly. "Get dressed, and we'll go."

It takes her less than two minutes, excitement in every step she takes. We move outside, the crisp air instantly waking my senses. Harper bounds, her footsteps light across the earth.

She throws a glance over her shoulder, grinning mischievously. "Are you coming or crawling?"

"I'm pacing myself," I answer dryly, pretending annoyance. Truth is, I enjoy seeing her so carefree and joyful, like the weight of the last few days is momentarily forgotten.

We wander deeper into the woods, sunlight filtering through the branches, casting patterns of gold across the trail. Harper effortlessly skips over exposed tree roots and fallen branches, occasionally spinning around to taunt me.

"You know, for someone so big and tough, you're pretty slow," she teases, hands on her hips, eyes sparkling.

I raise an eyebrow, fighting the urge to smile. "I'm conserving energy."

We hike for another hour, and I know the trail continues up to one of the lookouts on the mountain, but when we get to a meadow in the clearing, she stops and admires it.

"This is beautiful," she whispers.

"I agree," I say—however, I'm only looking at her.

She turns and sees me, shyly smiling. We hold an unspoken conversation, and I feel emotions streaming out of her in waves. I watch her, heart pounding. This is uncharted territory, but as her smile lingers, I can't bring myself to care.

As things between us grow too intense, she clears her throat. "Last one to the cabin owes the other dinner."

Before I can protest, she's already sprinting away, hair flying behind her, fluttering in the wind. Shaking my head, I chase after her, deliberately keeping a few paces behind. Her cheeks are flushed, eyes bright with adrenaline and laughter.

"Come on! Don't go easy on me," she hollers, so I pick up my pace.

When I try to push past her, she kicks her foot out and trips me.

"Cheater!" I say as I tumble to the ground, but it's more of a maneuver than a complete stop, and I pop back up.

"Oh my fucking God, are you a Terminator?" she yells, sprinting as hard as she can.

"Yes!" I say as we emerge from the forest's edge, the cabin coming into view.

Harper runs as fast as she can, and while I can easily pass her, I let her push forward, crossing her imaginary finish line on the porch.

Harper raises her fists victoriously. "Yes!" she shouts, spinning around, breathless. "Dinner's on you, Calloway!"

I catch up to her, stopping close, unable to suppress my smile, not even breathless.

Her joy is contagious, and for a moment, we're both free of every heavy thought, every worry that's been weighing us down.

"Congratulations," I say, chuckling. "You earned it."

She grins, stepping closer, her gaze softening. "You're terrible at losing on purpose, you know."

I shrug, pretending to be innocent.

She studies me knowingly, eyes full of unspoken emotions, as we step inside the cabin.

The afternoon drifts by in a haze, and by the time the sun starts dragging low across the trees, the world around the cabin softens into that lazy kind of quiet I can only ever find here. This is easy. Real. But also a dream in a way I'm trying not to think about too much.

I chop more wood, making sure we have enough for the next few days, as Harper stretches out on the porch swing, wrapped in one of the cabin's old quilts, her bare feet peeking out the bottom. I stack the logs on the porch as she watches the sunset, looking half-wild, half-angelic, with her hair a mess from the breeze. A smile touches my lips as I step inside, grabbing snacks, thinking about how her cheeks are sun pink from the sunshine she soaked in earlier.

She needed it. We both did.

I nudge the door open with my shoulder, carrying two sodas and a big, half-smashed bag of cheese puffs under my arm. Classy as hell.

"You planning on staying out here all night?" I ask, passing her on the porch.

Harper lifts her head lazily, and that slow, sexy grin is already forming.

"Are you volunteering to carry me inside, Calloway? Because you'll have to wrestle me for the privilege."

I chuckle, handing her the soda as I drop onto the swing beside her. "Harp, if you want my body on top of you, just ask."

She scoffs as she opens the cola with a hiss. "You actually wish!"

The swing rocks beneath us, the old chains creaking in rhythm. For a few minutes, we just sit there, sipping and watching the sunset torch the sky in molten golds and purples.

Without thinking, she nudges my knee with her foot, trying to annoy me. I catch her ankle before she can pull it back, my hand curling around the warm skin.

"You're gonna fuck around and find out."

She wiggles her toes at me, grinning. "I think I already have."

God help me, she's not wrong.

I don't let her go right away. My thumb brushes the inside of her ankle—a small, thoughtless motion—and suddenly, everything feels sharper, clearer.

"Even if I annoy you, I know you'll miss me when this is over," she says.

I look right at her and say low, "I will."

For a second, the swing keeps rocking, and neither of us says anything.

Then she sits upright, bumping her shoulder into mine. "Careful, Calloway. That almost sounded like feelings. We both know you don't have those."

I huff out a laugh, raking a hand through my hair. "Don't panic, Sleeping Beauty. I'm not proposing."

"Yet."

She laughs—really laughs—and I can feel the tension ease between us, even if her words are wrapped with truth.

Whatever this is lingering between us is waiting to capture us both.

"It's been a long time since I trusted anyone enough to want them close," I admit.

Harper doesn't speak right away. She doesn't tease my words away or press for more information. She just lets my words float around us, like a firefly in the night.

"I like that," she admits.

A few minutes later, she shifts, snagging the bag of cheese puffs. Without warning, Harper grabs a handful and pelts me with them.

"What the hell?" I duck as neon-orange puffs bounce off my chest and arm, leaving dust in their wake.

"You're getting way too sentimental," she says, laughing, her eyes sparkling like the damn sunset. "Consider this an emotional intervention."

I reach down, grab a rogue puff, and flick it back at her with deadly aim, nailing her square in the forehead.

She gasps like I mortally wounded her. "That's assault with a cheesy weapon!"

"Self-defense," I say, deadpan, grabbing more ammo.

Within seconds, cheese puffs are flying back and forth across the porch.

The swing rocks dangerously. Harper's laughing so hard that she's crying, trying to dodge and throw at the same time.

Finally, she surrenders, collapsing into my side, breathless and grinning.

"You're a menace, Calloway," she says, poking me in the ribs half-heartedly.

I wiggle away from her, not wanting her to realize how fucking ticklish I am.

When I glance at her, I tilt my head, catching her gaze, as something heavier stirs under the playful wreckage of our little war.

"You fucking love it," I say, voice rough around the edges.

"You're right about that," she admits, before she tucks her face against my shoulder, like she's hiding from her admission.

But I felt the electricity streaming between us and saw the sparkle in her eye.

I know, with bone-deep certainty, that I'm not just falling for her. I'm already hers. And somehow, she's mine. Neither of us is brave enough to admit it, but eventually, we won't be able to deny it.

11

HARPER

The smell of strong coffee pulls me out of sleep before the sunlight does.

For a minute, I lie there, half buried in soft blankets, listening to the creak of the porch swing just outside the bedroom window.

I don't move. Because the second I do, I'll have to admit last night actually happened.

The laughter. The way Brody caught my ankle like he didn't want to let go. How he looked at me like I wasn't just another mission he was stuck babysitting, but something he couldn't seem to walk away from.

I roll onto my side with a groan, dragging the quilt over my head like it might muffle the memory.

It was the magic of the sunset. Or maybe the playfulness of the cheese-puff fight got to our heads. Except … I felt the undeniable electric charge streaming between us. The one that's always there, like it's lurking in the shadows, waiting. Underneath the jokes, there was something bigger than us both, and the thought of that scares the hell out of me.

I sit up, the quilt puddling in my lap, and run my hands through my hair as thoughts of Brody fill my mind. The two of us is what

I've always hoped for, something I dreamed about as a lovesick teenager. Brody was always my secret crush, the uncatchable one.

Nope. Not even going there. Not when we are stuck in this cabin together for God knows how long. I have absolutely zero chance of surviving if I start acting lovesick. I push the thoughts away.

I shove my feet into a pair of socks and shuffle toward the kitchen, determined to drown out last night with caffeine and denial.

Brody's already up—because, of course, he is—and judging by the trail of fresh wood chips tracked across the floor, he's been outside, chopping things. Probably to work off whatever emotional slipup he'd made. A fort protects his heart, one I haven't been able to overtake.

I catch myself smiling at the thoughts. They're uninvited, those traitorous little things.

No. No smiling about Brody Calloway. No letting him get under my skin either. I'm here to clear my head, not lose my heart. But even still, I can't help the fantasy of it all. Micah already feels like a distant memory. I will erase him from my mind completely.

I grab a mug from the cabinet and fill it full of coffee, ignoring how my hands feel lighter than they should.

Somewhere in the back of my mind, a scandalous little voice whispers, *You make that man forget his rules.*

And even worse, he makes me forget mine too.

By the time I wander outside, the sun is creeping higher. The grass still has dew, but eventually, it will disappear.

I spot him immediately—Brody Calloway, an emotional disaster, pretending to be one with the earth.

He's at the edge of the property, raking piles of leaves that honestly don't need raking. His shirt is rolled up to his elbows, his jeans are dusted with dirt, and there's a determined set to his shoulders that screams, *Leave me the hell alone.*

Subtle. Really subtle, Calloway.

I cross my arms and lean against the porch rail, watching him for a few minutes. It's not just the way he's attacking the yard like it pissed him off that concerns me, but how he won't even glance toward the cabin. Like if he doesn't look at me, he can pretend he didn't feel the shift between us last night.

I *should* let him have his little retreat, but watching him rake the same patch of grass over and over like he's fighting demons? Yeah, that's not happening. I see through him like he's glass, and I won't allow the self-torture.

I hop down the porch steps and saunter toward him, calling out casually, "Careful, Calloway. Keep that up, and you'll start a turf war with the squirrels."

Brody doesn't stop raking, but I catch the twitch of his mouth, the almost smile he's fighting like hell to bury. He jabs the metal rake into the ground and finally looks at me, wiping his arm across his forehead.

"What do you want, Harp?" he asks, gruff but not mean.

I pretend to think about it, tapping my chin. "Well, I'm actually here to make a proposal."

He eyes me warily, like he already knows he'll regret whatever comes out of my mouth next.

"A challenge," I announce, "since you're obviously dying for a distraction."

Brody holds the handle of the rake tightly. "You want to compete again? After I let you win?"

"Yep," I say, deadpan, noticing his usual pleasantries have disappeared. "I actually demand a rematch. Higher stakes. No pity wins. Understand?"

He chuckles low under his breath, and damn it, the sound buries itself under my skin. "And what are these high stakes you're proposing, Harp?"

I grin. "Best out of three. The loser has to do a dare. No backing out, no whining, and no rules."

His jaw flexes like he's considering it, weighing how badly he wants to avoid whatever conversation we're not having.

I can see the exact moment he caves because he wants to win. He's just as competitive as I am.

"Fine," he says. "Explain."

"We'll play three games, and whoever wins two out of three, well, wins one single dare."

"Great. Prepare to lose," he says.

I bounce on my toes, already acting as if I won. I step forward, digging my finger into his chest. "Prepare to be humiliated."

Brody shoots me a look—one that's hot and heavy as he grabs my wrist.

His thumb brushes across my racing pulse, and his brow quirks up as if he feels it.

"You're dangerous," he says under his breath, like he doesn't want me to hear.

I freeze for just a second. It's playful and honest. Brody releases me and is already turning away like it meant nothing, but I know better. I'm not dangerous because I could hurt him physically, but because I matter. Way more than either of us planned. I shake it off, jogging after him and throwing him my best smirk.

"Don't worry. I promise to go easy on you this time." I snort beside him, amused.

When I glance over at him, he's already watching me with that unreadable look. Something that feels a little too much like trouble.

Brody leads me inside and grabs a worn deck of cards that looks like it's been shuffled thousands of times, along with a checkers board and some dice. It's like he's assembling weapons for a game war.

I stretch my arms overhead, then pop my fingers, giving him a smug little grin as we sit on the rug in the living room. "You ready to get your big bodyguard ego bruised?"

He tosses me a smirk. "Sweetheart, my ego's bulletproof. You're about to be humbled."

I fake a gasp, hand to my heart. "Such confidence. But more than expected from a Calloway."

Brody's mouth twitches up into a smirk. "Keep it up, Harp. Trash talk is all you'll have left when I'm done with you."

The air between us crackles—not the kind that usually comes before a fight, but the hot, simmering kind that's loaded with more. I ignore it—or at least I try to as I square my shoulders.

"All right, what's first? Card throwing? Checker stacking? Arm wrestling?"

Brody chuckles under his breath. "I'd break you in half if we arm-wrestled. Even your stubbornness has physical limits."

I flip him off with a cheerful smile, which earns me a slow, amused shake of his head.

We settle on a series of ridiculous challenges—a drawn-out game of checkers, which he won, followed by a competitive round of Go Fish. Right now, it feels more intense than any high-stakes poker game I've ever seen.

"Hopefully, Lady Luck is on my side," I tease.

Brody rolls his eyes dramatically, but I catch the flicker of amusement dancing behind his eyes.

"Harper," he says, voice dripping with playful suspicion, leaning forward to rest his elbows on his knees, "got any sevens?"

I scowl, handing over two sevens from my hand. "I swear, you're cheating. Do you have X-ray vision?"

He laughs, and the sound sends warmth fluttering through my chest. "Nah, I'm just that good."

"Or maybe you're the lucky one," I retort, refusing to admit he's getting under my skin.

"Mmm, luck has nothing to do with it." Brody wiggles his brows at me, shuffling his cards obnoxiously loudly.

"Hmm. Maybe I should make you streak around the cabin," I say, determined, knowing that if he wins this game of Go Fish, I lose overall. If I win, we tie, and I'll still have a chance of winning that dare. "Got any kings?"

His smile slips slightly, eyes narrowing. "You're kidding me."

I hold out my hand expectantly, grinning victoriously as he reluctantly hands over his single king.

"Thanks, *Bro*," I say sweetly, knowing he hates it when people shorten his name to that.

He growls, and I place my completed set of kings on the floor between us.

"I. Fucking. Win!" I do a little wiggle to rub it in.

Brody leans back dramatically, groaning as he covers his face with one hand. "My pride can't handle this."

"There's always a first time for everything," I tease, reveling in the victory. "Now we're tied."

Brody's scowling like a man personally offended by the laws of probability, which only makes me grin wider.

"Moving onto the next game," I say, snatching up the dice. "The first one to roll doubles wins. It's not too late to forfeit and admit I'm superior in every way."

Brody leans back against the couch, his gaze locked in on me.

"Keep talking shit, Harp," he says, picking up the dice and rolling. He gets a one and a six. "One minute, you're throwing dice; the next, you're trying to steal my soul."

I shrug, acting innocent. "I'm a woman of *many* talents."

He just watches me, that same look from last night lingering in his eyes. It's like he sees right through all the games and straight into the parts of me I don't show most people. It's thrilling.

I roll again and get a five and a two. We keep taking turns.

I shake the dice in my hand, then open my palm, placing a kiss on both.

He rolls his eyes. "Go."

I make an annoying show out of it, and when I roll double twos, I scream. "Victory," I say, standing up to gloat. "Now you'll kneel before me."

"Is that your dare?" Brody huffs a low laugh, tossing his hands in mock surrender.

"Hell no!" I say.

"Then give me your worst," he tells me.

I dust off my hands and take my time pretending to think about it. To be honest, I knew what I would ask him before we even started.

"No takebacks," I warn, pointing a finger at him. "No fake excuses."

He raises one dark brow. "Oh, I'm not afraid. Go on."

The image of him running around the cabin naked flashes across my mind so vividly that I laugh. Brody Calloway, cocky and barefoot under the stars, holding his cock. I nearly choke on my own tongue thinking about it. I wave it off before my brain short-circuits completely.

"I'll go easy on you this time."

He smirks like he knows exactly what I imagined, and for once, I'm grateful for him seeing me. Really seeing me.

"I actually dare you to give me one truth," I say, moving back in front of him on the floor. "No bullshit. No smart-ass comment. I just want one real thing about you nobody else knows. Our secret."

The smirk slides off his face because he realizes I played an Uno Reverse card. I know he's fearless when it comes to tasks, but not when it comes to talking. For a second, I think he'll dodge me and give me that cocky smoke screen he uses when things get too real. But Brody tips his head back, staring up at the ceiling, like he's looking for help, but there's nothing there to save him.

When he finally speaks, his voice is rough around the edges. "When I really care about someone, it scares the hell out of me because I know exactly what it'd feel like to lose them."

The words hit harder than I was ready for, knocking the air right out of my lungs. I don't say anything. I don't joke or offer some lame expression about time healing all wounds. I brush my fingers lightly against his, a silent *I hear you* he doesn't have to earn. For a long moment, we sit there as the soft hum of the ceiling fan fills the room.

I could kiss him so easily right now. It would take nothing. I could lean a little closer, place one hand on his cheek, and capture his mouth. We could forget the rest of the world exists. But I don't. Because some part of me knows, if I cross that line, there's no going back.

Instead, I give him a soft smile before I stand. Brody watches me with an unreadable expression as I reach my hand out to him. He takes it, and I pretend to pull him up, but—let's be real—I did nothing.

Without another word, I scoop up the dice and place them in his hand with a crooked smile.

"Come on, Calloway," I say lightly. "Let's see what your next roll would've been."

He rolls the dice and gets double threes. His mouth curves up into a smile.

"So close," he says with a smirk. "Next time, you're fucked."

"Promise?" I shoot back with a wink, and he shakes his head, laughing under his breath like he doesn't know what to do with me.

The late afternoon closes in around us, and the air in the cabin grows cooler as the house gets quieter. I stretch my arms over my head, yawning, the last of the adrenaline from our games draining out of me.

Brody leads me outside, and we sit on the porch swing and wait for sunset in silence. I like that I don't have to say anything when I'm with him, especially if I have no words to share. He understands, appreciates silence, and strives for it.

The day fades away, and afterward, he makes us fancy sandwiches with oven-baked fries for dinner. When we're finished eating, I rinse our dishes even though he protests.

Brody drops onto the couch like his bones have finally given up on him. His legs hang awkwardly over the armrest, boots planted on the floor because he's too damn tall for it. He tries to get comfortable, shifting around, folding one arm behind his head like it doesn't bother him, but I know better.

I hover in the kitchen for a second, chewing the inside of my cheek, before moving to the back of the couch and leaning over it.

"Hey," I whisper to him.

Brody cracks one eye open, looking at me like he's bracing himself for whatever I'll say. I shift my weight between my feet, instantly feeling weirdly awkward.

"You can sleep in the bed, you know."

Both of his brows go up. "That a dare or an invitation?"

I snort, rolling my eyes. "Don't flatter yourself, Calloway. It's logistics. You're gonna fold yourself in half on that couch like a damn lawn chair. If you're to protect me, you have to be at your very best. No more of this." I wait for a few long seconds. "Join me?"

He doesn't answer right away, but just stares at me, weighing his options.

I cross my arms and arch a brow. "Unless you're too scared? You'd be the first Calloway to be a fucking chicken."

That gets to him. He mutters something under his breath, pushes up off the couch, and follows me down the short hall toward the bedroom, grumbling the whole way.

Before we reach the doorway, he pauses, his voice low and gruff. "You have to stay on your side, Harp."

I flash him a grin over my shoulder, and he knows this is trouble.

"I can't make any promises."

Brody exhales slowly, like he already knows he's lost whatever game we're playing, but he follows behind me anyway. And just like that, the line between what we are and what we're pretending to be blurs just a little more.

12

BRODY

The door creaks behind me as I step into the bedroom, half expecting Harper to claim the entire mattress like she's a starfish.

Instead, she tucks herself neatly under the covers and props herself up on one elbow, grinning as if she's been waiting her entire life for me to show up. She pats the empty space beside her, slow and deliberate, as if she's inviting me to a death sentence. Crossing the line with her might be one. I'm not sure I'd survive Harper Alexander.

"Come on, Calloway," she says, her voice teasing. "I don't snore much. And I don't bite too hard."

I arch an eyebrow, shutting the door behind me without a word. Her grin widens, and it's pure mischief.

She knows exactly what she's doing. Hell, she's *counting* on breaking me down, but two can play that game. I reach for the hem of my shirt and pull it over my head in one smooth motion, tossing it onto the floor.

Harper scans up and down my body as if she's memorizing every tattoo I have, and I can't help but notice how she eye-fucks me.

The air surrounding us thickens, and I raise my brow. "See something you like?"

"Mmm."

Her smile says it all as she rests her chin against her fist, watching me strip out of my jeans. Then I'm left standing in a loose pair of black shorts that hang low on my hips. The room feels hotter and much smaller as she zeroes in on me.

"What are you waiting for?" Harper taps the mattress again, her fingers pulling down the comforter for me. "What's the matter? Afraid?"

"You're the one who should be worried, Harp." I give her a pointed look. "Don't cross the invisible line in the middle of the mattress."

"Is that where it's been hiding?"

I read the meaning behind her words. She's referring to the invisible line the two of us are teetering and have been for years.

"Hilarious," I say dryly.

"Look, I already warned you—no promises. I like to snuggle. Ask Billie." She snorts and tilts her head, as if she's daring me to do something about it. "Is this the center?" She reaches over, further teasing me. "Or is it here?"

"Don't test me, Harp."

I scrub a hand over my jaw, fighting the smirk creeping across my face as I move closer. As I slide between the sheets, the mattress dips under my weight, and I keep a healthy amount of space between us—not because I want to, but because there is no uncrossing that line once we do.

Harper hums under her breath like she can feel the tension radiating off me. "Relax, Calloway," she whispers.

"Easy for you to say," I tell her as I reach over and turn off the lamp.

"I'm harmless," she offers, but I can hear the smile in her voice.

"The fuck you are," I reply.

I glance over at her, letting my eyes trace down the slope of her bare shoulder peeking out from the blanket.

I swear I can feel that gorgeous curve of her lips tilt upward without even seeing it. I turn onto my back, staring up at the ceiling with two feet of space between us. I hug the edge of the mattress even though I want to be close to her. So little distance is left between me and the one damn thing I want but know I can't have.

She deserves better than me. Doesn't she? She deserves a man who isn't broken.

The night stretches around us, heavy with every word we're trying not to say. I'm lost in my thoughts, and God help me, I'm already losing this battle.

The room settles into a still silence that makes my ears ring. I can hear every creak in this old house, coupled with the rustle of sheets as Harper shifts, trying to get comfortable. I stay on my side of the bed as if it's a matter of survival, one arm slung behind my head. I focus on the wooden beams as if they'll offer me some sound advice about this entire situation—they don't.

The mattress gives slightly as Harper rolls closer, not all the way, but enough that the covers tighten between us. Enough that when she stretches out her foot, it brushes against my calf. My whole body goes rigid, every nerve suddenly aware of her. Neither of us moves. Not away anyway. I think she's still awake and testing the waters. Harper doesn't say anything, and she doesn't apologize or pull away. She just breathes, slow and steady, allowing the connection to linger between us, warm and reckless.

I squeeze my eyes shut for a moment, inhaling a breath that feels heavier than it should. Two feet of space didn't survive the first hour. At this rate, we won't survive the night.

I don't know how long we lie like that, trapped somewhere between exhaustion and desire, before her voice cuts through the dark.

"Brody?" It's soft, barely a whisper.

"Yeah?" My voice comes out raw.

There's a moment when I think she might back out and say nothing else. Maybe I can pretend she never said my name. Then she shifts again, and her hand brushes my arm under the covers, just the lightest touch, as if she needs to know I'm really there.

"I didn't want to be alone," she says, her voice low and a little shaky. "I've been having horrible nightmares about everything that's happened."

Something in my chest pulls tight. I turn my head toward her, even though I can barely make out her features in the dark.

"You're not alone, Harp," I say. Not tonight. Not ever, if I have any say in it. "I'm here. Always."

I'll make sure you're never alone again.

It's a promise that locks itself into my bones.

"You're safe," I reassure her.

Harper makes a soft sound, something like a sigh, and drifts closer, but doesn't fully touch me. She's close enough that I can feel her warmth beside me. I sense her breathing eventually even out, and it's steady against the hush of the room. She's already drifting, trusting me to hold the line between us. Trusting me to keep her safe.

I lie there, wide awake, staring into the dark, and make a second promise. One that's just for me.

If anyone tries to hurt her again, they'll have to go through me first.

What Harper deserves is protection, and it's the one thing I can offer her without failure.

THE FIRST THING I NOTICE WHEN MY EYES FLUTTER OPEN IS HOW perfectly Harper's body fits with mine. Her arm is draped loosely over my stomach, and the weight of her head rests just above my heart. I don't shift, not wanting to disturb this fleeting moment. My breathing aligns with hers, each inhale and exhale blending together in unspoken harmony. The early morning sunlight slips into the room, washing everything in golden hues, and it's almost too dreamy.

Today, I have to face reality, and I'm already dreading it.

Harper mutters something in her sleep, snuggling me tighter, as if she knows how temporary this might be. She's never seemed more delicate than right now, and I want to shield her from the world that awaits beyond these cabin walls. But I know we can't stay here, wrapped in something that feels so fragile that it could snap like a thread at any moment.

Exhaling slowly, I slide out from under her, careful not to wake her. She groans, her brows furrowing before relaxing again. A few seconds later, she slips back into her peaceful oblivion. I pause to watch her, memorizing her pretty face in the muted morning light and the way her long lashes curl on top of her cheeks. My heart beats unevenly, already mourning the loss of this moment. It's one I'll treasure for a long damn time.

I reach for a fresh T-shirt and slip it over my head. My footsteps creak over the old wooden floor as I make my way into the kitchen, the air growing cooler and emptier with each step away from her.

Before I settle myself at the small table, I make coffee and open my laptop. It's something I've avoided for the last few days while Harper became more comfortable in this space. Truthfully, I needed a break from the bullshit too.

The sudden brightness of the screen is harsh. I type in Harper's name, and the articles about her flood in relentlessly. The words that fill the page shatter the calm I felt just minutes ago.

HARPER ALEXANDER MISSING, FEARED IN DANGER

MICAH RHODES ISSUES DESPERATE PLEA FOR HIS FIANCÉE'S SAFE RETURN

REWARD FOR ANY LEADS TO FINDING HARPER ALEXANDER

MICAH RHODES BELIEVES HARPER ALEXANDER IS PREGNANT WITH HIS BABY

MY PULSE INCREASES AS I SCAN THE HEADLINES. I CLICK ON A VIDEO where he's acting like the upset man in love, but I know better. His grief is manufactured, and watching him turn Harper's escape into a performance makes me fucking livid, especially after what he did to her.

"If anyone knows anything, please, bring her home safely," Micah pleads, his eyes wet with perfectly timed tears. "Harper, I just want you back. I just want my family. I told you I would never let you go. I meant that."

The last sentence is a fucking threat, and an intense rage builds so quickly that I can barely breathe. The media feeds off his lies, tearing apart Harper's dignity and turning her into something she's never been—a weak, helpless woman.

My knuckles strain against the tight fists I've formed. I slam the laptop shut, and the sudden sound cuts through the silence. Leaning forward, I place my palms flat against the table and take a deep breath. I need to calm down, but seeing him makes me want to drive to the city and rip his fucking face off.

Harper doesn't know about this shitstorm yet, but I will have to tell her. I just hope the cruelty of the world doesn't crash down around her. It's a lot to take in at once after what she's been through.

Last night, lying beside her, I silently promised to give her safety. Now it feels carved in steel. I take a sip of coffee, and my breath steadies enough for me to face the fire, knowing I'm not finished yet. I log in to my secure email and quickly scan the new messages.

One of my informants—one who trades dangerous truths for large sums of money—emailed me.

I click open the message, and dread spreads through my veins at the sight that greets me.

Photos. Emails. Bank transfers. Micah Rhodes is far more than manipulative; he's corrupt. This may run deeper than any of us really knows, considering the photos clearly show him in back rooms, exchanging briefcases and shaking hands with known criminals.

All the evidence is full of hidden threats, wrapped in polite words—warnings about serious consequences if anyone crosses him. Bank statements show enormous money transfers, clearly revealing paths of bribery and shady deals tied to ruthless players. All information that's impossible to ignore.

Then one quick message jumps out at me:

If Harper won't comply willingly, then use force. She will make us a lot of money.

Fury rushes through me, sharpening my focus until it's just me and the brutal reality of what I need to do next. Micah has turned Harper's vulnerability into a weapon, publicly using mental warfare after he tried to destroy her.

Like a viper, I will strike back. He got one free pass; he will not get a-fucking-nother one.

Micah Rhodes believes he's untouchable, protected by power, cash, and lies. He has no idea how far I'm willing to go for Harper, the depths I'll dive to keep her safe. He's started a battle without realizing one crucial thing—I'm ready to go to war, and he has no fucking clue what I'm capable of.

I'm still staring at the screen as I click back to the articles. The weight of Micah's threats makes me want to lose control. I hear the faint creak of floorboards behind me, and before I can shut the laptop, Harper's voice, soft and sleepy, cuts through the quietness.

"What are you reading?" she asks.

I turn, instinctively blocking her view, but it's too late—her eyes are already scanning the brutal headlines on the screen. I forgot to close the fucking web browser.

"Oh my God." Her voice shakes, barely above a whisper, filled with disbelief. She steps back, her hand covering her mouth, fingers trembling. "Is this—are they saying I'm pregnant?"

I quickly close the laptop, but the damage is done. Her eyes, wide and hurt, flicker to mine. Shock floods her face, quickly replaced by confusion, then fear.

"He promised he would make her delete that photo," she whispers, as if she needs to defend herself. "Brody, I'm on birth control. I'm not pregnant. I swear, I—"

"Harper—" I start, but she cuts me off.

"Micah tried to convince me I was, even when I knew I couldn't be. He kept saying I was. I'm not. I'm *not*." Her voice rising in panic, she repeats it desperately, as if saying it enough times will make it true.

I stand up quickly, reaching out to steady her, pulling her toward me as her breathing gets shallow.

"Slow down. Breathe, Harp." I rub my hands up and down her arms, wanting to help calm her.

Her breath catches on a sob. "He told everyone, Brody. Everyone believes him. They think—"

"Listen to me," I say, cupping her face in my hands, keeping my gaze steady. "It doesn't matter what they believe. What matters is the truth. We'll get a test and figure it out right now. No matter what it says, I won't let you deal with this alone."

She nods, tears spilling down her cheeks. Her forehead rests against my chest as she cries soft, broken sobs that shatter my heart with each shaky breath. "I hate him."

"I know." I hold her tighter, smoothing my hand over her hair, wishing I could protect her from this pain. "I've got you."

She nods again, still trembling.

We get dressed quickly, our movements robotic. As we step outside into the chilly morning air, her body is tense. I help her into the passenger side of the Charger, closing the door before sliding into the driver's seat. The engine purrs to life, then rises to a roar as we hit the empty road toward town.

Harper stares out the window, and she's distant. The silence between us is uneasy, but I give her space, sensing the storm building inside her. When we finally pull into the pharmacy parking lot, I glance over at her, noticing how her fingers twist nervously in her lap.

"Stay here," I say, squeezing her hand. "I'll go in."

"Thank you." Her eyes meet mine, her vulnerability shining through.

Inside, harsh fluorescent lights buzz overhead. The air's sterile as I quickly grab two pregnancy tests and head to the register, ignoring the cashier's curious look. Minutes later, I'm back in the Charger, handing Harper the paper bag. She doesn't open it, just grips it tightly like it's her lifeline.

"Whatever it says, I'm with you," I promise. I glance over at her.

Her eyes search mine. "But what if—"

"No matter what, Harp," I repeat firmly. "I'm here."

"Do you promise?" She swallows back fresh tears as we drive toward the cabin.

"Yes," I say matter-of-factly, hating seeing her like this.

Fuck Micah. Fuck his manipulation. Fuck what he's done to her.

Harper's eyes stay fixed ahead.

Just after we make it up the twisting road of the mountain, she reaches over and slides her hand carefully into mine. I tighten my grip, offering whatever strength I can through that simple touch as I rub my thumb against hers.

"The truth will set you free, Harp," I say. "It always has. It always will."

13

HARPER

My heart pounds painfully, each beat echoing louder in the tiny bathroom, drowning out everything but the rapid rush of blood in my ears. The small plastic pharmacy bag feels heavy, weighed down by anxiety, fear, and memories of Micah I'd give anything to erase. He is still there, vivid, haunting me from the edge of my mind.

I grip the porcelain sink, blankly looking at my reflection in the old mirror. My face is pale, eyes wide, terrorized by shadows I can't quite shake. The version of myself staring back at me is fragile and close to breaking again. I am barely glued back together.

I knew he hadn't asked that girl to delete that picture. For all I know, he'd planted her there to continue his sick narrative.

The last time I took a test, Micah stood over me and watched. His voice was cold as he snatched the stick from my hand, ready to turn the result into another means of control. My stomach rolls at the memory, his harsh whisper echoing, *"I'll never let you go."*

A shiver crawls down my spine, and I draw in a shaky breath, fighting to regain control.

I remind myself firmly that Micah isn't here.

Instead, just outside the door, is Brody—quiet, patient, gentle Brody, who said, "Take your time," and meant it.

Brody, whose eyes are always calm, doesn't push or demand anything from me other than for me to be myself. He always waits, holding space for me without question.

It's almost impossible to believe someone like him has always existed in my life after everything I've been through. The creak of the old cabin floor outside the bathroom reminds me he hasn't left. He's still here, just waiting patiently for me. That type of simple kindness feels as foreign as it does precious.

I'm filled with gratitude and an overwhelming ache of something I can't quite place. How is it that in such a short time, Brody has made me feel safer than Micah ever did in months? And how terrifying is it that my heart is already starting to crave him and his presence?

I slowly open the bag, my hands trembling slightly as I pull out the tests. Such a small thing, yet it feels like it's holding my entire future hostage. I stare at them blankly for a moment, gathering strength I'm not sure I have.

I remind myself once more, *I am not alone.* Brody promised I wasn't.

As if he could hear my thoughts, he gives a light tap on the door. It startles me.

"Harp? You okay?" Brody's voice is soft.

Something about his tone—genuine concern and gentle warmth —finally pushes away the lump in my throat.

My voice emerges softer, shakier than I want. "Yeah, I'm okay."

There's a pause, and I hear the shift of his weight. "No rush. Just making sure you didn't fall into the toilet and needed a lifeguard."

I snicker, and a wave of gratitude hits me so hard that my eyes burn with tears. Such a simple thing—a kind word, patient understanding, a silly joke to take my mind away—but it changes everything, washing away lingering shadows of fear and slowly replacing them with hope.

I move closer to the door, pressing my palm against the worn wood, drawing strength from knowing Brody stands on the other side. "Stay close?" I whisper, my voice timid but full of trust.

"Always," he promises without hesitation.

In the heavy silence that follows, I finally unwrap both tests and do what needs to be done, hands still trembling. I set them down on the counter, forcing myself to breathe evenly, counting slowly as I wait.

I glance toward the door, knowing he's still there, patiently guarding my peace, and for the first time since Micah turned my world upside down, I allow myself the smallest flicker of hope that maybe, just maybe, I'm stronger now because this time, I'm not alone in the storm. Brody is thunder and lightning, and after the rainstorm, he brings flowers and rainbows. Brody is proof that clouds pass and there is life afterward—at least that's what he's shown me since being here.

The low hum of the cabin seems loud now, each passing second stretching until I can barely breathe. I stand motionless in front of the sink, my pulse racing, nerves fraying like a rope that's unraveling.

A soft knock echoes, and Brody's careful voice drifts through the door again. "Still doing okay, Harp?"

Something about his gentle persistence makes my throat ache. He's not demanding answers, not rushing me—just checking in. It's a type of support I've never known and a care I've never felt. I move toward the door, slowly opening it just a crack, feeling oddly fragile as our eyes meet through that small space.

Brody stands in the narrow hallway, leaning casually against the wooden wall, hands tucked into his pockets, his posture relaxed to hide any tension. But his dark blue eyes are filled with a concern that wraps around my heart.

"Hey," I say, my voice barely audible.

He smiles faintly, his eyes warm and reassuring. "Hi."

I look down, suddenly unsure of myself, fingers gripping the edge of the door. "Sorry. I didn't mean to take so long. I just ..." My voice trails off, as I'm unable to express the tangled emotions inside of me.

Brody shifts closer, careful but deliberate, closing some of the distance without pressuring me. "There's nothing to apologize for, Harper. Take all the time you need. I can stand here all night."

His simple kindness and unwavering patience are felt behind every word, and it cracks something open inside me.

I swallow hard, my eyes stinging. "I keep remembering the last time. With Micah." My voice breaks slightly on his name, bitterness mingling with pain. "He made me feel so ... helpless."

Brody's jaw tightens, his eyes darkening protectively. His voice is an anchor in my choppy emotions. "You're not helpless, Harper. You're stronger than he ever knew. He manipulated you. He probably kept a positive test to continue his sick narrative. I know about men like him. They find weaknesses to destroy women." His hand reaches forward, and his thumb brushes across my cheek. "You're an Alexander. You're indestructible."

I glance up, caught off guard by the raw sincerity in his voice and the ferocity in his eyes. I don't realize I'm moving until my hand reaches out instinctively, my fingertips brushing against his wrist, seeking comfort and connection.

"I'm glad you're here with me," I whisper. "I don't know if I could face this alone."

His gaze softens even more, the last traces of his carefully held distance fading. Slowly and gently, he takes my hand, threading his strong fingers securely through mine; the warmth of his touch sending comfort rushing through me.

"You don't have to face anything alone," he says, his voice powerful but sincere. "Not anymore. Not ever again, if I can help it."

My throat tightens as emotions tumble through me—relief, gratitude, and something deeper, something more profound that I'm almost too scared to name. I step a little closer, leaning lightly against the doorframe, drawing strength from the silent certainty in his presence.

"Will you stay right here?" I ask, looking up into his eyes, trusting he'll understand exactly what I mean and how desperately I need him close.

He squeezes my hand, his thumb brushing against my knuckles. "Always."

I nod, swallowing back tears, feeling his response sink deeply into my heart, rooting itself in the place Micah's cruelty once occupied. Brody is everything Micah never was—steady instead of controlling, patient instead of demanding, comforting instead of manipulative. And for the first time, that doesn't terrify me.

With one last squeeze of my hand, Brody leans back against the wall again, giving me space. His presence remains solid under the shaky ground beneath my feet. As I step back into the bathroom, letting the door remain slightly cracked, I breathe deeply, drawing strength from the gentle promise Brody made me years ago—that he would always tell me the truth. It's one he's never broken. And right now, the truth is that I'm not alone, not anymore.

My stomach twists, and anxiety builds relentlessly. I know logically that it's just a test, a simple result—positive or negative. But logic isn't what's strangling me right now. Instead, I'm trapped by memories sharper than glass, vivid enough to leave emotional scars I've tried to forget. But it's been less than a week since I escaped Micah, and it's clear that mental and emotional damage has been done.

The last time I stood like this, in a brightly lit bathroom, Micah watched my every move, impatient with bubbling anger. His voice was sharp as a knife, each word cutting deep as he ripped the test from my grasp.

I shudder, hugging my arms around myself, desperately trying to push the echo of his voice away. It's too easy to fall back into that moment. I remember his eyes, cold and accusing, stripping away every ounce of dignity I tried to hold on to when he forced me to believe I was pregnant.

I beg the memories to fade, but they cling to me, whispering doubt and self-blame into every silent second. My chest feels tight, my breathing shallow and uneven.

Then, just outside the bathroom door, I hear the creak of the old wooden floorboards where Brody is waiting. He doesn't pace impatiently or demand an answer. He's just there, giving me space while staying close enough to be a lifeline. That's the way it's always been with him. He's always close but still so far away.

I focus on the rhythm of his breathing—calm, unhurried. It grounds me, pulling me back from the cliff edge of anxiety. The memories of Micah's hostility slowly fade, replaced by the comforting awareness of Brody's presence. The difference feels both terrifying and healing.

Drawing in another slow, shaky breath, I stop pacing and face myself in the mirror. My reflection stares back, calmer now but still vulnerable, still uncertain. For two long months, I let Micah define my worth and play with my weaknesses to mold new fears. But here, in this small cabin, I'm beginning to see glimpses of a different reflection, one that is stronger, safer, and whole. I deserve to be loved, even though no man has ever loved me.

I refuse to glance at the tests lying on the counter, and I demand my courage. I remind myself again that I won't be alone, no matter the result. Not this time.

My gaze drifts to the partially open door, and I see Brody's shadow stretched across the floor. He still waits, giving me room to breathe and find my strength. Something inside me settles gratefully into place.

"I don't know if I can look," I whisper, more to myself than to him, needing to hear my voice.

When he finally speaks, it's firm with gentle reassurance. "You need the truth, Harp."

Brody's right. I need it in all aspects of my life.

I find myself breathing a little easier, my heart rate slowing, and the fear that had its grip on me finally loses some of its hold. Because now, in this small bathroom, Micah's cruelty feels more distant. And Brody's strength, his unwavering presence, feels like something I can rely on.

This time, I'm not trapped. This time, I have a choice. Whatever happens next, I know I'll be safe.

My footsteps forward slice through the silence, and I know I have to do this. Right now. I step closer to the counter, and my gaze fixes on the tests.

Brody enters and moves behind me, not speaking, not looking. He just places his hand on my shoulder. It's a reassurance I didn't know I needed. The air is heavy with anticipation, and it smothers me. I swallow, gripping the counter with one hand, planting my feet before reaching out for one of the tests.

The result window stares back, clear and definitive.

Negative.

A sharp breath escapes me, more of a gasp than anything else. I stare at the simple line, relief surging through me in an overwhelming wave, so powerful and sudden that my knees almost buckle beneath me.

I glance at the second test. Same result. I sway slightly, gripping the counter tighter as dizziness washes over me.

Micah is a fucking liar.

Brody's strong hand is warm and firm against my lower back, keeping me upright. He moves beside me. "Easy. I've got you."

I lean into him instinctively, my heartbeat beginning to slow. My entire body feels lighter, released from a weight I didn't realize had been crushing me. I lift my eyes to meet his, not bothering to hide the tears burning in them, not caring that he sees every exposed and lingering fear.

"It's negative," I whisper. "I knew it. I fucking knew it."

His eyes hold mine, endlessly patient, and a smile softens his features. "That's good, Harp."

A sob slips free, catching me by surprise. Brody immediately pulls me closer, his arms wrapping around me. I bury my face in his chest, inhaling deeply, finding comfort in him. He doesn't speak again and doesn't fill the moment with unnecessary words. He holds me until my breathing evens out as the result fully sinks into every muscle. I cry, tears pouring out of me, because I knew the truth, the truth that Micah tried to twist.

Slowly, I pull back just enough to look up at him again, my face still damp, my breath shaky but calmer. I reach up, brushing away tears with a weak, embarrassed laugh.

"Sorry. Still Little Miss Disaster after all these years," I whisper.

"You're not." Brody shakes his head, a faint smile playing at the corners of his mouth, his eyes gentle and understanding. "You don't have to apologize to me, Harp. Ever."

I nod as he brushes stray strands of hair from my cheek. His fingertips linger against my skin.

"Feel a little better now?" he asks, still close.

"Much better," I answer, finally feeling a genuine smile curl onto my lips.

Brody squeezes my shoulder, guiding me carefully toward the door. "Come on," he says. "You could use some fresh mountain air. My mom always said it was healing."

He leads me out of the tiny room, into the open cabin space, and outside.

We sit on the porch swing, and I breathe easier now. He opens his arm, and I lean into his strong body, enjoying his warmth at my side. The moment isn't ruined with words, just fluttering heartbeats as the mountain breeze brushes my cheeks. He reminds me that he is my safety; this is comfort, and it's real.

And for once, I allow myself to fully lean into it, grateful beyond words for this man who stays by me, even when my world feels like it's spinning out of control.

Brody Calloway has saved me in more ways than one.

14

BRODY

It feels like we've both taken our first real breath in days. Harper sits curled on the porch swing, knees tucked under her chin, absently tracing the wood pattern with her fingertips. She's calmer but still too caught in her pretty little head. I watch her from the kitchen window, noting the tiny crease of worry that hasn't faded since she escaped Micah. I'd give anything to wipe it all away.

Glancing toward the pantry, I see a dusty bottle of tequila tucked at the back, still unopened. An idea forms, and I reach out, pulling the bottle into the sunlight and turning it thoughtfully in my hands.

"You know …" I say casually, stepping onto the porch and letting the tequila bottle swing from my fingertips as I move toward her. I lean against the railing, blocking her view of the backyard. "I think this calls for a celebration."

Harper looks up at me, eyebrows arching skeptically, and then she notices the bottle. "Tequila, Calloway? Didn't peg you as the type."

I grin, shrugging. "You clearly haven't been paying attention."

She gives me a laugh, shaking her head. "Day drinking won't solve my problems."

"No," I agree, tilting my head playfully. "But it's damn good at distracting you from them."

Her smile becomes warmer and more genuine. "Fair point. You're definitely an expert in distractions."

"Trust me, Harp," I say. "I have something in mind."

She tilts her head curiously, glancing between me and the tequila. "And what exactly would that be?"

I extend my free hand toward her. "Come on. You'll see."

Harper hesitates only briefly, her eyes sparkling with amusement as she slips her hand into mine. I pull her to her feet, then reluctantly let go, already missing the warmth of her palm against mine.

"Let me grab a blanket."

"Okay," she says.

I rush inside, pulling the quilt off the back of the couch and throwing it over my shoulder. I join her, and we step off the porch, then take the trail. Harper walks beside me, close enough that our knuckles brush lightly every few steps. It sends tiny jolts of electricity soaring through me each time.

My eyes drift over, and I take her in. Light catches her brown hair, and it frames her face in warm gold. She's stunning, effortlessly beautiful—so much more than even she realizes.

She notices me stealing glances, but doesn't call me on it, just smiles.

Her eyes brighten with curiosity. "Are you gonna tell me where we're headed, Calloway?"

"Patience, Sleeping Beauty," I tease, forcing my attention back to the path ahead. "You'll know soon enough."

She smiles, shaking her head, clearly amused. But she doesn't press further, trusting me to lead her into whatever awaits us.

The trail ahead is filled with the soft rhythm of our footsteps on fallen leaves and the muted whispers of the breeze through the branches. I don't speak. I rarely do. It's easier to just listen and observe while absorbing every detail around me. Especially when Harper is close.

I notice everything about her. The light freckles that brush her nose, the little dip in her bottom lip, and how her eyes sparkle when she's genuinely happy. Like right now.

Our shoulders brush as the path narrows, and heat climbs slowly up my spine. I let myself glance sideways just for a moment, taking her in one more time. Sunrays cling to her skin, touch the curves of her cheekbones, and dance along the honeyed strands of her hair.

I turn away, forcing myself to breathe, my jaw tightening as I fix my eyes forward again.

I don't look at her again—at least not directly. But I feel every tiny shift she makes, every shallow breath, every glance she steals at me when she thinks I'm not paying attention. She doesn't have to say a single word to pull me in, to draw me toward her like a moth to a flame. It's a dangerous kind of pull, one I'm done fighting.

The weight of the tequila bottle swings easily at my side, the thick blanket slung casually over my shoulder. I focus on the familiar trail, letting its winding path steady my heartbeat as we walk deeper into the woods.

When the trees finally thin, opening into a small, sunlit clearing, I slow to a stop. The pond sits perfectly still, reflecting the sky like polished glass, and I hear Harper's soft inhale of breath beside me. I glance toward her, watching silently as surprise brightens her expression. For a second, I forget how to breathe.

"This is incredible," she says, stepping forward, her eyes wide with awe.

Something inside me aches as I watch her relax, her expression unguarded for the first time since this morning.

I unfold the blanket, spreading it on the grass by the water's edge. Harper watches me, a faint smile playing on her lips, but neither of us speaks. Words don't seem necessary, not here, not now.

Slowly, deliberately, I pick up a smooth stone from the ground and weigh it in my palm. Harper eyes me, raising an eyebrow in question. My mouth curves just enough to acknowledge her curiosity.

"How about a game?" I ask, nodding toward the pond. "We take turns skipping rocks. Whoever's stone goes farther wins the round."

She tilts her head, eyes dancing with challenge. "And the loser?"

I lift the tequila bottle slightly, sunlight catching the glass and amber liquid. "Gotta take a shot."

Her lips turn into a playful smile, sending my pulse into overdrive. Without breaking eye contact, she leans down to pick up a rock.

"Guess I'm getting trashed," she says. "I've never done this."

I raise an eyebrow, my mouth twitching into a smirk. "Already admitting defeat? Didn't peg you for a chicken."

Her eyes widen slightly, like she's offended. Harper straightens her spine as her competitive fire sparks to life. "Oh, you're on, Calloway. But just think how embarrassing it'll be when you lose to someone who's *never* skipped a rock in her entire life."

I take a step closer, lowering my voice into a warning. "I won't go easy on you, Harp."

She leans in, and a mischievous smile curls at the corner of her lips as she whispers playfully, "Oh, I know. And that's *exactly* how I like it."

Heat rushes through me at the challenge in her voice. Harper steps toward the edge of the water, looking at the stone in her hand with exaggerated concentration. Her lips press into a firm line, eyes narrowing at the pond like it's personally offended her.

I hold back a grin, amused by the intensity she puts into every small thing she does.

With a quick flick of her wrist, she tosses it. It arcs awkwardly, hits the water with a dull splash, and sinks immediately without a bounce. Harper stares at the ripples with exaggerated betrayal, then spins toward me, her cheeks flushed and eyes narrowed accusingly.

"Was that even a skippable rock?" she asks.

I try to keep my expression neutral, shrugging innocently as I move beside her. "It looked perfectly skippable to me."

She groans and holds out her hand. Chuckling under my breath, I twist open the tequila and hand her the bottle. Her fingers brush mine, and our eyes briefly lock as she takes two big gulps. Any time we touch, my pulse kicks up a notch, heat pooling low in my gut. I look away quickly, focusing instead on picking up a rock from the ground.

"Watch closely," I say, stepping forward. "It's all in the wrist."

I skim the stone over the water, watching it skip smoothly several times before finally sinking far beyond Harper's attempt. Glancing back, I raise an eyebrow. Her mouth falls open in playful disbelief.

"Are you a professional?" she asks.

I shake my head. "You'll never know."

"Right," she says, more determined than before to beat me.

She grabs another rock—this one is much bigger—and she tests the weight in her palm. She tries another toss, mimicking my earlier motion, but the stone sinks quickly once again.

She glares at me, gulping another shot of tequila. "You might have to carry me back to the cabin at this rate."

I chuckle. "Wouldn't be the first time."

I grab another rock, and it skids over the water with such a practiced ease that she gasps.

"How are you doing that? What the hell?!"

"Here," I say, plucking a stone from the ground. I step behind her and place my hand on her wrist, showing her the motion. "It's all about the angle of attack." My voice is steady and casual, but inside, my heart hammers against my ribs.

Every nerve in my body feels in tune with how close we are. Warmth radiates from her skin. I'm careful, moving slowly, guiding her arm back and forward again, showing her how to release at just the right moment. We stand close enough that I feel the hitch of her breath and notice the goose bumps that coat her arms when my chest brushes against her back.

"You're thinking too much," I say near her ear, my voice lower. "Just feel it."

She tilts her head slightly, turning her face toward mine. Our eyes lock for a breathless instant. My pulse spikes, tension winding through my chest, as desire dances against the invisible line that keeps us apart.

Then, slowly, she turns forward again and flicks her wrist just as I taught her. This time, the stone skips—one, two, three, and even four times before disappearing beneath the surface.

Harper spins around, her face glowing, her eyes bright with excitement. "Did you see that?"

I step back with a smile, creating space, sucking air into my lungs as I try to regain composure. "Not bad."

She lifts an eyebrow, her mouth curving. "I'd say it was pretty damn good actually."

"Oh, don't get cocky," I tell her.

Her confidence sparkles in her eyes, and it almost undoes me.

She picks up another rock and repeats the process, and it skips even farther. I grin proudly and force my gaze away, silently reminding myself to breathe. I toss another rock, and it doesn't go nearly as far.

"You didn't try!" she says.

"Uh, yes, I did," I tell her, taking the bottle and chugging, needing to relax.

After we're both too buzzed to care anymore, we sit on the blanket, soaking in the sunshine. The cool breeze brushes over our skin. Harper's so close to me that I can't concentrate on anything else.

"I needed this," she admits. "I don't know if I want to ever leave this place."

I turn to her, watching her hair blow, and smile. "I always feel like that when I come here," I admit. "My sister and I used to do this when we were kids. Brandy was undefeatable."

Harper's smile slightly falters. "I admire you. You've been through so much, and you're so resilient."

"I could say the same about you," I mutter as we both reach for the tequila with a laugh.

Two more gulps from each of us, and we lie back on the blanket and watch the fluffy clouds pass by.

Harper eventually turns her head toward me, and I meet her eyes. Our faces are inches apart, and I imagine sliding my mouth across hers.

"What do you think would've happened had you kissed me the night of Billie's eighteenth birthday?" she asks as if she could read my thoughts.

I think about the question. "I probably would've hurt you."

Harper's brows furrow. "What?"

"I was twenty-six and didn't know what I wanted in life. You were obsessed with me. I would've used and discarded you like I did everyone else back then. I was running away from too many demons."

"And now?" she asks.

The silence draws on between us.

"You're my purpose, Harp."

I can't help but study her lips, feeling the magnetic pull between us as we inch our faces closer. Harper's eyes flutter closed, and her breath hitches, but I carefully pull away.

"Not like this," I mutter. "Too much tequila encourages people to do things they usually wouldn't."

Her gaze pierces through me, and she groans, lying back on the blanket with frustration. "Still the unwanted one."

I burst into laughter, my vision blurring from the booze. "Shut the fuck up. You're the woman everyone wants and can't have. The girl who almost got away."

"Right." She rolls her eyes.

I take her hand in mine, interlocking our fingers together. "It's not a lie," I say, reminding her of our pact.

She lets out a slow breath, then moves closer to me. I open my arms, allowing her to lie on my chest, and hold her. Words evade us, and I imagine a life where we could be together.

The two of us stay just like this for only God knows how long, and if I had the ability to freeze time and live in this very moment forever, I would.

15

HARPER

My eyes flutter open, adjusting to the morning glow of sunrise. For a moment, I lie still, savoring the peaceful silence, and a smile touches my lips. Memories of yesterday by the pond flood back—the closeness we shared, the way Brody looked at me, the almost kiss that still tingles on my lips, even though it never happened.

My pulse races, and a warm, restless ache spreads through me. I've thought about kissing Brody Calloway more times than I care to admit. I have years of fantasies of us being together. But yesterday was different. Yesterday was real.

"You're my purpose, Harp."

I release a slow, shaky breath as my need becomes impossible to ignore. Glancing toward the closed bedroom door, I listen carefully to the sounds in the cabin. Silence answers back, and I know Brody's probably already awake, sitting somewhere quiet, sipping his coffee, and staring thoughtfully into the sunrise. A thrill slides beneath my skin at the thought of him waiting for me.

Unable to resist the restlessness simmering inside me, I slip silently from beneath the sheets and move toward the bathroom. The door clicks shut behind me as I step into the shower, turning the water to a comforting warmth. Steam fills the room quickly, surrounding me, and I undress, stepping under the stream. The water eases the tightness in my shoulders, but does nothing to calm the fire building between my legs.

Closing my eyes, I lean back against the cool tiled wall, water cascading down my skin in hot streams.

I let myself drift into the fantasy I've had for years—Brody's broad, strong hands exploring my body; his fingers tracing my ribs, gripping my hips, pulling me against him with the possessive urgency I've always craved from him.

A soft gasp slips from my lips as my palms begin to move, mimicking the path I want Brody's hands to take. My fingertips brush the curve of my breasts before teasing the sensitive peaks as I think about his hungry mouth capturing me.

Pleasure rises slowly, my breathing turning shallow as I picture his blue eyes locked on mine, his expression full of desire and need, which matches my own.

My hand trails lower, slipping between my thighs, finding slick, aching heat as I imagine Brody's deep voice whispering against my skin, telling me how beautiful I am, how I'm his purpose.

Intense pleasure sparks through me, my breath hitching as my fingers circle my clit. I can barely stand as I fantasize about taking the kiss we nearly shared yesterday. I slide a finger inside, feeling my walls clench tight. I need him. It's a need so damn deep and raw and passionate.

Intensity builds quickly now, and the impending orgasm tightens low in my stomach as my breathing quickens.

I whisper his name, desperate beneath the rushing water, imagining Brody's muscular body pinning mine firmly against the wall. His strength is protective, possessive, and perfect. My hips arch instinctively toward my hand, and my pleasure rises higher, deeper, brighter as I return to my clit, giving myself everything I want from him.

My body trembles, and I can't hold on much longer. As my eyes slam shut, the orgasm rips through me. I let out a soft cry, shuddering as I fall over the edge. Powerful waves wash over me, leaving me trembling, my knees weak, and chest heaving beneath the steaming spray.

I lean against the wall, trying to catch my breath, not remembering the last time I came so hard.

Suddenly, there's a knock on the bathroom door, jolting me from the lingering haze. My heart leaps into my throat, eyes flying wide.

"Harper?" Brody's voice calls through the door, concerned. "Everything okay in there?"

Flushed and panicked, I press a hand to my racing heart, quickly gathering my voice. "Yeah." I clear my throat. "Yeah, everything's fine," I manage, squeezing my thighs tightly together, as if to hide the truth, even from myself. "Just dropped the soap. Sorry."

There's a slight pause, and then I hear the unmistakable smile in his voice when he asks, "You sure about that?"

Embarrassment mingles with a fresh thrill of excitement.

I bite my lip to keep from laughing, trying to sound more convincing. "I'm fine! Really."

He chuckles through the door, his voice dropping into something warmer, sexier. "Well, if you ever need any help next time … just let me know."

My breath catches again—for entirely different reasons—and I bite my lip, wishing he would. I cover my face with my hands, wondering if he heard my desperate whimpers.

"I'll remember that," I tease. I envision the sparkle in his eyes and the smirk I'm sure he's wearing right now.

His footsteps fade down the hallway, and I turn off the water and step out, wrapping myself in a soft towel. The reflection in the mirror shows flushed cheeks and eyes bright with desire, longing, and uncertainty. I stare at myself for a long moment, acknowledging the truth I've avoided for years—Brody Calloway has always been the man I wanted. But after yesterday and everything that's happened between us, I realize that fantasies aren't enough anymore. I want the real him more than ever.

I dress quickly, slipping into soft leggings and an oversized T-shirt, my skin still tingling from my shower.

As I make my way to the back porch, where he is, anticipation dances within me, as I'm unsure of what to expect. Will he tease me or pretend our exchange yesterday never happened?

When we returned to the cabin, both drunk, neither of us discussed it. We fell asleep in each other's arms, and that was it. Completely platonic.

Stepping outside, I'm met with cool air and the sight of Brody leaning casually against the railing with a steaming mug of coffee in his hand. His gaze shifts toward me, and a slow, knowing smile lifts the corner of his mouth. I try to hide the butterflies that swarm me when our eyes meet.

"Good shower?" he drawls, eyes glinting playfully as he lifts the mug to his perfect lips.

"Would've been better with an extra pair of hands," I say teasingly, surprising myself with my boldness, cheeks burning even hotter.

Brody says nothing, but his gaze locks on to mine, eyes blazing with an inferno simmering beneath his hard exterior. He must've heard me.

My breath catches in my throat, heart racing wildly under the intensity of his stare. The air between us buzzes with unspoken words and possibilities, so charged and overwhelming that I have to look away.

I lean against the railing beside him, crossing my arms over my chest, letting our comfortable silence settle.

The forest hums around us, morning sunlight filtering through the trees, painting the wooden porch in soft patches of gold. Brody's presence beside me makes my heart race faster with every passing second.

Awareness of just how close we are buzzes through me when his tattooed arm brushes against mine.

"Did I just hear your stomach growl?" Brody asks.

I laugh. "Yes. I'm super hungry," I say, nudging his arm with my elbow to hide the hitch in my voice.

He tilts his head slightly, eyes still locked on mine. "Want pancakes?"

"That would be awesome," I say, grateful for the shift into something easier.

He raises an eyebrow. "Have you ever made them before?"

"No." I laugh, shaking my head. "I'm just here to look cute."

"You're doing a good job," he offers.

The sound is music to my ears. I don't think I've ever seen him smile so much, which makes my heart skip.

"You can handle the cooking, and I'll handle the syrup."

Brody's smile widens, his eyes dancing with mischief. "How about I teach you how? We'll go nice and slow." His voice carries a touch of intimacy that's not lost on me.

I smile with a racing pulse. "Careful, Calloway. I can read between the lines."

"Counting on it," he says warmly, shooting me a flirty wink as he hooks his finger with mine and leads me into the cabin.

My heart lifts at the simple touch as I follow him inside. I'm grateful for his ability to ease awkwardness and how effortlessly Brody makes me feel wanted and undeniably alive.

Warm sunlight streams through the cabin windows, bathing the kitchen as he pulls ingredients from the pantry. I lean against the counter, watching him. The grace of his movements and how comfortable he is around me makes me smile.

"Come here," he says, glancing over his shoulder at me, wearing a playful smirk.

I raise my brows. "I'm only here for moral support."

Brody sets down a bowl, and I look at all the ingredients on the counter: baking powder, flour, eggs, salt, milk, vanilla, oil, and sugar.

"Teach me your ways, pancake king."

A pleased smile spreads across his face, and his eyes meet mine briefly. It's too intense, and I force myself to glance away.

"First, we need to mix the dry ingredients." Brody grabs a measuring cup from the cabinet and a spoon from the drawer, placing them in front of me.

"Great. Let's do it," I say as he gives me the measurements for each item.

Brody leans his back against the counter and watches me, but he's super patient.

"You're a natural," he offers. "These are gonna be the best damn pancakes we've ever eaten."

"I find it impressive you have the recipe memorized," I say, but then I remember him mentioning that his mother loved breakfast.

"When I was a kid, there was an entire summer where I wanted pancakes for every meal," he admits.

"*Every* meal?" I ask as he pours the oil, vanilla, and milk into the bowl.

He hands me an egg, giving me a chance to crack it.

"Oh, yeah. Loved them," he says.

He watches me as I smack it on the flat counter, then press my thumbs in, opening the shell. The egg plops out with no shell. Brody holds up his hand, and I give him a high five.

"Look at you. Gonna be a chef by the time we leave here."

Laughter rolls out of me. "Okay, let's not get ahead of ourselves. I can crack an egg and skip a rock. Changing the world."

He chuckles. "Both great skills to have."

Once everything is in the bowl, he hands me a mixing spoon. "Now, there is a trick to this. You cannot overmix the batter. You stop when everything is incorporated. Got it?"

I nod, doing exactly what he instructed. When I stop, he glances in the bowl with a nod, then turns on the skillet. While it heats, we steal glances at one another.

"How big do you like them?" He waggles his brows.

I smirk. "Minimum six inches. But I think size matters."

Brody clears his throat.

"Oh my God, are you blushing?" I ask.

"No. *Pfft*," he says. "Are you kidding?"

"You are!" I tease him, reaching over and poking his side, making him squirm away. "Brody Calloway! Are you ticklish? Damn. It's soooo over for you."

I chase him around the kitchen.

He holds up a spatula and points it at me. "Harp! We have pancakes to make. The skillet is hot!"

I scrunch my nose. "You've only been saved because I'm starving. We might have to revisit this soon though."

"Harper Alexander! Don't start no shit, won't be no shit," he says, moving toward the stove.

I stand beside him, and my eyes trail over the tattoos on his forearm. I notice the Calloway Diamonds logo and a beautiful clock.

"This tattoo—it's an homage to your family."

"Yes. Easton drew it," he shares as he pours batter in palm-sized circles in the iron skillet.

The kitchen immediately smells like cake, and my mouth waters in anticipation.

I can't help but slide over the tattoos that peek out from the top of his shirt and go up his neck.

He notices me staring and lifts a brow. "This is a very important step. Keep your focus." He winks.

I shake my head as he continues, "Pancakes need patience and the right amount of heat. Watch for them to bubble."

I tilt my head thoughtfully, biting back a grin. "So, you're saying you like to take things slow?"

Damn, I'm brave today.

His gaze flickers to mine, heat flashing briefly in his eyes before he reins it in. A smile spreads across his lips. "Good things come to those who wait."

A soft blush rises up my neck, and I zero in on the bubbling batter. "That's why I'm letting you handle the timing. I wouldn't want to mess things up."

He can also read between the lines.

Carefully, he slides the spatula under a pancake and flips it. The side that's facing up is a golden brown.

He places his hand on the small of my back. "Grab some plates?"

"Sure," I say, placing them on the counter.

After another minute, he starts piling pancakes, then repeats the process until we each have a fat stack.

Brody removes the butter from the fridge, and I grab the syrup. We move to the table, and I watch as he puts little pads of butter between each layer. I follow his lead.

"All right, syrup queen, show me your skills."

Laughing, I drizzle syrup generously over both stacks, aware of his gorgeous eyes on me. Feeling bold, I swipe a fingertip through the sweet syrup pooling on my plate and slowly bring it to my lips, tasting it. His eyes darken slightly, watching me carefully.

"You're trouble," he says, amusement and something deeper coloring his voice.

I grin, my heart fluttering under his gaze. "But you like trouble, don't you?"

"Mmm. Fucking love it." Brody's eyes soften.

For a moment, we hold each other's gaze. Butterflies swarm inside me as his words sink in.

"Then I guess you're in luck," I whisper teasingly as we sit across from one another at the small table for two. "Because I'm the best kind."

"No one is denying that."

We each cut a sliver, and I lift my fork, the syrup dripping onto my plate. At the same time, we pop them into our mouths, and I moan. Not that I could help it. They're incredible. My eyes widen, and he swallows hard.

"Sorry, they're orgasmic," I admit. "Basically, these are the best pancakes I've had in my entire life. Now I understand why you wanted them for every meal."

He smiles, almost like he's remembering an old memory.

Breakfast passes in easy conversation, the gentle hum of our voices filling the cozy kitchen. We linger at the table, plates empty, mugs half-filled with coffee. I lean back in my chair, feeling more relaxed and carefree than I have in years, as the warm morning sunlight washes over us.

Glancing down, I remember my lack of a phone and clothes—everything I left behind at Micah's. A small frown tugs at my lips as I consider my reality. I look up slowly, meeting Brody's concerned gaze across the table.

"You okay?" he asks, reading me perfectly.

"Yeah." I sigh, fiddling with my fork. "I left my phone, clothes, and favorite weekend bag at Micah's. I feel a little ... lost and out of touch with the outside world."

He reaches across the table, his hand covering mine.

"Things are replaceable. You aren't," he says, thumb brushing reassuringly over my knuckles. "We'll need to go into town to get more groceries soon, and we can get whatever else you need."

"Really?"

"Of course." Brody's mouth lifts into a reassuring smile. "Buy the whole fucking town if you want. We'll do whatever makes you comfortable. Anything you need."

The intensity of his words sinks deep into my chest, easing the anxious flutter.

"Can we go in a few days? I think I need to mentally prepare to leave."

"Whenever you're ready, Harp. No pressure."

"Thank you," I whisper. "I don't know what I'd do without you."

Brody gives my hand a gentle squeeze before reluctantly pulling back, his eyes still warm. "You don't have to find out."

I offer him a light, playful smile. "So, shopping spree?"

He pushes his chair back as he stands, grabbing our plates. "As long as you promise not to bankrupt me with your wardrobe demands."

Laughing, I rise, too, nudging him with my shoulder as we move toward the door. "Impossible, Calloway. You have more money than either of us could spend."

"I've given a lot of it away," he admits.

"And somehow, you still have hundreds of billions," I say.

He smirks. "It's damn good to be a Calloway."

I watch him rinse our dishes and realize with certainty that no matter what happens from this point on, as long as Brody is by my side, I'll be okay.

16

BRODY

Twilight wraps around us like a whispered secret. We watch episodes of *Frasier* and toss cheese puffs into each other's mouths during commercial breaks. Even though Harper smiles, I can sense her anxiety rising. I can see it in how her shoulders tense and the way she gets lost in her head.

"You good?" I ask, turning down the volume and facing her.

She shakes her head. "Lost in thought. Trying to replay everything that happened and figure out what was real and what wasn't, you know? My life wasn't mine for two months, and I was fed so many lies," she says, glancing at me with a fragile expression.

An ache settles beneath my ribs. I close the distance between us carefully, my voice low and reassuring as I ask, "Do you want to talk about it?"

She exhales, tension visible in her shoulders. "I don't know."

After a few moments, I speak. "Harp, at some point—not right now—I need to know more about what happened. If you can share anything that you remember about things he said that seemed off, it would be helpful while I substantiate a case against him. Micah's a very bad person with ties to dangerous criminals. The information I have so far is extremely unsettling, especially knowing you were alone with him."

She tenses, her eyes drifting away from me. "He was so good at lying and making me doubt myself when things didn't seem right. I'd ask questions, and he'd tell me I was overreacting or was paranoid."

I tuck loose strands of hair behind her ear, studying her. "That's how manipulation works. I'm so fucking sorry you went through that. I want him to pay for what he did to you and other women. This is a pattern, Harp, and he needs to be stopped before he seriously hurts someone else."

She hesitates. "There was something—a note from a cashier in Newport the day he forced me to parade that pregnancy test around the store." She takes a shaky breath, clearly unsettled by the memory. "It said, *That man almost murdered my daughter. Leave him now!*"

Her words land heavily between us.

"Did Micah see it?"

"No. I flushed it in the toilet right after I read it." She swallows hard. "It shook me. Between that and the fake pregnancy test, Billie's warning text, the manipulation—" Her breathing quickens as her anxiety spirals higher, distress clouding her features.

I nod. "I texted you from Billie's phone when she told me what happened."

Harper's mouth drops open before she gives me a half-smile. "I should've known. Your words are the only ones that seem to rattle me. Always saving me."

I give her a soft grin. "Always. But it's never a burden."

Silence stretches on, but I let her speak when she's ready.

"He promised he'd never let me go. It was a threat, Brody."

Her breathing grows ragged, and I twist my body to hold her cheeks in my hands.

"Hey, breathe. Look at me, Harper."

Her gaze meets mine, her eyes glassy.

"You're safe now. He never had you, and I'll be damned if he ever gets close to you again. Do you understand?"

"Yes," she whispers.

I rub my thumb across her cheek, then wipe away a few tears that spilled. With each passing second, I grow more furious, remembering that vengeance for what he did is still mine.

Her eyes desperately hold mine as she battles with herself. "This is overwhelming."

"I know, Harp." I keep my tone calm and steady, anchoring her. "We'll figure it out. Together. He will get what's coming to him. For you and Billie. Enough is e-fucking-nough. He needs to be stopped because he will continue down this destructive path, and I'm so close to figuring out how to end him legally, even if I want to put a bullet between his eyes."

"Death is the easy way out. He deserves to watch his life clock run out behind bars." Harper's breathing evens, and the panic leaves her eyes.

"If you ever need to talk through any of this, I'm a great listener."

She laughs. "No shit. I've spent hours with you where you said no more than two words."

I smile and shrug. "I'll never judge you."

"Thank you," she says as she visibly relaxes.

A yawn escapes her, and I can see exhaustion on her face.

A long silence fills the room, and her breaths turn soft and steady.

"You should go to sleep."

"You're right," she says, no longer fighting it.

Harper has been lost in her head all day, and I gave her space while she read one of the thriller novels from the bookshelf. But I was only at arm's length from her the whole day.

I stand, and she follows me into the bedroom. She crawls under the blankets, and I sit on the edge of the bed.

"You're not joining me?"

I shake my head. "I have work to do, unfortunately. I'll stay with you until you're in dreamland. Deal?"

"Okay. Will you tell me a bedtime story?" She smiles in the dim light, eyes half closed. "Something to distract me."

A chuckle escapes me as I think about the innocence of her request. "A bedtime story, huh?"

She nods sleepily. "Make it a good one."

I lean back against the headboard and clear my throat. "Once upon a time ... there was a very stubborn princess. Her name was Little Miss Disaster."

Her smile widens a little, her eyes fluttering closed as she whispers playfully, "Sounds familiar."

I laugh, continuing in a gentle, teasing tone. "She loved napping so much that the whole kingdom called her Sleeping Beauty. But she had a problem—she snored like a baby bear."

She reaches over, finding my side and tickling me. I scoot away from her.

"I do not snore."

"Oh, she definitely did," I whisper dramatically. "But luckily, there was a brave knight who didn't mind. He was too busy making sure no trolls disturbed her royal naps."

Her smile fades into a gentle sigh. Her breathing deepens, her body relaxing into the mattress, completely at ease.

My voice lowers even further, barely above a whisper. "And that knight promised himself he'd always protect her, no matter what. So, he rescued her from an evil motherfucker's castle. He thought she'd kick and scream the entire way, but she didn't."

When I'm certain she's fully asleep, I lean over and press a soft kiss on her forehead. "Night, Harp."

I slip from the bed, careful not to disturb her peaceful rest. The tenderness in my chest sharpens into urgency as I move to the living room and reach for my laptop.

Harper might not be ready to unpack everything, but I have to act because time is running out. I will uncover and expose the truth about him.

The cabin is silent now, and the only sound is the soft hum of my laptop. I settle on the couch and rub my eyes before pulling up a secure internet connection. The browser opens, and my fingers move swiftly over the keys. The message from the cashier in Newport replays on an endless loop in my mind.

That warning feels darker, less like a single incident, and more like a sinister pattern.

I type quickly, scanning sketchy databases and encrypted forums, probing into anonymous threads where people discuss things too dangerous to say openly. Within moments, results flood my screen, threads titled vaguely, cryptically. I focus on one in particular: *Missing Women—Newport, Rhode Island.*

I pause, recalling the newspaper headline I glimpsed in the coffee shop, the one I brushed off at the time. I search the internet for missing women in Newport and see what comes up.

Another Newport Woman Reported Missing

Authorities Still Searching for Answers for the Four Missing Women

Newport Jane Doe #2 Identified

I find a few forum posts about it from the locals, and I scan anonymous messages, filled with vague hints and fearful warnings.

One comment immediately stops me:

She was spotted with someone from a powerful family. Vanished overnight. There was no real investigation, and the police brushed it under the rug. Everyone went quiet after that. They'll never find her.

Another user responds hesitantly, as if afraid to type the words:

I've heard whispers about someone prominent in Newport targeting pretty women, thirty-five and under. He's connected enough to erase evidence and cover his tracks. Girls just disappear, and nobody dares question it. I wonder if his fiancée knows.

My pulse quickens, dread filling my chest.

A third post, short and fearful, cements the darkness seeping into my bones:

People who dig into him vanish too. He's untouchable and powerful enough that even mentioning his name is dangerous. No one messes with him due to his profession. Local police and judges are in his pocket. He'll never pay for what he's done.

I sit back slowly, exhaling.

The dots connect—Harper's note, the missing women, the eerie headline from the newspaper at the restaurant. It all points to something disturbing, buried under Newport's pristine surface.

Micah Rhodes is a murderer.

My gaze flicks toward the bedroom, where Harper sleeps, unaware of what she narrowly escaped. This is far deeper than any of us imagined. Her confusion, panic, and fear were her internal alarm bells screaming for her to get out, but she was already too far in.

Determined to not let this happen to anyone else, I grab my phone and quickly type a message to Asher and Nick. After I rescued Harper, Asher and Nick agreed to help me take Micah down. The three of us have the skills and contacts to settle this once and for all. I could text my cousins, but that's a last resort. I want them to enjoy being married and not get involved in potentially dangerous situations. It's personal for Asher and for Nick too.

BRODY

We need to meet ASAP. In person. Contact Weston for info.

ASHER

Consider it done. Tomorrow.

NICK

See you then.

Their replies come fast, both confirming without hesitation.

Setting the phone aside, I close my laptop, my eyes fixed on the darkness.

Sleep won't come easily to me tonight. But I'll hold my ground, ready to defend Harper from whatever threat lurks. I will unravel every fucking secret Micah holds until he faces the fire for what he's done. As I lean back against the cushions, my heart thuds unevenly, anxiety threaded through my pulse. Even with the cabin wrapped in silence, my thoughts race, every uncovered detail pressing hard on my chest.

It would've taken me longer to put these pieces together if it wasn't for Harper. Sure, I knew he was a pile of dog shit and was making dirty deals in back rooms, but what he's currently involved in is much deeper than I thought. Micah Rhodes has to be stopped. Now.

Harper and Billie both deserve peace, safety, a life untouched by this motherfucker. I don't know the details of everything he did to Harper, but the thought of it makes my jaw clench in frustration.

Suddenly, as if summoned by the ache deepening inside me, a memory of Eden rushes forward, and it's bittersweet, strikingly clear despite how long it's been.

EDEN SITS CROSS-LEGGED ON MY COUCH, LOOKING AT ME WITH THOSE gentle eyes, her voice warm.

"We were always temporary, Brody," she says, regret softening her words. "But you deserve more than this. You deserve someone who can be everything you need. I'm not emotionally available."

I shake my head, stubbornly denying her logic. But Eden smiles, almost knowingly, leaning forward to touch my cheek briefly with her fingertips.

"Harper," she says, her gaze steady. "You're clearly in love with her. Maybe you should finally give her a chance."

"Are you breaking this off?" I ask.

"Brody, why are you fighting this? We were a fling. That's it. I care about you, but I cannot be with you in the capacity you want. You know who you should spend the rest of your life with. It's not me."

I BRUSHED HER SUGGESTION ASIDE, TOO TANGLED IN COMPLICATIONS and fears. But tonight, as I sit alone, Eden's words carry new meaning, heavier than before. She knew what I always refused to see.

Harper has always been there, waiting, holding a piece of my heart I've never admitted was hers.

My breath catches at the thought, at the regret of not listening sooner. But maybe now, it's finally time to honor Eden's memory— to trust her wisdom, even in death, and actually let Harper in.

Pushing to my feet, I move slowly back toward the bedroom, pausing in the doorway. Harper lies curled on her side, the moonlight tracing her face. Her breathing is deep and peaceful, the earlier anxiety erased by sleep.

I slide into bed beside her, settling close without disturbing her. Almost instinctively, she shifts toward me, her body seeking mine. When her hand finds my chest, her fingers curl into my shirt, and I relax. It's been so long since I've felt this.

Harper is exactly who I've always needed—and I'll fight the whole damn world before I let anyone take her away from me.

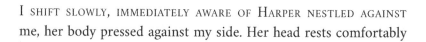

I SHIFT SLOWLY, IMMEDIATELY AWARE OF HARPER NESTLED AGAINST me, her body pressed against my side. Her head rests comfortably in the curve of my shoulder, one arm loosely draped over my chest. I'm growing used to waking up like this. I lie still, savoring how perfectly she fits against me. It feels dangerously good, dangerously right.

As if sensing me, Harper moves closer with a soft sigh. Her hair tickles my skin, her breath warm against my neck, igniting something deeper inside me. The tension I've held at bay suddenly tightens, making my pulse quicken and my body ache with desire. My jaw clenches as I fight for control.

Slowly, Harper's eyelashes flutter open, her sleepy eyes meeting mine. For a heartbeat, we just stare at each other, the intimacy stretching between us as I push hair from her face.

"Morning," she whispers, her voice soft and husky with sleep, sending a rush of heat through me.

"Good morning," I reply, knowing today is a new day, a new beginning.

Her eyes glance down, then widen when she notices what's causing the sheet to tent upward. A soft, amused snicker slips from her lips before she bites back a grin.

"Really?" she teases, her eyes sparkling playfully. "You always wake up, ready for battle?"

I chuckle, embarrassment mingling with amusement. "Hey, I can't help it." I arch a brow at her. "You've been rubbing against me for hours."

Harper's mouth drops open, and laughter lights her eyes. "I have not!"

I grin slowly, tilting my head in challenge. "You absolutely have. You're lucky I'm such a gentleman."

Her eyes narrow playfully, her cheeks coloring deeper. "Oh, really? A gentleman?"

"Always." I lean a fraction closer, removing some space between us. "Even when provoked by certain stubborn women who snore and sleep half-naked."

Her mouth falls open in mock outrage. "I do not snore. You keep saying that—"

"It's cute," I tease, enjoying her flustered expression. "I'm all about honesty, babe."

She huffs out a soft, incredulous laugh. "I think you're confusing honesty with fantasy, Calloway."

"Hmm," I say, allowing my gaze to linger on her lips. "If you say so."

Her breath catches, humor fading as the charged silence stretches on. The laughter from moments ago gives way to something deeper, something neither of us has been ready to name yet. But we both feel it wrapping around us in the morning sunlight.

"Asher and Nick know we're here and are flying in for a quick visit. We have some very important things to discuss in person."

"Today?" she says.

"Yes." Before the moment slips away, I continue, "You're so fucking pretty right after you wake up."

"Thanks." Harper ducks her head shyly, but the smile tugging at her lips reveals she likes my compliments. When she looks back up at me, her gaze is full of something I can't quite place.

"You're not so bad yourself," she whispers. "Especially when you're honest."

"I've got nothing but truths for you," I say, warmth spreading through my chest as I take in this moment.

She eventually slides out from the sheets and moves across the room. Before leaving, Harper glances back at me with a smirk. "I'm awake, right?"

I smirk. "If we're dreaming, please don't wake me up."

17

HARPER

I pace restlessly in front of the cabin window, my pulse racing with every distant echo of helicopter blades growing louder. I tug nervously at my sleeve, the knot in my stomach tightening. Nick and Asher will be here at any minute, and despite Brody's reassurances, I can't shake the anxious flutter in my chest.

I'm nervous about seeing Asher. I'm so afraid he's disappointed or mad at me for inviting Micah into his home. The last time I saw him, his eyes were wild, and he was so fucking pissed. I've never seen him so enraged.

I stop pacing, pressing my forehead against the cool glass, breathing deeply.

"Harp." Brody's calming presence fills the room, steadying me without words.

I glance back at him, standing near the kitchen counter, his eyes locked on to mine.

"It's going to be okay."

He moves closer, but he's careful not to crowd me. His fingers brush mine lightly, offering comfort without pressure.

"Eventually," I whisper, leaning into his touch. "I just don't know how to face Asher after everything that's happened."

Brody grabs my hand; his thumb strokes my knuckles. He holds my gaze. "Asher's coming because he cares about you and Billie. He doesn't blame you. No one does."

I draw in a shaky breath, trying to absorb his strength, hoping he's right. Since I escaped Micah, Brody has been my only contact with the outside world. However, I needed solitude, more than anyone knows, while I worked out shit in my head.

The helicopter's powerful hum suddenly fills the air, rattling the windows slightly and breaking our moment. My heart thumps nervously, the anxious flutter returning.

Brody squeezes my hand one last time. "Come on."

Together, we step onto the porch, the crisp mountain air washing over me, clearing my head just enough to breathe. I shield my eyes from the sun and the dust swirling beneath the spinning blades as the helicopter settles onto the grass in the clearing ahead. Anticipation and dread tangle inside me. Figures inside begin to move.

I brace myself, heart hammering in my chest as the blades slow and finally stop, leaving a sudden stillness that fills the clearing. Dust settles slowly, drifting like golden particles through the sunlight. The door swings open, and my breath catches as Nick steps out, followed closely by Asher.

My nerves ease slightly at the sight of Nick's familiar, reassuring smile, his gaze immediately finding mine. He crosses the clearing with purposeful strides, pulling me into a comforting hug without hesitation.

"God, it's good to see you, stepsis," he says, relief in his voice. "You scared us, Harp. You good?"

"Getting there." I squeeze him tightly. We only became stepsiblings last year when his mom married my dad. Before then, he was my brother's best friend. Their relationship is still on the rocks, but I've forgiven him for being a dipshit. Nick has a kind heart and he's a good man at his core; he just makes dumb decisions with his dick.

Asher steps up behind him, calm and steady as ever, giving me a gentle nod. "We've got your back. You're not dealing with this alone."

Relief floods me, and it's almost overwhelming. But just as I start to relax, another figure emerges from the helicopter, one I wasn't expecting.

Billie.

My pulse spikes, and shock freezes me in place.

My best friend hesitates when our eyes lock together. Hers are filled with relief, worry, and something softer that makes my breath hitch. And before I can react, Zane climbs out behind her, my brother's familiar frame instantly recognizable, and he gives me a nod. Easton and Weston quickly follow.

"Everyone is here?" I whisper.

My heart swells painfully. They all came for me, even after all the chaos I caused.

Billie closes the distance quickly, reaching me in a rush. Without a word, she pulls me into her arms, holding me tight as my emotions fracture open. Hot tears blur my vision, slipping silently down my cheeks.

"Billie, I'm so sorry—"

"Don't you dare apologize. I was just terrified of losing you." She holds me tighter, cutting off my apology, her voice firm and filled with emotion. Her words break through the last of my defenses.

I cling to her, shaking as the weight of the guilt and uncertainty finally releases from me.

"I thought I'd lost you too," I admit.

She pulls back slightly, cupping my face between her hands, her eyes shining with sincerity. "You're family, Harp. We don't break that easily. Will take a lot more than a mediocre fucking man to destroy what we have."

I nod, choking back fresh tears, relief washing over me as Zane steps forward, pulling me into his arms.

"Sis," he says.

My brother's strong embrace steadies me, reminding me I've always had a safe place with him. Easton and Weston both offer smiles, their presence reassuring me that we're in this together. My eyes find Brody, and he offers me a comforting smile.

Right now, I'm surrounded by the people who love me the most, and the realization sinks in—they're here because they care; because, despite everything that's happened, they still want me to know I'm not alone. And for the first time in months, I actually believe the bonds that hold us together can withstand even the harshest storms.

Billie's expression shifts, her eyes welling with fresh tears. Her hand flies to her mouth, and a broken sob escapes, shattering the quiet.

"Hey," I whisper, immediately reaching for her hand.

She shakes her head quickly, tears slipping down her cheeks, even as she tries to laugh them off. "Nothing's wrong. I just—" She squeezes my fingers, her voice breaking. "I'm so happy you're okay. I missed you so much, and I just want my best friend back."

Her words hit me straight in the chest. Without hesitation, I pull her back into my arms, holding her tightly, like if I let her go, she'll disappear. "You never lost me. I'm right here, and I'm not going anywhere."

We stay wrapped together, crying until our tears finally slow.

When we pull apart, I offer her a smile. "And you know what? There's a bright side to all this chaos."

Billie bursts into laughter. "Of course you'd find a silver lining."

She wipes her eyes, raising an eyebrow curiously as we sit on the porch swing together. Brody and the boys stand in a circle as he explains a number of things that neither of us can hear.

I instinctively look over at him and feel warmth flooding me. The calm confidence radiating off him awakens something deep inside me that's been simmering for years.

Billie tilts her head knowingly, a slow smirk curving her lips as she follows my gaze. "Hmm, interesting choice of view."

Heat rushes to my face. "It's not … I mean, it's just …" I stutter, shaking my head, a shy laugh slipping out. "He makes me feel safe. Really safe."

Billie's smile widens, mischievous and teasing. "He always has. How's that crush?"

"He's Alcatraz, impossible to break through … still." I nudge her lightly, laughing. "Nothing's happened. We haven't even kissed."

"Have you tried?" Her expression softens.

I tuck my lips into my mouth, remembering our moment by the pond. "Denied. Do not pass go. Do not collect two hundred dollars."

A cute little smirk plays on Brody's lips when our eyes meet again. My brother notices, and his brows furrow as he looks between us.

I glance back at Billie, breaking the connection.

"You've had a thing for him for as long as I can remember. Maybe this happened for a reason. Maybe it's finally time you two gave each other a real chance."

I meet her gaze, my heart fluttering at her words. I catch Brody's eye just briefly before he turns away. Maybe it really is time.

The late afternoon sunlight spills golden across the clearing, casting warm, shifting shadows through the trees. Voices drift toward us from the yard, where Zane, Easton, Weston, and Asher talk low with Brody and Nick.

I still can't believe my closest friends and family are here, together, protecting and supporting me despite everything.

"You can tell me anything," Billie says. "You know that?"

"I know," I say. "And same."

Zane stalks toward me across the grass and steps onto the porch, his expression gentle and protective. "Hey, Harp," he says, stepping closer and lightly touching my arm. "Can we talk for a sec?"

"Sure," I say, sensing the seriousness beneath his casual tone.

He guides me away from Billie, toward the opposite end of the porch.

For a long moment, Zane simply looks at me, his blue-gray eyes searching my face intently.

"Are you really okay?" he finally asks. His voice is filled with genuine concern. "Don't give me the easy answer just because everyone else is here. I need the truth."

I swallow hard, knowing my brother would fight an army with his bare hands for me. "I'm getting there. It's been a lot, but I'm feeling more like myself every day."

His shoulders visibly relax, and the tense lines of his face soften. "Good. You had me scared, little sis. I'm so fucking glad Brody was there."

"Me too," I whisper.

Zane quickly shakes his head, squeezing my shoulder. "I just want you safe. Whatever you need, whenever you need it, you call me. I'm always here for you."

"I promise I will," I tell him, noticing the flicker of vulnerability in his gaze. I give him a soft smile. "How are you? How's Autumn?"

My brother got married last fall to the love of his life, Autumn. He met her at a coffee shop when he went to Cozy Creek to escape the world.

A warm smile spreads across his face. "She's incredible. The love of my life. I didn't realize how good things could be."

I study him carefully. "And you and Nick?"

He doesn't answer immediately, but his jaw tightens, and the pain in his eyes isn't lost on me.

It's a touchy subject, considering he and his previous fiancée ended things because she had been cheating on him with his best friend. Nick sometimes lets his dick think before his head. My brother said Nick was dead to him after that, but marrying that evil woman would've been a mistake.

Zane was supposed to find Autumn, and I smile, thinking about how damn cute they are together.

"It's complicated. He broke my trust, and I don't know if I can forgive that, but I'm trying. I can't promise it'll ever be the same between us, but we're working through it." He exhales slowly, glancing away. "He was my best friend. That's not something I can just easily forget."

I take his hand, squeezing it firmly. "People make mistakes, even huge, messy ones. Forgiveness is possible. I know it was super fucked up, but Nick is a good guy. Just kinda dumb sometimes."

"He is a dumb fuck. But also, when did you become the wise one?" he teases and glances over at the guys, who are deep in conversation. He adds, "We'll see what happens."

My brother's eyes land briefly on Brody, who's chatting with the others, his strength steadying me, even from a distance.

Zane clears his throat, eyes twinkling as he nudges my shoulder. "Speaking of complicated … Brody Calloway, huh?"

My cheeks flush instantly. "Shut up."

He grins warmly, lifting a hand in gentle surrender. "Relax, Harp. If I trust anyone with you, it's him. He's a Calloway. They don't do anything halfway. And if I recall, you've always had a thing for him. Bet you get married."

I tilt my head at him. "Isn't it usually my job to hand out love prophecies?"

He chuckles, eyes brightening with affection as he leans in, speaking near my ear. "Yeah, well, maybe it's finally your turn."

He straightens, his eyes sincere, the teasing fading into something deeply heartfelt. "You deserve happiness, Harp. Brody's a good guy. If that's what you want, you've got my full support."

A wave of emotion hits me unexpectedly, gratitude and relief mixing inside me. I pull my brother into a tight hug, closing my eyes briefly, soaking in his familiar strength. My brother is my rock, the only reason I survived my mother's death. He protected me through it all.

"Thank you," I say, not realizing how much I needed to hear that.

"Doesn't mean I won't give him hell and fuck him up though," he says with a laugh and a smirk as we pull away. "Now, try not to get into any trouble after I leave. Okay?"

"I'll try," I tell him. "No promises though. Trouble is my middle name these days."

"It's always been," he reminds me.

Zane guides us to where everyone is gathered, their laughter and easy banter drifting comfortably in the cool mountain air. Easton checks his watch, glancing briefly toward the waiting helicopter, then shifting his gaze toward his car parked on the gravel nearby.

Brody follows Easton's eyes, his mouth curving into an easy smirk. "Yes, your fucking car is still in one piece."

Easton chuckles, shaking his head in amusement. "You read minds now?"

"Something like that." Brody shrugs, his gaze steady but playful.

Weston elbows his brother, a mischievous glint in his eyes as he glances from Brody to me. "Maybe you two should just elope and get it over with. I'm sensing fireworks."

Billie shakes her head, smacking Weston's arms, but I know he's just giving Brody a hard time because it's obvious he's different. Happy, even. I think we both are.

"Behave," she warns him with a mock stern look before turning back to me with a soft smile. "Actually, Harp, before we go, I brought you something," she says. "Wait here."

She jogs to the helicopter and returns with a weekend bag stuffed full. "Thought you might need some clothes."

I squeeze her tight, nearly crying when I see the brightly colored fabrics inside the bag. "Thank you so much."

Brody takes it and jogs it inside the cabin for me. He's gone for less than thirty seconds.

"Can we take a picture of us together? You know, to post something casual online and let everyone know you're fine and just taking some personal time?" Billie asks.

"That's a good idea," Asher agrees with a nod. He's a marketing expert who helped us navigate a treacherous path with Bellamore when Billie's ex tried to destroy our company. "It could ease some of the pressure. Everyone thinks you're a missing person right now, but thankfully, since you didn't marry that stupid fuck, there is nothing he can do but talk."

"If you think it will help," I say, adjusting my hair. "Do I look like shit?"

"No," Brody says, and everyone turns to him. He shrugs with a smile but doesn't deny it.

Billie pulls out her phone, stepping close and wrapping an arm tightly around me. "On the count of three, say Little Miss Disaster."

I burst into laughter just as she snaps the photo.

"Gorgeous," she says, showing me.

We look happy, like we're teenagers again without a care in the world, even though everything outside of this cabin is so heavy.

I hug her tight, and she whispers in my ear, her voice only audible for me. "About that pregnancy test?"

"Hell no," I tell her, my voice louder than I intended. "Was a setup. He planned it, like he knew I was getting ready to run. I'm not pregnant." I tap my arm where my implant is. "Old Faithful is still going strong. My reputation, on the other hand ..."

She chuckles, but her relief is visible. She meets my eyes with a protective spark. "We'll fix this. I promise. Whatever it takes. Asher and Nick will help."

Emotion rushes through me, and I hold on to my best friend, the sister I never had. The helicopter's engine starts and sends the blades into a slow rotation, the rumble filling the space. When we pull apart, Billie's eyes shine, her determination easing any lingering fears inside me.

We exchange goodbyes, and I actually don't want them to leave, but there is nowhere for them to stay. Everyone moves toward the helicopter.

Easton reminds me they're all just a phone call away.

Weston shoots me another teasing grin, mouthing, *Elope*, dramatically, earning an amused shake of the head from Brody.

Zane pulls me into another firm, brotherly embrace. "Stay safe, Harper," he says. "Remember, whatever you need, I'm here for you."

"I will," I whisper back, hugging him one more time.

Nick and Asher finish their conversation with Brody, then give me waves as they load up.

Brody stands beside me as they lift off, wind tossing my hair around.

Stillness settles over us as the helicopter grows smaller and disappears behind the trees.

Brody grabs my hand and squeezes it. "Want to sit by the firepit tonight?"

I exhale slowly, feeling the weight vanish from my shoulders. "Sounds perfect. I'll grab us a drink."

"Grab the bottle." He smiles.

I move across the grass, take the porch, then step inside the cabin. The peaceful silence wraps around me as I reach into the cupboard and pull out the bottle of tequila. I smile, and it brings back several memories. Through the window, I watch Brody carefully arrange logs and kindling.

Today was exactly what I needed.

Seeing Billie, feeling her arms wrapped around me again, talking to her, and laughing—it's something I didn't realize I so desperately missed until that very moment. And Zane's protectiveness, his belief that things would somehow get better, soothed places in my heart that had been raw. My family and friends showing up for me humbled me deeply. We're in this together. All of us.

Stepping back outside, bottle in hand, I feel the comforting heat as the fire begins to take hold, crackling against the dusk. Brody settles into one of the chairs beside the flames, his steady gaze lifting immediately to mine. The warmth of the fire dances across his face, highlighting the strong lines of his jaw and his perfectly sculpted cheekbones.

"Come here, Harp," he says, his voice low.

I move to him without hesitation, allowing him to guide me onto his lap. His strong arms wrap easily around me, holding me securely against him, and I sink into him. The tension in my body melts away.

We pass the tequila back and forth, sipping in comfortable silence. He steadies me, and effortlessly, he makes me feel safe.

Brody's arms tighten around me ever so slightly, like he knows exactly where my thoughts have drifted, what storms linger beneath the calm surface. Without speaking a single word, he lets me know I'm safe, that he understands. I relax fully against him, savoring the gentle strength that surrounds me.

I tilt my head slightly, glancing up into his eyes, my voice barely above a whisper as I say, "Thank you."

He studies me, his gaze warm and curious. "For what?"

"For being here," I say, feeling the emotion swelling in my chest. "For not forcing me to talk about things before I'm ready. For just knowing exactly what I need."

"Always." His expression softens, tenderness flooding his features as he reaches up, tucking a loose strand of hair behind my ear.

My breath catches sharply, and before I can stop it, words slip from my lips.

"You're going to fall in love, Brody Calloway. And when you do, it'll change everything you've ever known about yourself." My eyes widen in surprise, and I cover my mouth. "Whoops."

"Did you just give me one of your famous love prophecies?"

I squeeze my eyes shut and nod. I open one eye to peek at him.

"Well then, I'll drink to that." Brody just gives a slow, easy chuckle, lifting the tequila to his lips, his eyes shining warmly in the firelight. He doesn't question or deny it. Instead, he just smiles, a knowing smile, as if he already knew, as if I merely confirmed something he'd accepted long before tonight.

My heart skips, and butterflies flood through me as I rest my head against his chest again, feeling the steady rhythm of his heartbeat. I close my eyes, savoring the peace that settles over us.

I know without a doubt that I'm not alone. I have an entire army behind me, people who love me unconditionally.

And most importantly, right now, I have Brody, and he has me.

18

BRODY

The next morning, Harper sits across from me, her expression softer than it has been in days. Something in my chest eases at the sight. Yesterday's reunion—Billie holding her close, Zane's careful protectiveness, the strength she drew from being around those who cared the absolute most—has left a calm I haven't felt since I rescued Harper.

She glances up and catches me looking at her. She tilts her head, raising one eyebrow in challenge, a teasing smile tugging at her mouth. "See something interesting?"

"You could say that," I reply, not bothering to hide the amusement in my voice.

Her cheeks flush a faint pink, the color spreading down her neck, and I smile deeper.

"You seem better today. Happier."

She nods, eyes drifting toward the window, lost in thought for a moment. When her gaze returns to me, she offers a sincere smile. "Yesterday meant more than I realized it would. Having everyone here reminded me that people still believe in me and care."

"You were never alone, Harp," I tell her firmly. "Not then. Not now. Never."

Gratitude and something warm flicker behind her careful expression. Silence hangs between us, but it's easy and comfortable. I watch her, sensing she needs something more than just sitting around the cabin today. Something away from this space where we've both processed too many heavy moments lately. An idea sparks in my mind, one I've been holding on to for the perfect moment.

I push myself away from the table, standing. "Let's go hiking. Not to the pond. Somewhere different."

She's instantly intrigued. "Yeah? Sounds like fun."

"You'll love it," I promise, already imagining the excitement she'll have when she sees where I'm taking her.

She studies me, curiosity dancing in her gaze. "So mysterious, Calloway."

"Always," I reply.

As Harper moves toward the door and slides on her shoes, I watch her, taking in the subtle confidence returning to her steps and the gentle sway of her hair down her back. I promised myself I'd never let anyone get too close again, never lower my walls enough to feel this. But as Harper glances back at me, her eyes bright and trusting, I know I've already lost that battle. Fuck, with Harper, I've lost the war. And right now, I couldn't care less.

I smirk as I hold a hand out to her. Her fingers lock with mine. The simple touch sends a slow pulse of heat through my veins. We walk together down the trail, and there is nowhere else I'd rather be.

This time, I openly steal glances of her, and we exchange smiles when our eyes meet. The anticipation of Harper's reaction hums beneath my skin as we navigate the path. I crave her reaction when she experiences something new. The urge to impress her—to show her something meaningful, something uniquely mine—is stronger than I'd like to admit.

The trail winds downward through tall pines and thick underbrush. She rubs her thumb gently across mine, causing my pulse to quicken, but I keep my expression calm. I've become an expert at hiding how her simple touch affects me.

"We're almost there," I say.

Her eyes flicker up to mine, curiosity dancing in their depths. "Almost where?"

"Patience, Harp." I offer a wink but reveal nothing.

She huffs, pretending to be irritated, but her grin gives her away. "Fine. Keep your secrets."

I lead her onward, weaving through the trees until the soft rumble of water echoes in the distance. I feel her awareness sharpen, her curiosity intensifying as the sound grows clearer. Finally, the trees part, revealing a secluded waterfall tumbling down a cliffside.

The water glistens silver in the sunlight as it cascades into a deep, clear pool below. It's beautiful, completely untouched, and hidden away on the mountain. It's a place I discovered the weekend I escaped here, the weekend Eden died. I've not been back. Until now.

Beside me, Harper draws in a soft, awed breath, her lips parting. She turns to me, her expression softening into something breathtaking.

"Brody," she whispers, stepping closer, eyes never leaving mine. "This place is like a dream."

"That's a good way to put it. Especially with you standing here in front of me," I admit, my throat tightening at the raw emotion on her face. "You're the first person I've shared this with."

"I feel special." She moves even closer, eyes searching mine intently, filled with unspoken meaning.

Her gentle words almost undo me. I reach up, brushing my thumb along her cheekbone, feeling the warmth of her skin beneath my touch. Harper leans subtly into my palm, eyes fluttering shut momentarily to savor the contact.

"You are special, Harp," I whisper. "I'm glad it's you."

Her eyes drift open slowly, locked on to mine. Neither of us moves or speaks. We stand in a charged moment, the unspoken words between us nearly too loud to bear.

Finally, I let my hand fall away, stepping back to break the intensity. I gesture toward the water, offering her a small, playful smile. "Come on. Let's get closer."

Her eyes linger with emotion. She steps beside me, our shoulders brushing again, and this time, I don't pull away. We walk toward the waterfall together, silence settling around us, filled with possibility and an understanding that something powerful between us has shifted.

Sunlight shimmers through the cascading water, sending prisms of color dancing across the smooth stone walls of the hidden cave. Harper pauses just inside, her breath hitches as she takes in the magic of the secluded space. Tiny droplets sparkle on her skin and hair, capturing the filtered rays of sunlight, and my pulse quickens as I watch her take it all in.

"Wow," she whispers, eyes wide with amazement. "This is breathtaking."

I nod slowly, unable to look away from how the shifting light plays across her face, illuminating every delicate feature. I can't help but agree with her assessment, but I'm not referring to this place, but rather her.

I step closer, removing some of the space between us. "It felt right, bringing you here."

Her eyes meet mine, warmth flooding her expression. "Thank you. It's perfect. Magical."

The sound of rushing water is muted, and nothing but a gentle curtain separates us from the outside world. Harper steps forward slowly, mesmerized, and I instinctively move with her, guiding her across the slick stone floor of the cave. The footing is slippery beneath us, and she stumbles forward.

"Careful," I say, catching her around the waist, pulling her close to my chest.

"My hero."

Harper's sharp intake of breath echoes around us, her hands grip my shoulders as she steadies herself. She looks up at me, sparkling blue eyes, chest rising and falling rapidly as she realizes how close we are. My heartbeat crashes against my ribs, the sensation of her pressed against me igniting something inside me that I've been trying to suppress for weeks, years even.

"You okay?" I whisper, my voice barely audible.

"Better now," she breathes, her voice trembling, her gaze locked on to mine.

The world narrows to the soft rise and fall of her chest, the warmth of her body molded against mine. My gaze dips to her lips, soft and slightly parted, inviting me closer in a way that shatters any remaining resistance I have left. Slowly, my hand rises to cup her cheek, and my thumb brushes her jaw. Harper's eyes drift closed, a soft sigh escaping her as she leans into my touch.

My pulse thunders in my ears, and an unfamiliar ache spreads through my chest.

Suddenly, the fragile thread of my control snaps.

I lean in, my lips brushing hers softly at first, a gentle touch, but the instant our mouths meet, something uncontrollable erupts inside me. Harper gasps, her fingers gripping the back of my neck, pulling me closer. The kiss ignites, spiraling us both into something raw, urgent, and necessary.

Her mouth opens beneath mine, a sweet moan slipping past her lips as the kiss deepens. Heat floods my veins, electrifying every nerve, and suddenly, I'm drowning in the sensation of her. Her warmth, sweetness, and hunger are unlike anything I've felt in years. Her body arches into mine, pressing closer, fueling the fire between us as she threads her fingers through my hair. I savor every inch of her mouth, overwhelmed by how perfectly she fits against me, by how much I craved this very moment.

"Brody," she breathes again, her voice ragged, and it sends chills down my spine.

Her moan fills the space and awakens the sleeping dragon inside me, flaring back to life. Desire and longing mix together in an unstoppable wave that crashes over us.

I grip her tighter, deepening the kiss, needing her in ways I can't fully comprehend, yet understanding how long I've waited for this, waited for her. Our tongues twist together, and her soft whimpers are nothing more than a surrender to this, to us. It nearly undoes me. We're dangerously close to losing control, passion building to a sharp, reckless edge, and if we don't stop, we'll fall off the cliff together.

My heart slams painfully in my chest. I'm alarmed by the intensity of our emotions. Slowly, I pull away, breathing heavily, my forehead resting against hers.

"Harp," I rasp, the ache of longing bleeding into my voice, "there is no rush."

"I know," she whispers, her voice shaking slightly, eyes still closed. "You just make me want to lose control."

The feeling is fucking mutual.

We linger, holding each other close, breathing in the hush behind the waterfall. The gentle mist settles against our flushed skin, cooling the intensity to ground us in the moment.

When Harper finally opens her eyes, the softness and vulnerability in her gaze steal my breath. She smiles faintly, shy and sweet, her fingertips tracing down my face.

"You feel it too, don't you?" she whispers, barely audible.

"Yes," I admit, pressing my forehead against hers again. "I do."

I swallow hard, feeling every wall I've built to protect my heart crumbling to ash. I'm still breathing hard when I pull away. Not because I want to. Hell no. If I had my way, I'd keep kissing her until the sun dipped below that rock ledge and the cave filled with shadows.

But I know that if we don't pump the brakes now, we're going to cross a line there's no coming back from.

Harper's eyes stay locked on mine—bright, breathless, daring.

There's a flush on her cheeks that matches the teasing curve of her swollen lips.

"Do you always stop when things start getting good?" she asks, voice light but laced with something more.

I exhale slowly. "Just trying to keep us from setting the whole forest on fire."

Her grin spreads. "Your control is impeccable. Or is it?"

Fucking temptress.

Harper moves out of the cave, then takes a step toward the pool's edge and lifts her shirt in one slow, fluid motion. She tosses it onto a dry rock, then shimmies out of her leggings and panties, not bothering with modesty.

I cover my eyes. "What are you doing?"

"It's called living a little!" She dives into the large crystal-blue pool of water with a loud, "Woohoo."

A beat passes. Then her head pops up, and a radiant smile waits for me as she treads water.

"Come on!" she calls out. "You scared?"

I arch a brow. "Of what?"

"Of me. Of this. Of skinny-dipping." She swims around, laughing, and kicks lazily in the water. "Unless you're a chicken! But I'm telling everyone when we get back to the city." Her voice echoes through the forest.

I cross my arms, watching her. "What the fuck did you just say?"

She grins, eyes glittering. "Chicken!"

That does it. I yank my shirt over my head, kick off my boots, and strip with quick efficiency, muttering something about reckless women and how they're going to be the death of me.

Then I dive in after her, water rushing around me like a jolt to the system. She squeals as I resurface near her, and her laughter wraps around me like a second current, pulling me in, deeper than the water ever could.

"Now admit I'm not."

"Guess you proved me wrong." She smirks, swimming toward me until we're just inches apart.

The warmth from the sunshine covers us as the mood turns more serious. Her blue eyes glimmer, her dark hair is slicked straight back, and droplets of water cling to her sun-kissed shoulders like scattered pearls. There's fire behind her eyes as she coaxes me to come even closer. And I do.

"If you keep looking at me like that," she says, her voice hushed but electric, "I might think you have a crush on me."

I lick my lips, studying hers. "What if I do?"

"Do you?" Her smile tilts, like she already knows.

Silence streams between us.

"Mmm. The non-answer answer—love those," she whispers, closing the last space between us.

My fingers find her waist beneath the water. She doesn't flinch. She leans in.

"What do you think?" I ask, breath ghosting across her lips.

Her lashes flutter as her eyes close. "I can only hope."

I don't wait another second. I kiss her again. It starts soft, like we're testing the edge of something too big to name. But her lips part with a sigh that undoes me, and before I know it, we're clinging to each other, mouths urgent, bodies tangling in the water like we've been trying not to fall for years. She presses closer, fingers threading into my hair, her body molding against mine with no hesitation. No walls. Just heat, skin, and want.

I can't get enough of her. Of this. Of us. Her name's on my tongue, and I want her, need her more than I need air, when lightning strikes nearby in a loud crack.

Our eyes jolt open just as thunder slams overhead like the sky's being ripped apart.

Harper clutches close to me. We're both panting, eyes wide, lips kiss-bitten. We're drunk on one another, lost in the high of finally fucking crossing the line.

"Well," I say, trying to catch my breath, "that's one way to kill the mood."

But she isn't looking at me anymore. Her gaze lifts toward the sky, where mist rises and sunlight cuts through the shadows like a spotlight. A rainbow has formed from the mist of the waterfall, and she smiles.

Floating there—fluttering just above the surface—is a butterfly. Pale yellow, wings delicate and shimmering like it doesn't belong to this world at all.

Harper goes completely still, and a soft smile touches her lips. It's smaller than before, but deep.

"What is it?" I ask, voice low.

She doesn't answer at first. Just keeps watching the butterfly until it drifts higher and disappears into the trees beyond the falls.

When her eyes meet mine, they're a little brighter than they were a moment ago.

"Nothing," she says. "Just ... the universe. Those little signs show up when I least expect them."

And for once, I don't need the full story.

The storm rumbles in the distance, the fire between us still smoldering, but now wrapped in something gentler. Something bigger than the whole fucking sky.

I steal another kiss, and she whimpers against me as I thread my fingers through her wet hair.

Before the kiss deepens further, I pull away. "We should be responsible and head back," I mutter reluctantly, not wanting this moment to ever end. "Mountain storms move fast."

"Always so logical." Harper sighs, but grins.

We swim to the edge, and I pull myself out of the water. When I turn around, Harper's eyes are focused on me.

I glance at her over my shoulder as I gather our clothes. "Like something you see?"

She chews on her plump bottom lip. "We're past like."

Harper confidently steps out of the water, and I glance away, giving her privacy.

"You can look," she mutters, running her fingers through her soaked hair. "I want you to see what you've been missing out on."

My eyes slide from hers, down her body, and I absorb every small detail—the graceful curve of her neck, the soft strands of hair still damp from the waterfall. Her beautiful breasts and little pink nipples that are pointed like peaks. I slide down her stomach and notice a tattoo on her lower hip.

"Wait, you have a tattoo?"

She laughs, taking her clothes from my grasp. "Yes."

"What does it say?" I bend down to look at the cursive writing.

She grins. *"Little Miss Disaster."*

Laughter howls out of me as we dress.

"Guess my nickname for you is permanent then?"

"Kinda stuck forever," she tells me. "I did try to kiss you, then puked on you. I earned it."

"If at first you don't succeed," I say, not finishing, because I'm so damn glad she didn't give up on me.

Need and want simmer below the surface of our stolen glances. I can feel it in the charged silence, in every smoldering glance Harper sends my way as she pulls on her shirt.

The first faint raindrops begin falling onto the leaves, and I can hear the whoosh of rainfall and wind in the distance.

I hold my hand out for her, and we start along the winding trail back toward the cabin. Our footsteps are muffled by the soft forest floor as the world around us darkens beneath the gathering storm clouds.

"Seems like I'm always running from a storm, figuratively and literally," Harper says, glancing upward as another low rumble vibrates overhead.

"It's not you. The weather is unpredictable this time of year. I should've looked at the radar. This is why I'm not spontaneous," I reply, matching my steps to hers. "If we keep this pace, we'll return before the heavy stuff hits."

She gives me a faint smile, bumping her shoulder playfully against mine. "Just know there's no one else I'd rather be caught in the rain with."

I chuckle, casting her a sideways glance. "Fucking same."

Harper looks up at me, eyes sparkling with amusement, and her lips turn up into a mischievous smile.

"What?" I ask, raising an eyebrow at her.

"Nothing," she says, a faint blush coloring her cheeks as she glances away, biting back a grin. "Just trying to get the image of your perfect ass out of my head."

"Good luck." I shake my head slowly, my laughter gentle and deep as we step around a cluster of tree roots, our path growing steadily narrower. "I'm what dreams are made of."

"There's that Calloway cockiness I've missed," she counters.

I lift a brow at her, and she shrugs.

I let myself relax, allowing her laughter and teasing to fill spaces in me I thought were permanently empty.

Our silence is comfortable, easy, as the distant roll of thunder grows closer. More raindrops fall, tapping more steadily through the canopy above.

The cabin comes into view just as the bottom falls from the sky. The rain feels like ice against my hot skin. Harper quickens her pace, reaching out to tug my hand lightly. I pick her up and throw her over my shoulder as I sprint to the porch.

"Brody!" she yells while laughing. "You can't pick me up like a caveman and just throw me over your shoulder whenever you want to."

I smack a hard palm against her ass before I set her down under the shelter of the porch roof of the cabin. "Just did. What will you do about it?"

The sky opens up, rain cascading heavily, drenching everything we just left behind.

"Might have to put that strength to work in other ways, like in the shower and up against a wall," she mutters, biting her bottom lip.

"You should stop that," I warn, knowing the little control I have left is dangling on a severed rope. It will inevitably snap, but when?

"What will you do about it?" It falls from her mouth like a challenge.

Her hair is damp, and her eyes are bright with exhilaration. My breath stalls in my chest at the sight of her being so carefree, beautiful, and alive.

"What?" she whispers, holding my gaze.

I step closer without thinking, removing all the space between us. I lean in and whisper in her ear, "You're breathtaking."

Her fingers cling to my shirt as she looks up into my eyes. "I'm tired of lines and rules," she says as rain pounds steadily around us, closing us off from the world.

My fingers brush hers gently, her gaze dropping briefly.

"I'm trying really fucking hard."

"I know," she whispers, and a breathless silence settles between us, heavy with anticipation and promise.

I wish I could explain my hesitation, and one day, I'll be able to fully articulate my fears, but I can't. Not yet.

Harper smiles, almost shyly, as if she can read my mind, and she doesn't push me to speak. She never does.

"We should get inside," she mutters.

My chest tightens as she pulls away. "You're right."

She moves toward the door, casting me a final glance full of hope, almost like she can envision our entire future together. Through her silence, I know Harper's not giving up on me, and, fuck, I'm not giving up on her either. We'll make it through this storm together.

19

HARPER

The storm outside rages on. Wind-driven rain pounds the cabin's roof in relentless waves. I step into the bedroom, tugging off my damp shirt and shivering slightly in the cool air. Brody's in the kitchen, brewing coffee. The rich aroma drifts down the short hall, filling the cabin as The Beatles play on his phone. He's such an old soul.

I open a random dresser drawer to see what's inside, temporarily needing something dry and warm to chase away the chill. I stare into the drawer in confusion when I see women's clothes, folded neatly, in careful stacks. My heart skips as I slowly lift a faded gray tank top. My fingers tremble slightly, and a strange sensation tightens my chest.

I remember Brody's USMC jogging pants in my dresser drawer, planted to test the fragile, insecure men. The way I feel right now isn't based on insecurity, but curiosity and a hefty dose of jealousy. I dig further and see a pair of shorts from Bellamore's summer line, almost six years ago. I know because I designed them.

I glance toward the doorway, my pulse fluttering with uncertainty. I don't have the right to feel jealous because I'm the one who's here right now. An unsteady ache nudges me forward, and my thoughts drift to how secluded the cabin is and how special this place seems to be to Brody, and suddenly, I need to know whose clothes these are and why they're still here.

"Harper?"

I jump, spinning quickly toward Brody's voice. He stands in the doorway, holding two steaming mugs of coffee, his expression shifting from casual ease to tension as his gaze lands on the cutoff shorts in my hands.

A shadow flickers briefly in his eyes before he carefully adjusts his features. His jaw tightens, and the muscles in his shoulders go rigid. The quiet that follows is broken by the rain pounding against the roof.

"Who do these belong to?" I ask, keeping my tone light, forcing my voice to sound steadier than I feel. I hold up the shorts, my heart hammering at the guarded look settling on his face. "They have great taste."

Brody remains silent, stepping forward slowly to set both mugs on the bedside table. His movements are measured and cautious, as though he's preparing for battle.

When he finally meets my eyes again, his voice is low, edged with vulnerability he rarely reveals. "They were Eden's."

My breath stalls at the sound of an old friend's name.

The air between us grows heavy. Carefully, as if this moment were porcelain, I lower the shorts and fold them back, placing them into the drawer. My fingers tremble as I let them go.

"Eden Banks?" I whisper, my voice tight.

My heart twists in confusion. Eden and I were friends, connected through Billie and casual coffees, conversations about Bellamore, and the future we assumed was endless. Her life was cut too short five years ago. I'm speechless as I understand the magnitude of what Brody has carried for so damn long.

"I ... I didn't realize you two ..." I say.

Brody remains still, his dark gaze steady on mine, shadows

deepening in his expression. He releases a slow breath, as if trying to gather his words carefully before speaking.

"No one knew," he finally says. "Except Weston and Billie."

My throat tightens slightly. "Asher?"

"He knows now, but he didn't back then," he replies, pain weaving through his voice.

Brody crosses the small distance between us, sitting carefully on the edge of the bed. His gaze drops to his clasped hands, knuckles tight as he gathers strength.

"Eden and I ... we were ... brief. It was complicated. Just a fling. She wanted it to stay secret. It ended a week before she was killed."

Silence stretches between us, broken only by the rain and my racing heart. I step closer without realizing it, sinking down beside him on the mattress. My shoulder brushes against his as I search for words.

"You never told anyone," I say, pain flickering in my chest at the thought of Brody dealing with this alone for years on top of everything else he's endured. "You've kept this bottled up?"

"Who would care?" He gives me a faint, weary smile, the kind that doesn't reach his eyes. "I promised her it would stay between us. After she died, telling anyone felt like betrayal. It became easier to hold it in."

I reach out slowly, resting my hand on his forearm, feeling the tension radiate through him. "You didn't deserve to carry that alone. Eden wouldn't have wanted that for you."

His eyes find mine again. "I thought I could handle it. Then, over time, keeping secrets became second nature. Easier, safer for everyone."

I grab his hand, turning to him, interlocking my fingers with his. "You protect everyone around you. But who's protecting you?"

His lips part, but no sound emerges; the question catches him off guard. His eyes drift downward again; his expression moves into quiet resignation. "Me."

"No," I say firmly, my voice steady despite how my heart aches for him. "You deserve to have someone be there for you, just as you've been there for everyone else. I'm so fucking sorry. I can't imagine."

Brody lifts his gaze again, watching me silently for a long, intense moment. The lines in his face begin to soften, gradually replaced by gratitude. "You're the first person I've ever told."

I smile. "Thank you for trusting me."

Tenderness flickers across his face as he reaches out, tucking a loose strand of hair behind my ear. "You're the easiest person in the world to trust, Harp. Always have been."

"I won't tell anyone." It's a whispered promise.

"Thank you," he offers.

The air between us grows warm and charged again. But this moment isn't about passion; it's about two hurt people finally laying down all their burdens and choosing to trust despite having every reason not to.

We sit close enough to share the comforting rhythm of each other's breathing while the storm continues outside, washing away years of carefully built walls between us.

Neither of us says a word while the steady drumming of rain fills the silence around us, smoothing the edges of Brody's confession. Our words linger between us as our thoughts wander. I never realized the weight he'd carried behind his guarded exterior. His sorrow runs much deeper than I could've guessed.

He slowly draws a breath, shifting his body toward mine on the bed, the mattress dipping under his weight. "I've spent years convincing myself that everyone I cared about was better off if I stayed at a distance. I lose everyone I love." His voice breaks slightly on the last word.

His tone shakes something loose inside me as I recognize the unbearable sadness in his words.

"I'm not going anywhere," I whisper.

Brody stares down at our entwined hands, his thumb brushing over my knuckles. "It's safer for everyone—and maybe for me too—

if I keep those I care about at arm's length. I'm fucking terrified because the world keeps proving me right."

My throat tightens, tears prickling behind my eyes. I squeeze his hand, trying to pour every ounce of comfort and reassurance into that simple touch. "Losing people isn't something you caused. None of it was your fault."

When I meet his eyes again, I see years of hidden grief reflecting back at me. How did I miss this?

I reach up with my free hand, cupping his cheek. His eyes flutter closed at the touch, leaning slightly into my palm, as if craving contact but still afraid to embrace it fully.

"I'm here," I whisper, brushing my thumb over his cheek. "You don't have to go through this alone. Not anymore. Not ever again."

His eyes open, meeting mine, and I've never seen him in this light before. His gaze traces over my face, searching, as if committing every detail to memory.

"You've always been able to see straight through me, Harp. Even when we were younger. It always scared me, but right now, I'm more grateful for it than ever. To be seen is the greatest gift a person can give to another."

"You see me too," I whisper, leaning forward, our foreheads touching. "Whatever ghosts you're facing, we'll greet them together, okay?"

Brody exhales, tension visibly leaving his shoulders.

For the first time, he lets go, allowing me into the guarded space he's always kept closed. I breathe against him, realizing that he's not just healing me while we're here, but maybe I'm healing him too.

He breathes out. "Coffee's getting cold."

I stand, grab my mug, and tug him into the living room, leaving the emotions behind us. The rain is steady against the windows, creating a comforting rhythm that mirrors my heartbeat.

Brody moves toward the fireplace, arranging logs before striking a match. Fire engulfs the dry wood, and warm, golden firelight spills across the cabin walls, flickering and washing away the shadows in his expression.

I curl up on one end of the couch, tucking my legs beneath me, and watch him, noting the care and patience in his every movement. Even the smallest gesture seems full of intention, every touch deliberate.

He finally settles on the opposite end of the couch, leaning back against the cushions and stretching out his long legs. He's thoughtful, staring into the fire. I watch him closer, no longer shy about studying the subtle shifts in his features.

"Are you okay?" I ask, my voice hesitant.

He glances over at me, his eyes softening as they meet mine. "Yeah, I think I am," he says, lips curving upward.

He watches me closely for a long moment, and my heart flutters. The silence between us is filled with unspoken meaning—an acceptance of everything we've been through, everything we've shared, and how we'll make it through to the other side together. The warmth in his eyes sends a flutter of butterflies through me.

"Harper," he says, as though my name holds a thousand unspoken promises, "thank you."

A faint smile touches my lips.

"Thank you for today. For being here. For not letting me run away from myself, even when I want to."

"I'm not going anywhere. How does it feel to be stuck with Little Miss Disaster?"

He laughs, and the sound lights a fire within me. "Perfect," he whispers, holding my gaze. "Because I don't think I could survive letting you go."

The honesty in his words steals my breath, leaves my pulse racing, yet somehow calms me, all at once.

I nod, my throat tightening with emotion as a few tears spill down my cheeks. "Me neither."

"Come here," he whispers.

I scoot toward him, and he wraps his strong arms around me,

holding me tight against him, as if I'll disappear. My fingers grasp his T-shirt as I inhale his skin, not wanting to let him go.

We fall into comfortable silence, snuggled together as the fire crackles. The rain sprinkles against the cabin windows, leaving long streaks.

Today, we've found one another, and everything is right in the world.

20

BRODY

The next day, we step onto the front porch, and I close and lock the cabin door behind us. Harper stands close beside me, her presence comfortable, yet it's charged with something new and exciting. Even the slightest glance from her sends warmth rushing through me.

"Ready for this?" I ask, twirling the keys to the Charger around my finger.

"It feels weird, being dressed and going out," she admits as the sunlight catches in her golden-brown hair, pulled up into a messy ponytail. "But I'm ready. Can't stay hidden in the cabin forever."

I link my pinkie with hers, making my heart beat a little faster each time I test these new boundaries. She fully laces our fingers together and squeezes in response. It feels natural, right, like this has been a long time coming.

I open the door for her, and she slides in. Our eyes meet as I walk around the front of the car, then slide in behind the steering wheel.

We buckle, and she turns to me.

"Out of everything in Easton's garage, why did you choose this specific vehicle?"

I crank the engine, letting it roar, feeling the rumble and power under my fingers. I smirk. "You know exactly why."

"Fucking around and finding out suits you," she admits.

"This car should've been mine. Had I been five minutes earlier to bid on it," I admit as I back out of the driveway, kicking up gravel.

Her head falls back with laughter. "Ah, so it's personal too."

"It always is with me," I tell her as we head down the mountain, taking the switchbacks carefully.

Harper rolls down her window, closing her eyes and breathing in the fresh mountain air. I do the same, forcing myself to focus on the road instead of on her.

"This is true freedom," she whispers dreamily as she stares at the winding road ahead, surrounded by tall trees.

She reaches for my hand again, and I give it to her. This closeness feels like something we both need, something that's safe. Her thumb absently strokes my thumb, and it causes my body to hum with electricity. It's strange how something so simple can be so meaningful. It's like every touch we exchange holds a silent promise.

"What are our plans today?" She glances at me.

"Groceries and whatever else you want to do." I offer her a reassuring smile.

She laughs. "I never thought something as simple as going to town could feel like an adventure."

The warmth of her laughter stirs something deep inside me. "Every day is an adventure with you, Harp."

Her cheeks heat as loose strands of her hair blow freely in the breeze. "Wait, are you getting soft on me?"

"Never." I smirk, glancing sideways at her. "You just tend to bring out the best in me."

"I like that option," she says as sunlight streams across her face.

Being here with her like this feels like a dream, like something I've only imagined. Right now, it's our reality.

"Why are you looking at me like that?" she asks.

"You're breathtaking," I whisper. "A masterpiece."

She lifts my hands to her lips and presses a soft kiss on my knuckles. "You make me feel pretty."

"You are."

Everything between us feels so delicate and balanced. I glance down briefly at our joined hands and think about how we got here.

"What are we doing?" She turns to me, giving me her full attention.

I stare at the fluffy clouds overhead, thinking deeply about that question. "I don't know."

Her eyes narrow. "Okay, so if I wanted to put myself back out there when we returned to the city and I started dating other people, would th—"

"Fuck no." My brows furrow. "Absolutely fucking not."

"That's what I thought." She snickers, amused with herself.

"You have no idea what watching you with that piece of shit did to me."

I swallow hard, and her face softens.

"I can't imagine," she admits, knowing she's never had to witness me with anyone.

My relationships have always stayed secret. It's not that I've hidden them; it's just easier without public scrutiny.

"Do you know why I gave him a chance?"

I shake my head.

"Because he acted like he saw me for who I was at my core. In reality, you're the only man who ever has," she admits so fucking freely.

"Harp," I whisper, "I'm so fucking sorry he tricked you."

"I'm not. While I want him to get what he deserves," she says with confidence, "his actions made me see what was right in front of me all along, and I will forever be grateful for that."

A chill runs over me. "You somehow always see the bright side."

We park on Main Street, and I open the door for her. She steps out onto the sidewalk, wearing a cute pink dress that buttons in the front.

First on our list is getting her another cell phone so she can have contact with the outside world. We step inside the electronics store and buy the smartest phone they have, and the first thing Harper does is sync it to her cloud account.

As her pictures load, she lets out a sigh of relief. "I was so scared that I'd lost everything."

She holds the device tightly in her grip as we leave.

At the end of the block is a small grocery store. I hook my pinkie with Harper's, and we walk down the sidewalk toward it. At the front is a line of metal carts, and I grab one.

She waggles her brow at me as I push it around. "Hot."

"Hush," I tell her as she randomly eye-fucks me.

Every item that draws her attention, she plucks it off the shelf and tosses it inside the cart. She grabs junk food—snack cakes, bags of chips, popcorn, chocolate—as I mentally plan actual meals and get essentials.

"Don't tell anyone, but I'm really just a kid with adult money," she mutters, throwing in a massive bag of extra-cheddar crackers and Oreo cookies.

"As long as you still eat your fruits and veggies, I see no issue," I tell her with a wink.

"Happy one of us is responsible." She nudges me with her elbow.

Once the cart is full and we have enough for the week, we go to the front to check out. We don't get too much because I know we'll have to return to the city soon. While I want to stay in the cabin with Harper for an eternity, she won't be able to stay hidden forever. Bellamore needs her, and the public has been highly concerned about her after Micah made it seem like she was a missing person. That will be solved soon though.

As I load everything on the conveyor belt, she snatches up different candy bars, and then her eyes widen. "Shit, I'll be right back. I forgot one thing."

A minute later, Harper returns with a box of tampons. "Just in case."

She plops it down on the belt as our food is packed into the thermal grocery bags I picked up so we could spend more time in town if Harper wanted.

However, I'm leaving what we do for the rest of the day up to her. The last thing I want is for her to be overwhelmed. Being isolated can do that to a person.

My hands are full of the bags, and she tries to take some from me, but I shake my head at her. "I've got it."

"So, I guess I'm just supposed to stand here and look pretty while the circulation gets cut off in your hands?"

"Exactly. And you're doing a fucking great job."

"Thanks," she tells me. "I don't remember the last time I shopped for food. I usually have it delivered to my penthouse."

"Because you're spoiled," I say.

She gasps like she's offended, then tucks her lips into her mouth because she knows she can't deny it.

"And you deserve to be," I add. "If you were mine—"

"I can be yours. When you're ready," she says, and we both know right now that whatever this is going on between us, there are no labels.

I unlock the trunk, and we load the groceries inside.

I grab her hand, pulling her close to me. "You just got out of a shitty relationship, Harp," I explain, giving her a sweet smile. "I can't be your rebound."

"Brody Calloway," she tells me playfully, "I've had a crush on you since I was thirteen. You don't fit the rebound mold. And not to mention, I've not been dicked down by you so how could you even consider it that?" She shrugs.

I shake my head, but I can't help the laughter that spills out of me. "I don't know what I'm going to do with you."

"I can think of a few things," she offers. "Actually, I can make a list."

"Not. Helping."

Harper glances at the cozy Sugar Pine Springs Diner, nestled between a boutique and an antique shop. "Oh, can we eat?"

"Whatever you want," I tell her.

"Whatever I want?" she asks, playfully tucking her hands into her pockets and biting her lip.

I grab her hand, leading her down the sidewalk. "You're making it very hard to be a gentleman."

She waggles her brows, and her eyes slide from my lips down to my dick.

"Harp," I whisper, trying to hold back a smile as we enter, but I fail.

A bell jingles overhead, and a younger woman instantly greets us. "Whoa. You're like the perfect couple."

"I agree," Harper says, lifting her brow at me.

I playfully shake my head at her, but I like her pushing this. It shows me that she's not just going with the flow. I'm her prize, and, fuck, I'd be lying if I said she wasn't mine.

"How 'bout a booth for y'all?" the woman asks with a twang as she grabs two laminated menus that are front and back.

"Perfect," Harper answers, and we're led across the space.

The diner is packed with locals. No one is paying attention to us. While in Sugar Pine Springs, we're invisible, just two regular people without pasts or family expectations or paparazzi.

Harper glances back at me, her smile bright. Without thinking about it, I remove the space between us, placing my hand on the small of her back.

She slides into a booth by the window, sunlight pooling across the tabletop, and instead of taking the seat across from her, I scoot in beside her.

She settles against me, and I wrap my arm around her. Whatever this is, it's growing at a rate that neither of us can control.

The server walks up, and we quickly order coffee and water,

then tell her to give us the breakfast special that has a little of everything—from sausage to hash browns to a stack of pancakes.

When we're alone, Harper pulls her new phone from her dress pocket. I watch her, enjoying how loose strands of hair frame her pretty face and how she absently chews her lower lip as she scrolls. My gaze lingers, noticing small things, like how her long eyelashes sweep softly against her cheeks, and how the corners of her mouth tug into a small, secretive smile.

Feeling my stare, she glances up, catching me. "See something interesting, Calloway?"

"*Very,*" I reply, holding her gaze a heartbeat longer. I lean slightly toward her, whispering in her ear, "Just wondering how long I can get away with staring before you call me out on it."

A delicate color that matches her dress spreads across her skin. "Maybe I won't say anything ever again then."

"Because you like it." I rub my fingers on the outside of her arm and watch goose bumps form. I've always done that to her.

"Maybe I do," she whispers back, her eyes holding mine for longer than necessary.

The moment is filled with anticipation as I consider kissing her right here, and even though I want to, I don't. Instead, I glance out the window, scanning the perimeter, making sure nothing is out of place.

I relax as I drink my coffee, and suddenly, Harper's brows furrow. Her happiness is replaced by a scowl.

"Harp?" My voice lowers instinctively. "What's wrong?"

She hesitates, biting her lip again, before slowly turning the phone toward me. I lean closer, seeing Billie's Instagram post. It's the photo of them together, and it's hard to believe it was just a couple of days ago. I read the caption.

Don't believe what you see. Harper is happy, safe, and let's not forget to mention ... single. She's taking some much-needed personal time.

The comments are full of praise and congratulations, with people saying they hated Micah. He's being called an obsessed liar, which is more truthful than any of them knows. While I know she doesn't like this type of attention, seeing her supporters stepping up to bat for her is good for her. Even so, I sense her rising unease and feel the subtle stiffening of her shoulders as her jaw tightens. Harper has always dealt with anxiety, and it's something I instantly recognize. I always have.

I lean close and whisper into her hair, "You're okay. You're safe."

She types in Micah's profile, and the past few pictures that he posted are of the two of them together. My fist clenches, and so does my jaw. She clicks on the photo, and below it is nothing but people telling Micah he's a piece of shit.

"Hey," I say, clicking the button on the side of her phone. "You don't have to go down that rabbit hole right now, okay?"

She nods as she sets her phone down. "You're right. Seeing his face made it feel real. I hate this so much." Her voice is full of hurt.

"Hey." My voice drops, and I give her my full attention. "The world will eventually know the truth about him."

"I hope it sets me free, Brody. I'm scared I'll always be a prisoner to Micah." Harper takes a slow breath, leaning into my shoulder, eyes fixed thoughtfully on her coffee cup. "Each reminder forces me to relive it again and again. I think he would've killed me."

My nostrils flare at the thought, and I have no doubt he would've severely hurt her when he got the first chance. Especially considering the state I found her in that night I took her from that fucking prison of a home.

I give her a soft smile and turn my body toward her, where I'm almost facing her. "You know what brings me an immense amount of joy?"

She finally lifts her gaze, meeting mine. "What?"

"Revenge."

We stare at each other, and a sly grin slides over her perfect lips.

"Every time your subconscious brings his beady fucking eyes to the forefront, know that justice will be served on a silver platter. I promise," I say. "He fucked with the wrong ones this time."

"Please," she whispers, shaking her head. "Don't fight this battle."

"We're past that, Harp. This is war," I admit. "I owe him for Billie. And for you. He's hurt people I care deeply about, and no one gets a free pass when it comes to that. Do you understand?"

She sighs. "If I asked you not to, would you?"

"I'm sorry, but no. You and Billie deserve peace. The only way you will ever get that is if Micah is behind bars or dead. His choice, I guess."

"I want you to be safe. I can't lose you." She lifts her coffee cup to her mouth and drinks.

"You won't. This is almost over. I promise," I tell her, knowing that the boys are doing everything they can to uncover all of Micah's lies.

Easton, Weston, Asher, and Nick are the most intelligent humans in the world, with connections that run parallel to mine. Nick is a man no one should mess with, a man many underestimate, but he is a secret weapon.

Our food is delivered, and our table is full of different plates.

As we eat, I glance out the window and notice dark clouds rolling in, blotting out the sun as Harper finishes her coffee. She glances outside, her brow creasing slightly as a low rumble of thunder vibrates through the glass.

"Looks like the storm caught up to us," she says. "It always does."

Her words are more ominous than I'd like.

Harper grabs the syrup and covers her stack of pancakes with it. She cuts into them and takes a bite, and her eyes light up.

"How are they?" I ask.

She swallows down the bite. "Yours are better."

Laughter escapes me. "Don't flatter me."

"Whatever, pancake king. It's the truth."

We eat until it's hard to breathe, and as I hand our server my card, the rain begins to pour outside, coating the large windows in streaks of water.

We stand, and I grab her hand and lead her to the front. "Stay here. I'll grab an umbrella."

"Okay," she tells me, eyes shining just for me.

Fuck, I want to kiss her again, but I hold off. I step outside.

The first drops of cool rain pound against me. It quickly turns to sheets, pouring relentlessly down. By the time I reach the Charger, my shirt is plastered against my chest, soaked through. Shaking the water from my face, I retrieve the umbrella tucked beneath the seat, pop it open, and hurry back toward the diner entrance.

Harper stands just inside the doorway, arms folded across her chest as she watches me approach, her lips curled into a gentle, amused smile. I hold the umbrella up as she steps out, carefully keeping it over her.

"You didn't have to do that," she says, laughter coloring her voice as she leans into my side.

"I don't mind," I answer, meeting her gaze, suddenly aware of how close we're standing beneath the small canopy of the umbrella. "Besides, I couldn't let you get wet."

"I'll keep my comments to myself," she says, biting her lip as she turns to me.

She tilts her face upward, her eyes softening, searching mine as rain pounds steadily against the fabric overhead, creating a private cocoon that isolates us from the world. Her hand slips into mine, intertwining our fingers naturally, pulling me even closer, leaving me breathless.

Slowly, inevitably, the distance between us vanishes. My heartbeat quickens. With awareness building into something raw and undeniable, I lift my free hand to cup her cheek, my thumb brushing lightly across her rain-speckled skin. Her breath hitches at my touch, her lips parting in anticipation.

Without hesitation, our mouths finally meet—soft, warm, tentative at first. But as she melts into me, the kiss deepens naturally, her soft sigh drawing me further into her. Harper's hand clutches my soaked shirt, pulling me closer, as if needing more—more of me, more of us, more of whatever this is we've found together in the storm.

The rain continues to pour, splashing onto the pavement around us, but beneath this small umbrella, all I feel is her warmth pressed firmly against me, her lips parting beneath mine, our bodies fitting perfectly together. Every wall I've built around myself crumbles under her kiss and the urgency in how she clings to me.

We finally pull back, foreheads resting together, our breaths mixing unevenly as I stroke her cheek with my thumb, eyes locked on hers.

"Brody," she whispers, voice soft and awed, barely audible above the rain.

The world tilts on its axis.

"I'm falling for you," she confesses as I brush a strand of hair from her face.

"I'm here to catch you," I say with a smile.

For another lingering moment, we stand wrapped together beneath the steady downpour, unwilling to let go. Nothing else exists beyond the safety of the umbrella, beyond the woman pressed warmly against me.

Finally, taking her hand, I lead Harper toward the car, my heart beating heavily, fully aware there's no turning back from this.

21

HARPER

Rain drums steadily against the cabin windows, a soothing rhythm, blending with the warmth radiating from the fire. Brody stretches across the rug, the flames casting warm shadows along his face. His presence fills the room, as it always does, and I feel safe.

I tuck my legs beneath me, wrapped snugly in a thick wool blanket, as I steal another glance at him. The memory of our kiss in the pouring rain lingers—the quiet intensity in his eyes, the way he cradled my face like I was fragile and precious. My heart flutters because I feel like I'm living in one of my fantasies—well, almost.

He looks up, catching me watching him, and a faint smile tugs at his lips. "Want to watch TV? It'll probably rain for the rest of the night."

"No," I tell him.

"Cards?" he asks, resting his arm on the couch. "If I recall, you used to be really good at rummy."

I arch an eyebrow, shocked that he remembers that. It was one of my mother's favorite games, and when she was going through her chemo treatments, that was how we'd pass the time.

"I don't think you can handle losing."

He laughs, pushing himself upright and stretching toward a wooden cabinet under the bookshelves beside the fireplace. He digs around and turns back with a well-worn deck of cards. "You're going down, Alexander. There's just enough luck involved, so you can't accuse me of cheating when you *lose*."

"Oh, you think you're that good?" I tease, scooting down to the floor with him.

Brody leans toward me, shuffling the cards like a pro, his eyes glinting with amusement. "You have no idea."

"Fine then, let's make it interesting," I challenge, my heart racing as I meet his gaze. "Each hand you lose, one item of clothing disappears."

He stops shuffling the deck, his eyes locked on mine, momentarily surprised before a slow, heated smile curves his lips. "You're feeling bold tonight."

Heat pools in my stomach. "I have nothing to lose."

"Other than your clothes," he says, his gaze darkening slightly as he hands me my cards. "Careful, Harp. You're playing with fire."

"Good. I crave the burn," I state, arranging my cards as my pulse quickens.

He shifts to sit closer to me. "You're trouble."

"And you spell that *H-A-R-P-E-R*."

He chuckles as the sounds of the crackling wood fill the comfortable silence that randomly falls between us. Each time our eyes meet across the cards, butterflies flutter. Each playful glance holds a whispered promise of forever. My strategy is half-hearted; my attention is too consumed by the stubble along his chiseled jaw and the mesmerizing way the light of the flames dances across his high cheekbones. He's beautiful.

Brody slides a card from his hand and glances at it before looking at me. "Based on the cards you've picked up, I think you need this one."

I shrug. "Lay it down, and let's see."

Brody discards a queen, giving me the exact card I need.

I clap my hands together and let out a, "Woohoo."

"Ugh."

"You're making this too easy," I tease, placing my meld on the floor and winning the hand.

"I knew it." He shakes his head with mock regret.

"Rules are rules," I tell him, my eyes not leaving his as he slowly tugs his long-sleeved thermal shirt over his head.

He reveals tattooed muscles and strong shoulders. My breath catches, and of course, he notices. He notices everything.

"Don't get too distracted," he warns. "Or you'll be naked within the hour."

"Is that a promise?" I ask with a laugh as I gather the cards and shuffle.

Brody grabs a notepad and a pen so we can keep score. When he stands, I can't help but notice the package in his joggers. I force myself to glance away as my cheeks heat.

"You look guilty," he says with a laugh.

"Just be glad you're not a mind reader," I tell him.

"Oh, but I'd love to know what you're thinking right now."

I smirk. "I'm sure you would."

The next round plays quickly, but this time, Brody lays down his meld first, eyes twinkling victoriously as I sigh and discard my losing hand.

"Fair's fair," he says, a teasing challenge in his voice.

I hesitate only briefly before sliding the blanket from my shoulders and pulling off my sweatshirt, leaving just my tank top.

His eyes sweep over me, lingering with heated appreciation. "Oh, you're wearing layers. Not fair."

"Based on my calculations," I say, "as long as I win the next two, you'll be in your birthday suit."

"Ah, did you count my socks?"

My brows furrow. "*Cheater.*"

He snorts, and it's so damn adorable, him being so carefree, that I can barely handle it.

We continue the game, each round stripping away our barriers. With every discarded card and soft laugh, our glances linger longer, our breathing deepens, and the space between us shrinks.

I win the next hand, and Brody reaches for his sock, giving me a mini striptease, twirling it over his head before tossing it at me.

"Ew, stinky-boy socks!" I tell him, unable to hold back my laughter as I sit on the floor in my bra and panties.

His eyes slide up and down my body, and my heart pounds against my ribs. I love being under his gaze. Heat pools low in my belly, and I'm unable to tear my gaze away from his.

His dark blue eyes hold mine steadily, burning with raw intensity.

"You're beautiful," he whispers.

I lean forward, shooting my shot, brushing my lips against his. Electricity races through me. "I need you."

"You have me," he confesses.

Emotion tightens my throat, but I don't look away. I can't. The moment is too real, too perfect, as our gazes lock, the crackling fire fading into the background. We both feel it—the shift, the surrender, the unstoppable pull between us. His breathing matches mine—shallow, uneven, edged with the same aching need.

"Brody ..." I whisper, my voice trembling with vulnerability and want. "Tell me to stop."

His gaze drops briefly to my lips before returning to my eyes, filled with fierce tenderness. "No."

I breathe, my heart nearly bursting. "Okay."

And this time, when we come together, there's no hesitation—only surrender.

Brody's mouth claims mine, soft yet demanding, sending a surge of heat cascading through my veins. His lips are warm, tasting faintly of chocolate. This kiss is different—no pauses, no hesitation. Instead, it's deep and purposeful as we take our claim.

His big hands find my waist, gripping lightly before sliding slowly up my stomach, tracing gentle circles against my skin. Every careful touch sends shivers through me, awakening a deep need that I've never experienced before. I melt into him, my arms twining around his neck, my fingers sliding through the softness of his hair as he guides me onto his lap.

Not once do we break our slow, intoxicating kiss.

He groans as I settle against his thick cock, our bodies aligned, heat building like a storm between us. I feel his heartbeat racing beneath my fingertips, matching the rhythm of my own pulse, fierce and relentless.

My lips slide from his mouth to his ear and down his neck. My tongue traces the tattoos that stretch up toward the base of his neck.

"Fuck," he growls as I pull away.

I'm breathless and slightly dizzy as he rests his forehead against mine, eyes closed as he fights for control. I trace my fingers along the rugged line of his jaw, marveling at the strength and vulnerability etched into every feature.

"This feels right," I whisper, my voice trembling as my heart hammers in my chest. "Like it was meant to be."

His eyes open, filled with emotions he usually keeps locked away. "You're inescapable." His voice is rough, raw, stripped bare.

I shake my head, cupping his face between my palms. "All I want is you, exactly as you are right now."

He exhales heavily, his voice dropping lower, full of emotion, as he says, "I haven't let anyone get close to me in a long time. I don't know if I'm capable—"

"You are," I interrupt firmly, pressing a lingering kiss to the corner of his mouth, then another along his jaw, feeling him tremble beneath my lips.

His fingers grip my hips, pulling me closer, his breathing uneven as he fights his internal war. "If you need me to stop, just—"

"I need this. I need you," I whisper firmly, lifting my gaze to meet his.

Slowly, his resistance crumbles, replaced by a burning resolve that sends delicious heat racing over every nerve in my body. He reaches up, carefully threading his fingers through my hair, tilting my face toward his. "I want you, Harper. Completely. But only if you're ready."

"I'm more than ready." I breathe out.

Brody kisses me again, deeper this time, hungrier, and every last wall between us falls away.

His strong hands slide beneath my thighs, lifting me effortlessly. The world spins around me as he lays me down on the plush rug. My pulse pounds so hard that I can feel it in my throat, racing with anticipation and nerves. I've imagined being with him just like this countless times, always believing it wasn't possible. I was so fucking wrong.

But now he's here, his weight pressed above me, blue eyes dark with desire and longing. My breath trembles as I reach up, tracing the line of his jaw, memorizing every rugged contour, every tattoo. The flickering firelight paints him gold, and I'm suddenly overcome by the reality of this moment.

I'm about to be with Brody Calloway, the man I've wanted since before I fully understood what that even meant. The boy I stared at as a teenager, sneaking glances at gatherings, my pulse racing every time he smiled or laughed or brushed past me. I tucked those feelings deep inside, carefully guarding secrets beneath casual smiles and lighthearted teasing.

But right now, with his gaze locked on to mine and heat radiating from his skin, I no longer have to hide. This dream is real.

Brody lowers his mouth, feathering gentle kisses along the hollow of my throat, trailing warmth that makes me shiver beneath him. My fingers tighten in his hair, holding him close, afraid that if I let go even for a second, I'll wake up. Afraid this perfect fantasy will slip through my fingers like water.

"Little Miss Disaster," he whispers against my skin, as though he fears shattering me with the slightest pressure.

I burst into laughter as his words send warmth flooding

through me, filling every lonely, uncertain place inside my chest. All those years spent imagining what it might be like to belong to him, to be seen by him—it's nothing compared to this reality. Nothing prepared me for the intensity in his eyes or the tenderness in his touch.

"I've dreamed about this," I admit, my heart fluttering nervously at my own vulnerability. "About you."

His breath catches, eyes darkening with an emotion I've never seen before. He looks at me like I'm precious, like I'm something he never dared hope for either.

"You deserve better than dreams, Harper," he mutters, pressing his lips to my collarbone with care. "You deserve it all."

My eyes sting, emotion thick in my throat, but before I can reply, his hands glide beneath my bra, removing it, his touch igniting sparks that scatter like a kaleidoscope. The heat of his fingertips along my ribs sends shivers of longing cascading through me, awakening desires deeper and more powerful than I've ever experienced.

My breath quickens, anticipation merging into a dizzying rush. His eyes drift slowly down my body, filled with admiration. Under his gaze, my skin tingles, flushed and alive, because he makes me feel like a treasure. Every brush of his fingertips feels like a promise —one I never imagined Brody could offer to me.

With gentle urgency, he eases my panties down my hips, his hands trembling slightly, betraying his careful control. I watch him closely, feeling empowered and desired beneath his gaze, suddenly realizing how deeply he's affected too. This moment is just as significant for him as it is for me.

He moves lower, trailing kisses down my stomach. But as he goes farther down, anxiety stirs in my chest. My pulse quickens, uncertainty gripping me.

"Wait," I breathe, my voice shaking as his lips brush along my hip bone, teasing dangerously close. "No one's ever ... I've never had someone ..."

He pauses immediately, lifting his gaze to mine, understanding softening his eyes as he senses my hesitation. His palm settles against my inner thigh, warm and reassuring, grounding me instantly. "Do you want me to stop?"

"No," I say quickly, my cheeks heating at how eager the word escapes me. I swallow thickly, heart racing. "I just—I don't know what to expect. No one's ever ... done *that*."

He presses a soft kiss against my thigh, his eyes holding mine, voice low and soothing as he says, "We'll take it slow. If you're not comfortable, just say the word."

"Okay." Warmth spreads through my chest, my breath steadying at his patient reassurance.

I trust Brody completely, and the care and respect in his eyes only deepen that trust.

A slow, devastating smile curves his mouth, and heat flares in his gaze. "I've waited a long time for this moment," he admits, voice rich with emotion, kissing along my skin. "Can't wait to taste you."

I exhale shakily, tension giving way to pure anticipation, my body trembling as he parts my thighs wider. He lowers his mouth, eyes locked on to mine, and when his lips find me, they are soft and achingly gentle.

I let out a sigh, and the world melts away to nothing. He moves slowly at first, his lips exploring me with soft strokes. My breath catches in my throat, heat flaring through my body.

Brody grips my thighs firmly, holding me open as he sinks deeper into the embrace. His mouth moves over me with growing confidence, his tongue sliding through my folds, teasing and exploring every inch of me, desperate to memorize how I respond to his touch.

"Oh God," I whisper, fingers tangling in his hair, hips arching involuntarily toward his mouth as the orgasm builds so damn quickly. The sensation is overwhelming as electric pleasure races up my spine. "Feels so good ..."

He groans against my sensitive skin, the vibration making me shudder beneath him, breathless and helpless as he guides me toward a climax I've never reached before. My pulse races, pleasure building deep in my belly, threatening to spill over with every flick of his tongue, every deliberate swirl over that sensitive spot.

"Mmm. My new favorite flavor," he murmurs hoarsely, pressing deeper kisses along my most intimate area. "Better than I ever imagined."

I shiver as the sound of his voice, which is so damn full of desire, nearly pushes me over the edge. I lift my head, meeting his smoldering gaze as he continues his sweet torture. His eyes hold mine fiercely with possessive desire as he moves his tongue in slow, sensual strokes that send sparks through every nerve in my body.

"I've thought about this," he whispers roughly. His growl vibrates with intense hunger, his breath hot against my skin. "Tasting you, making you mine ... God, Harper, do you have any idea how long I've wanted you?"

"Tell me," I say in a hushed tone.

"Years."

His admission ignites a fire inside me, and I lose myself completely to him. The intimacy, the trust, the feeling of him worshipping me sends me spiraling higher, sensations overwhelming me until I'm panting, gasping his name, begging for release.

"Please, don't stop. I'm so close ..."

He slides a finger carefully inside me, moving and curling slowly, perfectly timed with each teasing stroke of his tongue. My body shudders, and my back arches off the floor. My legs tremble as I desperately race toward the edge.

"That's it, Harp," he encourages, his voice a low rasp against my heated flesh. "Let go for me."

His voice, his touch, the relentless rhythm of his mouth send me falling over the ledge. The orgasm steals my breath away. Ecstasy explodes within me, hot and consuming. My cries echo through the cabin as wave after wave of pleasure washes over me, and my entire body trembles in his hold.

Brody guides me through every shudder, coaxing me back down from that dizzying peak. He presses kisses against my thighs, whispering praises against my skin until my heart finally slows, until I can breathe again.

I blink up at the ceiling, my vision blurry. I lift myself up on my elbows, staring at him.

"It's never felt like that before," I admit breathlessly, drunk off the intensity. "I didn't know it could feel like that."

He slowly moves up my body, eyes burning with possessive tenderness as he captures my mouth in a slow, deep kiss. I can taste myself on his lips, feel the strength and restraint in his muscles.

"This is just the beginning, Harper," he whispers roughly against my lips, his voice filled with promise. "We have all night."

"I hope we have forever," I confess, running my fingers through his messy, dark hair.

"We do," he confirms, kissing me again. "We fucking do."

22

BRODY

Harper's palms press into my chest, gentle but firm, guiding me onto my back against the welcoming warmth of the rug. My heart pounds like a drumbeat beneath her fingertips, each uneven thud echoing deep inside my chest, awakening places that have been dormant for far too long.

She hovers above me, her hair cascading down her bare shoulders, eyes luminous and locked on to mine. In that silent moment, vulnerability pulses between us. It's a language that I haven't allowed myself to speak in so long that I nearly choke on the intensity of this. My defenses are stripped away, and Harper leaves me with nothing but raw need for her. It's an aching, primal, and I need her more than I need air.

Slowly, she sinks down onto me, inch by torturous inch, and she takes control until all of me is buried deep inside her. She doesn't move, allowing her body to adjust to me. The sensation of being with her like this is nearly blinding. A sharp breath tears from my chest as pleasure and emotion intertwine, blending into a single feeling that nearly undoes me.

Harper moves slowly at first, her hips rolling delicately. My fingers grip her hips, enjoying how she perfectly fits me, as if she were shaped for me alone.

My throat tightens. I'm overwhelmed by how long it's been since I allowed myself to feel anything even remotely close to this. But even now, it's deeper, more intense than anything I've ever experienced. With Harper, it's not just physical in how our bodies connect, but emotional, almost spiritual. I want to worship her as I get lost in her gaze. She sees every scar I carry, but she still looks at me like I'm something precious, like I'm something worth protecting, something she wants.

My breath hitches as she slides up and down me, every shift of her body rips control from my grasp. Pleasure builds uncontrollably, but I fight it back, desperate to savor every second with her. This is the first time of many, and it's something I never want to forget.

"Harp," I rasp, my voice hoarse. The rough edges of my buried emotions scratch my throat, and I can't put into words how fucking good this feels to finally cross the line we've been teetering on for years. My fingers guide up her body, so fucking desperate to memorize the silkiness of her skin, the curve of her waist, and the heat radiating between us.

She leans forward, her lips ghosting over mine, her breath trembling against my mouth. "I belong to you, Brody."

The confession rips through me, powerful enough to shatter any lingering barriers I foolishly believed I could keep. I place a hand around the back of her neck, guiding her lips down to mine, desperate to kiss her—to imprint myself onto her, to promise without words everything I feel but can't articulate. She's stolen my heart.

I cup her face, meeting her eyes with intensity. "I'm yours too," I confirm, admitting a truth I've held on to for far too long. "For as long as you want."

Her eyes glisten, filled with wonder, trust, and something

deeper, something unspoken that grips my heart so tightly that it's almost painful. Forever.

Her hips begin moving again, finding a rhythm that destroys any rational thoughts I have. I groan out, gripping her tighter, losing myself in the intoxicating trust she's always reserved for me.

I'm so far gone, every wall I've built collapsing beneath the weight of what she makes me feel. It's terrifying, exhilarating, and undeniable. I've guarded myself for years, denied myself even the hope of feeling like this again. But right now, with Harper, every fear fades into insignificance, drowned beneath this intimacy.

My fingers trace over her skin, and I commit every curve, every breathless whimper to memory. Her soft gasps and moans surround me, drawing me deeper into her depths. I'm drowning in her, in every stroke of our bodies. The way she makes me feel only reinforces the unspoken truths that are screaming in my head. I need her. Not just for tonight, but until my last breath. Harper is my person, my other half, and it scares the fuck out of me. It always has. But I'm willing to accept it now.

I let go completely, fully surrendering to this gorgeous woman, to the wild beauty of this moment, to a future I stopped believing was possible. Her eyes flutter closed, her head tilting back as I guide her faster, deeper, until we're both clinging desperately to each other, breathing erratically and in sync, moving as one, racing to the end.

As she cries out, she shudders around me, squeezing me so fucking tight that I forget my name. My release tears through me, and it's powerful enough to blur my vision. My breath catches, my eyes sting, and my heart is exposed like never before.

A whispered promise pours from my lips without hesitation. "You're mine, Harp."

She leans down, her mouth brushing against my lips, and she whispers back to me, "Always."

And just like that, with one simple truth, my world reshapes itself entirely around her, around us, around this. It feels like space and time have ripped open as the intensity of these truths fully consumes me.

After we lose control, she collapses onto my chest, as if every last ounce of energy has left her body and only my arms can hold her steady. I wrap myself around her, pulling her closer, feeling the rapid beat of her heart against the erratic beat of mine as we stay joined together.

Time slows around us, and I hold her, never wanting to let go. She's breathless as my hands trace lazy circles down her back. We stay suspended in this haze, clinging to the moment that consumed us. I don't feel like the same man I was before, and I know there is no going back from this.

The cabin is silent, except for our breathing and the crackle of the fire. Harper's heartbeat slows against my chest, and I hold on to her like I'm afraid reality might shatter this moment. I close my eyes, memorizing everything—the smell of her skin, the weight of her body pressed against mine, the sigh of contentment she releases against my neck.

She shifts, lifting her head just enough for her gaze to meet mine. Her hooded eyes are bright, shining just for me. Reaching up, I brush back a loose strand of hair from her cheek, my thumb rubbing across the flushed softness of her skin.

"You okay?" I ask, suddenly unsure. "Did I—"

She quickly presses a finger to my lips. "I'm perfect," she whispers. "You were perfect."

A relieved smile touches my lips, and it eases the knot of anxiety I didn't even realize had formed. "It's been ... a while," I admit carefully, studying her face closely. "I wasn't sure—"

"I know," she interrupts, her fingers trailing down my jaw, her touch featherlight, brushing away all my doubts. "You made me see stars."

My heart pounds hard in response to her confession.

"I hope you made a wish." I give her a grin, resting one arm behind my head.

"Oh, I did. I've been searching my entire life for this. For you. Exactly how you are," she tells me.

I don't think anyone has ever seen me this clearly, this honestly —without judgment, without expectation. I've been living behind walls for so long, wearing a thick armor I thought was impenetrable. But somehow, Harper slipped through every barrier I'd made like they never existed.

She studies me, eyes traveling slowly over my face, and a smile forms as she memorizes me, just like I did with her moments ago. Her gaze trails over my tattoos, fingertips carefully following the inked lines. Tingles spread under her touch, each careful stroke peeling away layers of my past, revealing parts of myself that were always reserved for her.

"Do these all have stories?" she asks, looking up at me with curiosity.

"Some of them," I admit, following her gaze to the ink on my arm. "Some are memories, some reminders. And some ..." I pause, choosing my words carefully. "Some are things I thought I'd lost forever."

Her eyes lift slowly, and they're full of understanding. She leans closer, pressing a kiss against my collarbone, lingering there for a long, quiet moment. "You deserve happiness, Brody. You deserve to hold on to good things."

Harper doesn't just see me; she sees through me—straight into the hidden places I've protected from the outside world. The realization is both terrifying and exhilarating because I know I can never escape her. I don't want to.

"I'm actively working on that," I whisper, sliding my hand up her back.

Her eyes are serious as she presses her palm over my heart. "I'm not going anywhere."

She read between the lines; of course she did.

I cup her face, guiding her eyes firmly to mine, needing her to hear my words. "I'm not either. I will always protect you. I will always keep you safe."

The promise hangs between us, solidifying the bond already tightening around us, cuffing us together. Harper nods, accepting my truth without hesitation, and I feel immediate relief, knowing that's exactly what she wants.

She feels the same, and I want to scream it from the rooftops.

Harper settles her head back against my chest, drawing circles over my skin. I breathe in the scent of her hair, feeling my heart pound steadily beneath her fingertips.

After a long moment, she whispers, "Real-life you is way better than fantasy you." Her voice is a blend of playfulness and sleepy satisfaction.

I chuckle, the rumble vibrating through my chest. "Good to know fantasy me takes the back seat."

She tilts her head slightly, peeking up at me with a mischievous look in her eyes. Her smile is playful in a way that's uniquely Harper. "We can do this again, right?"

"Fuck yes." Laughter falls out of me, and happiness chases away shadows that have lingered for too long.

She chuckles, and the sound is music to my ears. "Great. So, should I apologize for keeping you really busy now or later?"

I tilt her chin upward, painting my lips across hers.

"Already addicted, huh?" I whisper against her mouth, feeling her smile.

"Yes," she admits.

"Me too."

Harper stands, and we clean ourselves up, then lie on the couch naked. As I hold her, I run my fingers through her hair, and she moves closer. Her breathing slows as sleep threatens to claim her. As I drift toward sleep, surrounded by Harper's warmth, I promise myself that I'll always hold on to the good things, to Harper, no matter what it takes.

Her breathing evens out against my chest, and her body relaxes. I carefully shift beneath her, scooping her up as I rise from the cushions. She stirs slightly, mumbling something unintelligible about floating. Her eyes flutter briefly before settling closed again.

"I've got you," I whisper, pressing a kiss against her forehead as I carry her toward the bedroom.

"My hero." Her arms tighten around my neck, and it's the simple trust she has for me—that she's always had—that nearly undoes me.

I set her onto the mattress, sliding the covers over her before joining her.

She snuggles into me. Our bodies mold perfectly together, and we're the best big and little spoon on the planet.

The tension I've always carried melts away, replaced by bone-deep relief that love exists for me. The emptiness is exchanged with Harper, and right now, my heart is overflowing with hope, with something strong enough to silence my loudest fears.

I brush my lips against her hair as my arm snakes around her waist, breathing in the sweet smell of her skin as I close my eyes.

Tonight, nothing can touch us, and I let myself believe that I deserve every ounce of happiness Harper brings into my life. Nothing else matters but this.

I WAKE TO HARPER'S BODY DRAPED ACROSS MINE. THE FAINT SCENT of her skin fills my senses, and I cherish it. I replay every moment from last night, every whispered confession we made. It wasn't a dream. It happened.

Harper releases a sigh as she holds me closer. My breath catches as I study her plump lips and her long eyelashes. It's as if she's always belonged here with me, as though the jagged pieces of my life are finally smoothing around her.

I didn't realize just how much I'd craved her and how monumental it would be to share this kind of intimacy until now.

Harper didn't give up on me and showed me that falling in love was possible again.

Her eyelids flutter open, blue-gray eyes lifting to meet mine. She gives me a sweet but shy smile.

"Morning," she whispers.

"Morning," I say back, brushing a loose strand of hair from her face, enjoying how pretty she is when she wakes up. "Sleep okay?"

"Better than okay." She stretches, the slow arch of her back pressing her body even closer to mine. "The best."

I chuckle. "Great. If you could leave a review ..."

"Five out of five stars. Absolutely recommend." Her fingers trail along my skin, brushing over the tattoos etched permanently on my arm, tracing each one like it's a story she's determined to know by heart.

I don't think I'll ever be able to get enough of these quiet mornings with her.

"Did you imagine this was possible?" she asks, her voice barely above a whisper. Her eyes search mine. "Us?"

I thread my fingers with hers, holding our joined hands close against my chest, right above the steady rhythm of my heart.

"Only in my dreams," I admit, the confession slipping from my lips with ease. I feel raw and exposed, but I push forward, wanting to share the parts of myself that I hide from the world with her. "Even when I knew I shouldn't."

She tilts her head curiously. "Why shouldn't you?"

I hesitate, sorting carefully through my fears before finally giving voice to the one that's held me back the longest. "Because losing you—losing *this*—would be the one thing I don't think I could survive."

She leans forward, pressing a kiss against my chest, her lips lingering over my heart. When she lifts her head again, her eyes shimmer with certainty. "I'm not going anywhere, Brody. You don't have to carry that burden anymore."

Something inside my chest loosens, relief flooding through me in a powerful wave, washing away the last shadowed fragments of my doubts. I reach up, brushing my thumb across her cheek.

"Promise me," I whisper, my voice full of emotion.

"I promise." She breathes without hesitation. "I'm right here, and I'm not letting go. Ever."

I catch her lips with mine, pouring every ounce of trust, longing, and affection into it. She sighs against my mouth, deepening the kiss, melting willingly into my arms as our tongues lightly twist together. When we break apart, our breath mingles in unison.

Harper whispers, her voice wavering with emotion, "Thank you for letting me see you. Really see you. You've always kept everything so hidden. But this feels different. Like you trust me."

I cradle her face, studying her. "I do trust you, Harp," I admit. "More than I've ever trusted anyone."

Her eyes sparkle with admiration, and it nearly undoes me. She leans forward, brushing another soft kiss over my lips, as if she's trying to seal my words with a stamp of approval. The intimacy of that moment—the promise of something deeper—settles into my bones, weaving itself into the very fabric of who I am.

We linger, savoring this new sense of trust, comfort, and connection that was forged in the fire of our past. Harper's breath is warm against my skin. My arms tighten around her protectively, and we fall into a comfortable silence, wrapped securely in each other's arms.

She's the kind of partner I've always needed, even if I'm not quite ready to put words to that feeling yet. Harper drifts off again, and I enjoy the way her presence calms every anxious thought that used to haunt me.

My fingertips trace slow patterns along her body as I memorize the delicate slope of her back, the smoothness of her skin, and the rhythm of her heart beating against mine. Time slows and stretches lazily around us.

This is the life.

Outside, the rain has finally stopped, leaving a peaceful stillness, only punctuated by the occasional dripping of water from the trees onto the cabin's metal roof. It feels surreal to be here, holding Harper like this, and I'm at peace.

Eventually, my phone vibrates on the nightstand, jolting me back to the present. I reach for it, glancing at the screen while trying not to disturb Harper.

Nick is calling me.

Carefully, I untangle myself from her and slide out of bed. She grumbles, and I pause, brushing my lips over her forehead.

"I'll be right back," I say.

Her brow smooths again as she slips back into sleep.

I tug on a pair of boxers and step into the hallway, closing the bedroom door behind me before answering.

"Calloway," I say.

There's a brief pause before he responds, voice unusually tense. "Brody. Sorry to interrupt your ... break, but we've got a major problem."

Tension stretches across my shoulders, and I straighten as I move into the kitchen to start a pot of coffee. "Explain."

"Micah Rhodes." The name lands heavy, and Nick's voice is tight with frustration. "Billie's post didn't exactly have the effect we'd hoped. The public's torn. Last night, there was a shitstorm of posts, mostly lies, as Micah crashed out. A lot of them think Micah's the victim. He went live on Instagram, hysterical, threatening legal action against Bellamore. And now they've got paparazzi swarming headquarters and digging around, trying to find Harper."

"Fuck," I whisper.

"That's not all," he says. "There was a picture of you two that was shared. You were kissing in the rain. Like, real fucking romantic, Brod, but not the look Harp needed, and people are trying to figure out your location."

I exhale, pinching the bridge of my nose.

"Micah is furious. Commenters have stated different places

where they think you are." Nick hesitates briefly, concern clear in his voice. "He also released a statement this morning, accusing Harper of cheating while pregnant and painting himself as the wounded fiancé. After that pic got leaked, it's working. Relationship scandals are a PR nightmare. Oh, there is one more rumor that the baby is actually yours."

My jaw clenches as a sudden wave of anger boils beneath my skin. "I'm going to fucking kill him."

"No, you're not." Nick's voice softens slightly, a rare moment of emotion breaking through. "Billie and Asher are working overtime to do damage control. But you both need to be ready to leave soon. It will get worse before it gets better."

I close my eyes as I lean against the counter, and Harper's peaceful face flashes through my mind.

"I won't let him hurt her," I tell him.

He releases a relieved breath, as though those words were exactly what he needed to hear. "I know you won't. And we're here too—Zane, Asher, Easton, Weston—all of us. But watch your back, Brody. Rhodes doesn't play fair."

"Neither do I," I confirm with more gruffness in my tone than I intended.

"Good." Nick pauses briefly, and then his tone shifts, becoming cautiously curious. "How's she doing?"

My chest warms at the memory of Harper tangled in my arms, her sleepy smile, her whispered promises. "She's good. Better than good."

"Love to hear it," he says. "I'm sure Zane already gave you the lecture, but if you fucking hurt my sister—"

"Stepsister," I correct him.

"I'll fuck you up," he finishes.

"I hope you would."

He chuckles. "Tell her I'm glad she has you. We all are."

"I will." I smile, knowing I have everyone's support with this relationship, but I'm determined to take things slow.

"Keep me posted," Nick says finally, tension lingering beneath his tone. "And stay safe."

I hang up, turning my gaze to the hallway. The weight of this news settles heavily in my chest, and the brief peace of the morning is overshadowed by our harsh reality.

Micah Rhodes is ruthless, dangerous, and desperate, and I know he won't stop until he finds Harper.

I push down the surge of anger and frustration, letting determination take its place. I won't let him win.

He won't touch Harper again—no matter what it takes, no matter what it costs.

I step back into the bedroom, easing silently onto the bed.

Harper shifts, reaching for me, and I move close. My chest eases when she settles against me; her presence grounds me, as usual.

"Everything okay?" she mutters.

"It will be," I whisper, pressing a light kiss into her hair, holding her tighter. I close my eyes, breathing her in.

"Mmm. You're a dream come true," she whispers with a happy sigh.

"You are too." I kiss her forehead, knowing things are about to change.

23

HARPER

I blink awake slowly, awareness trickling in with comforting warmth. Brody's arms are still wrapped around me. I let my eyes drift shut again, savoring the feeling of him—solid, safe, mine.

I breathe him in, inhaling the familiar scent of his skin—woodsy and clean, mingled with something that's uniquely him. Carefully, I lift my head, leaning back just enough to study his peaceful face. Even in sleep, he has a strength etched in his chiseled jaw and the curve of his perfect lips. And in this quiet moment, there's something rare he rarely lets anyone see.

I lift my fingertips to his face, tracing featherlight lines along his jawline. I take my time memorizing each rugged contour, enjoying the vulnerability in his neutral expression. My thumb grazes across his lower lip, and my pulse quickens as heat stirs within me, settling low in my belly.

My fingers move downward, tracing along his bare shoulder, feeling the muscles flex beneath my touch. Desire mixes with need, and I can't help myself.

His eyelids flutter open slowly; blue eyes meet mine. He blinks, and his gaze slowly focuses on me.

"Morning again," he whispers, voice gravelly, and it sends a delicious shiver down my spine.

"Morning again," I reply, grinning, my heart skipping as he continues watching me with intensity. "We fell back asleep."

"It's good to catch up on rest," he tells me as his hand moves to my waist, brushing over my naked skin beneath the sheets.

His gaze holds mine, and it's filled with the same need that pumps through my veins. I lean in, capturing his lips.

Brody responds with a groan, pulling me closer, deepening our kiss with unhurried ease. His mouth is warm, his fingers wrap possessively around my hip, and I shift him onto his back, taking control as I remove his boxers.

"Harp," he says, his voice rough, vulnerable.

The sound makes my heart race as desire tightens in my core.

"I want you," I whisper against his throat, pressing kisses down his neck, feeling his pulse quicken beneath my lips. "Right now."

He carefully lays me down on my back and slides his strong body between my legs. Our eyes lock as he exhales, waiting outside of my entrance. I'm so fucking wet and needy for him that the anticipation alone is too much for me to bear.

He grips my hip as he slowly guides himself into me. My breath hitches, pleasure rippling through me as our bodies slowly join. He goes slow, giving me time to adjust to him as he stretches me wide. His hands move to my waist.

"Are you okay?"

"Yes," I whisper.

He gives me another inch and then another. My breathing grows ragged, and I feel as if he'll rip me in two. I nod, and he moves until our ends completely meet, until we're fully connected.

His eyes lock on to mine, heavy-lidded, blazing with unguarded emotion. "God, Harp," he rasps, his voice a deep, hoarse whisper. "This is everything."

My heart soars, body trembling as he slowly and carefully thrusts in and out. I gasp; the sensation almost overwhelms me as the intensity builds between us. He finds a slow, perfect rhythm; our bodies move effortlessly, instinctively.

Our breaths mingle, eyes locked. Every movement is filled with trust. Moans escape me as pleasure winds tighter, stronger, drawing us closer to release. I grip his shoulders, surrendering to this man who holds my heart in his hands.

"Brody." I gasp as the orgasm rushes through me in powerful, electric pulses.

His eyes darken, and he groans, his grip tight as he finds his own release. My name tumbles from his lips. "My Harp."

Breathless and trembling, he kisses me so damn sweetly, pouring every emotion into me as he hovers above me. He presses a kiss against my forehead, breathing into my hair. "You make me feel alive."

Joy and warmth flood my chest.

"Same," I whisper, smiling against him. "I could get used to this."

His arms tighten around me, holding me even closer. "Good," he says. "Because I don't ever want to wake up without you again."

I lift my head, eyes meeting his, feeling the sincerity and depth of emotion behind his words. I feel the same.

Brody and I slide out of bed and take a quick shower together.

After we get dressed, I walk into the kitchen and see that there's a pot of freshly brewed coffee. He must've made it when he woke up earlier.

Brody snatches two mugs from the cabinet and fills them full.

"It's still hot," he says, handing me one of the steaming mugs. "Best part of waking up is …" A teasing smile tugs at his lips. "You."

I blush as I take a sip. "Us," I correct.

He moves closer, and I lean into him, enjoying slow mornings where we can just be. It's peaceful, and this time with him is something I'll cherish for the rest of my life.

Brody's phone vibrates on the counter, and I see Asher's name pop up on his screen. I glance up at him, and tension settles in his shoulders.

I know that look, and I know something's wrong.

"What's going on?" I ask, remembering he slipped out of bed to answer his phone this morning.

He sighs and reaches for his phone. "Someone snapped a picture of us kissing in town. Micah's on a rampage and is playing the wounded fiancé card."

Seconds later, he's showing me the proof. The photo takes my breath away—the two of us kissing passionately beneath the umbrella in the rain. It's sexy, and it makes me smile, but that fades quickly when I read the comments. I'm being called a cheater, a liar, a skank, and a whore, among many other things. My hand shakes because Micah isn't just coming for me; he's determined to destroy my reputation. Some people defend me, and my heart aches with gratitude, but this isn't enough.

"What the fuck?" I whisper. "Why are they saying that's my engagement ring?" I hold up my hand, clearly showing that the infinity ring is on my right hand. It was my mother's, a good-luck charm. Micha's ridiculous ring is in Brody's bedroom, sitting at the bottom of the drawer next to the bed.

"They'll spin the narrative however they can. You know how this goes."

My pulse spikes, and I feel like I might have an anxiety attack.

"Hey," he says quietly, his voice careful and controlled. "We'll figure this out." He pauses, jaw tightening even more, frustration flickering behind his blue eyes.

"There's something else," he says. "There are rumors about the baby being mine."

I blink, caught completely off guard by a sudden, vivid image that flashes through my mind—my belly rounded, Brody's hand resting over it, pride glowing in his eyes. A surprising warmth spreads through me, unexpected but undeniably comforting. The thought doesn't bring an existential dread.

I quickly shake away the thought, cheeks heating. "The baby rumors piss me off the most."

"I understand," Brody says, watching me carefully. "The bigger the drama, the more the gossip columns are encouraged to talk about it. I'm really fucking sorry."

I nod slowly, trying to process this new complication. Strangely, though, the sting of Micah's lies feels distant now, overshadowed by that beautiful vision still lingering in my mind. Carrying Brody's child doesn't seem frightening; in fact, the thought fills me with a quiet sense of rightness.

He notices my expression change and tilts his head at me. "What is it?"

A small smile tugs at my lips, despite the chaos. "A baby with you doesn't feel like a nightmare."

His expression softens, surprise flickering in his eyes before warmth floods his gaze. He steps closer, tucking hair behind my ear. "Maybe one day. When you're ready—because I know you're not."

"Thank you," I say, the genuine sincerity in his words melting something inside me, replacing all my fears. I lean into his touch. "I just hate that they're turning this—us—into something ugly."

Brody shakes his head. "It's about perspective, though, isn't it?" He glances down at the picture of us kissing. "I think that's very fucking beautiful."

"You're right," I tell him. "And I'm supposed to be the one who finds the bright side."

He smirks. "I'm a changed man."

A chuckle escapes me. "That's what we call the power of the pussy."

Instead of being upset, we laugh together, and he pulls me into him.

We dance barefoot in the kitchen, and I tilt my head up to meet his gaze.

"Tell me something real," I say as he spins me around.

"I can't imagine a future without you in it," he says.

"Neither can I," I admit as my breath catches.

Brody leans down and captures my mouth, and he tastes like mint and coffee.

"We'll make it through this. After storm clouds come flowers and rainbows."

I smile. "It's the only thing that keeps me hanging on."

After we eat brunch, the day stretches out in front of us. It's easy, and it offers a sense of calm despite the shitshow that waits for me outside of this cabin.

Brody suggests we spend the afternoon relaxing, away from screens and messages and the relentless gossip columns. I couldn't agree more.

Eventually, I wander toward the built-in bookshelves lining the far wall of the living room. Fingertips brush over the worn spines of books that have been read several times. The shelves are filled with thriller novels, old notebooks, and magazines. My attention catches on a thick, leather-bound photo album, tucked neatly among it all.

"What's this?" I glance at it.

Brody's eyes look at the album, and a faint smile tugs at his lips. He stands from the couch and walks toward me. "Family photos."

I look up at him. "May I look?"

He nods, sitting beside me as I settle on the couch, the leather cool beneath my fingers. His thigh presses against mine, and it's comforting. I lift the cover, revealing pages filled with memories of smiling faces, holidays, birthday parties, and everyday moments, made precious with the passing of time.

I study each picture, careful not to rush, allowing Brody space to process whatever feelings surface. He remains silent at first, his breathing steady beside me, but I can feel him tense.

"That's my mom and dad," he finally says, pointing to a candid picture of a laughing couple, eyes bright and carefree. "They were high school sweethearts. Together forever, right up until the very end."

I glance at him, noticing his faint smile, tinged with sadness.

"They look really happy."

"They were." His voice grows gentle. "They had the kind of love we always hear about but never think is real."

"My parents were the same way," I admit. "It bothered me for a long time and made me think there was something wrong with me because I'd never be able to live up to what my parents had."

I give him a small smile, reaching for his hand and squeezing it. "Then Zane fell in love, and I realized I wasn't doomed after all."

This makes Brody laugh because my brother is a known hard-ass. "You're not doomed, Harp."

"You're not either," I tell him.

Brody leans back slightly, eyes distant. I carefully turn the page, coming across a picture of a young Brody, his smile wide and carefree, holding up a fish by the pond. I enjoy the innocent joy on his face and know that the young boy had no idea what was in store for him.

"You were really cute."

He chuckles. "*Were?* I'd challenge that."

"True." I grin, nudging him with my shoulder. "Now you're a wet dream."

He rolls his eyes but laughs. "We used to come up here as a family. Fishing trips, hikes, Fourth of July. This cabin was our safe haven. My mom didn't come from money like my dad did. This place was part of her inheritance, and she refused to get rid of it. Dad wanted to build something big on the property—a huge mansion that overlooked the town—but Mom said no. Humbled him."

"Typical Calloway," I say with a gentle laugh. I reach out, covering his hand with mine. "I love it here. The simplicity of it is something I'll cherish."

"I love you being here." His eyes meet mine, and they're full of warmth and gratitude.

"Thank you for sharing this with me," I offer.

Brody draws in a deep breath, leaning closer and pressing a kiss against my temple. "There's no one else I'd rather share this with."

The album rests open across our laps, each photograph becoming a bridge between us, connecting his past, grounding us to the present, and illuminating the fragile hope that maybe, despite all the darkness we've faced, our future might hold the kind of love our parents had. A type of love neither of us thought we'd ever find.

BRODY AND I STAND SIDE BY SIDE AT THE KITCHEN COUNTER, ingredients spread out in front of us. Preparing dinner together is a normalcy I'm growing used to.

Brody effortlessly chops vegetables, the knife moving swiftly. I watch him, impressed by how domestic he looks right now.

He offers me a smirk. "See something interesting?"

I don't look away. "Just something I want."

"Mmm. Well, tonight, you're dessert." His tone drips with gentle amusement, his eyes glinting with teasing mischief. "I even have whipped cream."

I laugh. "Where will you put it?"

"All over you, and I plan to lick it off," he counters smoothly.

"Can we have dessert first?" I ask.

He stops chopping and stares at me. "You'll ruin your dinner."

"Tease!" Rolling my eyes, I bump my hip against him.

His laughter is rich, and it makes my heart flutter.

"This feels right. Easy," I say, dropping my gaze as I slowly dice bell peppers exactly how he showed me.

When I glance back at him, his expression is thoughtful, and his eyes are sincere. "It does."

Silence settles between us for the next ten minutes, broken only by the sounds of our meal preparation. Tonight, we're making skillet beef tips with steak, peppers, onions, mushrooms, and garlic.

Brody drops the seasoned steak into the cast-iron skillet, and the aroma immediately drifts through the cabin. My mouth waters in anticipation.

"Once this is browned, we'll take it out, then cook the veggies until they're translucent," he explains. "This is one of my favorite meals."

"Yeah? You're my favorite meal," I tell him, reaching into the cabinet and pulling down two wineglasses.

Thankfully, we picked up a bottle of red from the store when we went.

"You're such a bad fucking girl," he mutters as I uncork it and fill our glasses nearly full.

I swirl the liquid around as he removes the meat from the pan.

"You enjoy it," I tell him with a chuckle.

"I do," he says.

I move closer to him, and we lean into each other's presence.

"Brody?" I finally speak again, my voice barely above a whisper, after I take another sip of wine.

He glances at me.

"All of this—I don't think I could've handled any of it without you."

He leans over and kisses my forehead. "You're stronger than you think, Harp. Give yourself more credit."

He continues stirring the veggies and cooking them until they're done, and then he dumps everything into one skillet.

"Wow, good job, Chef. This looks incredible," I say, standing on my tiptoes to grab two bowls from the cabinet.

We load our bowls full, and I realize I've won the lottery with him.

"You can cook. You clean. You're an incredible lover. Honestly, I'm glad you built a barrier around yourself for me."

Laughter rolls out of him. "I'm a catch. What can I say?"

"Love that Calloway cockiness. I expect nothing else," I tell him, shooting him a wink. "But it's true. You are a catch."

After dinner, the cabin settles into a quiet calm, punctuated only by the gentle crackle of the fireplace and *The Golden Girls* on TV. Brody sits beside me on the couch with the bottle of wine on the coffee table.

His phone rings, and he makes a face when he sees it's Billie.

"She's probably going to give us hell for that photo," I tell him. "Answer."

Brody puts it on speakerphone, and Billie is hysterical.

His brows furrow. "Hey, hey, what's up?"

"They took her!" Billie screams into the phone. "They took her right outside of the office."

"Billie. Calm down, please. Explain. Took who?"

"Mia! We were walking into Bellamore, and some man took her. They threw a cover over her head, and I think they thought it was Harper. I've called the police, and ... and ... they could've taken me, too, but I ran, Brody. Like you told me. I ran and locked down the building."

My eyes are wide, and my heart is racing.

Mia is our chief marketing officer at Bellamore, and she has the same build and hair as me. We've been confused for one another in the past. But still, this doesn't make sense. I don't understand.

"Where are you? Are you alone?"

"No, no," she says. "Asher's with me. I have security following me now. It's gotten so bad and out of control. I'm so scared." Billie sobs, and I'm spiraling and freaking out.

"Who do you think is responsible?" he asks.

"Micah," she whispers. "I saw him."

My heart feels like it might beat out of my chest.

"Please stay safe. Please protect Harper. I have to go," she says, then ends the call without listening for his response.

Brody stares at his phone, his nostrils flaring. His jaw clenches tightly, and he looks at me. I see the storm swirling in his eyes.

"What does this mean?" I ask, stressed and worried.

Brody is lost in thought. "I have to find more information about Micah. I've been digging deeper after what you told me. There's something here ... I just haven't quite figured it out yet. The fact that he took Mia—what the fuck!"

He's livid in a way I've never seen before. Unease floods along my spine as he grabs his laptop. Brody opens information that contains names, dates, and cryptic messages, sending a wave of dread through me.

My gaze catches on a name in an email—Blaire Bowers.

A memory jolts through me, sharp and vivid. I straighten abruptly, a chill slithering down my back. "Blaire Bowers—Brody, I know that name."

He immediately turns, his expression sharp with urgency. "From where?"

"She sent him a text message the morning we had brunch in Newport." My voice trembles slightly, my pulse quickening as memories flood back, disjointed and frantic. "Micah was on a call with someone in Newport. After he ended it, she texted him, and I saw it. I don't know what the message said, but it was her name."

Brody's jaw tightens visibly, fury flashing through his eyes. "He had contact with her."

"Yes." I swallow hard, anxiety knotting in my stomach. "At the time, I thought he was cheating."

Brody clicks rapidly, pulling up another tab, revealing a photograph of a smiling young woman with long, dark hair and blue eyes. Underneath, bold letters declare she has been missing from Newport for two weeks.

"That's her?" I whisper, horror gripping my throat as I realize our similarities. "Oh God, she's missing?"

He nods grimly, fingers tightening into fists. "She's not the only one. There's a list of women. Most of them had some kind of connection to him—personal or business. There have been whispers online for a while now, but everyone is afraid to name."

The realization hits me with brutal force, a sickening twist of guilt and dread churning inside me. "How did I not see this?"

Brody reaches out, gripping my hand, grounding me. "He's a master manipulator."

I shake my head slightly, breath shallow as another memory resurfaces. "He always took these strange, secretive calls. He'd step outside, away from me. He'd be furious afterward, snapping at anyone around him. Once, he said something about 'keeping the situation contained,' and I thought it was some work scandal, not ..."

"Not kidnapping or possibly worse," Brody finishes, his voice rough with fury. "He's more dangerous than any of us realized. And this is just the tip of the iceberg."

His eyes hold mine. "I will uncover the truth. These women deserve justice."

I squeeze his hand, drawing strength from him. "I can't lose you."

"Never." Brody's promise burns brightly in his dark blue eyes. "Everyone is working to take him down."

I feel both comforted by Brody's presence and haunted by the shadows Micah has cast over our lives. This revelation is darker than I ever imagined it could be.

"This ends soon," Brody says with determination in his voice. "We have to find Mia."

"This is my fault," I whisper.

"No," he says, wrapping his arm around me and kissing my forehead. It's the only thing that brings light to this darkness surrounding me.

A chill runs down my spine as I realize that could've been me.

Micah has to be stopped before he hurts someone else.

24

BRODY

Normally, easy mornings would bring me a sense of calm, but right now, a tight knot twists in my gut. Harper carefully folds her clothes, placing them in the weekend bag Billie brought for her when she visited. She moves slowly, like she's trying to delay the inevitable—we're leaving. Being in the city with more protection is the safest option, and I will always choose Harper's safety first.

I watch her from the doorway and focus on the way the sunlight catches in her hair and splashes across her cheeks.

It's moments when I can't stop admiring her that I'm reminded exactly how far I've fallen. Every instinct screams at me to shield her, to pull her back into my arms, to keep her locked safely here, away from everything dark. But our reality waits for no one, and this place is no longer safe with Micah on the loose.

Harper's pretty eyes meet mine across the small bedroom. She pauses, fingers lingering on a folded sweater.

"What's on your mind?" I ask, knowing she's lost in thought.

I move to her; my heart lurches at the fear lingering in her eyes.

"Just thinking about things," she says.

Since last night, when we received that frantic call from Billie, Harper has been on edge.

My smile fades, replaced by seriousness. "No matter what comes next, we'll walk through the fire together."

Harper steps closer to me, wrapping her arms around my waist. "I'm really scared."

"I know," I say, holding her against me. "I've got you."

She leans forward, resting her forehead against my chest, breathing as I wrap an arm tighter around her waist, holding her close.

Her voice is muffled. "I wish we could stay here. Just you and me. Everything feels simpler here."

I rest my cheek against her hair, memorizing her scent, her warmth, and the steady beat of her heart. "Me too. But we'll carry a piece back with us and come visit when it's safe again." I smile. "We've changed here."

She nods, pushing back just enough to meet my eyes. "You're right. We have."

Silence settles around us. We both know the peace we feel here is fragile and temporary, but we cling to it, savoring the last precious minutes we have left.

Finally, reluctantly, I press a kiss to her forehead. "Finish packing. The helicopter will arrive soon."

Harper sighs, stepping back, gathering her folded clothes. "I'm almost done. What will happen to Easton's car?"

"He's scheduled a transport to deliver it back to the city."

"Oh," she says.

I watch her for a few seconds longer before moving into the living room. Bags are scattered on the floor, one is packed with clothes, and the other holds my gear. I systematically check my inventory of weapons, my mind already racing forward to what awaits us in the city. Micah, the public fallout, the uncertainty of Mia—it's overwhelming. Being here is the true calm before the storm that's waiting for us on the horizon.

Harper deserves peace and to feel safe. She should be able to live her life without shadows looming. If it costs me everything, I'll make damn sure she gets that. Because protecting Harper Alexander isn't just another promise I made to my cousin. She's become my everything.

She's the person who's awakened parts of me I thought died years ago, who's reminded me there is a life waiting for us that's worth fighting for.

I haul the last bag onto the porch, setting it down with a thud as the familiar distant chop of helicopter blades grows louder. Harper steps out behind me, eyes lifted toward the sky, squinting in the sunlight. A breeze catches in her hair, lifting it around her face. She looks like a woman who's ready to face whatever waits beyond this mountain—stronger, steadier, healed in ways I've only begun to understand.

"There it is," she says, stepping closer as the chopper crests the tree line and descends toward the clearing. Her hand slips into mine, squeezing.

I squeeze back. "Ready?"

Harper nods once. "I have no choice."

I lean in close, pressing a quick kiss against her temple. "This is almost over."

The helicopter settles smoothly on the grass, blades still spinning. I gather our bags, and we move across the yard. When we're twenty feet from the door, a noise cuts through the rhythmic pounding of rotor blades.

It's the sound of a distant engine, faint, but it's growing louder. Something about it feels off. Wrong.

I tense, immediately scanning the winding mountain road visible between the trees. Dust kicks up, clouding the air as a sleek black car comes into view, speeding toward the cabin at a dangerous pace.

Harper stiffens beside me, her fingers tightening around mine. Her voice is edged with sudden panic. "Brody, that's ..."

I already know. A cold chill slices down my spine.

Micah Rhodes.

I turn, urgency filling every movement as I drop my duffel full of guns. I cup Harper's face. "Listen to me. You're getting on that helicopter. Now. You hear me?"

She stares at me, eyes wide and frantic, already shaking her head. "Brody, no—"

I grip her shoulders. "You have to go."

Her eyes fill with panic, and she roughly grabs my arms, yanking me with her. "Come with me. Please."

I keep my voice calm even though I want vengeance. "Harper, please get in the helicopter. You have to trust me."

Tears stream down her face, fear bright in her eyes. But finally, with trembling lips, she nods quickly, understanding that arguing now means risking everything. "Please be careful."

"I promise." I grip her hand one final time, tugging her quickly to the helicopter and helping her inside. My heart pounds violently as Harper settles into the seat, eyes never leaving mine as I buckle her in swiftly.

"Brody—"

"I'll come for you," I say, offering her one last reassuring smile.

Before she can protest again, I slam the helicopter door shut, patting it twice to signal the pilot.

I move to my duffel, pulling out handguns and extra clips, just as Micah's car skids to a stop behind Easton's car. Dust settles around, and anger flares in my chest.

Harper desperately presses her hand against the glass, eyes wide with panic, pleading silently for me to join her. She's screaming at the top of her lungs.

My heart clenches, but I force myself to step away. The helicopter blades spin faster, lifting the craft upward as Harper's tear-streaked face stares down at me through the window.

Turning, I face Micah's car head-on. The helicopter rises

LYRA PARISH

quickly above the clearing, but I know Harper can see every detail unfolding below.

This is what it means to protect someone you love.

Micah steps out of the car, eyes hidden behind dark sunglasses, his posture casual. Deadly anger roars inside me, and I glare at him.

I straighten my stance, my voice cutting through the fading noise of the helicopter above. "You really shouldn't have come here, Rhodes."

My fingers curl around the familiar weight of the gun. I pull it swiftly, aiming at Micah's head. I won't miss—sharpshooters never do. My pulse pounds heavily in my ears as every fiber of my being screams to end this now, to make sure he never gets another chance to hurt another woman or Harper again.

Micah freezes; surprise sweeps across his arrogant features before his expression quickly settles back into a calculating calm. He lifts his chin slightly, a defiant smirk meeting his lips as he challenges me, almost as if he's silently daring me to take the shot.

A metallic click to my side splits the tense silence from the tree line, and my blood runs cold as I recognize the unmistakable sound of another weapon chambering a round.

Reluctantly, I glance sideways, my heart dropping as Nick steps from the woods, gun pointed directly at me.

"Nick," I growl, confusion and frustration lacing my voice, "what the fuck are you doing?"

His expression remains cool, eyes locked firmly on mine, though a muscle twitches visibly along his clenched jaw. "Stopping you from making the biggest mistake of your life."

My jaw tightens painfully. "You don't understand—"

"I understand perfectly," he interrupts, eyes blazing with intensity as he keeps the gun locked on me. "Get in your car, Rhodes. Leave right now," he yells.

I keep my weapon pointed at Micah.

Micah hesitates, weighing his options as his gaze flicks rapidly between Nick and me.

"Did I fucking stutter?" Nick steps forward, the threat in his voice unmistakably clear.

Then he swivels abruptly, shifting the barrel of his gun toward Micah, voice hardening to lethal steel as he says, "If you don't get in your fucking car right now, I'll blow your damn head off myself and end this." His voice rises, echoing with a promise that even Micah can't ignore. Nick pulls the trigger; a bullet whizzes through the trees. "You think I'm fucking joking? I'm a great shot."

Micah steps back abruptly, running a hand through his hair, as if regaining control. He meets my gaze one final time, his voice cool and utterly devoid of emotion, saying, "This isn't over, Brody. Harper belongs to me. One way or another, I'll make sure she remembers that."

My fist clenches tighter around the grip of the gun, but I hold myself in place, refusing to rise to his bait.

"The next time you fucking dare come near her, you won't walk away. That's a promise. Where is Mia?" My voice remains dangerously calm, my eyes never leaving his face.

Micah smiles, and I see pure evil. "Not sure what you're talking about."

Micah gives me one last glare, then turns toward his car. The engine roars to life, tires spinning violently, sending a spray of dirt and gravel, as he speeds away, leaving a cloud of dust hanging heavy in the air.

I watch until his vehicle disappears down the mountain road, every muscle in my body still coiled with rage. Before I can even exhale, I spin toward Nick, my gun trained firmly on him, my heart hammering violently in my chest.

He mirrors my stance, gun aimed steadily at my chest. Neither of us blinks. The air between us is tense, crackling with anger.

"Why the fuck would you do that?" I shout, my voice ragged and vibrating with rage.

Nick's eyes are blazing wild. "Because ending him ends you and Harper, you dumb fuck."

We stand locked in place, the forest echoing with our harsh words. Nick lowers his gun, though the intensity never leaves his expression.

"You pull that trigger, and it's all over, Brody," he says, his voice steady. "He wins. You lose. Harper loses you."

My chest heaves as I lower my gun, the weight of Nick's words sinking into me, shattering the adrenaline-driven rage that consumed my thoughts. He's right; I nearly crossed a line I could never come back from.

"You don't think he's trying to trap you? No telling who he told he was coming up here." Nick shakes his head, frustration and concern written on his face. "Get your shit together. We can't protect her if you go rogue."

I exhale heavily, dragging a shaking hand down my face, forcing myself back into control. The helicopter has vanished beyond the tree line, taking Harper to safety. But even as relief loosens the tightness in my chest, dread quickly fills the emptiness it leaves behind. I'm not with her right now. I can't protect her if we're apart.

Micah's threat echoes chillingly in my mind—a cold, stark warning that he's far from finished.

Unfortunately for him, neither am I.

25

HARPER

My pulse pounds violently in my ears as the helicopter jerks upward, and my breath catches, strangled by fear. I'm helpless, trapped behind cold glass, forced to watch the distance stretch between Brody and me. The earth falls away, swallowing the last solid connection I have to him, my palms pressing against the window, as if I could somehow claw my way back down to him.

"Brody!"

My scream dissolves instantly, devoured by the relentless roar of the rotors. He stands below, rigid as stone, facing Micah head-on, weapon drawn. Even from this height, I can see revenge radiating from him, a violent promise held in every muscle of his body.

My breath fogs the glass, and I smear it away, unwilling to lose sight of him for even a heartbeat. I ache to be on the ground beside him, standing united, but instead, I'm powerless, suspended above this nightmare, every cell in my body screaming to go back.

Movement below jerks my attention, sending ice shooting through my veins. Brody turns his head, and I see sunlight glinting off the metal in his hand. My heart slams brutally against my ribs as terror slices through me like a blade.

"No," I whisper, trembling fingers pressing harder into the glass, as if that could somehow bridge the distance. "Brody, don't—"

Micah halts abruptly, a moment of hesitation before his familiar arrogance returns, and he moves forward again, every step a taunt. My fists tighten into helpless balls, nails digging into my palms, drawing tiny, crescent-shaped marks of pain. This can't be happening. Not again. Not now, not when I've just found everything that matters.

Then the world shifts violently, shattering what little composure I had left.

A second figure emerges from the trees, stalking silently toward Brody, a dark silhouette unmistakable against the bright clearing. My breath catches, terror exploding white-hot through my chest, squeezing my lungs painfully tight. A gun is aimed directly at Brody's back. He's outnumbered.

"Brody!" I scream as if he could hear me, my voice cracking on his name. I pound against the window, as if my desperation can shatter it. Tears spill hot and uncontrollable down my cheeks, blurring everything into a distorted nightmare.

A rush of adrenaline pulses through me, and the helicopter banks away, pulling the terrible scene from my sight. A violent wave of nausea surges through me, bile rising harshly in my throat as I fight the devastating helplessness flooding every nerve ending.

I grab a barf bag, feeling as if I might fill it.

"We have to go back," I plead brokenly to the pilots. My voice is weak beneath the deafening thump of rotors. "Please, you have to land. You have to—"

"I'm sorry, Ms. Alexander. We have orders from the Calloways," he says firmly.

My heart splinters into painful fragments, my hands trembling violently as I fumble for my phone.

My pulse pounds erratically, panic fogging my vision. I can't think—I can't breathe—but instinctively, my fingers move, shaking as I type out a message to Billie.

Brody's in danger. Micah found us. Please, send help.

I hit Send, clutching my phone, but an error flashes cruelly across the screen: **Message Failed to Send**

I realize I have no cell service.

"No ..." My voice breaks into a raw sob, and I choke on the anguish rising in my throat. "Come on. Please, please go through."

I lift my phone higher, moving it around the confined space, but the signal bars remain empty, hopelessly blank. Frustration and despair smother me, leaving me hollow and alone.

Brody's down there alone, fighting for me, risking everything for us, and I'm helpless to stop it.

What if he's hurt? What if they shot him?

"Please be okay," I whisper into the emptiness around me, my voice nothing more than a shattered plea, a prayer to whatever forces might listen. "Please, Brody ... be okay."

Hours pass, and I feel numb, like a shell of myself. My body feels weightless, floating somewhere outside of myself. Inside, my thoughts and the what-ifs unravel faster than I can grasp them. Brody's face is burned into my mind, determination mixed with something darker. I squeeze my eyes shut, but it only sharpens the image. My pulse throbs so violently in my temples that it hurts.

Why didn't I fight harder? Why didn't I insist that he stay with me and drag him onto this helicopter myself?

The stark notification on my phone stares back coldly: **Message Failed to Send**

A sob releases from me. It's guttural and raw. I blink rapidly, wiping tears from my face, my heart twisting painfully in my chest.

"Please," I whisper again, clicking the message.

Still nothing—no service, no way to reach Billie, no way to know if Brody's safe.

A thousand terrifying scenarios flood my mind, each worse than the last. What if Micah hurt him? What if that other figure ...

Air catches painfully in my lungs, and I grip the seat belt, my knuckles turning stark white. I battle the surge of helplessness and guilt crashing over me. The city skyline looms closer as the helicopter slices through the air. I can't explain the soul-deep terror that's currently tearing me apart. No one could possibly understand the nightmare we narrowly escaped or the even darker one unfolding back at the cabin.

Brody's words echo suddenly. *"I'll come for you."*

Fresh tears spill down my cheeks, hot with frustration. He made me feel safe, protected. But now he's back there alone, facing danger without me—because of me.

The helicopter banks, descending rapidly toward the rooftop landing pad at the top of Park Towers. The city rushes closer, a concrete maze filled with unknown threats, and life feels empty without Brody by my side. Reality sets in that I'm here, and he's there, completely out of my reach.

As soon as the skids touch solid ground, I unclip my seat belt, my heart pounding. The door slides open, and a blast of cold city wind whooshes through the cabin. I'm already moving, practically stumbling out, my legs weak and unsteady beneath me as I get out.

"Ms. Alexander!" a voice shouts, urgent and concerned. Two men in suits rush forward, extending a hand to steady me. They're carrying my bags. "Are you all right?"

I can't answer. Anxiety grips my throat again, and I shove past him, needing to find Billie, Asher, someone, anyone who can help. My phone finally vibrates in my hand, and I freeze, hope flaring painfully in my chest as I move inside the building. I stand in the hallway, glancing down at my phone, noticing I have three missed calls from Billie, along with texts. I open them.

BILLIE

Harper, are you okay?

BILLIE

Nick called. Micah found you guys?

BILLIE

Harper, please answer me!

BILLIE

Let me know when you land.

My heart leaps painfully at the name—Nick. How would he know? Confusion mixes with chaos, and I can't seem to put the pieces together.

My fingers shake as I dial Brody's number, pressing the phone hard against my ear, needing any sign that he's okay. Each ring feels like an eternity.

"Come on. Please answer," I whisper, my voice cracking, eyes filling rapidly with fresh tears. I can't lose him.

It clicks abruptly to voicemail, his steady voice—calm, reassuring, so heartbreakingly familiar—filling my ear. "It's Brody. Leave a message."

"Call me. Please tell me you're okay." I choke back a sob, disconnecting quickly and dialing again. "Please, please, pick up," I plead to no one, my voice trembling.

Straight to voicemail again.

My heart beats hard, and a fresh wave of dread has my knees buckling. I quickly scroll to Nick's number, clicking on it with numb fingers as I search for answers.

His phone rings once, twice, and then I get his voicemail.

Nick's smooth, confident tone is completely at odds with the chaos inside me. "It's Nick. You know what to do."

"Call me immediately!" I demand.

I end the call, tears blurring my vision. Suddenly, the phone vibrates in my hands, Billie's name flashing brightly across the screen.

"I'm heading to my penthouse," I say before she can even speak. "Micah found us. Brody stayed behind to face him. Someone else showed up as I was lifting off. They had a gun on him. I don't know what happened. I couldn't—"

"Harper," Billie interrupts, voice steady. "Where are you?"

"At the top of the building, standing in the hallway. Security is watching me," I tell her as a guy in a suit pretends like he can't hear me.

"Wait for me. I'm on my way up there," Billie says.

She has a penthouse here but doesn't use it anymore. Maybe she started using it while I was gone.

She clears her throat, bringing me back. "Listen to me. Easton and Weston have a security detail heading to the cabin now to make sure no one is hurt. We know Micah was there; Nick called earlier, saying he was there to back up Brody because he had a feeling about something. We haven't heard from either of them since."

"Nick was there?" I shake my head; none of it makes sense. "Someone pointed a gun at Brody. What if Nick is hurt too? What if they were both ambushed?"

"I'm coming. I'll be up there in less than five minutes," she says as I sob uncontrollably.

I sink to the floor in the hallway and wait for her.

"It's going to be okay." Brody's reassurance echoes in my mind, but beneath it simmers an inescapable dread.

The thought of losing Brody is terrifying and very, very real. But all I can do now is helplessly wait. My heart is suspended somewhere between hope and fear, and there is nothing I can do.

My fingers tighten around the phone, and I force myself to speak. "How do you know Nick was there?"

"Nick mentioned it to Asher a couple of days ago. He said he had a feeling Micah would find you. He told Asher he was heading there, just in case."

Confusion transforms into disbelief. "After Mia went missing?"

"Yes," Billie says with an exhale, and an edge of uncertainty slips into her voice. "He's been tracking Micah, but I don't know any details. He just said he was going to make sure you were protected. He's really fucking stubborn, and he likes to take things into his own hands."

"I know," I tell her.

I've known Nick since I was a little kid because he was best friends with my brother.

"After that picture of you two swallowing each other's tongue was posted, there was speculation that you were in Sugar Pine Springs. Nick acted immediately."

I laugh, but then my breath catches. "None of this makes sense."

Seconds later, Billie rushes to me, with Asher following in her shadow. As soon as she sees me, she pulls me to my feet and holds me tight. For a long moment, we cling to each other; the tension slightly eases.

"Are you okay, Harp?"

"No," I say truthfully, my head pounding from stress. I squeeze my eyes shut against a dizzying rush of emotions. Nick's involvement adds another layer to an already dangerous situation. "Why wouldn't Nick have told us? We could have been prepared—"

"Brody is always prepared to protect you," Billie confirms, placing her hands on my shoulders and looking into my eyes. "It's why you're safely in New York right now."

My voice is barely audible as I whisper, "I'm so scared something bad happened."

"I know, but right now, we have no answers," Billie replies. "Let's get you to your place, okay?" She's gentle and kind.

"Will you stay with me? I can't be alone," I tell her as I cling to that fragile thread of hope.

"Yes," she says without hesitation.

Asher picks up the duffel bags that are by my feet, and Billie takes the weekend bag and leads me to the elevator. She's my anchor in this storm.

"I won't leave you until Brody shows up," she whispers, grabbing my hand and squeezing it. "We'll get through this."

I meet her eyes, swallowing past the lump still lodged painfully in my throat. "Are you worried about him?"

"No," she says confidently. "Nick is a fucking punk, but he's not going to hurt Brody. Trust me."

"I know what I saw," I say, and I feel like I'm hyperventilating.

"Breathe. Brody knows how to handle himself. You have to trust that."

"I can't lose him," I choke out. "Not now."

"You won't," she says. Certainty rings in every word as the elevator doors slide open. She guides me out. "Brody could take on Nick and Micah at the same time with his eyes closed. They're bitch boys."

Asher chuckles and mutters, "I'm telling him you said that."

"It's true. I've seen him fight five dudes at once. He's one of the best shots. Completely lethal. And he's like a cat with nine lives," she tells me.

I press my thumb against my door. It unlocks, and I step inside. It feels weird being home.

"Let's get you settled."

Billie guides me into my penthouse, and Asher sets the bags down on the floor. I peer out the floor-to-ceiling windows that overlook Central Park. The sun hangs lazily in the sky, and I glance at the clock on the wall. It's just past six in the evening, and soon, it will be dark. Hours have passed, and I've heard nothing.

Asher gives me a soft smile, but I see concern in his eyes. He squeezes my shoulder, and then they lead me to the sectional that's close to the gas fireplace. Billie presses a button, and the flames come to life. I stare at them, thinking back to the cabin and the time I spent with Brody over the past couple of weeks.

"How about some tea?" Billie asks. "Always makes you feel better."

I'm reminded of Micah and how he drugged me.

I burst into tears, covering my face with my hands. "So much has happened."

Billie sits next to me and places her hand on my back. "Harp, what can I do? Want to punch Asher?"

"Hey!" he says.

"He can take it," Billie tells me. "Just one hard punch, anywhere you want. I'll make it up to him later."

"Do I get a vote?" he asks.

Billie shakes her head and smiles. "He deserves it for giving me hell for years. I'd suggest below the waist."

Laughter spills out of me, and it's the first time I've cracked a smile since earlier today.

"Ah, there's my bestie. Now, want some coffee? I'll order pizza and Chinese, and we can have a buffet while we wait for Brody to arrive," she says.

I study her. "You're not concerned."

She shakes her head and gives me a soft smile. "Not at all."

"Okay. I'll take coffee," I tell her, then turn to Asher. "You're safe."

"Thank fuck," he tells me.

"For now," I add.

Our bags are on the floor, and I stand, walking to Brody's to dig inside it. Right on top is his cell phone, turned off. That means he has no way to reach the outside world, and the thought of that makes me spiral again. I hold it in my hand while Billie watches me from the kitchen as the beans grind.

"What is it?" she asks.

"His phone," I tell her. "I guess that explains why he's not answering."

Minutes later, Billie returns with a steaming mug of coffee, placing it carefully in my hands as she settles beside Asher. The chemistry burning between them is impossible to ignore. I watch how Asher naturally holds her close to him, along with the way Billie's eyes soften when she meets his. They're perfect together, and I'm so damn glad they ended up together.

"What?" Billie asks as I blow on the steaming liquid.

I smile. "You're totally meant to be together."

Asher smirks, and they share a silent conversation. "It was inevitable."

He presses a gentle kiss to her temple, leaning back comfortably as Billie's fingers intertwine with his. An ache spreads through my chest.

Asher stands, bending over to slide his lips over Billie's. "I'm going to grab my laptop from your place. I'll be right back, okay?"

Billie nods and watches him as he moves to the door. The two of us are alone, and I don't even know where to begin.

"What is going on with Mia? What happened?"

She starts at the beginning, explaining how they went to lunch together, and when they returned, someone took her. Billie hasn't been to work since it happened and is lying low, staying at Park Towers because they have the best security in the city due to who lives here.

"I feel guilty, like this is all my fault," Billie confesses. "He wouldn't have targeted you if it wasn't for me."

"And he wouldn't have targeted Mia if it wasn't for me," I tell her. "I'm so sorry. I allowed the vampire in. He would've killed me, Billie. Women are missing because of him. Handfuls of them. I'm so scared."

The color drains from her face. "What?"

"You didn't know?" I ask, studying her.

She shakes her head as the realization of what we're dealing with etches across her face. I can see her anxiety rising. We sit in silence, watching the flames lick up the side of the fireplace. I'm lost in my head, and the only thing that pulls me out of it is a knock on the door. I nearly jump out of my skin as Billie stands to answer it. She looks out the peephole, then swings it open, allowing Asher in. He stops, gives her a sweet kiss, then continues to the kitchen.

She settles back on the couch next to me.

"To have someone look at me the way Asher looks at you—

that's the dream, isn't it?" I say, sipping the coffee, nearly begging the warmth to seep into my chilled bones.

Billie's eyes are filled with quiet certainty as she squeezes my hand. "Brody does, Harp. He always has."

My heart flutters at her words; emotions rise, and I don't know how to handle them. I blink rapidly, forcing back fresh tears, and Billie shifts closer.

"You two have always had something special. It took you too long to see it, but it's there, burning so fucking bright." Billie's voice is gentle and sincere, thoughtful and understanding. "Trust that."

I nod, leaning into the comfort of my best friend's presence, absorbing the reassurance in her words. I didn't realize how much I'd missed this, missed her. Right now, she's the glue that's holding me together.

"Brody's probably already on his way here now," Billie says with certainty.

"I hope you're right," I whisper quietly, my voice barely audible.

Asher pops into our conversation. "She always is."

It causes me to laugh because it's true.

Billie glares at him. "And don't either of you ever forget it."

When I look at the two of them, I believe my own happily ever after is possible and that Brody will find his way through the storm to find me. I cling to her words, desperately wanting to believe Brody's safe.

The evening fades into night as I lie back on the couch and watch *The Golden Girls*. Billie watches it with me while Asher continues to work. We order food, and I barely eat because I'm too upset. I want sleep to take me under, but it refuses. Every time I close my eyes, the image of metal in Brody's hand, Micah's arrogant smirk, and the shadowed figure stepping from the woods appear in my mind. My heart won't stop racing. Anxiety claws at me relentlessly.

With a frustrated exhale, I finally sit up, wishing the couch would suck me in. Billie's steady breathing drifts from the other side of the couch. I stand up, placing a blanket over her, and exhale a long breath. The dim light from the lamp casts shadows along the walls.

A quiet tapping on keys draws my attention toward the kitchen island, where Asher is now sitting. His face is illuminated by the glow of his laptop screen.

He glances up, eyebrows lifting slightly. "Can't sleep?"

I shake my head, moving toward the refrigerator to grab a bottle of water. "Every time I close my eyes, it's just ..." I trail off, unable to voice it again, the memories still too raw.

Asher nods with quiet understanding, turning his gaze back to the screen. "I understand how that is."

I sit in the chair across from him, and he looks up at me.

"How did you learn about Brody and Eden?" I bluntly ask.

His expression softens, and he smiles. "He told you I knew?"

I nod. "How?"

Asher swallows hard, and he hesitates, but his resolve breaks on his exhale. "I learned it through an old letter."

He gives me a sad smile. "Eden wasn't the type to settle down with anyone, Harp. She and Nick were very much alike in that manner—stubborn, but unable to commit. If you're asking because—"

"I'm not jealous. At our age, past relationships are a part of life. I was just curious—that's all. We were friends. Not close, but I knew I could count on her. So did Billie. She wanted us to succeed in our business and told us she'd do whatever she could to help us during our many coffee chats. Seems as if you picked up the slack," I tell him.

He nods, grinning. "I'll always have your back."

He glances back at his laptop.

"What are you working on?" I ask.

Asher's jaw clenches tightly, and his eyes are shadowed with seriousness. "I'm tracking Micah's movements—who he's been talking to, where he's going. Patterns, anything to stay ahead of him."

"Find anything useful?" I ask, chugging water down, hoping it will cool the inferno burning inside of me.

"More than I'd like." His voice carries a calm determination that steadies me. He studies me closely. "Look, I know you're really fucking worried right now, but don't be. That man is tougher than nails. He got shot and lived ... twice. Fought in wars. He's a badass. He'd tear the world apart before he let anything happen to you."

A small smile touches my lips. "I know, but that's also what scares me. What if he tears *himself* apart instead?"

Understanding fills his eyes. He leans back slightly, watching me carefully. "You know, Billie taught me that, sometimes, the people who've seen the darkest shit in life love the hardest. Brody's like that too. He's been through hell, Harper. He's lost more than anyone should, but it made him into someone who knows exactly what he has to do to protect the people he cares about. Not someone I'd want to be up against. He's like a fucking Terminator."

Laughter bursts out of me. "I thought the same thing."

Asher smiles. "Because that shit is true."

His words steady me.

"I don't know how you and Billie did it," I admit. "How you made it through everything—all the chaos, the media, the lies."

Asher glances toward the couch, where Billie sleeps. "You have to refuse to let fear win. You look it in the face and tell it to fuck off and keep going. When you find someone who's your reason for everything, giving up isn't an option. You fight until the very end. If it's meant to be, you make it out to the other side together. Maybe a little scorched, but alive." His voice carries conviction, the kind forged through battles fought and won together.

I watch him silently for a long moment, absorbing the strength he radiates.

"Brody loves you, Harp," Asher adds, his eyes steady on mine, "in a way that doesn't ever break."

I inhale, the tightness in my chest loosening slightly. A glimmer of hope fills the hollow space left behind by fear. "Thank you, Ash. For staying, for helping. For being here."

He gives me a grin. "You're Billie's best friend. The two of you are a package deal. I'd do anything for you. So would Nick, Easton, and Weston. Especially Brody. You have an army standing behind you, and there is a light at the end of this dark-as-fuck tunnel."

I nod, his words etching into my bones.

For the first time since flying away from Brody on that mountain, I let myself truly believe that strength and love will be enough to bring him safely back to me.

26

BRODY

I grip the steering wheel until my knuckles turn white, the leather creaking beneath my tense hands. I'm fucking livid.

Easton's sleek, vintage car growls beneath me as the tires rip across the winding mountain roads. The trees blur outside the windows, nothing but streaks of green and gray under the pale slice of sky. Every mile stretching between me and Harper twists at my nerves.

I should've been on that fucking helicopter. I should've been right beside her, keeping her safe. Instead, I let Micah *fucking* Rhodes get too close—close enough that I pulled my gun, felt my finger twitch against the trigger.

If Nick hadn't stepped in ... well, Micah would've disappeared.

My jaw clenches, teeth grinding against each other, anger throbbing like a heartbeat in my veins. I refuse to even glance at Nick, who's sitting beside me, lounging casually in the passenger seat like this is some goddamn road trip.

Nick shifts slightly, deliberately stretching his legs and sighing loudly, breaking the tense silence that's been building like a thunderstorm. "You're welcome, by the way."

I bite down harder, fighting the urge to throttle him right here. I imagine myself slamming the back of my fist into his face, knocking him out completely. "Don't. Fucking. Start," I growl.

"Oh, I think I've earned the right to start," he says, smug amusement clear in every word. "Saved your ass back there. Didn't even get a thank-you. Typical fucking Calloway."

I breathe through my nose, keeping my eyes locked on the road. "You stopped me from finishing it."

He snorts, unbothered by my anger. "You mean, I stopped you from landing yourself in jail, dumbass. You pull that trigger, you don't see Harper again. Ever. And we don't find Mia or the other missing women. Sorry, but we need Micah alive."

I don't respond—don't need to. He's right, and he knows it, which only makes the burn, combined with his cocky-as-fuck attitude, even worse. Anger is simpler than admitting he saved me from my recklessness. Easier than admitting just how deeply I lost control the second Micah stepped into that clearing.

Nick lets the silence hang just long enough to become uncomfortable before nudging me again. He's relentless in his baiting—a total Banks trait. "So, tell me exactly how long you've been in love with Harper? Asking for research purposes."

Heat spikes dangerously in my chest, crawling up my throat. I grip the wheel even harder, knuckles aching now. I cannot fuck this up—it's something I repeat to myself. "None of your damn business."

"That long, huh?" He chuckles, clearly amused by the rage crackling off me. "Damn."

I force air through clenched teeth, refusing to let him see how far he's crawling under my skin. But Nick Banks is nothing if not persistent. He shifts again, obnoxiously relaxed as he taps an absent rhythm on the door.

"Got to hand it to you, Brod. Didn't think you had it in you," he muses, eyes glittering with that irritating spark of mischief. "To risk it all like that. Guess she's worth it."

"She's my purpose," I snap before I catch myself, the truth slipping through the cracks in my armor.

The car fills with abrupt silence. Nick's gaze narrows, his playful edge softening into something serious. He watches me carefully, measuring the weight of what I just admitted. For once, he doesn't have some smart-ass comeback. Instead, he nods and then looks away, leaving my words floating between us.

I wish I could read his fucking mind as my heart hammers inside my chest, and the realization of my admission sinks deeper into my bones. Harper isn't just someone I'm protecting anymore; she's everything worth fighting for, worth risking it all. And today, for a split second, I almost crossed that line and ruined everything.

Nick clears his throat. "So, you and Harper ... wow."

"Careful." My jaw tightens, and I finally spare him a brief, enraged glance.

He lifts his hands defensively, palms up, but he smirks, loving that he's annoying me. "Relax. I only ever saw her like a sister. Zane's my best friend—I wouldn't do that to him."

"Nah, you just fucked his fiancée." I look him up and down pointedly, voice flat and cold.

He barks out a surprised laugh, shaking his head. "Ouch. Tell me how you really feel, Calloway."

I shift my gaze forward again, but the tension eases just slightly, replaced by something closer to respect. "I just did."

"Zane and I are working through it. As you know, love can make you do stupid-as-fuck things." Nick leans back into his seat, staring thoughtfully into the darkness beyond the windshield. "Anyway, there are other ways to destroy Micah Rhodes—ways that don't land you behind bars. Ways that make him face every goddamn consequence. One day, you'll thank me. I'll be waiting."

My fingers twitch; curiosity replaces my anger. "What do you know?"

"Enough to bury him," Nick replies firmly, the hard edge returning to his voice. "But that's a conversation for tomorrow, when we're with Asher. He's better at playing the long game than I am."

I nod, accepting that much. My heart rate eases into a controlled thump.

For now, at least, Nick's right. Ending Micah without killing him and making him suffer the way he's made others suffer is what Harper deserves. What every woman he's hurt deserves too.

"Do you know where he took Mia?"

Nick shakes his head. "That's what I'm trying to figure out. I will. I just need more time."

Silence stretches between us, and I have nothing else to say.

Eventually, he settles deeper into his seat, yawning dramatically. "Wake me up if you decide to crash. Preferably not into anything."

I don't bother responding, jaw tight as I stare into the endless road ahead of us. Harper's smile visits my thoughts, and then I remember the fear in her eyes as the helicopter lifted her away. She was panicked, screaming at the top of her lungs. My heart constricts as I relive that.

I press hard on the gas, increasing my speed. I'll drive eleven hours straight to find my way back to her tonight if I have to.

Stars sprinkle across the sky as clouds move overhead. A heavy mist clings to the highway, and we drive a few hours in a downpour. Fatigue pulls at the edges of my consciousness, but adrenaline mixed with anger keeps me alert.

Beside me, Nick shifts restlessly, stretching his legs out as far as the cramped car allows. He sits up and glances at me. "Are we ever gonna stop, or is your plan just to torture me into submission?"

"I'd prefer unconsciousness," I say flatly, eyes never leaving the road.

He chuckles dryly. "Careful, Calloway. I might start to think you don't like me."

"You'd be correct."

Nick snorts, amused rather than offended. "Damn, someone needs a nap."

"Then take one," I reply.

Nick stops talking, but the silence never lasts long with him. He clears his throat. "I'm gonna need to take a piss soon."

"Be my guest," I say, smirking.

He taps his fingers rhythmically against the dashboard. Nick lets out a deep laugh. "You know, I forgot how much fun you are. But, hey, if you want to kill Rhodes so badly, we could lock you two in a room together, and you could bore him to death with your brooding."

I refuse to let Nick get to me, even though every fiber of my being wants to throat punch him. Nick watches me closely, clearly sensing just how close I am to the edge.

Eventually, he sighs deeply. "You ever think maybe Harper wouldn't want you risking everything just to prove a point?" he asks, carefully treading the line between serious and casual. "You know, if roles were reversed."

His words sink into the chaos in my mind, but I don't give him the satisfaction of admitting he's right. Instead, I offer him a stony glare.

"Just saying. Harper deserves justice, sure. But she also deserves you."

The quiet sincerity lurking beneath his sarcasm unsettles me. I swallow back the tightness in my throat, focusing on the endless stretch of road again.

Finally, grudgingly, I admit, "I know."

"Glad we can finally agree." Nick smirks lightly, glancing at the stars above. "I really would appreciate a pit stop. This car is nice as hell, but it wasn't built for road trips or anyone over six feet."

I check the fuel gauge, knowing we'll need to stop for gas soon anyway. A few miles ahead, I see the faint glow of a neon sign for a twenty-four-hour gas station. I pull off, and the car rolls to a stop by the pump.

Nick gives me an exaggerated sigh of relief. "Thank God. Now I won't have to tell Easton I pissed inside his car. However, I'd have loved to see the look on his face."

"I'm not stopping because of you." I put the car into neutral. "You're driving the next shift. If you can drive a stick."

Nick shakes his head. "You forget I didn't grow up with a fucking silver spoon in my mouth, Calloway. Sometimes, all of you could use a hefty dose of fucking reality to humble you."

Ignoring him, I step out; the late-night air washes over me, easing the edge of exhaustion just slightly. When I reach instinctively for my phone, my heart sinks when I realize I left it in the duffel bag Harper took with her onto the helicopter.

"Fuck," I mutter under my breath.

Nick raises an eyebrow, catching the frustration in my tone. "What's wrong now?"

"My phone," I admit. "It's with Harper."

Nick shrugs, unsurprised. "Left mine in the city after texting Asher my plans. Didn't want anyone tracking me."

I glance at him. "You're telling me we have no way to communicate with anyone?"

Nick offers a carefree grin. "Raw-dogging life. Asher knows I was meeting you. He'll be waiting for us."

I grind my teeth, irritation deepening. "You're reckless as hell, Banks."

"Probably why we get along so well," he quips, smirking as he rounds the car, heading toward the gas station's front door. "Want anything?"

"Some duct tape," I holler.

He flips me off and steps inside.

As I fill the car with fuel, all I can think about is Harper. Nick's casual confidence isn't misplaced because I know Billie and Asher were waiting for her to arrive and will keep her safe until I return to the city. But that doesn't stop my current need to hold her, to know she's unharmed, and to make sure she knows how fucking sorry I am for scaring her.

Nick returns with a bag of snacks, and he's holding two cups in his hands. "Coffee for Cranky," he tells me as he jerks the keys from my hand and slides behind the wheel.

I finish pumping the fuel, and he starts the engine, revving it. I slide into the passenger side and glare at him.

"Careful. My ass is on the line if something happens to this car," I explain. "Anything happens to it on your watch, and you're paying Easton for it." Frustration simmers deep beneath the surface.

A smirk touches his lips as he peels out of the parking lot, kicking up loose gravel. The bastard is driving it like he stole it.

Mile markers pass us, and I keep my eyes focused on the road, knowing Harper is waiting for me. It's the only thing that keeps me calm in the chaos.

I replay everything that happened and saw actual fear on Micah's face, and I think he knew I'd pull the trigger without flinching. He won't escape unscathed next time. He'll pay for everything he's done, but I'm trying hard to trust Nick's approach, knowing he's right.

Harper deserves real justice, and if Nick, Asher, and I can serve it, we will.

"Fuck," I whisper as Nick takes curbs at NASCAR speeds.

One thing that sucks about vintage cars is that oh-shit handles weren't a thing back then.

"I need this car in my life," Nick admits, finally cracking the quiet.

I see he's going eighty-eight miles per hour.

"Any faster, and we'll time-travel back to New York," I say, referencing *Back to the Future*.

He glances at me. "If you're that unhappy, you could always walk back to the city. But then that means denying you the pleasure of my incredible company, and we couldn't have that, now, could we?"

"You're more annoying than Asher. Do you know that?" I clench my jaw.

"Yeah," he says proudly as I take a drink of my coffee.

Nick eyes me, his voice softer, deliberately testing, as he says, "You know, Calloway, I've been thinking about how fucking jealous you get when it comes to Harper."

My gaze pins him in place. "Excuse me?"

His expression turns smug, entirely unbothered. "You're protective as hell. Borderline obsessed, actually. I get it; she's fucking stunning. Sweet. Sassy as hell too. Competitive. Jesus, don't even get me started."

Something hot and dangerous tightens in my chest.

He lifts a brow, clearly enjoying himself now. "Relax, Romeo. Even though your hate-filled glares are adorable, I'm immune. You know, I could've dated her several times."

I scoff. "Don't flatter yourself. You're not her type."

"Trust me, I'm everyone's type." Nick laughs, genuinely amused by how pissed he's making me.

"You're an asshole, Banks."

"So I've been told a few thousand times." He shrugs, entirely unapologetic.

"Wake me up when we need gas," I tell him, closing my eyes. "Until then, maybe shut the fuck up."

He laughs. "No can do, Brod. You're stuck with me for another three hours. Lucky you."

Even though he acts like a dickhead, he does keep his mouth shut, and I'm grateful.

Sleep pulls me under like quicksand, and Harper's pretty face swims in and out of focus in my fragmented dreams. Her laughter, the sweet press of her lips, the warmth of her skin—each memory flickers, bright and perfect. Adrenaline jerks me awake, my heart hammering painfully in my chest. Blinking hard, I sit up. Streetlights blur past the window, casting shadows across Nick's tired profile. His eyebrows lift.

"Is Sleeping Beauty awake?"

The nickname almost makes me smile, but I hold it back as I rub a hand roughly over my face. Exhaustion scrapes my eyes like sandpaper, but then again, it's been a long fucking day. "How far out are we?"

"Ten minutes, tops," Nick replies, his voice carrying a rare note of seriousness.

A wave of anxiety rolls through me. Harper's so close, but she still feels so far away. My hands curl into fists against my thighs, tension rushing through every muscle in my body, and I try to relax. I've never needed to see someone as badly as I need to see her now. I need the simple reassurance that she's safe, whole, untouched by the ugliness that unfolded on the mountain.

"She's fine, Calloway," Nick says, reading me easily. "Billie and Asher are with her, guaranteed."

"Doesn't stop me from fucking worrying," I mutter, my voice strained.

He smirks, glancing sideways at me as the engine of the car roars and bounces off the buildings. "That's part of your charm. Personally, I find it exhausting." His expression softens. "Listen, I meant what I said. We'll end this asshole. But we do it right. Justice, not revenge. Understand?"

I swallow hard, the weight of his words pressing into me. Reluctantly, I nod. "I get it."

"Good. Didn't want to keep repeating myself for your stubborn ass." He seems satisfied enough.

My pulse accelerates the closer we get, an urgency simmering like firewater beneath my skin.

When we finally pull into the underground garage at Park Towers, I barely register Banks parking Easton's precious car like he's a stunt driver.

"Who the fuck are you?" I ask.

His eyes narrow. "Some would say their worst nightmare."

We get out of the car, and Nick drops the keys into my hand. I head straight for the elevator, leaving Nick behind. My pulse pounds in my temples, anxiety and anticipation crashing together with each ascending floor, until I finally stand before Harper's penthouse door.

I knock, the sound echoing harshly in the silent hall. My breath feels like it's trapped tight in my lungs.

The door swings open, and I nearly growl with irritation at the sight of Asher standing there, arms spread wide, lips puckered sarcastically.

"Welcome home, sunshine. Miss me?"

"Fuck off," I mutter, shoving roughly past him.

And then my world stops.

Harper stands frozen in the kitchen, the golden glow of lights washing over her. My heart clenches violently at the sight of her—safe, unharmed, stunningly beautiful. For one suspended heartbeat, we simply stare at each other, the air stretching thin and fragile between us.

Her eyes fill rapidly, tears spilling silently down her cheeks as a sob escapes from her. Her fingers release the wineglass she's holding, and it hits the floor, shattering into glittering fragments.

"Brody," she whispers, her voice cracking with raw, desperate relief.

I close the distance in three rapid strides, catching her as she rushes toward me, her body colliding against mine. My arms wrap around her, pulling her flush against my chest; her warmth and scent capture me completely. My throat tightens, and my overwhelming emotions nearly bring me to my knees. She clings to me, trembling, small hands gripping my shirt, as if afraid I'll vanish if she lets go.

"I thought—" she chokes out, shaking her head as if the words physically hurt. "Brody, I thought ..."

"Shh," I whisper, pressing my lips to hers, breathing her in deeply, soothing her with slow strokes along her back. "I'm here. I'm right here. I told you I'd come for you."

She pulls back just enough to look up at me, her tear-filled eyes searching mine. My chest aches at the fear still lingering behind her gaze, and I wish I could erase its shadows.

"You're safe," she whispers, fingertips grazing my jaw, as if to reassure herself I'm real. "You're really here."

"I'm here," I repeat, cupping her face and brushing tears from her cheeks. "I'd have driven for days to see you."

Her breath catches on a sob, relief and love brightening her gaze until it nearly blinds me. I press my forehead against hers, breathing in the quiet intimacy of this moment, understanding how fucking right she feels, back in my arms, where she's always belonged.

I don't hesitate. I don't pause; I simply close the tiny distance remaining between us, my mouth capturing hers in a kiss that obliterates every ounce of fear. The kiss deepens instantly, urgently, possessively, and it's filled with desperation and love as overwhelming relief courses through both of us. Harper's hands slide up, fingers tangling in my hair, holding me as I hold her, both of us refusing to let go. The room dissolves around us, fading into nothing but stolen breaths and trembling sighs. My pulse races, heart slamming roughly against my ribs, every nerve in my body sparking to life like an uncontrollable wildfire. This—her—burns me to ash.

We break apart, foreheads pressed together, completely oblivious to everything else.

I smile against her lips. "I've been waiting all day for that."

Harper's laughter fills my chest, soothing the sharp edges of fear that haunted me during the drive. I press another kiss against her lips, savoring the warmth of her body pressed against mine.

"Wow," Billie whispers from somewhere behind Harper. "Fireworks like I've never witnessed."

Harper pulls back slightly, her cheeks flushing pink as we both glance over to find Billie and Asher watching us with raised eyebrows. Asher chuckles beside her, arms crossed casually as he leans against the counter, clearly entertained.

"I forgot you were here." Harper laughs as she grabs my hand.

"Don't stop on our account," Asher adds, eyes sparkling with amusement as he cleans up the broken wineglass. "This is better than cable."

Before I can fire off a comeback, heavy footsteps echo in the hall, and Nick bursts through the open doorway, breathless and grinning widely as he takes in the scene. "Damn! Did I miss the big reunion?"

"Yes," Billie announces firmly, quickly stepping forward with a laugh. She grabs Nick by the arm, steering him back to where he came from. "Time to go, Bankses. Both of you."

Nick tries to protest, but it's playful.

"See you tomorrow," Asher says as Billie loops her free hand around his arm, too, determinedly guiding both of them out of the room. Asher barely resists, flashing me a teasing grin as Billie pushes him through the doorway.

The door clicks shut firmly behind them, leaving Harper and me alone. Silence settles around us, and Harper lifts her face to mine again, eyes sparkling with laughter and relief.

"I thought they'd never leave," she whispers, warmth radiating from her gaze as her fingers brush my cheek.

"Me neither." My voice is thick with gratitude as I lean into her touch. "Everything is finally right in the world."

"Yes, it is." Harper pulls me into another perfect kiss, chasing away the fears that followed me back to the city.

"Are you okay?" she whispers, searching my face and arms, making sure I'm unscathed.

"I love you," I say, the words falling freely from the deepest corner of my soul. "I love you so goddamn much, Harper."

Her voice trembles, broken and beautiful. "I love you too, Brody. I always have."

27

HARPER

B rody tips my chin upward so our gazes lock. My heart squeezes when I see the unguarded emotion swirling in his eyes, like a storm finally calmed. His thumb brushes across my lower lip, sending warmth cascading through me.

"I missed you," I whisper, my voice barely audible. My fingers curl into his shirt, holding on to him, afraid he might vanish if I let go. "I was terrified I'd lost you."

"I'm so fucking sorry," he offers. He leans down, pressing a kiss against the corner of my mouth. "You're stuck with me."

A quiet laugh escapes me, mixing with a sob that catches in my chest. The relief of having him here, safe, nearly undoes me. His arm tightens around my waist, holding me closer even if it doesn't feel close enough.

"You must be exhausted," I say, noticing the dark circles under his eyes. I'm full of both guilt and gratitude. "Come on. Let's get you cleaned up."

Brody nods, eyes never leaving mine as I lead him toward the bathroom, our hands intertwined. His grip grounds me in the present, and all the worries I had hours earlier vanish. The silence between us is filled with unspoken words and reassurances that are louder than any words we could exchange.

My heart is still pounding hard, but with each beat, I remind myself that Brody is here with me and safe. I lean into him, savoring his familiar scent, mixing faintly with lingering sweat, as I help undress him, then I do the same.

The heavy, relentless fear begins to ease away as we step under the warm stream together. I grab a loofah and wash him meticulously, memorizing every curve of his muscles, every deep line of his tattoos. I was so worried I'd never get to be with him again that I don't want to take a single second for granted. I tilt my head back, looking up at him through damp lashes, my gaze tracing every familiar line of his face. The deep crease between his brows, the faint stubble shadowing his jaw, the tired circles beneath his eyes, reminding me of the day he's had.

"I didn't think I'd be able to sleep without you by my side," I whisper, my fingers brushing his cheek, needing the physical proof that he's whole, unhurt.

His eyes soften, warmth flooding through the exhaustion. "I already told you once, I don't ever want to wake up without you by my side again. If that means driving through the night, then so be it."

A lump rises in my throat, and I pull him closer, pressing my lips urgently to his again, the kiss deepening instantly, fueled by desperate relief and overwhelming love. His hands slide over my back, holding me flush against him, our bodies molded perfectly together.

"I was so scared," I confess against his lips, my voice trembling slightly, vulnerable and raw.

"And I'm so fucking sorry for that." Brody pulls back just enough to meet my eyes.

Something powerful and comforting fills me at his quiet certainty, steadying my pulse, calming the storm of lingering anxiety. I finally breathe deeply, the air no longer tasting of panic.

I brush my fingers along his jaw, noticing how tension still lingers in his shoulders. "Relax."

His mouth curves upward, and relief meets his eyes. "You read me so well."

He threads his fingers through mine as steam rises around us. The glass of the shower is fogged as the heat washes away the remnants of stress.

My breath catches as his strong arms wrap around my waist, pulling me against him. I lean back, savoring the sensation of his warm skin pressed to mine, comforted by the rhythm of his heartbeat.

"You have no idea how good this feels," he says against my ear.

His fingers trace slow, soothing circles along my waist, each touch causing butterflies to swarm me. Peace shines through—a silent acknowledgment of what we've survived.

"I think I have a pretty good idea," I tell him, pressing a kiss to the hollow of his throat. "I feel like I can finally breathe again."

Brody's arms tighten slightly, holding me as if he can't bear the thought of letting me go ever again. His fingers drift upward along my back, brushing over my neck before cradling my face. The look on his face steals my breath, and I lift onto my toes to meet him halfway, kissing him beneath the water.

Our lips move desperately, each kiss deepening as reassurance transforms into need and want. His hands slide lower again, and he grips my ass, pressing my body flush against his. Our breaths mingle as our tongues twist together.

When we finally break apart, Brody leans his forehead against mine, exhaling. "God, Harper, I don't know what I did to deserve you."

I smile, resting my fingers against his cheek. "You fought for me when no one else did."

His deep blue eyes are intense with sincerity. "I always will."

The shower rinses away the remaining fear, leaving nothing but certainty and love in its wake.

Eventually, Brody turns off the water and reaches for a towel, wrapping it around me first. He dries me, taking his time. Every stroke is protective, as if he's wiping away every trace of anxiety I felt earlier.

I take my time drying him, too, wiping away streaks of water that trail down his chest. Once we're dry, he gathers me up in his arms and carries me to my bedroom. It's not the first time Brody has ever been at my place, but it's the first time we've been here alone. I sigh, hanging on to him, my head resting against his shoulder.

"I can walk," I say, though I make no move to pull away.

"And I can carry you," he tells me firmly as he sets me on the bed. "I'm not letting you out of my arms again tonight."

The promise in his words settles deep inside me, and as I stare up at him, I realize that's exactly where I want to be.

Brody's eyes hold mine. The lamp by my bed casts a warm glow in the room. The way he's looking at me, as if I'm his everything, steals the breath from my lungs. My heartbeat quickens as he moves onto the bed, settling beside me, the mattress dipping beneath his weight.

Without hesitation, I reach for him, and he moves closer. Each touch is careful, gentle, reaffirming how we feel about one another. His muscles tense slightly under my fingertips, his breath catching as I trail downward, memorizing every familiar contour.

"Harp," he whispers. My name spills from his lips like a quiet prayer.

I lean closer, brushing a lingering kiss against his chest, trailing up to his mouth. He exhales when our eyes meet.

"I thought I'd lost this," he confesses. "You. Us. Today, on the mountain—"

My fingers press against his lips, silencing him. I shake my head, eyes burning with sincerity. "You didn't. You never will. We can talk about this later, okay?"

Relief swirls in his eyes, and I can't help but kiss him. Our mouths collide in a sensual kiss, each second deepening our connection beyond words.

His hands glide over my skin, lingering at my waist, drawing me flush against him. How he holds me makes me feel cherished, treasured, as though nothing else exists beyond this.

Brody hovers above me, and I lie beneath him, his gaze carefully tracing my face, absorbing every detail. His eyes hold a silent question, seeking my reassurance, ensuring I feel safe. My heart melts at his care, and I nod, fingertips brushing along his jaw.

"This is exactly where you should be," I whisper, my voice barely audible, but he hears me.

The last traces of uncertainty fade from his eyes. Brody lowers himself, his mouth finding mine again, our kiss growing deeper, more urgent, emotions finally breaking free, carrying us forward. He enters me with care; each movement carries longing and love. My body arches toward him, my fingers gripping his shoulders, needing to feel every long inch of him.

We move together, building a perfect rhythm gradually. Our hearts and breaths align, creating an intimacy so powerful that I can feel it in every nerve, every cell of my whole damn body. I've never felt so connected to another person. It's like our souls have intertwined, and there's no undoing it.

"I love you," he whispers as he moves in and out of me. "Fuck, so much."

"Love you." I'm so damn close that I don't know how much more I can take before he unravels me.

Our gazes lock as I come undone below him, his name spilling from my lips as pleasure crashes through me. My back arches off the bed as my eyes squeeze tight. Brody follows moments later, his breathing uneven as he slams into me, losing himself.

"Now, everything is right in the world," I say to him, repeating the words he said earlier.

After cleanup, we stay wrapped in each other's arms. Our heart rates begin to slow, and breathing returns to normal. His fingers comb through my hair, and it feels so damn good. For a long moment, neither of us speaks, simply absorbing the magnitude of what we've shared.

Finally, Brody nuzzles his nose against mine and captures my lips. When he pulls away, his gaze is serious but somehow soft. "One day, I'm going to marry you, Harp."

My breath catches, my heart stuttering in my chest. "You want me as your wife?"

"Fuck yes." Sincerity is clear in his eyes as he cups my cheek. "That's the truth."

Emotions bubble inside me, and I'm filled with overwhelming joy. I smile, leaning in to kiss him again, sealing the promise between us—because I know, deep down, he means every word.

We're tangled together beneath the sheets, limbs tangled, and I feel safe. His fingers drift lazily along my body, tracing patterns on my skin as he closes his eyes.

I study the peaceful expression on his face, the way his dark lashes rest against his cheeks, and how his breathing steadies. I never dreamed this could be my reality—Brody here, beside me, loving me openly, without hesitation.

His eyes flutter open, immediately finding me staring at him. A cute smile touches his lips. "See something you like?"

"I see something I love," I admit, tracing my fingers along his collarbone.

His eyes brighten with amusement, and he leans over and kisses me. "I can never get enough of you."

"This all feels so fragile," I say, my voice barely above a whisper.

His gaze is steady, reassuring. "We're as tough as diamonds."

My eyes burn with sudden tears, and I quickly blink them away.

He wraps his arms tighter around me, pulling me against him. "You're everything to me."

I absorb his words as warmth floods my veins. "You're everything to me too."

The world suddenly feels distant and unimportant in the

sanctuary we've built. It's a moment so perfect that I'm almost afraid to breathe, scared I might somehow shatter it.

Brody's voice breaks the silence that temporarily covered us. "I've never been good at imagining the future, Harp. It's always been easier to live moment to moment. But with you ..." He pauses, a smile playing on his lips. "With you by my side, I can finally see my entire life play out like a movie. It's clear as day."

My heart leaps in my chest; his admission jolts something awake deep inside me.

I lean up, looking directly into his eyes, my voice trembling just a little as I say, "Tell me what you see."

His gaze is even more full of warmth, promise, and sincerity. "Us. Going on adventures. Building a life together. Having a family. Sharing love that lasts until my very last breath."

The certainty in his words causes tears to stream down my face. "I can see it too."

His lips brush mine so damn sweetly that I can't handle it.

"It's confirmed then," he says, and the weight of his words settles warmly in my chest.

My head rests on his chest, and my breathing finally grows even, mirroring his. The future feels closer, brighter, and infinitely more possible. I soak in the steady rhythm of his heartbeat beneath my ear. It's become my favorite sound.

His fingertips trail along my back, each stroke drawing me closer to the edge of sleep. I exhale, savoring how right this feels, how effortlessly our bodies mold together, as though we were made for this.

Brody's lips press against my hair, and the sweet gesture sends butterflies fluttering in me. "I didn't know peace like this existed."

We hold each other quietly, the moment heavy with unspoken truths. Both of us silently acknowledge how far we've come, how much we've overcome to be right here. I close my eyes, breathing him in, feeling the rise and fall of his chest. My heart settles into an easy rhythm, matching his, as exhaustion begins pulling me under.

Just as I'm drifting toward sleep, Brody's voice breaks through, his words like a caress against my hair. "You're my sanctuary."

His words pierce me straight to the core.

I lift my face, brushing my lips along his jaw, whispering with absolute certainty, "You're mine too."

In that simple, powerful exchange, I let go completely, sinking into sleep, secure in the comfort of Brody's arms, knowing without a doubt that we have finally found the place we both belong—with each other.

28

BRODY

A firm knock echoes from the front door. It's too loud, too impatient, and it cuts through the early morning solitude. I glance at the clock next to Harper's bed and see it's barely past six. It's too damn early to deal with the Banks brothers.

"Ugh," Harper whispers.

"It's Asher and Nick. I'll be back."

She nods and rolls over, but her breathing is steady. I lean over, kissing her bare shoulder, drinking her in as the sun rises. The memory of last night's confessions is still fresh, and her *I love you* still hums under my skin. Reluctantly, I slip quietly out of bed, going to her dresser and opening every drawer until I find my joggers. I pull them on with a smirk as the knocking comes again, sharper this time.

I take the stairs down to the front door as they continue to pound.

"Fuck," I mutter, walking barefoot across the living room.

I yank open the door with more force than necessary, glaring at the two men standing casually in the hallway, both wearing that cocky-as-fuck Banks grin.

"I really can't stand either of you," I admit.

Asher smirks, holding a laptop under his arm as he leans against the doorframe. "Morning, sunshine. Did we interrupt something?"

Nick grins beside him, holding two steaming cups of coffee. "Aw, he still looks cranky, Ash. Maybe we should've let him finish getting his beauty sleep because we're dealing with the beast."

"Why are you here so early?" I snap, stepping aside to let them in.

"Some of us have to work today," Nick says in his full voice as he moves past me.

"Keep it down. Harper's still asleep."

Asher strolls past me. "I'm sorry my brother is a dickhead."

"I'm the entire dick," Nick tells him. "Give me some credit."

"Ugh," I reply dryly, following them into the kitchen.

Nick sets down the coffee cups, sliding one toward me as a peace offering. He takes an exaggerated sip of his, watching me over the rim.

"Let's skip your usual brooding and get straight to business," Nick says, making himself comfortable on a stool.

Asher raises a brow at me, settling himself next to his brother. "Brooding is his best quality. Don't take that away from him. It took years of being an ass to pull it off."

"Fuck off, both of you," I mutter, taking a grateful sip of the coffee despite my irritation. The caffeine does little to ease the tension. "Did you find anything new?"

Asher's expression sobers instantly, his eyes sharpening. "More than we expected. Turns out, Micah has been busy—very fucking busy. Nick, show him."

Nick grabs the laptop and types in a few things, then scrolls rapidly before turning the screen toward me. My blood goes cold as I see surveillance images—grainy but unmistakable—of Micah Rhodes.

"His car was spotted an hour and a half north of here after he took Mia. I just haven't figured out exactly where, but I know who will know."

My jaw tightens painfully, anger flaring white hot beneath my ribs. Another victim. Another life Micah will try to ruin because he can.

"Has the public been made aware that Mia is missing yet?" My voice is clipped, barely controlled.

Asher shakes his head grimly. "No. Bellamore's keeping it quiet for now. We need to act fast. I'm afraid of what he'll do when people start searching for her. Based on his pattern, it's grim."

I exhale, running a hand roughly through my hair, my pulse spiking as urgency takes hold. Harper is safe in the next room, but Mia's situation is different—every second counts.

"We have another big problem though. Micah's father has the police department in his pocket. They could tip him off if we call the authorities."

I stare at Nick, understanding what this means. The three of us hold a silent conversation.

"This has turned into a rescue mission," I say, and Asher exhales.

Nick's gaze meets mine, serious and unflinching. "If we go there and find Mia, it's enough evidence to put Micah in prison for a very long time."

Asher slides the laptop around and opens folders, showing files upon files of evidence that he's found regarding the missing women in Newport. "There are at least twenty missing between Newport and the city. Mia doesn't deserve to be another one of Micah's victims."

I click through surveillance photos, transaction records, and partial transcripts of conversations. Each piece of evidence the Banks brothers have found is just another nail in Micah's coffin. I sift through the documents, my jaw tightening with every new revelation.

"How long have you been tracking him?"

Asher leans forward, elbows resting on the counter, eyes narrowing thoughtfully. "The moment Harper started dating him. But after you rescued Harp, we doubled down and went to the dark web. Nick made some calls, asked for some favors, and turned over every goddamn rock he could find."

Nick shrugs modestly, though a smirk tugs at his lips. "I might've pissed off a few people along the way, but it was worth it. Turns out, Micah has powerful friends in high places—people who prefer to stay anonymous. I can relate."

I flip through more information; frustration boils even hotter. "And these 'friends' protected him?"

"Until now," Nick replies smoothly. "Let's just say, after he showed up to confront you, his friends no longer think he's worth the risk. This morning, Micah pulled large sums of money from several accounts, and I think he's getting ready to run. His lies and deceit are falling around him like a house of cards."

"But not fast enough," I say.

Nick nods, his expression sobering again. "After he left Tennessee, he returned to the city and was seen entering an investment firm that I have confirmed is helping him. They have the answers we need."

"Give me the firm name," I tell him, and then I glance at Asher.

Nick interrupts. "We'll visit them tonight," he says firmly, with no room for argument. "Once we find where Mia is, I've coordinated the rescue with one of my friends at the FBI. He's waiting for my confirmation and an address."

I glance toward the stairs, half expecting to see Harper standing there, listening. But the penthouse remains quiet, peaceful. It's a stark contrast to the chaos stirring within me.

Asher catches my gaze. "Don't worry. Billie won't let Harper out of her sight. They're stronger together. Easton and Weston are staying behind to protect them. We just have to stay safe."

Nick chuckles, breaking the tension. "Aw, look at how in love you two are. Kinda gross."

I roll my eyes at him as Asher closes the laptop.

"We need to finish this. Tonight," I say.

Asher stands, sliding off the stool, determination hardening his expression. "I agree."

Nick nods. "Great. Tonight then. The sooner we move, the sooner we get Mia home—and put Rhodes behind bars."

As Asher scoops up his laptop, Harper comes down the stairs, wearing pajamas. She narrows her eyes at Nick and Asher.

"What happened?" she asks, her voice full of worry.

I move to her instantly, pressing a reassuring kiss to her forehead. "We're going to find Mia."

Harper pales visibly, her gaze locking on mine. "When?"

"Tonight. It's turned into a rescue mission," I say firmly, cupping her cheeks. "Before he hurts her."

She nods, understanding but clearly torn. Harper's eyes soften, worry still clear, but trust wins out. She squeezes my hand, turning her gaze briefly toward Asher and Nick. "The three of you are going?"

"Yes," Asher confirms.

Nick tips an imaginary hat, the faintest smirk on his lips. "We're going to threaten some bastards, fuck up Micah, save Mia, then watch him get arrested. Bing, bang, boom. Easy."

"What time will we meet?" Asher asks.

"Before sunset," Nick confirms.

Harper glances between them as they move toward the door.

"Have a good day, Harp!" Nick calls out. "Also, I got your voice message. Let me know when you plan to fuck me up so I can be prepared."

She shakes her head at him. "Sometimes, I wonder why my brother ever liked you."

Laughter roars from me.

"Good one, Harp," Asher tells her as he follows his brother out the door.

It clicks closed, and when we're alone, I turn to her.

She looks me up and down, smiling. "You found your pants."

"And they fit exactly how I remember."

"They look better than I remember." Harper falls into my arms, and I stand there, holding her in the early morning sunlight. The silence captures us. "I don't like this."

"I know," I say, stealing a soft kiss. "But it's almost over."

WE SPEND THE DAY TOGETHER, LOUNGING AROUND, AND I CAN'T HELP but notice how she holds on to me. When night falls, Asher texts me and lets me know he and Nick are downstairs waiting for me in an SUV. I grab my bag of weapons and swing it over my shoulder.

Harper kisses me like tomorrow will never come. It better.

"Please, please come back to me," she says.

I kiss her nose, then capture her lips again. "I will. I promise. This is a cakewalk. I love you, Harp."

"I love you. Please hurry. I'll be waiting." She walks me to the door.

Billie is on her way and should arrive at any minute.

We share one final look—silent understanding, a promise exchanged without words—before I turn toward the door, prepared for whatever comes next.

The drive is tense, silence heavy inside the SUV as we navigate Manhattan traffic. I needed to drive to keep my mind busy, so Nick got out and forced Asher in the back. My fingers tap restlessly against the wheel, adrenaline and urgency pulsing beneath my skin. Nick's directions are clipped and precise.

I glance at Asher in the rearview, unable to ignore how his fingers fly rapidly across his phone screen. Every so often, he mutters under his breath, clearly coordinating something. He and Nick both have connections and resources that interconnect with mine, but his contacts can make things happen fast, without red tape or hesitation.

280

Nick glances briefly at me from the passenger seat, eyes sharp. "You good?"

"Yeah," I reply shortly, jaw tightening as we roll to a stop at a red light.

He chuckles, shaking his head. "A man of few words. Shocker."

"Maybe you should take notes," Asher chimes in from the back, tone dripping with sarcasm. "Could be a good look for you."

Nick's lips twitch with amusement. "You're both so serious; lighten up."

"I just want to make it back to my fiancée, unscathed," Asher counters smoothly, glancing up from his phone.

From the rearview, I see the concern etched on his face.

I exhale, cutting off their banter. "Where exactly are we going?"

Nick's amusement fades. "Micah's been funneling money through a small investment firm, so we're going to pay them a visit. He used the company to cover his tracks, buy properties under false identities, and I believe that includes a house upstate. If we confront them and get someone to talk, we can nail down the exact location of where he's hiding Mia."

The memory of Harper's terrified face back on the mountain claws at me, and I tighten my grip on the steering wheel. If I find Rhodes first, I might tear him apart with my bare hands.

"And if they won't cooperate?" I ask.

Asher meets my gaze in the rearview mirror, voice ice cold as he says, "They'll cooperate."

The determination in his eyes leaves no doubt. This isn't business anymore; it's deeply personal for him, too, especially after everything Micah put Billie and Harper through.

We pull up outside a sleek glass-and-steel building that blends seamlessly into the upscale buildings surrounding it. My heart pounds steadily as I park the SUV and kill the engine.

Nick glances at me, his expression grim. "Let's keep it professional, gentlemen. We need actionable intel, not more headaches."

Asher scoffs, adjusting his jacket. "Speak for your-fucking-self."

We exit the SUV swiftly, moving through the bustling lobby like shadows, drawing curious stares from late commuters. My pulse remains a steady drumbeat as we step into the elevator, moving rapidly toward the top-floor offices. When the doors slide open, a sleek reception area greets us. I step forward first, posture rigid with barely restrained anger. The receptionist looks up, startled by our sudden arrival.

"I'm sorry, do you have an appointment?" she asks.

"No," I reply shortly. "But we need to speak with whoever's in charge. Right now."

She hesitates, eyes flicking nervously from me to Nick and Asher behind me, clearly weighing her options.

Asher steps smoothly forward, placing his business card firmly on her desk, his tone dangerously calm. "Tell them it's urgent. I promise they'll want to hear what we have to say."

She picks up the card, her eyes widening in recognition. Asher is known as the Boogeyman of Business and can destroy any company's reputation if he wants. Most in the city are scared of what he can do. Without another word, she quickly picks up the phone, dialing with trembling fingers.

The clock ticks louder with each passing second.

Mia is counting on us. Harper and Billie are counting on us.

Micah Rhodes won't see us coming.

Within minutes, we're ushered into an expansive corner office. Its large windows reveal an incredible view of downtown Manhattan. At the desk sits a well-dressed man in his late fifties, clearly used to this. His gaze narrows suspiciously as we enter, taking in our expressions carefully before gesturing for us to take the empty seats in front of him.

"I'm Garrett Vaughn. What's so urgent?" His voice is calm but cautious. He glances up at the clock on the wall, making note of the time.

I watch him, keeping my gaze directly on his.

Nick closes the door behind us, subtly positioning himself to block any easy exit. I lower myself into one of the chairs, leaning forward, locking eyes with Vaughn.

"Micah Rhodes," I say coldly, skipping pleasantries. "He's one of your clients. We need everything you have on him. Now."

Vaughn's eyes harden. "I'm sorry, but client confidentiality—"

"Your client has kidnapped *another* woman," Asher interrupts, tone deadly serious as he drops casually into the seat beside mine. "Mia Karrington, the chief marketing officer of Bellamore. There are handfuls of women tied to him who have disappeared, and trust me, you do not want your company tangled up in this. It's enough to destroy you."

Vaughn visibly pales. He swallows hard, trying to regain control. "I hope you have proof because that's a very serious accus—"

"We have plenty," Nick cuts in smoothly from behind us. "More than enough to send Micah away for life and drag your firm down in the process if you keep stonewalling."

The man's gaze flickers nervously between us, hesitation clear in every subtle movement. My fists clench; impatience takes hold.

"Every minute wasted is a minute Mia might not have," I growl. My voice is barely restrained. "You really want that on your hands?"

The color drains further from his face, beads of sweat gathering at his temples. Finally, he exhales a shaky breath. "I wasn't personally involved. Rhodes insisted on absolute secrecy. He used one of our junior associates, Trevor Merewood, to handle most of his transactions."

"Where's Merewood now?" I demand.

"Gone," Vaughn admits reluctantly, shaking his head. "He resigned days ago. Cleared out his desk without explanation."

Frustration boils hot in my veins. Days ago is when Mia was taken. How fucking convenient.

"We'll need access to his records. Every file, every transaction involving Rhodes—every-fucking-thing," I say.

Vaughn hesitates, voice uncertain as he says, "This isn't standard protocol—"

Asher leans forward, tone dripping with icy threat. "Let's make this really fucking easy for you. You either cooperate fully, or tomorrow morning, your firm's name will be splashed all over the news, permanently tied to kidnapping, extortion, and whatever else we uncover. The FBI is involved, and either you help us or I will ruin you. And trust me when I say, I'll sleep incredibly at night, knowing this company no longer exists."

It's not a threat; it's a promise.

Vaughn freezes, eyes wide with fear. After a brief stare down with Asher, he finally nods stiffly. "Follow me."

He leads us swiftly from the office, down a quiet hallway, lined with closed doors, finally stopping at an empty office. Quickly unlocking the door, he flips on the lights, illuminating rows of filing cabinets and a lone desktop computer.

"Everything Merewood left behind is here," he says. "Take whatever you need, but I never saw you here."

"Agreed," Nick replies smoothly, moving swiftly to the computer. "This will stay strictly confidential. I appreciate your cooperation, Mr. Vaughn."

"Don't ever let me catch you wrapped up in this type of bullshit again," Asher warns, staring at him before he leaves us in the office.

Nick immediately sits down, placing a USB drive into the computer. He works so fast as he downloads every file from their database, clicking between windows so quickly that I can't keep up. I look between him and Asher.

"You're hackers. Both of you," I whisper.

"You didn't see shit, Brod," Nick warns.

Asher is amused by the whole operation as he oversees what Nick does. My pulse races with fresh urgency as I flip through files in the cabinets, desperate for any hint that could lead us directly to

Micah's safe house. Every second counts now. We're running out of time.

An hour passes in tense, heavy silence, broken only by the quiet hum of the computer and the rustle of paper as Asher helps me sift through countless documents. My eyes blur from scanning over financial records, transaction statements, and obscure, coded notes.

"Anything?" I snap, glancing toward Nick, who's still typing away on the computer.

He rubs a hand over his jaw, his usual smirk replaced by concentration. "Micah's actually really good at covering his tracks. But Merewood got sloppy near the end. I've got something here about an off-book property purchase upstate. Cash transaction. Remote area. I think this is it."

I move toward him, leaning over his shoulder, scanning the transaction records glowing on the screen. My pulse kicks up as I go to the Maps app and look at the house from above. "This is it."

Asher steps beside me, eyes narrowing. "He's repeating his patterns. The place must be isolated enough that he thinks no one will find him."

Adrenaline rushes through me. "We need to move. Now. This might be our only shot. If he's got Mia there, he'll be on high alert. We hit him fast and hard," I say, my voice clipped. "No warning."

Asher nods, determination in his eyes. "I'll coordinate with the authorities. One misstep, and Rhodes could panic. He's desperate now, which makes him more dangerous."

"Already on it," Nick replies, grabbing his phone and stepping toward the doorway to make the call.

Asher watches him briefly, then turns back to me, his expression grim but resolute. "You ready for this?"

"More than ready." My voice is edged with anger and urgency. "He's not hurting anyone else."

Asher grips my shoulder, silently conveying his solidarity. "We end it tonight, Brody."

I hold his gaze, grateful for the unspoken understanding. "Tonight."

Nick returns quickly, pocketing his phone. "They've got a team mobilizing that will meet us near the property once we confirm Mia is there. This stays quiet until we have Mia. If we show up and the house is empty, we keep searching. There is no room for crying wolf in this situation. We need solid evidence, or Micah will continue to escape. He has too many people in his pockets."

"Let's go." I'm already moving toward the door, impatience driving my steps, every nerve in my body tightened like a coil. "We're running out of time. Less talky, Banks."

We exit the firm and ignore the startled glances from employees as we rush toward the elevators. My pulse races faster with every step, knowing that everything—Mia's safety, Harper's peace of mind, our entire future—depends on what happens next.

Tonight, we're taking Micah Rhodes down. And I'll make damn sure he never harms anyone again.

THE SLEEK BLACK SUV SLICES THROUGH TRAFFIC, NICK AT THE wheel, navigating the chaos of Manhattan like a race car driver. Asher sits up front, coordinating with his friend at the FBI through clipped phone calls, confirming their tactical approach and planning the extraction.

I'm quiet, rigid in the back seat. My fists are clenched so tight that my knuckles ache. Every passing second is torture. My heartbeat is a relentless drum as Harper's pretty face flashes through my mind.

"Hey." Nick's voice interrupts my thoughts from the front seat, his gaze flicking up briefly to meet mine in the rearview mirror. "You okay back there?"

"Fine," I reply.

"Yeah," Nick says dryly, taking a sharp turn that jolts us all sideways. "You're the picture of Zen."

Asher snorts, still focused on his phone. "He's about five seconds from punching through the door and sprinting there like a fucking Terminator."

"Not helpful," I mutter.

Asher looks back at me with a smile. "If you need a pep talk, I can put Billie on speaker."

"Jesus," Nick groans, rolling his eyes dramatically. "Don't threaten us like that."

Despite myself, a low laugh escapes me, easing some of my tension. Nick grins, clearly satisfied that he broke me.

"That's better," he says, checking the GPS on the dashboard. "At least we know you're not fully robotic yet."

"Close enough," Asher says, shooting me a look. "If you need a motivational speech, I'm sure I could come up with something."

"I'm motivated enough," I say.

My jaw tightens when we leave the city behind. The glowing lights are replaced by darkness as the SUV barrels steadily toward our target.

Nick navigates onto the interstate, and silence falls again.

Asher finishes another call, finally lowering his phone and sighing deeply. "I'm going to owe my friend a huge favor," he announces. "He's got a team and is going rogue to help us."

"Great," I say. "Rogue FBI agents. Just what we need."

"Focus, boys. Micah won't make it easy," Nick warns. "Cornered men make desperate moves."

"So do we," I tell him.

I lean back into the seat; my gaze is focused forward. Harper's fear, Billie's panic on her twenty-first birthday—it all blends into raw, simmering rage that demands resolution.

Justice, not revenge, I repeat to myself, even though I want blood.

29

BRODY

The SUV speeds down the dark highway, headlights cutting through the thick night. We've been on the road, traveling west for over an hour. Heavy clouds cover the moon, making the darkness feel more oppressive than usual. Shadowy trees zoom by, and Asher's face lights up every now and then from the blue glow of his phone as he quickly types out messages.

I clench my jaw and focus straight ahead. Deep down, I know we're doing the right thing. Sure, we could've called the local police to check out the property, but the bodyguard in me, trained to protect, knows that cops get bogged down in red tape, especially when Micah has so many people in his pocket. The last thing we need is for anyone to tip him off.

"What's on your mind?" Nick asks.

"We can't let Micah get away this time," I reply.

Nick nods, clearly thinking the same thing. "He's gotten out of trouble too many times in Newport."

Asher looks up from his phone. "That's why we're dealing with this ourselves first. If we go to the cops right away, they'll hesitate, ask questions, and take their sweet time. By then, Micah could move Mia somewhere else. Or worse."

I can't shake the image of the woman in Micah's grasp. She looks so much like Harper, and that fucking infuriates me. It very well could've been Harper instead.

Asher sighs, running a hand through his hair. "Just so we're clear, if this goes sideways, it's our asses. Are we ready for that?"

"That's why we don't let it go sideways," Nick says confidently. "We find Mia, deal with Micah, and then hand him over. Easy-peasy."

"Easy-peasy," I repeat, knowing this is anything but.

A tense silence falls over us, broken only by the sound of tires on the asphalt.

"Relax, Ash," Nick finally says with a smirk. "You've got me and Brod. What could possibly go wrong?"

"I appreciate your optimism," I say with a hint of sarcasm. "But I just want to get this over with."

Nick presses down on the gas a bit more, and the SUV lunges forward. Every second counts, and this time, we can't afford to fail.

Eventually, he turns off the paved road and onto a narrow gravel path, hidden by overgrown branches and thick brush. The headlights slice through the dark woods, casting long shadows on the trees. Gravel crunches under the tires, the noise way too loud in the heavy silence.

"Kill the lights," Asher whispers from the passenger seat, his eyes scanning ahead.

Adrenaline pumps through me, and I crack my neck, getting ready. I used to live for trouble like this, but now that I've got a future waiting for me, I'm not sure if I want to keep putting myself in danger. Once I get Mia out, I'm done. This will be my last mission, and then I'm focusing on protecting and loving Harper. Retiring from this life feels right.

My eyes narrow on the dim outlines of the road.

We creep forward until the house pops up in the dark, looking like a ghost in the faint moonlight filtering through the pines. Boarded-up windows and peeling paint make it seem abandoned, but I spot fresh tire tracks on the grass. Someone has been here recently.

Nick parks under a shadowy canopy of trees on the other side of the brick wall. He cuts the engine, and silence wraps around us again.

"It's quiet," Nick finally says. "Too quiet."

"Exactly why we need to move fast," Asher replies, still focused ahead. "Let's fucking end this."

His words remind me that Harper, Billie, and Mia are caught up in Micah's vendetta. It's our fight now, and I can't back down; I have to face it, end it. I won't let Micah slip away again.

Nick catches my eye in the rearview mirror. "Ready?"

Asher turns slightly, his face set with determination as he pulls out his gun and loads it. "We do this fast. No mistakes."

The weight of responsibility sinks deeper onto my shoulders. "Let's go. Be invisible," I say, pushing open the door.

We hop out of the SUV and carefully shut the doors. Each move is smooth and seems almost practiced. Gravel crunches under our boots as we take the driveway toward the house. The cool night air brushes against my skin as we hustle forward. My heart's steady, but I'm overly aware of any noise or movement around us. I've trained for moments like this, and while it's not ideal, I know I could handle it solo. Having Nick and Asher with me just means we'll get Mia out safely. Hopefully.

I take the lead, signaling with simple hand gestures for Asher and Nick to spread out and create a tight perimeter. We fall into our positions seamlessly.

Once closer to the house, I can see how run-down it is. Ivy creeps up the walls, every window boarded up, and the front door looks heavily barricaded. I scan for other ways in. Nick points toward a side entrance, barely visible. Asher gives a quick nod and carefully moves to cover our flank. I follow Nick, my footsteps steady as we approach the door. My grip on my gun tightens instinctively, muscles ready for action.

We pause just outside, pressed against the wall. A faint glow seeps out from beneath the slightly open doorway. That means the house has power—not completely abandoned then.

Nick looks over at me. *Ready?* he mouths.

I nod firmly, exhaling, knowing this will take us less than an hour.

We hang back at the side entrance. Adrenaline races through me, but I keep my breathing steady. Nick shifts beside me, ready to jump into action, and on my other side, Asher's tense silence is electric. The light spilling from the doorway looks eerie, like a warning for whatever's waiting inside.

My military training kicks in.

Micah isn't a soldier. He's dangerous, reckless, and desperate, but he doesn't have combat training. I hold on to that thought; it sharpens my focus. It's an edge we can use.

Nick gives a countdown with his fingers, starting from three. I take a deep breath, getting my head straight as he hits one. Then he quickly swings the door open and slips inside smoothly. I follow him, gun up, scanning the dark space quickly.

The room is small, cramped, and lit by a single bare bulb hanging overhead. Dusty furniture fills the place, clearly abandoned ages ago. It's dead silent, broken only by our careful breathing and my racing heart. Asher shuts the door behind us. The house feels like a tomb. The stale air almost chokes me, and every creak under our feet echoes around us.

Nick heads toward the next doorway, signaling us to follow. We fall into line, and the weight of my retirement feels heavier with each step.

I'm set on ending Micah's reign of terror tonight.

We clear the first room quickly. The next one is a kitchen, dimly lit by a flickering yellow bulb. It's empty too. He's around here somewhere—I can feel it—and a chill of dread settles in my bones. Suddenly, Nick stops, spotting something at the back wall. He tilts his chin, pointing out a faint outline, partially hidden behind an old pantry shelf. It's a door.

My pulse races with excitement. Everything in me knows that whatever's behind that door will lead us right to Mia and then to that motherfucker.

Asher moves stealthily toward it, careful of the creaky floorboards; his movements are calculated. He glances back at me, eyes asking. I give a quick nod, and he pulls the pantry aside just enough to fully reveal the doorway.

A shadowy stairwell is behind it, and it goes down into pure darkness. Every muscle is tense with anticipation, as we're just moments away from facing whatever's down there.

I step up, taking the lead. It's my responsibility, my fight—one I've been waiting over a decade to end.

I glance at Asher and Nick. Their faces are hard but supportive; they're ready to follow wherever this goes. The bond we've built over the years, even though they're total pains in my ass, gives me strength.

I head down the stairs, overly alert, picking up on every little sound or movement. Each step creaks under my weight, loud in the heavy silence, but I can't help it. Asher and Nick follow behind me, guns ready, keeping an eye on my back as we go deeper into the depths of the basement.

The air gets colder and thicker, smelling like mildew and something else—something familiar. I think I hear a whimper, barely there but unmistakable, sending a surge of protectiveness through me.

Mia.

Anger bubbles just beneath the surface, sharpening my senses and only gearing me up for what's ahead.

I pinpoint where I think I heard it from and signal to Nick and Asher behind me. We carefully move deeper into the basement, weapons raised and senses on high alert.

292

Every step gets me closer to Mia and to Micah Rhodes. Can't fucking wait.

I push down the surge of anger rising inside me. My eyes scan the dimness, taking in the shadows. Nick moves past me. He narrows his eyes, quickly checking every corner and potential hiding spot. The room feels abandoned, with dusty furniture and forgotten items scattered around. It's a snapshot of life before Micah brought his bullshit here.

I stay alert as Nick suddenly pauses. He signals with two fingers toward the far end of the room. My heart races, adrenaline kicking in as I follow his cue. Behind an old, rusty fridge, a small space comes into view. It's a partially hidden doorframe, barely visible under layers of dust and grime. It's the perfect secret entrance— easy to miss unless you know exactly what you're looking for.

This has to be where they are.

Asher quickly joins us, his face darkening as he realizes what the hidden doorway means. He locks eyes with mine, and we know Mia's here. And where Mia is, Micah's not far behind, ready for trouble.

"Make the call as soon as you can," I whisper to Asher, and he nods.

Nick gestures again, his movements sharp and calculated. He steps up, pushing the fridge aside, trying not to make any noise for anyone who might be listening on the other side of that door. The scraping sound is soft, but it feels way too loud.

Asher moves next to me, his gun aimed at the entrance. He gives me a quick nod, letting me know he's ready. I keep my weapon raised; my military and security training grounds me. My hand is steady; my mind is focused.

Nick carefully turns the doorknob, inching it open. The hinges creak, but luckily, it's quiet enough not to draw attention. Beyond the doorway is a long, dark hallway.

I take a deep breath, bracing myself for whatever's lurking inside.

Nick goes first, moving silently down the narrow hall. I follow right behind him; each step feels heavy. Asher watches our backs, covering us as we slip farther into the hidden room. The air grows damper and musty, mixed with a metallic smell that makes my stomach turn.

Suddenly, a scared whimper breaks the silence, faint but unmistakably real.

My throat tightens, and I clench my jaw, knowing we're closer than ever. We're moments away from facing the nightmare Micah is forcing this poor woman to live. I lift my hand for Nick and Asher to move carefully. We step closer and closer, the faint sounds of Mia's frightened breaths guiding us.

I want to reassure her, but I don't know if Micah is close by.

A muffled sob comes from the corner, shaky and scared. Each sound hits me hard, pushing me to bring her home safely and finally make Micah Rhodes pay for all the pain he's caused.

Adrenaline sharpens my senses. One wrong move could ruin everything. I grip my weapon tighter, ready for the showdown just ahead.

I click on my tactical flashlight, and it cuts through the darkness, lighting up the space as we reach the end of the hallway. The room feels large but somehow cramped because of the low ceiling. I scan the room slowly, each second dragging on, until I finally spot a figure huddled against the far wall.

Mia is curled up, knees pulled to her chest, her wide eyes filled with fear. She's trembling under my gaze, her dark hair a mess around her pale, scared face. She sits in her bra and panties, and she's filthy. My breath catches when I realize how similar she looks to Harper—those same striking blue eyes full of fear, the same delicate features. I vaguely remember meeting her a few years ago.

For a moment, I freeze, caught between the present and memories of Harper's own fear. A wave of anger rises in me; protectiveness grips my chest.

I relax my stance, lowering my gun. "Mia," I say, my voice calm, crouching down to her eye level. "I'm Billie's cousin. We came to save you."

She flinches at first, pressing back against the cold wall, her eyes darting to Asher and Nick, who are just out of the flashlight's beam. Her breathing picks up, fear spiking, but she stays quiet, trying to trust me.

"It's okay," I assure her, keeping my tone steady and soothing even though my muscles are tense. "Come with us. We're getting you out of here. Micah can't hurt you anymore."

At the mention of Micah, she shudders, shaking her head, tears slipping silently down her cheeks. Her voice breaks into a small, barely audible whisper. "He said no one would ever find me ..."

"We did," I say, holding out my hand. "I know you're scared, but you've got to trust me. Can you do that?"

She studies my face, looking for some reassurance. After a tense moment, she finally gives a small, unsure nod. A wave of relief hits me, and I extend my hand, palm up.

"I'm going to help you up," I tell her, keeping my voice gentle, not wanting to overwhelm her fragile trust. "Stay close."

Mia's shaking hand reaches out to mine, fingers cold as they brush against my palm. I grab her hand, helping her to her feet. She sways a bit, her legs shaky, and I steady her, trying to keep her out of sight as much as I can.

Her eyes lock on to mine, wide and vulnerable, wearing the same expression Harper had when I rescued her. It brings me back, and anger nearly blinds me.

I glance at Nick and Asher, giving them a quick signal. They're still by the hallway, weapons drawn, eyes sharp. Their tension matches mine, confirming we're all in this together.

For a moment, it's quiet around us.

Mia reaches for my hand, and I let myself feel a sliver of hope.

Maybe, just maybe, we can all get out of here safely.

30

BRODY

Adrenaline surges, razor-sharp and cold, as Mia takes a trembling step toward me. Relief softens her terrified features for an instant, then shatters like glass as a dark figure explodes from the shadows in the corner.

Micah lunges forward, grabbing Mia roughly by the arm. She cries out, a high, panicked sound that echoes painfully in my chest. Before I can react, Micah yanks her against his chest, pressing a gleaming blade to her throat. My pulse spikes, fingers tightening around my weapon as anger and dread clash inside me.

"Back off!" Micah's voice is harsh, his eyes unhinged. "One step closer, and she dies!"

Mia's wide blue eyes meet mine; sheer terror is etched into her face. My stomach twists painfully as the haunting resemblance to Harper floods my vision. For one paralyzing moment, I see Harper's face—her fear, her vulnerability when I rescued her from this fucking monster. Rage rises, and it's white hot, threatening to consume every shred of reason I have.

I swallow hard, forcing my voice into a calm, steady tone. "Micah, let her go. She's got nothing to do with this."

He laughs, the sound bitter, broken. "Nothing to do with it?

She's everything to do with it. She's here because of you—because of Harper and Billie."

"This won't fix anything," I say, cautiously lowering my gun in a deliberate motion, maintaining eye contact. I raise my other hand, palm open, showing my cooperation. "Let her go, Micah. She's innocent. Your fight's with me."

Micah's jaw clenches, his grip tightening around Mia, making her whimper. Every muscle in my body screams to intervene, to protect her, to end this swiftly and violently. But I hold myself back, knowing any sudden move could be catastrophic.

"Harper ruined my life," Micah snarls, the blade trembling dangerously close to Mia's delicate skin. "And you ... you destroyed and took everything I had left. You took it all, Calloway."

"Then take it out on me," I urge, stepping forward, every movement careful, measured. "You've got me. Let her walk away, and I'll do whatever you want."

"Brody." Asher's tone is sharp, but I silence him with a slight shake of my head.

Micah hesitates briefly, clearly weighing my offer; desperation and rage fill his eyes. "You think sacrificing yourself makes you a hero?" he sneers bitterly. "You're nothing but Harper's little puppet. Her little fucktoy that she will leave for another man. When I close my eyes, I can still imagine my dick in her mouth, choking on me. How do my sloppy seconds taste?"

I swallow back my anger, focusing on Mia's trembling form, her shallow, panicked breaths. "You're right," I say evenly, meeting Micah's gaze head-on. "You win. Now let her go and fight with me."

Micah's expression shifts abruptly, confusion flickering across his face as he considers my offer, the blade wavering slightly. When he hesitates, I see my chance, but I wait for the right moment, unwilling to risk Mia's life. Micah is too unpredictable. His pupils are blown out too, which tells me I'm dealing with someone who's on something.

"Let her go," I repeat, my voice softer but no less firm as I hold

Micah's gaze. "You don't want her. You want revenge. You want me to suffer. You've got me right here."

His eyes narrow; suspicion fights with his desire to punish me. I sense the moment he chooses me and watch his grip loosen around Mia's waist.

He shoves her forward, and she stumbles, collapsing toward Nick, who catches her, pulling her quickly behind him and out of immediate danger.

But my relief is short-lived. In the same heartbeat, Micah pivots, his gaze locking on mine, eyes blazing.

"Now," he growls, stepping forward, fingers tightening on the blade, "it's your turn to pay."

But before I can fully react, Micah throws the knife toward my head, and I dodge it. As he steals my attention, he charges me, the force of his body slamming brutally into mine, knocking the gun from my grasp. It skitters across the basement floor, out of immediate reach. Pain jolts through my spine as we crash onto the hard concrete, my shoulder absorbing most of the impact.

Instinct and years of training instantly kick in. My muscles tense, responding with precision as Micah's fists slam against my ribs. I grit my teeth against the pain, feeling his desperation intensify his strength. He fights without discipline, without strategy; it's just raw, animalistic fury.

I find an opening, gripping his wrist and forcing him off-balance. Micah growls, his free hand clawing at my throat. His nails dig into my skin, breaths hot against my face.

"You should've stayed out of this," Micah hisses, voice strained as he shifts, knees digging into my chest. "You think you're a hero, Calloway? You're fucking nothing."

I ignore his bullshit, focused on finding a way to maneuver beneath him. My heart pounds in my ears, every breath tight. I twist again, planting my feet against the concrete, using my legs to shove us sideways. Micah loses balance, falling onto his back with a grunt of surprise. I shove my fist into his face, knuckles on flesh.

Asher's voice cuts through the chaos, urgent as he and Nick try to find a way to help. I can't make out what either of them is saying because I'm so fucking fueled by rage.

Micah bucks beneath me, his anger giving him unnatural strength. His elbow strikes my jaw, and stars explode in my vision. I shake it off, adrenaline dulling the pain. I pin him harder, pressing my forearm against his windpipe to restrict his airflow. But Micah doesn't give up. His eyes flash dangerously, fingers scrambling across the concrete. A wave of dread hits me as I realize he's reaching for the discarded gun.

Panic flares in my veins. I adjust my weight, fighting to keep him pinned, but Micah's fingers stretch closer, murder gleaming in his eyes. He manages a rough shove, creating just enough space to thrust his arm outward, fingertips brushing the cold metal barrel.

"Brody! He's got the gun!" Nick shouts, voice full of alarm.

Their guns are pointed at us, but there's no clear shot for them to take.

Micah's fingers wrap around the grip, his face transforming into a psychopathic sneer. Without thinking, I grab his wrist, forcing the gun upward and away from both of us. I put my other hand on his throat and squeeze tightly. I want to see the life drain from him, but he's stronger than even I anticipated.

We roll across the floor, bodies tangled in a struggle. Time stretches around us painfully, and my only goal is to disarm Micah, my grip tight around his wrist, keeping the weapon from turning back on us. I'm too hell-bent on us all walking away from this fucking nightmare.

"Let go!" Micah snarls, his voice full of rage.

I have to stop him. I have to end this, or none of us will walk out of this basement alive.

Every muscle strains as I wrestle Micah for control of the gun. Sweat slickens my grip. Micah's face twists with wild desperation, teeth bared as he fights to turn the gun back toward me.

"Brody," Asher's urgent shout pulls my attention. "Hold him!"

I clench my jaw, fighting with all my strength to keep Micah's arm locked upward, the barrel wavering dangerously above us.

"You're not walking away from this," Micah spits, muscles straining.

"Neither are you," I say through gritted teeth, channeling all my strength into this struggle.

Micah bucks under me, scraping his heels against the concrete for leverage, the sound echoing harshly.

In that split second, my grip slips just enough for Micah to jerk his arm downward, shifting the gun dangerously close to my chest. My heart slams against my ribs. With a final burst of strength, I force his wrist upward again. But it's too late.

A deafening shot rings out, echoing painfully against the concrete walls. Time slows as silence follows, broken only by the ringing in my ears.

Shock registers on Micah's face; his eyes widen, surprise replacing his rage. For a heartbeat, we freeze, both of us processing the sudden violence of that gunshot. The blast drowns out every other sound as time slows to a crawl.

I force myself to breathe, but my chest feels impossibly tight, as though a heavy weight presses firmly against it. I glance down as ice floods through my veins. This time, my hands and my shirt are smeared with blood.

"Brody!" Nick's voice cuts through my fight-or-flight haze.

But everything is too blurry and frantic.

31

HARPER

T he world is too still.

    I sit on the edge of my couch, fists clenched in the hem of my sweater, trying to breathe normally, like it's any other night, like I'm not waiting to find out if someone I love is safe. Billie's beside me, flipping through a magazine she hasn't looked at once. Her foot taps impatiently, but she hasn't said a word in twenty minutes.

Then my phone rings, pulling us both away. I rush and reach forward, nearly lunging for it.

I see it's Nick, and my heart jerks forward. I quickly answer and put it on speakerphone. "Nick?"

"Harper … Brody … there was a gun … he's not …"

His voice hits me like a slap in the face. It's ragged, breathless, and hysterical.

The call cuts out, and I stare at the screen. It's just silence.

He's not …

He's not … what?

Billie's brows are furrowed, and her jaw is set. I glance at her, growing as hysterical as Nick sounded.

He's not what? Breathing? Conscious? Alive?

A strange noise claws out of my throat as the phone slips from my hand and drops to the rug with a thud. I don't move to pick it up as panic rises in my belly. The edges of the room start to tilt, and my lungs seize.

"Harper?" Billie's voice snaps toward me.

But I can't respond. I can't speak. I can't even think. There's a buzzing in my ears, high and sharp, drowning everything. I'm already falling. Backward. Forward. Into a mental pit that I cannot climb out of. I stand up, needing to feel like the couch isn't sucking me in, but when I do, my knees hit the floor. Pain stretches up my legs, but it barely registers as a sob escapes me.

I can't breathe, and I'm having a full-blown panic attack. There is no air in this room. My hands press against my chest as I gasp to breathe.

Billie drops to the floor beside me. "Harper, look at me. Breathe. Okay? Just breathe. Count to ten."

I can't remember the last time I had a panic attack like this, where I felt like I'd die. My heart shatters, and I try to suck in air; noises release from me, and I feel like I'm drowning, actually suffocating.

"Harp, please. Look at me. Look at me," she repeats.

I try to meet her eyes, the tears blurring my vision.

Words won't form. My throat closes up. The world narrows to three things—Billie's hands gripping me, the ringing in my ears, and the memory of Brody telling me he's going to make me his wife, that we have a future together. My chest collapses inward. I can't do this. I'm not made for this life where the man I love is put into constant danger.

"Harper!" Billie shakes me. "You don't know anything yet. You hear me? You don't *know*."

I know this feeling. I know this silence. I know what it's like to have someone ripped out of your life mid-sentence. I know what it feels like to grieve a life I didn't get to live with someone who's ended too early. I think of my mother and the last time I saw her. Even then, I didn't know it would be the last time. I was only a kid, eight years old, and I didn't understand what was going on. And here I am, twenty-four years later, feeling the same despair, feeling as if my entire world is shattering around me.

My head drops, and I fold into myself, sobbing so hard that it hurts. The air still won't come. My nails dig into my arms like I'm trying to hold myself together by force alone. Billie holds me tight, hugging me like she won't let my dark thoughts swallow me whole.

"I can't," I cry. The words fracture; my sentences won't form. "I can't lose him."

Billie rocks us like I'm the one who's dying. And at this moment —this awful, breathless, breaking moment—it feels like I am. I feel like I might. I don't want to live in a world where Brody doesn't exist, where I don't get to wake up snuggled in his arms each morning.

The phone rings again, and it pulls me from my kamikaze spiral before I completely crash out.

I don't move. I can't. I feel as if I'm glued to this moment in time, stuck frozen by grief.

I hear it again, the sharp, happy ringtone, cutting through my sobs like a blade, but I can't bring myself to reach for it. My arms are heavy, and my breath is too shallow. My body is still caught in that last second before the world ended.

Billie grabs it from the floor, checks the screen, and freezes.

"Harper," she says, her voice shaking, "it's Brody."

The name hits me like a slap to the face and snaps me out of my spiraling thoughts. My heartbeat pounds loudly in my head as my lungs spasm for air. She hands it to me, and I look down at it, clumsy and desperate, fumbling to press the button, nearly dropping the device to the ground.

"Brody?" It's barely a whisper. My voice is wrecked.

There's static. A breath.

"Harp." His voice is rough and hoarse, but it's solid. He's alive.

I burst into happy tears as every muscle in my body collapses. A sob rips through me, and I try to pull myself out of the hysteria, wanting to crawl through the phone to hold on to him tightly.

"Are you okay?" I finally force out, sniffling. "Please."

"I'm safe," he says quickly. "I'm okay, Harp. I promise. I'm coming home to you."

My whole body shakes. I can't stop crying. I can't get enough air between the gasps. "Nick said—he said there was a gun. He said you weren't …" My throat closes around the words. "I thought …"

"I know. I'm sorry. The service out here is shit," he tells me, and he sounds exhausted.

I cradle the phone in both hands like it's my lifeline, and in a way, it is. "Are you hurt?"

"No. Just banged up. Nothing serious. Micah's in custody. Mia's okay. It's over."

I press a hand to my chest. "Come home."

"I am." He pauses. His voice drops lower. "I'm on my way to you. I'll be there in less than an hour."

A beat of silence stretches between us.

"It's over, Harp. You and Billie don't have to worry about this fuck anymore," he says, his voice raw.

"And Asher?" Billie asks.

"Asher is safe. We're all okay," he confirms.

"I'm waiting for you. Please hurry," I tell him.

The line goes quiet, not empty, not gone, just quiet. His call must've dropped.

I lower the phone, my chest still heaving, tears sliding down my cheeks. Billie holds on to me, eyes wide, hands wrapped around me.

"They're okay," I say breathlessly, my voice cracking.

My body trembles; the aftershock of everything is almost too much. I feel sick, like I need to throw up; the adrenaline is like poison in my blood. Billie exhales hard, relief shaking through her. We hold each other and cry, knowing that tomorrow will come, but Micah will never be able to hurt us again.

"This nightmare is over," Billie finally whispers. Hope is laced in her voice. "He can't hurt us."

I don't know how long we sit on the floor, holding each other tight. Time doesn't exist as I replay everything that's happened over the past two and a half months. I'm not the same woman I was; I can never be her again. I feel as if I've transformed, been burned completely to ash.

"Let's get off the floor," she says, her voice soft.

We move to the couch. I feel numb but calm as I cry. This time, I'm not mourning a life I thought I lost; I'm celebrating a miracle that Brody is still alive and that Asher and Nick are okay. The silence feels too loud as I sort through memories. Neither of us has words as we stare at the flames in the fireplace, licking up the sides.

Billie's phone lights up with a ton of text messages, and then a call comes through. She squeezes my hand as she talks to Asher, and I see the relief wash over her face, along with the love in her eyes. The call ends.

"They're fifteen minutes away."

I nod, glancing down at the time on my phone. "You should go meet him."

"Yes," she says, and I can see how emotionally drained she is. Billie grabs my hands. "I'm so sorry, Harp. I'm so sorry. Sometimes, I think that maybe had I done something differently, Micah wouldn't have targeted us."

She wraps me in a tight hug, and I shake my head.

"Hey. I hate that any of this happened, but without Micah, as much as I want him to burn in hell, I don't know if Brody and I would be where we are. I'm grateful for that. I'm grateful for you and your friendship and the fact that you didn't give up on me when I was too blinded by his charm to see the reality of my own horrible situation. Without you, I don't know if I'd be breathing right now. I owe so much to you."

We hold each other for a moment longer, and then we break apart, and she stands. I walk her to the elevator, my movements feeling too mechanical.

"Can we get together soon?" I ask, just wanting to hang out with my best friend.

"Yes," she confirms with a nod.

I give her a smile as the doors slide closed, then return to my penthouse. It's too quiet, too big, too empty. I miss the cozy feel of the cabin and how I felt safe and secure in that small space. I try to quiet my thoughts as I wait for Brody and light a candle. I even walk out onto my balcony and inhale the cool night air. The city hums with the hustle and bustle I'm so accustomed to, but I feel indifferent, being here, and for the first time, I understand why my brother escaped to Cozy Creek.

My body is still running on adrenaline and dread, caught between the moment I thought I'd lost Brody and the moment I heard his voice. I'm curled on the couch, knees to my chest, eyes fixed on the door like I can call him into existence. I wish I could snap my fingers and he'd magically appear. I replay everything—that crushing pressure in my chest, the ringing in my ears, the images of us.

Then I hear the elevator and the muted knock against my door. I stand before I can think, my bare feet slap across the floor, and my hand fumbles with the lock. When I open the door, I'm overwhelmed when I see him standing in front of me with messy hair.

He's backlit by light, his shoulders wide and solid, but his posture is just slightly off—like he's holding pain somewhere in his ribs and won't let it show. His jaw is bruised. His lip is cracked. There's dried blood on his shirt, and his eyes are wild.

Brody looks wrecked and relieved. The second he sees me, it's like the last thread that was holding him upright finally snaps.

He exhales, and it sounds like it's been trapped in his chest for hours. I wrap my arms around him, holding him tight, never wanting to let him go, never wanting to feel that way ever again. I sob in his arms, happy that he's here, that he's safe, that he's breathing.

"Harp, I love you."

"I love you so much," I cry out.

He pulls me inside with him, arm wrapped over my shoulders. I hold him tight, both hands needing to confirm he's really here and I'm not dreaming.

He catches me in his arms and pulls me into him without hesitation. My fingers curl into the back of his shirt, holding on to him with everything I have. My body shakes, and I don't even try to hide it. He smells like sweat and salt and something raw beneath the surface, like he just came through a storm and hasn't quite shaken the wind off yet.

"I thought I'd lost you," I whisper, my voice cracking. "I thought …" I can't finish. I press my forehead to his chest instead, listening to the steady thud of his heartbeat.

His arms tighten around me, one hand sliding up to cradle the back of my head. "I know," he murmurs, his voice rough and full of guilt. "I'm sorry. I'm so fucking sorry. It will never happen again."

I pull away from him and look up into his eyes. "I don't understand."

"I'm retiring. I'm done," he says. "I can't lose you, lose this life we have. It's not worth it to me. Before, I didn't have a reason to live. Sacrificing myself to protect the people I loved the most felt right. But now, the only person I want to protect is you and the life I dream of having with you. I'm fucking done, Harp. I never want to put you through that again. I won't. That was my last mission."

"You're serious?" I ask.

"Yes," he says, and I feel it in the way he holds me—like he needs me to survive this moment too. "Easton and Weston know."

I look up at him, and the second our eyes meet, something

inside me buckles. He brushes a thumb under my eye, catching a tear I didn't realize had fallen.

"I'm yours, Harp," he says again. "You're my purpose, and you will be for as long as my heart beats."

Happy tears stream out of me. He kisses me, pours everything that he is into me, into us, into the beautiful future that we both imagine so clearly. I take his hand, guiding him to the couch. He doesn't resist. He follows me, unsteady in a way that breaks my heart all over again. He says he's fine, but I can tell he's not. He's hurting.

Brody sinks into the couch and opens his arms, and I crawl into them without hesitation. This right here is the light at the end of my tunnel, and having him home safe is proof that we made it to the other side together.

The tension in his shoulders hasn't fully released, but he's trying. I can tell by his steady breaths that he's trying to soften the edges of whatever he's still carrying.

"Do you want to talk about it?" I ask, looking up at him.

He shakes his head. Silence takes over.

Brody doesn't just let me sit beside him, but he pulls me closer, his arm sliding behind my back, fingertips resting just above my hip, like he needs to keep touching me or risk unraveling completely. The penthouse is quiet, except for the low hum of the city beyond the windows. It's a faraway sound that makes me feel even more separated from the world.

I rest my head against his shoulder, letting the weight of the last few hours drip out of my eyes, piece by piece. My fingers lift his shirt. Every breath he takes feels like proof of something I still can't fathom—I didn't lose him. No matter how much Micah tried to ruin my life, I was allowed to keep Brody.

He lets out a breath like he's been holding it for days.

"I didn't know how deranged Micah was," he finally says, his voice quieter than I've ever heard it. "Until I saw Mia. When I looked at her, I saw you. And I realized if I didn't walk out of there, if something happened to me, that it would destroy you."

A sharp ache cuts through my chest. I lift my head, turning so I can really look at him. His eyes are rimmed with exhaustion, the bruise along his jaw already darkening. But beneath it all, there's that familiar vulnerability that gives me a glimpse of when we were in Sugar Pine Springs.

"I thought I'd lost you, and I had a horrible panic attack. I felt like I was dying," I whisper, reaching up to touch his face. My thumb brushes beneath the shadow of the bruise. "I broke. I couldn't breathe. I couldn't think. I've never felt anything like that in my life."

I wonder if that's how Eden's death affected him, but I don't ask. I can't.

Our eyes meet, and he doesn't speak for a second, just presses his forehead to mine, our breaths mingling in the narrow space between us.

"I never want you to experience that again."

"Thank you," I say, my voice trembling. "The way I feel about you isn't something I can undo. I can't live without you. I don't want to. And I feel selfish, saying that, but twice in the past few days, I've been faced with the reality of losing you, and I understand what you told me back at the cabin about not being able to survive that either."

Something flickers in his expression as he holds me, kisses me, and runs his fingers through my hair. "You won't ever have to live in a world without me, if I can help it," he says. It's a promise, and it does something to me.

My throat tightens, my body tenses, and before I can stop myself, I lean in and return my lips to his without hesitation. His mouth moves against mine with the same urgency he had when he pulled me into his arms, like we're both searching for something we thought we'd lost today. It's not desperate. It's not even about lust. It's about survival. It's about still being here and needing to feel something real after the chaos.

My hands slide up to the back of his neck, fingers tangling in his hair as the kiss deepens. He shifts beneath me, adjusting until I'm straddling his lap, my knees on either side of him. Brody's hands stay planted on my hips, holding me steady, grounding me. I break the kiss, only to rest my forehead against his again, our noses brushing as we breathe each other in.

"I just need to feel you," I whisper. "I need to know you're really here."

"I understand," he confesses, as if he hasn't fully recovered his ability to speak. "I need you always."

My heart clenches, and I nod because I can't find words for the way that makes me feel. My hands slide down his chest, over the ridges of muscle, and I memorize every inch like it might vanish again.

When I tug at the hem of his shirt, he lifts his arms, letting me pull it over his head. I toss it aside and press my hands to his skin, my palms flat against the warmth of his chest. His heartbeat thrums under my fingers. It's fast but steady, and I let out a breath I didn't realize I had been holding all night.

Brody reaches for me then, his touch careful but sure as he slips his hands beneath the hem of my sweatshirt and lifts. The moment it clears my head, his eyes meet mine, and something in the charged air changes.

His fingers trace a path along my ribs with a featherlight touch, as if he's memorizing something sacred. My body responds instinctively, leaning into him, aching to be close in a way that has nothing to do with sex and everything to do with *belonging*.

He kisses me again until the tears finally stop burning behind my eyes, until the fear vanishes, until there's nothing left between us but skin and breath and love. His hands move with purpose, but not urgency—like he's rediscovering every inch of me, not to take, but to remember. His fingers trail along the curve of my waist, up my spine, down my arms. Each touch is intentional, like he's asking me a silent question and waiting for my body to answer.

I kiss him deeper, my mouth parting against his as the last thread of fear snaps. All that's left is this—his warmth, his scent, the rasp of stubble against my skin, the steady beat of his heart. My thighs tighten around him as I straddle him, and his breath hitches as I roll my hips once, just enough to let him know I need more. He exhales my name like a prayer, his lips dragging along my jaw, down my throat.

Brody lifts me, guiding me backward until my spine meets the cushions, his body lowering to cover mine. We move like we're rediscovering how to exist in the same space again, like the closeness has to be relearned and rebuilt in this new freedom we have. Every kiss, every brush of skin stitches us back together until we're whole again, like we were at his cabin.

His hands skim beneath the waistband of my leggings, dragging them down inch by inch, his gaze never leaving mine. There's nothing rushed about it. No games, no facade. Just this. Just us.

When he finally pushes inside me, I gasp, my arms wrapping around his back as my body arches into his. It's not the kind of gasp that comes from pain or even surprise. It's the kind that says, *Finally.* Like my body's been holding a space for him, waiting for him to come home.

We move together like the world has narrowed down to this specific moment. We make love, losing ourselves in one another. We are all that matters. Our love keeps me going. Every thrust is deep, steady, grounding—not about taking or rushing, but about cementing what we have, making it permanent. Every stroke says, *I'm here. You're safe. We survived this.*

We stay close, his forehead pressed to mine, our ragged breaths mingling. Tears prick behind my eyes again, but they come from something that can only be felt deep inside as he breaks me open.

"I love you, Harp," he whispers, like he can't hold it in any longer.

My breath catches on the inhale, and he kisses me like tomorrow will never come.

"I love you, Brody," I say against his hot mouth that's desperate for mine. "I've been in love with you for a long damn time," I confess.

We keep moving like time bends around us. It's the kind of intimacy that doesn't burn but glows bright in the darkness.

Brody Calloway is my sunshine, and his love for me lights the way.

32

BRODY

I'm still inside her when I realize I could've died tonight.

Her legs are wrapped around me, her lips still parted from the last kiss, and her fingertips skim the sweat along my back like she's grounding both of us. Our bodies are pressed tight, skin to skin, heart to heart. The world narrows to the sound of her breathing and how she sighs my name like it's the only thing holding us together.

I keep moving, but it's now deeper, drawn out, like I can't stand the thought of letting her go. My body is aching in places I won't admit out loud. Bruises are layered deep under my skin, but none of it matters when she looks at me like I'm not broken. Like I'm hers.

Her hands grip my shoulders, not to pull me closer, but to *keep* me here. With her. In this moment. Where the fear has finally faded, and what's left is just us. We're unguarded, our movements raw, and something wraps around us that feels too big to name.

"I needed you," she whispers, her voice thick with everything we haven't said.

"You're all I could think about." My voice cracks as I lower my mouth to her shoulder, pressing a soft kiss there. Then another.

Then another. Each one is gentler than the last. "If that shot had gone any other direction—"

"I don't want to think about it."

She shuts me up with a kiss that's more desperate than the others. Her hands slide into my hair, her hips lifting to meet mine again. There's nothing frantic about it, but there's an undeniable urgency. There's meaning. Like she's writing something permanent into me with every breath and every movement.

I bury myself deeper inside her, and it hits me all at once. I've never made love like this. Never moved like this. Never needed someone the way I need Harper right now. It's not just the sex or the closeness, but the *knowing*. The truth of her under my hands, the way her body gives, welcomes, holds me like she's claiming me. It's understanding and seeing one another for exactly who we are.

I want to be claimed. By her. Only her.

Her legs tighten around my waist, and I brace a hand above her head, the other slides around the back of her neck. She's everything I never thought I deserved. And somehow, she's still here, still choosing me as we make love.

I feel it before she says anything—her body tightening, her breath catching. I hold her gaze through it, watching the way her mouth falls open, the way her brows pinch together as she clings to me like she's afraid she'll come apart if I let go.

"I've got you," I whisper, my voice hoarse. "Let go, Harp."

She breathlessly breaks in my arms, and I follow a heartbeat later, spilling into her with a groan that sounds more like surrender than release. My body collapses over hers, but I catch myself with one arm, not wanting to crush her, but I'm not ready to pull away.

Not ever.

For a long time, we don't move. We just breathe, staying tangled in each other. Our skin is damp, hearts still racing, as her fingers trace lines along my back. I know I'll never forget the feeling. The after. The way this doesn't feel like sex at all. It feels like survival, like coming home.

The room is warm, filled with the scent of Harper's skin and the echo of the way she whispered my name when I came undone inside her.

I lie beside her for a while, her fingers tracing patterns along my ribs, her legs tangled with mine, like we're afraid to let go. Part of me doesn't want to move at all. I want to stay right here, memorize the rhythm of her breathing and the way her chest rises and falls, but the ache in my shoulder is setting in now. My body's starting to hum with the pain of the night, and it reminds me I'm stitched together by adrenaline and determination.

I press a kiss to her temple, then shift to sit up.

"I need a quick shower," I whisper, brushing a strand of hair off her face.

She nods without speaking, her eyes heavy-lidded, watching me like she doesn't want me too far away from her. I stand, stretching, and the tight pull across my ribs reminds me of the fight in the basement. Being slammed down on the concrete floor. The loud sound of the gunshot in my ear.

My jaw clenches as I enter the bathroom, trying to shake the flash of Micah's face and deranged eyes from my mind.

The tiles are cold beneath my feet as I turn the water on and step into the shower. I let the heat pound against my shoulders. Steam rises around me, and I want it to erase everything I just walked through. I close my eyes and press both palms to the wall, letting the water run down my back, over my neck, across the bruises I haven't even looked at yet. My mind goes quiet, not because the fear is gone, but because there's nothing left to fight. The threat is over now that Micah's in custody. Harper's safe. I made it back in one piece.

The bathroom door swings open behind me, and it's followed by light footsteps.

Harper steps into the shower without hesitation, her presence sliding in next to me like she belongs there. She doesn't speak and just moves close. The heat of her body presses against my back for a breath, and she wraps her arms around me, hugging me as she kisses my back. After a few seconds, she takes the washcloth and soap, and I let her wash me. Her hands are careful.

She starts with my shoulders, working the cloth over each one. There's a carefulness in her movements that undoes me. She's not trying to distract or seduce. She's caring for me, and she touches me like I'm the only thing that matters. This isn't about scrubbing off blood or sweat; it's about showing me that I'm not alone in the aftermath.

I turn to face her, and when she reaches my chest, I cover her hand with mine.

"You don't have to," I mutter, unsure why I'm even trying to stop her.

"I want to." Her voice is calm. "Let me."

So, I do.

I drop my hand and let her continue, and she washes me in quiet circles. Her fingers linger where bruises are forming, where the skin is tender. When she sees the scrape along my ribs from Micah's fingernails, she presses a kiss before continuing, her lips warm, even beneath the heat of the water. I let my head fall forward, water running down my face as emotion overtakes me. I don't cry, but I feel close, completely overwhelmed by her gentle touch. I haven't allowed myself to be taken care of in years. I forgot what it feels like to be touched with gentleness, without expectation.

Her arms wrap around me when she's finished, her cheek pressing against my chest. We stay like that for a while—just breathing as I allow her to hold me.

"I thought of you the whole time," I say, staring at the marble tiles. "Every second, I thought of you."

Her grip tightens just slightly. "And you came back to me, safe."

"Because there was no other option."

We stay like that until the water cools, and even then, I don't want to leave.

Harper reaches for a towel and dries my chest before wrapping another around my shoulders. She grabs a towel for herself, then guides me out with a smile and a look in her eyes, like she'll never let me fall apart alone again.

The ceiling fan in her bedroom hums up above, and the sheets smell just like her. She's already in my arms by the time I even realize I'm lying down.

She's snuggled against my chest, her cheek resting just beneath my collarbone, her fingers lightly brushing the edge of the towel, still slung low around my hips. We haven't spoken in the last five minutes, but everything important has already been said. The silence between us doesn't feel heavy but earned.

Her bed in the Park Towers penthouse is too big for one person, but it feels right for two. She fits perfectly against me, like her body knows the shape of mine. Like we were meant to be. My arm is wrapped around her back, fingers moving in circles across her skin. Her breath is steady, and I can feel the weight shedding from us both with every inhale.

My mind tries to go back—to the sound of the gun, to the moment Micah's hand found the trigger—but Harper's hand slides up my chest and pulls me back into the present. She doesn't even know she's doing it; it's just instinct. Just her body telling mine we're okay now and that there's no more running or fighting to be had.

The image of her earlier, standing in her doorway, hair a mess, eyes full of panic and love and devastation, burns behind my eyes. She didn't ask if I was okay because she didn't need to—because she *felt* it. She *knew*. And the way she touched me after ... how she let me fall apart inside her without needing to fix anything ... I don't think I've ever been loved like that.

My chest tightens, but not in the way it did before. This is different. It's full. It's real. It's love.

She shifts slightly, her leg hooking over mine beneath the covers, and I smile into her hair. She smells like soap and steam and something that's just her. I kiss her there, right at the top of her head. She hums with an exhale, still half asleep but aware enough to melt closer.

For just a second, I think about Eden, and how she knew Harper and I belonged together. It's a conversation and a moment that has lived in the back of my mind for years. But tonight, I understand what she meant; I just didn't see it. And maybe, just *maybe*, that's how I honor her.

Harper exhales against my chest, and I feel it like a vow settling between us.

I tighten my arm around her just a little more, burying my face into her hair, breathing her in like she's the only real thing in the world—because she is.

And as I finally let my eyes close, I know one thing with absolute clarity. The nightmare is over. I let go of the weight I've been dragging behind me for far too long.

Harper and I made it through the darkest of storms. And now I get to keep her and enjoy the rainbows.

33

HARPER

The first thing I feel is his hot breath against the back of my neck.

It's the kind of morning where the light hasn't quite figured out how to fully fill the room, where everything is still covered in a golden hush. The sheets are tangled around us, half slipped down my hips, and his arm is heavy over my waist. One of his legs is hooked lazily around mine, his body curved protectively behind me —like even in sleep, he's making sure I don't drift too far.

The world could be ending outside those windows, and I wouldn't know. I wouldn't care.

I lie there for a moment without moving, afraid if I shift even a little, the spell I'm under might break. My fingers find the inside of his forearm and trace the edge of his tattoo. I don't need to see it to know exactly where the inked curves of the Calloway Diamond logo are. I've memorized every inch of him by now, not just with my hands, but with something deeper. I could close my eyes and still see the tattoos on his shoulder, the scruff on his jaw, and the base of his throat, where his breath catches when I kiss it.

There's a weight in my chest that's unfamiliar, but it isn't heavy. It's full. Not the kind of fullness that comes from fear or adrenaline or barely surviving, but the kind that settles in after everything else has moved out of our way—the noise, the tension, the ghosts.

Brody shifts behind me, his arm tightening around me just a little, like some part of him senses I'm awake. I smile, not turning yet, letting the silence linger for a little longer. But then he drags his nose along my shoulder, then presses his mouth into my hair, and I can't pretend anymore.

I roll onto my back, and his blue eyes that hold a new sense of calm find mine right away. He's barely awake. His dark hair is a mess, but he smiles like he was dreaming of me. That adorable Calloway smirk seems to undo me every time.

"Hi," I whisper, brushing a thumb across the stubble on his cheek.

"Hey," he says. He blinks once, then again, like he's making sure I'm real.

There's no rush to move, no need to fill the quiet. He leans in and kisses me, his lips brushing mine with a kind of longing that doesn't ask for anything. It just is.

When we pull apart, he sighs against my cheek and whispers, "Mornings are always better when they start with you."

I laugh. "That was dangerously close to romantic."

He smirks, one eye still half shut. "Don't get used to it."

I reach toward him, tickling him, and he giggles and tries to wiggle away. Then I see him make a face like he's in pain, and I immediately feel guilty.

"Aw, I'm sorry," I tell him, placing my hand over the curves of his abs. "I'll owe you one."

"Thanks," he says, cocky and macho, like he didn't just giggle like a kid.

I let my fingers wander through the mess of his hair, smiling when he hums with satisfaction.

"Your touch feels so good."

He's warm and completely relaxed, and it's such a contrast to the man who walked into my life, guarded and tense, ready to burn down the world for me. I can't help but stare at him for a moment longer, memorizing the way he looks when he doesn't think anyone's watching.

I've never felt this safe. Not just physically, but in the space between us. In the quiet, that always terrified me, but with him, it feels like home.

For the first time, I don't feel like I have to get up and outrun something because there's nowhere I need to be other than here with him, in his arms. We lie in the quiet, in the steady truth of us, and I'm exactly where I'm supposed to be, where I belong.

"Coffee?" he asks.

"God, yes," I tell him as he slides out of bed, putting on those old joggers I've kept since I was seventeen. I'm unable to take my eyes off him. "Hate to watch you go, but damn."

"Keep it up, and we'll stay here all day."

"Don't threaten me with a good time!" I tell him as he comes and steals another quick kiss.

His strong palm rests on my cheek, and when he pulls away, he's grinning.

When it's just me, alone in the silence of the morning, I stare up at the ceiling, smiling so wide that it hurts, that this is my life. I'm living the dream.

The strong aroma of dark roast pulls me out of bed, and I slide on a T-shirt and some tiny shorts. The scent drifts down the hallway like a promise. The city is just starting to stretch awake outside the penthouse windows.

Brody's in the kitchen, back to me, standing over the coffee machine with a level of concentration that makes me smile. His shoulders are relaxed, his hair still a mess from sleep, and the faint bruising on his back is obvious.

I just watch him for a few seconds, admiring every strong inch of him.

Brody showed up for me when my life was falling apart and held the pieces together like they were something worth saving. He helped me without asking for anything in return because he felt I was worth it.

When he finally turns, there's a softness in his blue eyes that he's always reserved just for me. It's private, like the way he touches me when he thinks I'm asleep or how he watches me when he doesn't think I'm looking. It's the small things he does that are louder than his words ever could be. His actions speak for him.

"Hey, Sleeping Beauty," he says, holding up a mug. "I added a splash of cream. Hope it's enough."

I accept the cup with a soft smile.

He places a kiss on my forehead and grins. "Let me know if it tastes like jet fuel because that roast is dark as fuck."

I act offended, cradling the mug in both hands, letting the heat soak into my fingers. "You're cute."

"Just cute?" he asks, sipping his own and leaning against the counter.

His eyes scan me—bare legs, messy hair, sleepy eyes—and something shifts in his gaze. Not hunger, not lust, just pure admiration. It's the look that says he sees me. I don't have to perform or be polished. I can just be.

I sit on the stool beside him and hold the cup tightly. "You have plans today?"

He nods. "I'm meeting with Easton and Weston to discuss me leaving."

"You're serious?"

"Yeah. Guess it's time to be a trust-fund baby," he says with a smirk, tilting his head toward me. "About time, right?"

I laugh. "What will you do in your free time?"

"You," he says, shooting me a wink. "I honestly haven't thought much about it. Maybe I'll volunteer for the Wounded Warrior Project. I just want to live for once in my life." He moves toward me and dips down to kiss me. "I have you to thank for that."

There's a beat of quiet between us then. Not awkward. Not heavy. Just stillness. And in that stillness, I realize how easy this feels. How natural. Like our lives have already started folding into each other without either of us noticing.

"You're welcome," I tell him, waggling my brows. "I will keep you plenty busy."

I sip my coffee and let the warmth settle low in my belly as my eyes slide over him. Strong and sexy.

Brody Calloway is a walking fantasy, and he's mine. Forever.

His fingers brush a strand of hair away from my cheek. "You're so pretty."

"You are too," I tell him.

Then he kisses me once, with certainty, and pulls back just enough to smile. "Let's go house-hunting. Something that's ours. That holds no memories of anything else. A place for our new beginning."

"I'd love that," I tell him, a grin taking over. "Moving kinda fast, huh, Calloway?"

His grin widens. "First comes love."

I can't help the smile that touches my lips, knowing this is true happiness.

"Now, I have to go meet my asshole cousins and let them make jokes for an hour," he says.

"Going like that?" I look him up and down.

He tilts his head at me. "What do you think they'd say if I walked into Calloway Diamonds headquarters like this?"

"You'd better not. I don't need my future husband being splashed around gossip magazines. Do you know how many spank banks you'd be added to? Absolutely not."

Laughter roars out of him. "I always forget you were the jealous type."

"*Pfft*, speak for yourself," I tell him, standing to capture his lips again. "But I am jealous. You're mine. And only mine. I'm willing to fight."

"Fuck," he whispers across my mouth. "Hot."

"You should text Lexi. I bet she'd happily give you some of

Easton's clothes. See if he notices when you show up in one of his tailored suits."

He nods, pulling his phone from his pocket. "Good idea."

Brody, Weston, and Easton are basically the same size. However, Brody is more muscular.

His phone vibrates, and he shows me the text.

LEXI

Only if you take a picture of his face when you walk in.

He types back to her.

BRODY

Deal.

Brody chugs the rest of his coffee, leaving a warm kiss on my lips as he heads toward the door. "I'll be back very soon. An hour, tops. Love you."

I grin. "Love you."

I watch him walk away, and this time, it doesn't come with the fear that he won't return. It comes with the steady truth that he always will.

I'm mid-sip when a knock rings on my door. I move to the door, half-expecting to see Brody, wondering if he forgot something. I look through the peephole and see Billie.

I pull it open and smile. "Good morning."

"Morning!"

She steps inside, holding a small white box in both hands, her oversized sunglasses pushed to the top of her head, jet-black hair perfectly disheveled in that effortless bob only she can manage. Her expression is casual, but there's a buzz to her—something under the surface, like she's carrying more than what fits inside the box.

"I brought you something," she says by way of greeting. Which, to be fair, she's done many times before.

I arch a brow and close the door behind her. "No Asher in tow?"

"Nah. I just saw Brody in the elevator, and he told me you'd taken the morning off since you had been kidnapped," she says with a wink.

"Okay, I wasn't technically kidnapped," I say. "Actually, when we tell the story to our kids, let's keep that one. Going with that psycho of my own free will isn't as exciting."

She cracks a smile and hands me the box. I open it to find a silk sleep mask, embroidered with metallic gold thread that says *Nap Queen*.

I snort, laughter bubbling up before I can stop it. "Okay, this is on-brand."

"Right?" She smirks, sinking onto the edge of my sofa. "Saw it in a boutique window and immediately thought, *That's Harp.*"

I set the box on the counter and lean against it, studying her. She's trying too hard to look casual, like she didn't come here with an agenda. There's a softness in her shoulders that makes me pause.

"What's going on?" I ask, reading her easily.

She knows me better than I know myself at times, and the feeling is mutual.

She exhales through her nose. "Nothing. I mean, it's something, but not dramatic."

"Everything okay?" I wait impatiently.

"Yes." Finally, she looks up at me, eyes wide and a little too shiny. "Asher and I are engaged."

For a second, the words don't register. They hover in the air between us, and I blink at her like I misheard.

"What? Oh my God! That's incredible! Like, it just happened?"

Her smile somewhat falters. "No. Weeks now. I just hadn't told you yet."

My gaze drops automatically to her hands. No ring. It confuses me, and she gives me a half-hearted shrug.

"I stopped wearing it until you knew. Everything got too complicated. Micah. You. The timing was off. It just never felt like the right moment."

Guilt surges through me, knowing I'm the reason she hasn't celebrated. "When did this happen?"

"The week before you got engaged to Micah, when we were in the Hamptons," she says. "Before everything."

My stomach twists. I think of the whirlwind that followed and how quickly everything spun out of control. My own pain became the loudest thing in the room, and I cover my mouth with one hand. "I'm so sorry. I ruined that for you."

"No." She shakes her head immediately, fingers reaching for mine. "You didn't ruin anything. I was never waiting for the perfect announcement or the headline. I have him. And I have you. That's all I'll ever care about."

Emotion swells in my throat, and it's too thick to swallow. I blink hard, trying to keep the tears from falling, but they visit anyway.

I squeeze her hand. "I'm so happy for you. Genuinely. You deserve real love. I'd love to celebrate with you."

She hugs me tight, then pulls away. "Now it's your turn."

I smile wide. "One day. Soon."

"Yeah?" she asks, giddy with excitement. "Harper Calloway. Has a ring to it, doesn't it?"

Her laughter is completely contagious.

"Seems like dreams are actually coming true," she says.

"We're both exactly where we're supposed to be," I confirm.

There's a silence between us that doesn't feel empty. Billie doesn't look away, and neither do I.

"I remember when you used to write *Harper Calloway* on everything. My brothers were assholes, but Brody ... match made in heaven."

I've never been more grateful for her than I am at this exact moment.

"I'm sorry for missing your birthday," I finally say, realizing we broke our tradition of having a shot of tequila together. "Micah wouldn't le—"

"No more apologies, okay? I'm just so damn grateful you're still here to celebrate the rest of them with me," she says. "No more survival mode. No more judgment. Only understanding. We're moving forward, not backward."

My eyes burn, and I blink fast, but it's no use. Tears, full of understanding and gratitude, fall anyway, sliding down my cheeks like they've been waiting for permission. I wipe at them with the sleeve of my T-shirt, laughing under my breath.

"I'm about to start my period. Forgive me. I'm emotional as fuck."

Billie reaches over and squeezes my hand. "I get it. I kinda owe you a thank-you. Since Asher and I haven't been public, we've been able to enjoy our engagement without the media speculating and starting shit. It always works out just the way it's supposed to."

I nod, my voice caught in my throat. "It does."

She smiles and laughs, and it reaches her blue eyes—the same color blue each of the Calloways has. "I still can't believe after everything Asher and I have been through, I'm marrying him. He's still a gigantic pain in my ass, but I love him."

Laughter bursts out of me. "I'm glad you have someone who challenges you. Don't see you being with anyone who would just roll over and do what you say."

I don't know how long we sit in the kitchen, chatting about everything that has happened or our relationships. At some point, I end up making a second cup of coffee, and before I finish it, there's a light tap on the door. Billie glances at me with brows raised, and I shrug.

I open the door, and Brody places a kiss on my lips.

"You're back already?" I ask, glancing at the clock, realizing I've been chatting with Billie for nearly an hour.

"It was a ten-minute conversation with twenty minutes of shit talking."

I smirk and take a step back, drinking him in. "Damn. Gucci looks good on you."

"This suit pissed Easton off beyond belief. Worth it," he says as he lifts a brown paper bag from the bakery I love that's close to Calloway Diamonds headquarters. He stops when he sees Billie. "You're still here?"

She shrugs. "Had a lot of catching up to do."

He sets the bag on the counter, and when I glance at him, he winks, mouthing, *You okay?*

The smile that spreads across my face feels unshakable—a confirmation that everything is perfect. I've finally found balance in my life.

He's trying to act casual and failing miserably at it. He searches Billie's face, then mine, then glances at the box I still haven't moved off the counter. "I can leave if I'm interrupting."

Billie shakes her head. "You're not; Harper knows the good news about the engagement."

Brody's eyebrows lift with practiced effort. He gives a mock gasp. "Wait. You're engaged?" The way he says it is a beat too slow.

I don't even bother hiding my smile as I glance at him. "You're a terrible liar."

A small breath releases from him as his eyes crinkle at the corners. "The main reason why I stick to telling you the truth."

Billie whips around to face him, eyes wide. "I can't believe you didn't tell her. Wow. Even I'm impressed."

He shrugs unapologetically. "It wasn't my news to share."

Billie stares at him for another second before a smile breaks across her face. "The two of you are perfect together."

"I try," he says, pulling pastries out of the bag, one by one, like he's done this a dozen times before. "The cinnamon rolls are still warm."

"Ooh, my favorite," Billie says, reaching for one without hesitation.

I lean back against the counter, watching them both, realizing this is my life. Brody catches my eye and gives me the smallest nod.

Everything really does feel okay now, and without having to say it out loud, I know it is.

"When are you proposing?" Billie directly asks him.

Brody's brows furrow. "Fuck off."

She scoffs. "No way to treat your favorite cousin."

He shrugs. "I dunno. Seems like Weston is taking the number one spot these days."

Billie actually looks offended as she snags a turnover and makes her way to the door. "I won't stop asking until you do it." She glances at me. "Got your back, Harp."

I giggle as she opens the door and leaves with a sassy swing to her hips. I turn to Brody, looking him up and down.

"Like what you see?" He adjusts the tie.

"I kinda want to peel that off of you with my teeth."

I watch him as he moves toward me, completely unhurried, unbothered, and at ease here, like he's always belonged. Maybe he has. Maybe this is the version of me that I was always meant to be. He runs his fingers through my hair and meets my eyes.

"How did it go?" I ask.

"Great. They were super supportive and very happy for us."

He dips down and captures my lips, taking his time as our tongues twist together. He moans against me, and I melt into him fully. My eyes flutter open, and I stare into his blues.

"What are you thinking about?" he asks, voice low.

I tilt my head, resting it on his shoulder. "How surreal this feels."

He presses a kiss to the top of my head and pulls me in closer, like he understands exactly what I mean. I close my eyes, holding him, and let myself feel this beautiful thing we've built in the aftermath. It's not perfect. It's not polished. But it's ours.

I no longer feel like I'm dreaming. No, I've finally woken up.

34

BRODY

ONE WEEK LATER

The city slides past my window in a blur, and the sun is already sinking low enough to cast everything in shadow. My driver picked me up ten minutes ago and is taking me across town. I tap my thumb against my thigh at the red light, not because I'm impatient, but because my nerves are starting to settle in places I can't shake loose. It's been a long time since I've felt anything like this.

I've been shot at, thrown into hand-to-hand combat with psychopaths, gone to war—and still, none of it feels as heavy as what I'm about to do. It's not fear. It's knowing that Harper deserves every ounce of intention I can give her. That means doing things the right way, not just for her, but for the people who matter to her. The ones who protected her when she didn't have a voice.

The bar Zane picked is tucked at the end of a narrow street downtown, half hidden behind ivy-covered brick and a matte-black door with no sign. It's understated and extremely private. It's the kind of place where real conversations happen.

I walk in and spot her older brother—CEO of Xander Resorts.

He's the kind of man who makes everyone feel like they're being unraveled when he's silent. He's seated at a booth near the back, already sipping a drink, posture casual but eyes sharp the second they lift and find mine.

I slide into the seat across from him. "Zane."

"Brody." He gestures to the server. "Would you like a drink?"

"Just water."

He raises an eyebrow but doesn't push. The server leaves us alone, and for a beat, neither of us speaks. The silence stretching between us is measured and intentional, like he's giving me room to prove I'm not afraid of it. It makes me a little nervous, but I thrive in the quiet.

He clears his throat. "You already spoke to my father."

It's not a question. I have.

"A few days ago. I wanted his blessing. He gave it willingly," I tell him.

Zane leans back slightly, fingers tapping the side of his glass. "Then why am I here?"

There's no accusation in his voice—just that razor-sharp curiosity that comes with being the older brother. The protector.

"Because you didn't agree with her relationship with Micah. I think your finger is on the pulse, and you know what is best for your sister," I say simply. "And because it matters to me that you're not just okay with this."

His gaze narrows, but he doesn't respond.

"I didn't come here because I need your permission. I came because I respect you, and so does Harper. And because if someone were going to ask me for my sister's hand, if she were still alive, I'd expect the same courtesy."

That lands with him, and his expression shifts, just slightly, but it's enough to know I've hit the right chord.

Zane swirls the liquid in his glass. "You don't scare easily."

"No," I say, a faint smile pulling at the corner of my mouth. "But I don't take responsibility lightly either."

LYRA PARISH

He nods once—a silent acknowledgment—and finally says, "Good."

Zane doesn't waste time with small talk. Once my water is in front of me and his drink's been topped off again, he shifts forward slightly with his dress shirt sleeves rolled to his elbows. His forearms are braced on the table. There's nothing hostile in his posture, but nothing open either. He's watching me. Calculating. The kind of look he's honed from years of sitting in board meetings full of people who rule the world.

"Why do you think you're good enough for my sister?" It's not said with sarcasm. It's direct and honest. A challenge that requires clarity.

I expected nothing less. Zane's a known hard-ass. Always has been.

I meet his steady gaze. "Because she deserves someone who understands exactly what she's been through and still chooses to show up for her anyway. I'm not here to fix her. I'm here to love her. Every day. Without flinching."

Zane's jaw tics slightly, like he wasn't expecting that answer, or maybe because it's the truth.

"I've seen what it looks like when someone tries to control her. Dim her down to keep her manageable. I'm not interested in being that man. I want Harper with all her sharp edges. Her ambition. That's who I fell in love with, and I want her light to keep shining."

For a beat, he just watches me, and then, finally, he speaks. "She almost didn't come back from what Micah did."

"I know. I watched her rebuild herself with shaking hands. I've seen the cost of survival written all over her."

"And you think you're built to handle that?" he questions, sipping his drink.

"I don't think," I confirm, giving him a smirk. "I *know* I am. I've walked through fire for her and with her. I've stood between her and the worst kind of darkness. Not because she needed me to, but because I couldn't live with myself if something happened."

332

He leans back, folding his arms across his chest, still unreadable. "Harper was my priority when we were kids. If you hurt her, if you ever make her question her worth—"

"You won't have to come looking for me," I interrupt. "I hope you'd fuck me up if I did any of those things. Know that I'll spend every day making sure she knows what it feels like to be safe, wanted, and loved exactly as she is."

Something shifts in his eyes, and it's recognition. It's the look of a man who's tested a theory and gotten a result he can live with.

Then his face cracks into a smile. "I think those are the most words I've heard you speak—ever."

I don't shift in my seat or glance away. I hold the moment because it deserves to be held—because when a man hands you his sister's heart, you honor it.

Zane leans back now, less guarded than before, but still every bit the older brother. Still the man who stepped into roles no one asked him to fill when they were kids and carried Harper through storms she never even saw after their mother passed away. I respect what he's done. I don't resent it. If anything, I get it more than he knows.

"I never expected to fall for her," I admit. "She's fire. Untouchable, impossible not to be drawn to, but wild. But somewhere along the way, she stopped being a mission and became my purpose. She was the reason I started thinking about the future again. I didn't realize how dark everything had gotten until she walked in and made the room feel like it had windows."

I pause, searching for the words that don't come easy, not because they're not true, but because they're real. "She makes me a better man. When I'm with her, I want to be who she sees. I don't know if you can understand that."

"I can." Zane exhales, like he's sorting through his own memories with his wife, Autumn.

The silence hangs between us.

"I don't take marriage lightly," I continue. "And I'm not here like it's a checkbox on a list. I'm here because she deserves a love that shows up for her in every room, in every fight, in every quiet moment after the storm. I want to be that for her. I already am."

His expression doesn't change, but something in his shoulders finally eases.

"I want to marry Harper," I say. "And I'd like your blessing, not because I need it, but because she deserves that kind of respect from the man who will be with her until the end of time."

Zane doesn't speak immediately. He just studies me for another long second, the kind where judgment and understanding live side by side. Then, finally, he sets his glass down and folds his hands on the table.

"All right," he says. "You've said what you came here to say. Now let me say mine."

The table between us feels smaller now, like the weight of everything I said filled the space. Zane leans forward, and I meet his gaze without hesitation.

"You're not wrong about her," he says finally. "Harper's always been the one who walked into a room and shone in her own special way. Even when she was a kid, she had this way of refusing to bend for anyone. She's strong-willed, competitive, and stubborn. A true Alexander."

His eyes don't leave mine. He's deliberate.

"I've spent most of my life trying to protect her from people who didn't know what to do with that kind of fire. Who either tried to tame it or use it for their own warmth. Micah was both. And it damn near killed her."

A pulse tics at the base of his jaw, but he doesn't look away. "So, understand this, Brody. When I say I accept this relationship, I'm not handing over a prize for you to flaunt. I'm acknowledging that you—out of everyone—see her for exactly who she is, and you still want to build a life beside her, and that you're not asking her to dim her light. That you're not trying to carry her out of the ashes and mold her how you please. I see that you're just standing there beside her while she rises, and you support that. It's exactly what she needs." He pauses, letting the moment settle before adding, "I have no issues with you or this relationship."

Relief hits me, and I exhale, not realizing I was even holding my breath. "Thank you."

Zane lifts his drink, but his tone sharpens, the edge returning. "But if you ever lie to her, clip her wings, or give her even a second of doubt about her worth, you'll find out just how much I still believe in revenge."

I chuckle. "Exactly what I expected you to say."

His mouth twitches like he might smile, but it doesn't make it all the way to his eyes. "Then we understand each other."

He offers his hand, and I shake it. It's not an overly warm gesture, but it's not meant to be. It's just a single moment between two men who love the same woman in different but equal ways— and who both understand the weight of that love.

We don't say much after that because there's no need. The handshake said the rest, and it was the acknowledgment I needed.

My phone vibrates, and it's a text from Harper. I read it.

HARPER

How much longer?

I smile and meet his eyes. "I have to go. Your sister calls."

I toss a couple of bills on the table to cover his drink as he finishes the last of it. As I stand, he does, too, but there are no extra words or back slaps or forced sentiment.

As we walk outside, he turns to me. "She's not easy."

I glance back with a smirk. "Oh, I'm not afraid of a little trouble."

He nods once, and his eyes soften. It's a final stamp of approval that's full of respect.

I step out onto the street, and when the warm evening air hits me, I know summer is among us. The noise of the city rolls over me, but I don't feel like I'm in the middle of chaos anymore. I haven't felt like that in over a week.

I return Harper's text.

BRODY

On my way back. Just finished my meeting.

HARPER

☺ Great! Come home to me.

Those words settle right behind my ribs. Because that's what she is to me.

Harper is my home, and where my heart lives.

35

HARPER

ONE WEEK LATER

The farther we drive away from the city, the calmer everything becomes—not just around us, but inside me. The skyline fades behind tinted glass, replaced by stretches of highway and the steady rhythm of asphalt under tires. Trees blur past like they're exhaling, and summer is upon us. The days are longer, the sun is brighter, and it's one of my favorite seasons, other than fall.

We're still hours from Sugar Pine Springs, but my excitement is ready to bubble over.

Brody's behind the wheel of Easton's vintage, blacked-out Dodge Charger, and the longer we're in it, the more it feels like he was born to drive this car. It's all dark chrome, deep engine purr, and intimidation. A "fuck around and find out" car, as Easton has coined it. This isn't Brody's sleek black Range Rover with its silent confidence; it's louder. Bolder. Un-fucking-apologetic.

I glance at him from the passenger seat, sunlight cutting across his sexy face, and raise a brow. "So … when exactly did Easton give you permission to take his firstborn?"

Brody doesn't miss a beat. "He didn't."

I sit up straighter. "You're telling me you *stole* his car again?"

"I prefer *liberated*," he says, adjusting the rearview mirror with one hand while the other rests casually on the stick shift. "It practically begged me to take it."

"Brody," I groan, but chuckle, "Easton's really going to lose his shit this time."

"He'll be fine," he says, totally unbothered. "He needs to loosen up and go iron his socks."

"To be a fly on the wall when he finds out," I mutter. "Poor Lexi. She's going to have to listen to this until her babies are born. That might be the only thing that pulls him away from complaining about it."

"He's out of town until tomorrow. We'll be on the mountain by the time he notices."

I shake my head as laughter escapes me while I settle deeper into the seat. The Charger hums beneath us like she knows exactly where we're going. The open road stretches endlessly ahead, and the uncertainty doesn't feel like a threat, but more like a promise as we race to our secret escape.

Brody glances over at me, his hand leaving the shifter to slide toward me. His fingers find mine easily, lacing them together without looking down.

"You good?" he asks.

I nod, thumb brushing along his. "It just feels different this time. It's exciting."

His mouth curves, just slightly. "That's because it is."

When we cross the Tennessee state line, the sun dips lower behind us. And somewhere between stolen cars, back-road laughter, and the rhythm of his thumb against my skin, I realize we're not running anymore. We're going home.

By the time we pull up to the cabin, the last light of the day is caught in the trees—burnt orange bleeding into deep purple as the sun sinks behind the mountains. The Charger rumbles to a stop, its engine growling low, like it doesn't want the ride to be over. Brody kills the ignition and rests his hand on the gearshift for a second longer, eyes on the cabin ahead.

It looks just like I remember the first time I laid eyes on it—wood weathered by years of Tennessee rain, the wraparound porch draped in shadows, a porch light glowing, like our past selves have been waiting for us to return to the comfort.

I step out of the car, shoes crunching against gravel, and breathe in the scent of pine and damp earth. The air is cooler here, thinner, cleaner. It wraps around me like a welcome, slipping into my bones and settling deep inside of me.

Brody circles to the trunk, grabs our bags, and walks beside me. I loop my arm around his as he leads the way up the steps. He unlocks the door, and my heart races with anticipation. We step inside, and the cabin is warm. The lamp next to the couch glows yellow, and I replay all the special moments we shared here. There's a faint scent of cedar and vanilla hanging in the air, and music plays low from a record player in the corner that I never noticed before. It's like it's been playing since before we arrived. But it's the flowers that catch my breath.

A simple arrangement sits on the kitchen table—wildflowers in a glass jar, not overly done, not staged. Just intentional, like someone didn't want to make a big deal out of it but did anyway. I glance at Brody, and he avoids eye contact, pretending to fiddle with the luggage straps like they're suddenly complex knots.

"Okay," I say, "what's going on?"

He glances up, face carefully blank. "What do you mean?"

"This." I gesture around the room. "The music. The flowers. Did you hire a romance consultant while I wasn't looking?"

"Just wanted to make it nice for you," he says too casually. "And I didn't want to go grocery shopping."

My brows rise.

"We're not leaving the cabin for two weeks. Just me and you,

Sleeping Beauty." He chuckles, finally meeting my gaze. There's something warm behind his eyes.

I step forward, my fingers brushing his as I take one of the bags from his hand and set it on the floor.

"This is beautiful. Thank you."

"You're beautiful," he tells me.

The silence between us stretches for a beat, and it feels like standing on the edge of something bigger than the Tennessee sky.

I turn toward the living room, running my hand along the back of the couch, and let the coziness wash over me. The last time I was here, I was half broken, full of fear, and unsure of everything. But tonight, I'm none of those things. I'm a changed woman because of Brody and his love.

The night settles around us like an exhale, and even though Brody drove the entire eleven hours, he still makes us dinner.

It's simple though—grilled cheese and tomato soup. I try to help, but he insists I don't lift a finger. I let him win, mostly because I like watching him move around the kitchen; it's sexy. He doesn't talk much while he cooks, just hums to the soft music on the record player. Every so often, he steals a glance and a kiss, and I breathe in every moment.

Once our food is ready, he sets it down on the two-person table we've eaten many meals at.

"Wow, this is the best grilled cheese. Thanks, Chef," I say, loving how gooey it is.

He smirks. "You're welcome, cutie."

We exchange stolen glances and silent conversations. I never force Brody to speak, not when I know he's comfortable not to. It's fine because I don't need words to communicate with him. His eyes say everything he doesn't.

After we finish eating, he rinses our dishes and then leads me outside with our fingers interlocked. The chill nips at my bare arms, but I follow him without hesitation. Wood is already stacked in the firepit, and he bends over to start it. A few seconds later, with a click, lanterns light up in the backyard, creating a warm, ambient light.

A thick blanket is draped across one of the two Adirondack chairs, and there's that same jar of wildflowers on the little side table, swaying slightly in the breeze. I stop walking because it's absolutely magical. The simplicity of it, the care in how it's laid out, makes my throat tighten.

"You did all this for me?" I ask.

"Of course. Seeing the look on your face right now? Worth it."

He loops his finger in mine and leads me to the waiting chairs. I sink into it, and he sets the blanket over me before settling beside me, so close that our knees touch.

I let out a contented sigh, watching the fire and enjoying the warmth. Above us, the sky stretches wide and open, stars poking through in clusters, bright and scattered and wild. There's no city glow to drown them out here, and it feels like they're sparkling just for us.

Neither of us speaks as we watch the flames flicker. He reaches over and his hand finds mine. I glance over at him and smile because he's so calm. But the longer I watch him, the more I see he's holding something in. I notice it in how his thumb keeps running the same slow circle against mine and the way his jaw keeps flexing, like there's something caught behind his teeth.

I reach for him with my opposite hand, my fingers brushing across his scruff. "What's on your mind?"

He exhales through his nose, a shaky laugh caught somewhere in his chest. His eyes flick to mine, and whatever he's been holding back starts to surface. "You know me so well."

Brody leans forward and kisses me. It's not hurried or hungry, just soft. And I don't know if I've ever been kissed beneath the stars. His forehead rests against mine, our breaths mingling in the cool mountain air. The fire crackles beside us, casting orange light along his jaw. I watch his throat bob as he swallows, and for the first time since I've known Brody Calloway, he looks nervous.

"I've been trying to figure out how to say this," he starts, his voice low. "But every time I run through it in my head, it sounds too neat. Too practiced."

"Don't overthink it," I whisper, fingers lacing with his.

He nods once and exhales like he's bracing for a free fall, and then he shifts out of the chair and moves until he's on one knee in front of me.

My heart stops. Actually stops.

His hands don't shake, but there's tension in his shoulders.

"I didn't think forever was something I'd ever get," he says, eyes locked with mine. "Not with my past. Not with the way I'd lived. I thought I'd always be the guy who showed up when things fell apart, never the one who got to build something of his own."

Tears rise fast and hot behind my eyes, but I don't blink them away.

"But then you came crashing into my life with your fire and your stubbornness and your impossible strength. And suddenly, I didn't want to be the man who only protected people; I wanted to be the man who deserved you. The one who got to love you out loud with his full chest, without apology, exactly as you are."

He reaches into his pocket and pulls out a small box. The leather is worn at the corners. He opens it, and inside is a simple, timeless ring—platinum band, oval diamond, nothing excessive, just elegant.

My mother's ring.

I gasp, and I'm so overwhelmed by happiness that I don't realize I'm crying until tears drip down my cheeks.

"Your father gave it to me," he says, confirming it. "He mentioned how important it was for you to have this ring."

"Brody ..." His name comes out cracked and full of emotion.

"Harp, you didn't save me, but you made me want to be saved. And I want a life with you. A home. A million slow mornings and quiet nights and every messy, real, beautiful thing in between. Please marry me. Please be my wife. Please let me protect you and love you until my very last day."

I can't speak, but I nod hard, fast, too many times. And then I'm out of the chair and into his arms, the blanket falling to the ground as I kiss him through the tears, through the laughter, through the shaking in both of our hands.

"Yes," I finally manage against his mouth. "A billion times, yes."

He slips the ring onto my finger, and I stare at it like a piece of my heart has finally returned to me.

We hold each other under the stars, the fire warm beside us, the trees swaying like they're witnesses. And as he presses his lips to my temple, I know this isn't a dream. It's my reality. We lie together until the fire burns down, and instead of adding more, Brody stands, lifting me into his arms and carrying me over his shoulder like a caveman.

"Brody Calloway!" I say with a laugh as his hand lands firmly on my ass. "I thought we talked about this!"

"We did," he says as he takes the steps up the porch and takes me inside.

The door closes behind us, and he sets me on my feet.

We're smiles and laughs as he takes my hand in his. He twists the ring with his thumb; the cool metal against my skin feels like it belongs there, like my finger has always been waiting for him.

I glance down at it again as he leads me to the couch and stacks logs in the fireplace. The wood immediately catches, and the diamond sparkles. When I look at him, I know that he's everything I've ever wanted and dreamed about. His smile hasn't faded since I said yes.

Brody moves into the kitchen, and I watch him as he pours two fingers of whiskey into mismatched tumblers.

He joins me on the couch with a cute grin and hands me mine. He lifts his glass. "To forever."

"And ever," I add.

We clink our glasses together and drink, his eyes never fully leaving mine.

Brody isn't just someone I love; he's the man I chose. And

tonight, under the stars, he chose me too. It's the greatest feeling I've ever experienced—to love and be loved while also being seen.

I set my glass down on the coffee table and move closer to him. The tips of my fingers brush under his shirt, against his skin. His breath catches, just slightly, the space between us stretching thin.

"I wished for this life with you."

His hand finds my waist, warm and steady. "Guess I'm proof wishes come true."

"I forgot how much of a smart-ass you are, Calloway," I joke.

He chuckles, then kisses me slower. His lips move against mine with the kind of hunger that isn't about urgency but meaning. My fingers lightly trace across the hard lines of his stomach. I love the way his groans sound against my mouth.

He pulls me close until I'm straddling his lap, both of us breathless. His hands slide beneath the hem of my shirt, palms rubbing up my back.

"You're going to be my wife," he whispers, his mouth brushing the curve of my neck.

"I can't wait."

He kisses me again, and this time, there's no holding back. My heart pounds so hard that I can feel it in my throat. He just proposed, and I said yes. His blue eyes are dark, hungry, and I can feel the bulge in his pants straining against the fabric, begging for my attention. My mouth waters as I think about having him for dessert.

I slide off him and drop to my knees on the carpet, my fingers trembling as I reach for his belt. The leather slides free with a hiss, and I can hear his breath hitch above me. My fingers fumble with the button of his jeans, and after I finally pop it open, the zipper comes down with a slow, zipping sound. His cock springs free, already hard as fucking steel, the thick vein running along the underside pulsing with every heartbeat.

"This cock is mine," I whisper, my voice thick with lust.

"Then own it," he quips.

"Plan on it," I say, tilting my head, wrapping my hand around his shaft, feeling the heat radiating from him.

I lick my lips, leaning in closer, my breath ghosting over the swollen head, where pre-cum is already beading. The scent of him is intoxicating—musky, primal—and my eyelids flutter as I take him into my mouth.

My tongue swirls around the tip, savoring the salty taste of him. His groan is deep, nearly a growl, and it vibrates through me as I take him deeper, inch by inch. My lips stretch around his girth, my jaw aching in the best fucking way as I work him into my throat. His hands grip my hair, not guiding me, just holding on for dear life as I sink down until my nose brushes against his pelvis.

"Fuck," he whispers.

I pull back, letting my tongue drag along the length of him before plunging back down, deeper this time. My throat opens up for him, swallowing him whole, and I can feel his cock twitch against my tongue as I suck him off like my life depends on it.

My hand joins in, stroking what my mouth can't reach, twisting and tugging in rhythm with my head bobbing. Saliva drips from my lips, coating his dick in a slick wetness. The sound of my mouth working him is obscene. It's wet, sloppy, and I can hear every fucking slurp, loving every guttural moan that escapes his lips.

"I'm so close," he warns, his fingers tightening in my hair.

But I don't stop. I *can't* stop. I want to taste him, feel him spilling down my throat.

My free hand slides into my panties, rubbing my clit, feeling the fabric already soaked with my arousal. The pressure builds as I suck him deeper, faster, my head bobbing until he's fucking my face, his hips jerking with every thrust.

"I'm gonna ..." he starts, but I cut him off by swallowing him whole again, letting his cock hit the back of my throat.

With a guttural growl, he comes. Hot, salty liquid shoots down my throat, and I swallow every drop, my mouth milking him until he's spent and trembling above me. When I finally pull back, my lips are swollen and slick, my chest heaving as I look up at him. His cock is still twitching, still hard, and I know this is just the beginning.

"Your turn," he whispers, his voice dripping with sin.

I smile, and the look in his eyes says it all. Tonight, he's going to rock my fucking world.

36

BRODY

Her mouth is swollen and wet, still glistening with me. She's on her knees between my legs, looking up at me like I'm pure sin, and the only thing I can think is how badly I need to ruin her. Completely. Thoroughly. One orgasm at a time, until she's shaking and wrecked and doesn't remember her own name, only mine.

She licks her lips like she's proud of herself. She should be. But this round? It's mine.

"Your turn." My voice is full of want and need.

She barely nods before I scoop her up with one hand under her thighs, the other around her back. She wraps her arms around my neck, laughing breathlessly as I carry her down the hallway toward the bedroom.

"Queen treatment," she says.

"Fuck yes," I growl. "I love having you in my arms."

The bedroom is dark, but I don't bother flipping a switch. I don't need to see her in anything but shadows and skin. I lay her down in the center of the bed, slow and deliberate, like I'm offering her up to myself. She props herself on her elbows, watching me as I strip off my shirt, and then I meet her eyes.

"Let me undress you," I say.

She lifts her hips and lets me peel her leggings down, dragging her panties with them, leaving her bare and beautiful in the middle of my bed. Our bed.

My gaze rakes over every inch of her. Her thighs are already glistening, her pussy flushed and swollen, begging for my mouth, my fingers, and my cock.

I kneel between her legs and drag her down the mattress until her ass is flush with the edge, and then I place her knees over my shoulders. She gasps when I spread her open, my tongue already flicking out to taste every drop of her.

"Brody!" she gasps, breath catching as I flatten my tongue against her clit and lick her slow.

She tastes like everything I've ever wanted—sweet. Fuck, she's soaked, dripping for me. I devour her like a man starved, my tongue working in circles, then fast flicks, then long, greedy strokes that make her hips buck and her hands claw at the sheets. Her thighs start to tremble around my head. I suck her clit into my mouth as she whimpers, her cries high, needy. It's a broken sound that makes my cock throb against the mattress.

"Keep going," she begs.

I slide two fingers into her tight cunt, curling them just right, dragging them against that spot that makes her see stars. Her body arches off the bed, and I know she's right there, suspended on the edge, ready to fall over. I can taste it. I can see it in the way every muscle in her body tenses.

"That's it, sweetheart," I mutter against her soft pussy. "Come for me."

As if I snapped my fingers, Harper shatters.

Her legs lock around my head, and she cries out my name like it's the only word she knows. Her pussy tightens around my fingers, wet and pulsing, as I ride it out with her, licking her through every wave until she's twitching, breathless, begging.

"I need to feel you." She gasps. "Inside me."

I rise up and drag my cock along her soaked entrance. "Your wish is my command."

I thrust into her in one slow, hard stroke.

She screams out in pleasure when I sink into her—tight, wet, pulsing around me, like her body was made to take every inch.

My hands grip her thighs, spreading her wider as I drive in deeper, grinding my hips into hers until I'm buried to the hilt. Her pussy squeezes around me like a fist, and I bite out a curse as I pull back and slam into her again.

"Fuck, Harp," I groan out, sweat already beading down my spine. "You feel like heaven, wrapped in sin."

Her head rolls back against the mattress, lips parted, eyes glassy and wild. "Don't you even think about stopping."

I shift her legs up, folding them toward her chest so I can go deeper, harder, the sound of skin on skin echoing in the room like a goddamn rhythm. Her guttural groans only encourage me to fuck her harder.

"You wanted to taste me on your knees?" I pant, thrusting deep enough to make her cry out. "Now I'm going to fuck you until you're a Calloway."

"Yes. Yes, please—"

Her voice breaks on the last word as I slam into her again, her breath catching with every stroke. I reach between us, rubbing her clit in tight, punishing circles that make her body jerk beneath me. She's already so close again. I can feel it in the way she trembles, the way her thighs start to shake, how her pussy clenches, like she's trying to drag me in deeper than I can go.

"You're going to come again," I order, voice feral. "On my cock."

Her eyes roll back, her lips parting in a silent scream as her body seizes around me, orgasm tearing through her like a lightning strike. She spasms beneath me, sobbing my name, her pussy milking me so tight that it takes everything I have not to come with her.

I grab her hips and flip her over before the last wave even

finishes, dragging her up onto her knees, her ass in the air, back arched like a fucking dream. I slide back into her from behind, gripping her hair as I drive into her again.

"Look at you. So fucking beautiful," I growl in her ear. "And completely wrecked for me."

"Only for you," she chokes out. "Only ever for you."

I thrust into her again, and again, and again, until I feel the pressure in my balls, in every fucking nerve in my body. She's tight, soaked, clutching me with every pulse, and I know I can't last much longer. I'm barely holding on.

"Come inside me. I want all of it," she gasps, holding the comforter with tight fists.

My whole body locks as I thrust deep and come with a roar, emptying into her in thick, hot waves. My cock twitches inside her as I ride it out, breath ragged, muscles burning. We collapse onto the bed together, tangled and heaving. Her body is pressed against mine, both of us slick with sweat, shaking with aftershocks. I bury my face in her hair and wrap my arm tight around her waist.

"Harp," I whisper, "you're going to be the death of me."

She laughs, satisfied, snuggling closer. She looks into my eyes and grins. "At least you'll die happy."

She's not wrong.

By the time we return to Manhattan, everything feels louder.

Even the air is hotter, more humid, like the city's already gearing up to test our patience this summer. The Charger glides into the private garage beneath my building, but I barely register the motion. Harper's next to me in the passenger seat, hair curled over one shoulder, sunglasses on despite the overcast sky, legs crossed like she doesn't realize how much she's ruined me. She's wearing the ring that was always meant to be hers. It's an oval spark of forever that holds more sentiment than any diamond ring I could've created for her. I catch her twisting it now and then, like she's making sure it's still there. I don't think I'll ever get used to how fucking beautiful she is without even trying.

Tonight, Asher is throwing a get-together—part cocktail party, part networking trap, part power play—but underneath it all, it's just his way of making sure people don't forget how he can ruin them if he wants. It's private. Exclusive. A cashmere-and-caviar kind of night. Everyone who's anyone will be there, except Easton and Lexi.

Easton texted me earlier, saying Lexi will deliver their triplets any day now, and she's on bed rest until the babies come. We're all pretending not to hover, but the truth is, none of us are more than one text away. If Lexi sneezes twice in a row, Easton will put the entire Calloway family on lockdown.

I reach for Harper's hand, leading her into the elevator. She's wearing a black satin dress, with a scandalous little thigh slit, and no back. She wore it just for me and knows exactly what seeing her so dressed up does to my self-control.

I lean in close, whispering in her ear, "If you're trying to make it impossible for me to focus tonight, you're doing a great fucking job."

"I am," she says boldly.

She kisses the edge of my jaw just as the elevator opens, and we step into Asher's townhome that's an entire building. And just like that, the temperature shifts.

People are everywhere—men in tailored suits and shiny shoes, women in heels that could kill a man if they were aimed in the right direction. Waitstaff move around the large floor with trays of champagne and charcuterie. Music hums from invisible speakers, just enough to let people talk without revealing too much. The last time I was here, Weston proposed to Carlee, and it feels like a lifetime has passed since then.

I spot Billie and Asher near the bar area. My cousin is wearing a midnight-blue gown, and Asher's hand is possessively resting on the small of her back, like he dares anyone to look twice. She lifts her glass when she sees us, her mouth twisting up into something that says she's ready to stir trouble.

Harper squeezes my hand. "Ready for this?"

I glance at her ring, then back up at her eyes. "I've already got everything I want."

When we move closer to them, Billie is already smirking like she saw the diamond on Harper's finger from a mile away, but she doesn't say anything.

"Happy you're back in the city," Billie says, hugging Harper. "I was scared you two were going to move there."

"We were gone for two weeks," Harper says.

"Two weeks too long," Billie tells her as I grab a drink from the tray behind her.

"You know you were occupied with Banks while we were gone," I say to her with a brow lifted.

"It's not a lie." Asher raises his glass in a lazy salute. "Welcome back, lovebirds."

Billie gives Harper a once-over. "You look radiant. That's either post-sex glow or a facial. Knowing you, it's both."

I glance at Harper's flushed cheeks and the way her mouth twitches with the effort to not give herself away.

I lean into her ear. "You want to tell them, or should I?"

She smiles, then lifts her hand subtly, just enough for the light to cast little rainbows from her finger.

Billie's mouth drops open a full inch before she recovers. "*Finally.*"

Asher grins and gives Harper a side hug. "Welcome to the Calloway club. Careful, they're cranky."

Billie gives him a playful smack, and I shrug.

"No lies detected," I say. "You're lucky I'm in a good mood."

We don't have long to enjoy the moment before I hear the unmistakable sound of Weston with his loud laughter and exaggerated storytelling. He rounds the corner with Carlee on his arm, grinning like he owns the room. He does. No matter what, Weston is the life of every party he attends.

"Are we celebrating something?" he calls out, eyes scanning the group of us as he approaches. He's wearing a green velvet blazer, no tie, and the kind of tailored pants that say *I know my angles*. His charm hits like champagne—bubbly, a little too much, but entirely effective.

Carlee has that effortless grace she always carries. Her hair is up, and her emerald earrings catch the light.

"Look who decided to show up," Weston says, squeezing my shoulder before pulling Harper into a full-body hug like she's his favorite person on earth. "You're glowing. What did he do? Or do I want to know?"

Carlee raises a brow at Harper, then at me, then back again. Her eyes narrow like a woman who can predict what Harper will say.

"You've got that *I said yes to something big* look," she tells her in a soft voice.

Harper lifts her hand again, slower this time, the smile stretching across her face. "Guess I'll be a Calloway after all."

She sticks her tongue out at Weston. There was a time when she tried to date Easton and then Weston, but they turned her down. The thought makes me laugh now.

"Yes! I knew it! Easton owes me a hundred thousand dollars!" Weston shouts, taking two dramatic steps back and throwing both hands in the air like he's been personally attacked by joy. "I love this for me and for you too! Congrats!"

Harper's laughing so hard that she has to lean into my side for support.

Carlee pulls Harper into a tight hug. "I knew it! Congratulations. So happy for the two of you. Truly."

I nod. "Thank you."

"No, thank *you*," Weston says, grabbing my hand and shaking it like I just saved a civilization. "Billie and I were both losing patience."

"I was not," Billie chimes in, sipping her champagne. "I was waiting with elegance and judgment. I knew it would happen. I'd wished it would."

Weston turns to Harper, takes both of her hands, and kisses the air beside each cheek. "Did you elope?"

"No! You're so annoying," Harper tells him, smacking him. "Control your brother," she says to Billie.

"Control him? *Pfft*. Impossible," Billie replies.

"She's right," Carlee agrees. "Weston has a mind of his own."

There's another round of toasts, and before I know it, someone's passed us new drinks. The mood in the room has shifted now—our announcement rippling outward through the party in low whispers and congratulations. Tonight was how we planned to announce that we were official, and it worked exactly as we'd predicted.

I glance at Harper, admiring her, and I take her hand in mine, kissing her fingers. Our eyes meet, and I shoot her a wink, ready to leave this fucking place. A small smile plays across her lips, like she knows exactly what I'm thinking, and I think she does.

The music shifts to something slower, sultrier, with a low drumbeat woven through it. As my eyes scan the room, I spot Nick near the back wall, half in shadow, nursing a drink and smirking at his phone, which makes his face glow bright.

He's leaning against a column, cocky as fuck, like he has nowhere to be and everything to hide, which is how I know he's up to something. Dressed in black on black, the collar of his shirt unbuttoned just enough to hint at trouble. He looks like the guy every girl here is watching out of the corner of her eye. The type of guy every father warns his daughter about.

Harper notices him, too, and drags me across the room with her toward him. "Didn't think you'd show," Harper says. "Know how much you love your brother's business parties."

He lifts his chin. "And miss the Calloway-Banks merger announcement? Please. This party's basically a shareholder meeting now."

Harper snorts beside me. "Don't be dramatic, stepbro."

"Ew, yeah, don't call me that. Asher was right. It's weird," Nick replies without hesitation. Then, his eyes gleaming, he adds, "Tonight I'm being well-behaved. For once."

That earns him a suspicious look from Billie, who's walking up beside Harper.

"You're grinning like someone who isn't," Billie says, tilting her head. "Which means you're either hiding something or freshly laid."

She's great at serving a hefty dose of reality. It's one of her best qualities.

Nick raises his brows in mock innocence. "Can't it be both?"

"God help us," Asher mutters.

Carlee steps in, watching Nick like a bored socialite, but I know who she is and why LadyLux matters. "He's been in a suspiciously good mood lately. I think he's seeing someone and won't admit it," Carlee says.

Nick just smirks. He doesn't confirm or deny. It's the best policy when keeping secrets.

Harper watches him for a second longer, head tilted slightly. She's known him longer than any of us, other than Asher. "You're different."

Nick's smile falters, just for a beat, but he catches it quickly. "New haircut."

I don't push him. Not yet. But something's changed.

And I have a feeling we're all going to find out exactly what that is very soon.

37

HARPER

ONE WEEK LATER

B illie's office smells like flowers, cookies, and magazines.
Sunlight filters in through the massive windows behind
her desk, catching on the glass-topped table we've turned into
ground zero for wedding planning chaos. Swatches of fabric are
laid out like battle plans. Mood boards lean against the wall.
There's an open bottle of champagne chilling in a brass ice bucket
beside a tray of pastries we've barely touched but insisted on
having delivered anyway.

Billie is lounging on the curved ivory couch in the corner. She's
barefoot, legs tucked under her, her oversized sweater half falling
off one shoulder, like she styled it that way on purpose. Her tablet's
in one hand, champagne in the other, and she's flipping through a
digital lookbook like she's vetting designers for Paris Fashion
Week. A curated spread of bridal magazines is fanned out on the
floor in front of her.

Across from her, Mia is perched in a leather chair, dressed in
head-to-toe cream and sipping champagne like it's a business
expense, which, knowing her, it probably is. I'm so happy to see her

smiling and well. Each time I look at her, I think about what Brody told me and how they found her. I still carry guilt, but I'm trying to heal from that. Therapy has helped a lot.

"As Bellamore's chief marketing officer," she says, holding up her tablet like a gavel, "I feel obligated to point out that a dual-wedding campaign could fuel an entire year's worth of brand expansion with coordinated content drops. We can interweave narrative arcs and launch a limited-edition capsule line in celebration. I've already mocked up a hashtag: #callowaywedding."

Billie sighs, setting down her glass. "You know Harper's going to want barefoot vows under a tree somewhere."

"Which will look *incredible* on drone footage," Mia says without missing a beat. "And I assume yours will be in a castle, Ice Queen?"

"Château de Villette," Billie confirms. "It's going to be cinematic."

I glance between the two of them, laughing into the rim of my glass. "Are either of you planning to let me make a single decision about my wedding?"

"Of course," they say in unison, and I expect nothing less.

"I want to get married in the same place my brother did in Cozy Creek—it was gorgeous. On top of the mountain this fall."

Mia leans forward, swiping through her notes. "This is perfect. A fall wedding. Oh my gourd!"

"Oh, stop," I tell her.

"You're a key part of Bellamore, Harp. Your wedding has brand equity. We can't just leave it to chance. I mean, do you want a dress reveal that breaks the internet or not?"

It's ridiculous. It's excessive. It's us. And it feels damn good.

Laughter escapes me as I glance at my best friend. Billie and I have built something bigger than a fashion house. Bigger than the brand. This feels like a celebration of surviving everything that tried to break us, and we did it in designer heels with a custom color palette.

"Harp wants something timeless," Billie adds. "And a man who looks at her like she's his whole world. Which she has. Other than that, she doesn't care."

That sobers me a little. Not in a bad way, just in the way simple truth always does. I glance down at my ring, replaying how Brody proposed to me and how his eyes sparkled only for me. The firepit is still in Tennessee, but the warmth of that night hasn't faded. I can still feel it in my chest every time I breathe.

Billie tosses a swatch in my lap. It's light-rose-gold satin, soft and expensive. "Thoughts for bridesmaid dresses?"

I run my fingers over the fabric. "If we're being dressed like champagne, I'm in."

Mia lifts her glass. "Cheers to that."

Laughter spreads through the space like silk, and it feels so easy.

As I look around, I know the storm is over and our wounds are healing. Eventually, everything that happened will be a distant memory, a scar that's forgotten. After it's all said and done, we're women who bled for what we built, and now we're planning new beginnings.

Mia's phone buzzes, and she excuses herself with a dramatic eye roll. She mumbles something about a campaign asset that can't wait until Monday, even though it definitely could. Billie watches her leave with a smirk, then turns back to me with a little sigh, sinking deeper into the couch.

For a moment, neither of us says anything.

The room goes quiet in that rare, gentle way it only does between people who are best friends. We've never needed words either.

The sunlight slants lower across the table, catching the edge of my ring again. I twist it on my finger because I still can't believe it's real.

"She suits this place," Billie finally says, nodding toward the door Mia just walked through. "You picked the perfect person for the job."

I set my glass on the table that's holding our swatches. "Mia's terrifyingly competent. I used to think she'd burn out in six months. Nope, she's as obsessed as us."

Billie glances over at me. "She's a great asset."

I lean back in my chair. "Do you ever look around and wonder how the hell we got here?"

"All the time," she says. "Especially after having two glasses of champagne before noon."

I study the way she's relaxed. It's in her posture, in the softness around her eyes. She still looks like she could cut through a boardroom with nothing but her tone and stilettos, but today, she also looks like someone who let herself believe in something again.

"I almost gave up on all of this," I admit, my voice lower now. "Not just love. Everything. The company. The idea that I could still be someone outside of the bad that happened."

Billie's expression shifts, and she's not surprised, just intrigued.

"I did give up," she admits. "A few times actually. But you … you never let me disappear. You never let me forget who I was."

"I believed in you. I still do," I say, remembering how hard she worked to save Bellamore after her ex tried to take everything away from us.

"You stood by me when I didn't believe in myself, Harp." She looks away, toward the window, like she's trying to hold back her emotions. "You stayed by my side anyway."

I nod, throat tight. "That's what we do, right?"

"Yes," she whispers. "It's what we do. Love you, Harp. Thank you for being my very best friend. I will walk through the fire with you."

I feel my emotions bubble. "It's mutual."

The silence that fills the room is the kind that lives in truth. In shared history. In all the versions of us that got buried along the way, and all the new ones we're still becoming.

She leans forward, her eyes on my ring now. "Brody's good for you. He doesn't try to take anything from you. He just shows up."

A smile touches my lips. "That's what Brody has *always* done best."

She reaches over and squeezes my hand once, then leans back with a little sigh. "All right, enough emotional vulnerability. Let's pick floral palettes before I start crying and have to fire someone for seeing it."

BY THE TIME BILLIE LAUNCHES INTO AN ARGUMENT OVER TABLE arrangements—"Round tables are elegant, Harper, not basic"—I slip out of her office and into the hall, needing a snack. Or air. I could be a little drunk. Okay, I'm tipsy.

I slide onto the bench beside the showroom window and pull out my phone. A new text is waiting, time-stamped five minutes ago.

> **BRODY**
> How's the day drinking on the clock?
>
> **BRODY**
> Should I send a rescue team or a pizza?

I smile before I can stop it.

> **HARPER**
> Billie is currently rage-pinning silk ribbon colors. Pray for me.

Three dots appear immediately, then disappear, then appear again. I can almost see him pacing our penthouse, shirtless and barefoot, pretending he's not waiting for me like I'm his plan.

BRODY

Tell her I'll forgive her for stealing you during your lunch break ... if she sends me a cake.

BRODY

Or you in nothing but frosting.

My cheeks flush as I bite back a laugh.

HARPER

That could be arranged.

He replies with a photo—him on the couch, shirtless, legs stretched out, a glass of whiskey in one hand and that lazy smirk on his face that says he knows exactly what he's doing to me.

BRODY

Remind me again why you're planning a wedding right now? Seems like a lot of work when we could be naked.

I roll my eyes, thumbs moving fast.

HARPER

Because I want flowers, vows, and a custom dress I get to cry in. And Billie will actually divorce me as a friend if we elope and don't tell her. She still hasn't forgiven Easton.

BRODY

Yes, she has.

HARPER

Doesn't mean she'll ever let him live it down.

BRODY

That's true. Hurry, future wifey. I miss you so damn much.

I tuck my phone to my chest for a second, letting the smile

linger. This is what it feels like to be wanted without urgency and to be loved without conditions.

My phone buzzes one more time, and I glance down at it.

BRODY

I love you.

And just like that, butterflies swarm inside me.

THE PARTY PLANNING SPIRALED INTO A THREE-HOUR DEBATE OVER china patterns, signature cocktails, and Billie's refusal to wear anything floral for any pre-wedding events. She mentioned Easton is on high alert—Lexi's due any day, and he's packed their hospital bag with color-coded backups like it's a military operation.

By the time I hug her goodbye and escape Bellamore, I'm tired, but not in a bad way. I'm happier than I've ever been.

It's late when I finally make it home. The lights are low when I step inside.

Brody's sprawled across the couch in a T-shirt, one arm slung over the back cushion, his expression relaxed and open in a way that still makes my chest tighten. *The Golden Girls* is on the TV, and he looks at me like he's been waiting for this moment all day.

"Hey," I say, kicking off my heels and moving toward him.

"Hey," he says with a smoldering smirk. "I ordered Thai. It's in the kitchen."

God, I love him.

I walk straight into his arms, sinking into his lap, letting my forehead rest against his neck. He holds me without question, without words, his hands running through my hair. I lie on him like that for a long time, just breathing, recharging, and reconnecting.

Brody pulls back slightly and taps his phone, eyes scanning the screen. "There's something you should see."

He turns the phone so I can read it, and for a moment, my brain doesn't register the words. I have to read it several times.

MICAH RHODES: SENTENCED TO LIFE IN FEDERAL PRISON WITH NO PAROLE. MULTIPLE COUNTS OF KIDNAPPING, MURDER, EXTORTION, AND WIRE FRAUD.

I STARE AT IT FOR A LONG MOMENT, AND IT DOESN'T HIT ME LIKE I thought it would. There's no rush of vindication, no cathartic sob, just a slow breath. It's anticlimactic, complete indifference.

"It's really over," I whisper.

Brody meets my eyes. "It was over the second you walked away from him."

"You mean the moment you carried me out of his place?"

"Yes," he agrees.

"The world knows the truth now," I say, my throat tightening.

His lips brush my temple. "This is his legacy."

I pull away from him. "Justice has been served. Thankfully."

"You're free, Harp. Billie is too."

"Only because of you. I'm so thankful." I fall against him again.

My fingers slide under the hem of his shirt to feel the warm, steady rhythm of his heartbeat, because right now, Brody is all that matters. Not the past. Not the pain.

Just this. Just us. And the life we're building together.

38

BRODY

When my phone rapidly buzzes on the counter, I'm mid-bite of an over-toasted bagel that Harper cooked for me for breakfast. She tried, so I'll eat it with a smile.

One look at the screen, and I know something's up. Weston's name flashes across it, his message in all caps, like he's already yelling through the text before I've even opened it.

WESTON

> IT'S HAPPENING!!!!

WESTON

> EASTON'S LOST HIS DAMN MIND!

WESTON

> BUT ALSO LEXI'S GIVING BIRTH. BRING
> CHAMPAGNE! FUCK IT, BRING BOURBON!

I blink, reread it once, then twice. "Harp," I call out toward the hallway, "Lexi's in labor."

There's a beat of silence, followed by the unmistakable thump of Harper's feet scrambling across hardwood. She appears in the doorway a second later, still barefoot, still brushing her hair back from her face, eyes wide with excitement. "Now?"

"Now," I say, grabbing my keys. "Weston's text was a full-blown emergency alert."

She grins and disappears into the bedroom again. I hear drawers opening and the zip of a garment bag being yanked free. I finish my coffee in three gulps and slide my phone into my back pocket.

By the time she's back, she's wearing shorts, an oversized T-shirt, and the engagement ring that still makes my chest tight every time I see it catch the light.

"You ready?" I ask.

She pulls on her shoes. "I was born ready. But also, are we stopping for snacks? Because Easton's going to stress-eat everything in sight."

"I'm more worried about Billie trying to reorganize the hospital."

"She will," Harper mutters. "And she'll do it in heels."

We pile into the Range Rover and head for the hospital. The morning traffic is light, which feels like some divine favor. The group chat is blowing up, and our phones are buzzing nonstop with replies in the group thread.

BILLIE

Easton is hyperventilating. Weston is flirting with the anesthesiologist to get updates. God help us all.

CARLEE

I have snacks and tissues. I'm emotionally prepared. Can't say the same for your brothers.

ASHER

I've got Billie. She's pacing like she's the one going into labor. Send backup. Anyone grab bourbon?

WESTON

Apparently, booze isn't allowed. I asked.

Harper's laughing beside me, scrolling and snorting as she reads me every new text. The sunlight beams through the windshield and hits her cheeks, and at that moment, I realize I don't just love her; I love all of it, and having her beside me in the excitement with the family she's inheriting. However, she's always felt like family, and she's always been a part of the Calloway chaos.

By the time we reach the hospital, it's already a scene. There are two nurses standing just outside the maternity wing, whispering like they've seen a ghost—or worse, a Calloway in crisis. Weston's voice booms from down the hall before we even turn the corner, followed closely by what sounds like someone knocking over a magazine rack.

Harper and I step into the waiting area, and it's exactly what I expected … chaos in designer clothing.

Weston is pacing in front of the nurses' station like he's waiting for a stock to drop or the second coming of Christ. He's wearing a camel coat, leather gloves, and sunglasses—indoors—gesturing wildly with a bottle of sparkling water like a microphone.

"Three babies," he says to no one in particular. "You understand? That's like … that's a trilogy."

Carlee's seated in the corner near the windows, calm and polished as ever, pulling various snacks from her enormous quilted tote like she's been tasked with catering the apocalypse. A nurse thanks her for the protein bars, and she smiles like she's their little helper. She's the only calm one here.

I glance at her, and she shrugs, completely unfazed. "My family is huge. I'm used to this."

Billie sits on the edge of the couch with her phone in one hand, and the other taps against her knee. Her light coat is draped over the armrest in a perfect fold. She's tense in that way only Billie can be—poised, dressed to kill, and seconds away from micromanaging someone into submission.

Asher sits beside her, scrolling through his phone with the dead-eyed calm of a man who knows the only way to survive is to let this play out. He's actually one of the most patient people I've ever met, until he's not.

"Welcome to the circus," Asher says without looking up.

"Lexi's still in labor?" Harper asks as we sit down beside them.

"Not sure. We haven't gotten another update yet," Billie says. "Easton's currently in a supply closet, practicing breathing exercises and contemplating the fragility of life."

"Weston's not helping," Carlee adds. "He's been running bets on who will cry first when the babies arrive."

I glance across the room just as Weston waves at us.

"My money's on me!" he shouts. "Or Brody. He's got that *sensitive, soon-to-be-married man* glow."

Harper leans into my side. "Do not engage. That's what he wants."

"I make no promises."

We fall into an easy rhythm after that—someone refills coffee, Asher pulls up a baseball schedule to distract Weston, Billie complains about the hospital's slow-as-hell Wi-Fi, and Harper grabs a pen and starts sketching something on the back of a discharge pamphlet. I watch her for a while. Her brow is furrowed, her fingers moving like they already know the future. She's calm and settled, glowing in that way people do when they're happy.

And for a moment, in the middle of the noise and the nonsense, I realize this is our version of normal now. I wouldn't trade it for anything.

The nurse clears her throat, pulling everyone's attention away. "Mama's doing great. All three babies are healthy—two boys and a girl. All breathing well on their own. No complications."

It's like someone presses play again on the entire room and raises the volume. Carlee gasps first, covering her mouth with both hands as tears spring to her eyes. Billie exhales, her shoulders finally dropping. Weston lets out a yelp so loud that it startles the nurse, and Asher mutters something that sounds suspiciously like, "I owe you five thousand bucks."

I can't stop smiling.

Harper reaches for my hand, and I take it without thinking, threading our fingers together. This is joy—the real kind. The unfiltered kind that makes everything else worth it.

"They're perfect?" Carlee asks, her voice shaky.

She and Lexi have been best friends since they met in college. They're as close as Billie and Harper.

The nurse nods with a smile. "They're beautiful. Mom's asking for some quiet before visitors, but Dad says he'll be out in a second."

Weston fans himself with a takeout menu, like he's just witnessed a miracle.

Asher claps a hand on my shoulder. "You ever think about what you'd do with three at once?"

"Pass out," I say.

Harper squeezes my hand. "You'd be a great dad."

I look down at her and smile. "Want to find out?"

Her eyes soften in that way that says she wants that future. One with cribs and midnight feedings and someone laughing in the background while we lose our minds together.

And right then, Easton walks through the doors.

He's pale, grinning, a little stunned, like someone just told him he's now the CEO of the moon and handed him three screaming interns. His hair's a mess, his shirt half untucked, but his eyes shine like the sun.

"They're here," he says, his voice hoarse.

We know that, but hearing him say it hits different.

"They're so damn small," he adds, rubbing his face. "And perfect. And *loud*."

Billie's already up and hugging him before he can continue.

Carlee wraps her arms around them both. Weston claps him on the back and then immediately starts suggesting names, like Rogue, Riot, and Moxie.

Easton laughs and takes it, arms around the people who care about him the most. I stand back, watching the moment unfold, thinking this is what family looks like. This is my family.

When we're finally allowed in, the nursery room is quiet. Not silent exactly because there's a low hum of equipment and the occasional beep of a monitor, but it's hushed, like everyone knows something sacred just happened.

Lexi is resting, propped up against pillows with a pink flush in her cheeks and that glazed, exhausted look only brand-new mothers have. She's wearing an expression that's equal parts disbelief and awe. Easton hasn't moved more than a foot from her side, his hand on hers, his other arm protectively looped around the tiny bassinet beside them.

There are three of them, all swaddled like little burritos while they sleep.

Two boys and one girl.

The boys are identical—at least from where I'm standing. They wear pale blue hats and have wrinkled little faces. Their pink mouths twitch in their sleep, like they're all dreaming of milk or mutiny. The baby girl is in the middle, dressed in soft lavender, already squirming a little more than her brothers. I can already tell she's going to be a handful and give Easton a run for his billions. The thought makes me smirk.

Harper steps closer, her hands clutching the edge of the bassinet as she stares down at them. I move beside her, wrapping an arm around her waist, watching her expression change from surprise and wonder to absolute awe.

"Do they have names yet?" she asks.

Lexi smiles, half delirious but proud. "Almost. We've narrowed it down to six hundred."

Easton grunts. "I was vetoed on anything starting with an *X* or a *Z*."

"You suggested Xander, Xavier, and Xenon," Lexi mumbles.

"Xenon is cool. Sounds like a superhero," he says.

"Or a printer," Weston tells him.

"Or a cult leader," Billie says, walking over to admire her niece and nephews. "Lex, please don't let him name the babies something ridiculous."

"I won't," Lexi confirms with a wink. "But if it were up to him ..."

Easton places a kiss on Lexi's head, and I love seeing them together. It's true love, the real kind.

Weston lifts one of the babies like he's holding Simba. "I've claimed this one," he announces. "We've already bonded. He blinked twice at me, which is obviously the Calloway family sign for *mentor me*."

"Put him back before Easton tackles you," Billie says, but her voice is warm beneath the sarcasm.

Carlee is already snapping photos, misty-eyed and beaming. "You should frame this," she tells Lexi. "It's your beginning."

I glance at Harper again. She's still staring at the babies like she's mesmerized.

"Do you want to hold one?" I ask, nudging her.

Her eyes flick to mine. "Can I?"

Lexi nods without hesitation. "Please. There are plenty of them to go around."

Harper reaches down and carefully lifts the baby girl, cradling her like she's held a hundred newborns before this. She rocks side to side instinctively; the baby snuggles into her like she knows she's safe.

I didn't think witnessing this would hit my emotions so hard. Watching Harper with that little purple-swathed bundle in her arms—her expression soft, her body quiet, her eyes shining—it punches something deep in my chest.

She catches me staring and raises a brow. "See something interesting?"

"This suits you," I whisper into her ear.

A smile tugs at her mouth. "Dangerous thing to say to a woman holding a baby."

We're not supposed to be in here this long, but no one's telling us to leave.

Lexi's eyes are heavy, but she keeps smiling every time someone leans in to grab her hand or whisper congratulations. Easton hasn't stopped watching her, as if he blinks too long, she'll vanish. One hand still grips the back of her shoulder, like he's afraid the moment might float away without him. A nurse peeks in to check vitals, sees us all still gathered, and just shakes her head fondly before ducking out. A minute later, she returns with a Polaroid camera.

"Want a group photo?" she asks.

It's chaos after that.

Weston tries to fix his collar in the reflection of the monitor. Billie is directing lighting from the edge of the bassinet like she's styling a campaign shoot. Harper brushes down Carlee's hair while simultaneously handing her a fresh lipstick. Asher's already planted himself behind Billie with one hand on her hip, waiting like this is just another boardroom headshot.

Lexi hands the baby girl off to Harper again. "She likes you," she whispers. "She stopped squirming when you held her."

Harper grins as the baby nestles under her chin, a breath escaping her tiny lips.

And me—I've got one of the boys now, swaddled in a powder-blue blanket, tucked carefully in the crook of my arm. He's impossibly small. My free hand slides instinctively to Harper's back, steadying her without even thinking.

The nurse positions us quickly, smiling like she knows she's watching a whole ecosystem of history form in front of her.

"Okay, big smiles," she says. "On three. One, two—"

The shutter clicks.

In that single frozen moment, I feel it all. Lexi and Easton, exhausted but radiant. Billie and Asher, smirking but unshakably solid. Weston pretends not to tear up as he holds his nephew tight. He's a big softy though. Carlee laughs while being supportive. Harper beside me, holding the future like it already belongs to her. And me, watching the people I love become something lasting, a legacy.

Lexi and Carlee hug each other for a long time, and Carlee whispers something into her ear.

"No way," Lexi says, holding her hands, and tears stream down her cheeks.

"Are you okay?" Easton asks as he starts to freak out. "Someone get the nurse. Lexi?"

"No, I'm fine," she says, grabbing Easton's hand. "It's the perfect time to tell them," Lexi encourages Carlee.

"I'm pregnant," Carlee announces.

The room bursts into excitement, and this is round three or four.

"Shh, shh," Carlee says. "Keep it down."

Billie's mouth falls open. "Oh my God. It was your pregnancy test in the trash at Easton's party."

Weston laughs. "Surprise! Now I'm crossing my fingers that we have four babies so I can outdo you, Easton."

"Shut. Up," Carlee tells him, her face paling. "One is more than enough."

We each offer our congratulations to them, and Harper hasn't stopped smiling. I imagine our children growing up together, getting into the same bullshit we all did. A smile touches my lips as I enjoy that vision.

Not long after, the energy in the room shifts again—this time quieter, more intimate—as my aunt and uncle arrive with their spouses. All of them are layered with different kinds of emotion, every one of them beelining for Lexi and the babies.

Billie's the first to nudge Harper and round everyone up. "Come on. The grandparents need this moment."

We take it as our cue to leave.

One by one, we slip out of the room; hugs and whispered congratulations are followed by promises to come back tomorrow to visit. I squeeze Easton's shoulder on the way out, and Harper kisses Lexi's temple with the gentleness only a friend can get away with.

By the time we reach the hallway, the door clicks behind us. And for once, there's nothing left to say. This is a brand-new chapter for Easton and Lexi, and for Carlee and Weston. For all of us. And I'm looking forward to the future.

39

HARPER

The penthouse smells like coffee and vanilla, and faint music drifts in from the kitchen—Brody's playlist, all oldies. The songs make me take a longer breath without even realizing it, and they remind me of being back at the cabin. I roll onto my side and stretch, feeling the delicious ache between my legs from the incredibly rough sex I begged for last night. Brody didn't hold back, and I think I might feel him for weeks after that.

My phone is still on the nightstand, face down, but buzzing with notifications. When I finally flip it over, it lights up with unread texts and photos that were taken yesterday at the hospital.

WESTON

> The caption for this photo is: Most Iconic Uncle of
> the Century.

He attached a picture of him holding two babies at once.

CARLEE

> You look like you stole them.

BILLIE

> He did.

WESTON

Blaze loved it.

EASTON

We're not naming one Blaze. Stop.

ASHER

Too late. I think Weston already monogrammed
some onesies.

They love trolling Easton because they know how easy it is to get a rise out of him. I smile and scroll through the pictures. Lexi is in bed, glowing and exhausted. Easton stands beside her, looking like he's been hit by a truck full of emotions. The babies, tiny and swaddled, are all sleeping like they didn't just rearrange the entire world by arriving.

I stop on one photo of me and Brody, taken by Carlee when we weren't looking. He's holding one of the boys, eyes downcast and focused. My arm is looped through his, my head tilted against his shoulder.

We look like a family. Not someday. Not maybe. Now.

I close the photo and place the phone back on the nightstand.

I hear the sound of a mug being set down in the kitchen, then Brody's voice humming. I don't call out. I don't move yet.

I just lie here, wrapped in linen sheets, smiling, trying to convince myself this is really my life.

A breath later, the bedroom door creaks open, and Brody appears in the doorway, holding a mug in one hand and wearing nothing but a pair of low-slung pajama pants that should be illegal.

He leans against the doorframe and looks at me like I'm his sunrise.

"I was going to let you sleep in."

"I know," I say, stretching lazily. "But I missed you."

He lifts the mug like an offering. "Forgive me. I brought coffee."

I sit up, the sheet slipping from my chest. His eyes slide down my half-naked body, and I feel fully seen and appreciated. He crosses the room, sets the mug down on the nightstand, and then slides into the bed beside me, reaching for my waist like it's second nature.

"Hi," I whisper.

"Hi," he says, brushing a kiss against my bare shoulder. "You look so fucking sexy. I just can't help myself."

His hand drifts lower, fingers skimming over the curve of my hip, and I don't stop him. I tilt into his touch, hungry, wanting to come undone together.

"You didn't come back to bed just to give me coffee, right?" I ask.

His mouth brushes the edge of my jaw as he kisses up my neck until he meets my ear. "I missed my favorite view."

His fingers slide beneath the sheet, warm against my skin, and when he kisses me this time, it's laced with something sweeter than urgency—it's gratitude. His tongue slides against mine, his hand gripping my thigh, pulling me closer, and suddenly, there's no air between us. No distance at all.

"You looked good with him," I whisper, breath catching as he moves back to the softness of my neck.

"Who?" he asks, smiling against my skin.

"The baby," I mutter, threading my fingers into his hair. "The picture."

He lifts his head and meets my eyes, and for a moment, everything goes still.

"One day," he says, rubbing his strong hand against my belly, "I'll give you a baby."

My heart flips, then lands, steady and sure.

I pull him back down to me, lips brushing his. "One day, I want that. When we're both ready."

"We'll get lots of practice until then." He smirks.

"Hell yes," I say. "Lots and lots and lots of practice. We'll be pros."

And just like that, the coffee goes cold on the nightstand,

completely forgotten as he slides between my legs. His cock is hard, thick, pressed right up against the curve of my thigh, like it woke up already desperate for me. I'm still half asleep, but my body is awake, ready, and wet. I ache for him, and I shift just enough to press back into him.

His hand slides down my side to my waist in a possessive but gentle way. His palm cups my pussy like it's his to hold. My nipples harden instantly as he flips me onto my back with one fluid motion, pinning my wrists above my head with one hand, the other skimming down to my thigh.

"I'm in control this time," he growls against my skin, nibbling along my jaw until his lips crash into mine.

I grin, loving every damn second of it.

He unapologetically claims me with his tongue, taking what he wants, and I give it all to him. I moan as my hips roll up instinctively.

"So fucking wet for me," he mutters against my lips when his fingers part me. He rubs gentle circles against my clit, adding just enough pressure to make me gasp. "You gonna be good for me today?"

"Wreck me." I breathe, knowing I'm still sore from last night.

"What do you need?" His voice lowers as he continues playing with my clit. "Say it."

"I need your cock ripping me in two." I moan, writhing beneath him, desperate now. "I need you to *fuck* me like I'm yours to keep."

"Oh, you fucking are," he says.

I buck into his hand, the orgasm building so fast because he knows exactly what my body needs. I nearly cry out when he pulls away, not giving me what I want.

I groan in frustration.

"Not yet," he says, that wicked smirk pulling at his mouth. "Greedy little thing."

"Maybe that will be my next tattoo," I whisper as he kisses his way down my body like a man memorizing a map. His lips trail over my throat, my collarbone, my breasts. His tongue flicks over one nipple before his mouth closes around it, sucking hard while his hand continues teasing that clit. He parts my thighs, opening me like a feast he intends to devour.

When he gets low enough to breathe against my pussy, I shudder.

"You want my mouth?" he asks.

"Yes," I gasp.

"Then take it."

I arch up into his face, rocking against him, but he's there, tongue lashing over my clit with a rhythm that drives me wild. Two fingers slide deep inside me, and I cry out, hips grinding helplessly into his face.

He groans into me, and I love the way his scruff feels against my soft skin. He works me in sync, tongue and fingers, relentless and merciless. He's making low, feral, hungry growls, like he's claiming every inch of me with his mouth.

The build happens fast, and it's impossible to outrun or hold back even if I wanted to.

"That's it," he encourages, flicking my clit just right. "Come for me. Let me taste you, Harp."

I fall apart with a scream, the orgasm ripping through me like fire. My vision goes white as my legs tremble and shake. I can feel myself pulsing around his fingers, soaking his mouth, but he's not done.

He flips me onto my hands and knees, grabs my hips, and drives into me in one brutal thrust.

"Fuck!" I cry out, the stretch overwhelming, but oh-so perfect.

His pace is relentless and deep. Every thrust slams into the spot that makes me see stars, the one that makes the world around me disappear. His hands grip my hips like he owns me. Fuck, he does. Every inch of me.

"Like being fucked so hard that you forget your name?"

I can't speak, so I just moan and nod.

Another orgasm builds again, but this time, it's fast and brutal. When he reaches around and rubs my clit in tight circles, I scream and shatter all over again, my pussy clenching around him like a vise. He fucks me through it and keeps going as I beg him to split me in half.

Another orgasm hits and then another, until I'm screaming his name, shaking, with my face buried in the sheets.

"Give me another one," I demand, and he chuckles as he drives into me.

I chase something sacred, and I worship these moments together.

He wraps my hair around his fist and slams into me until I come again. I've lost count. I don't even have words left. Just sounds and pleasure and him. Brody's muscles tense, and he buries himself deep inside me. He whispers my name like a prayer, his cock pulsing inside me as he comes. He collapses over me, panting, his chest against my back, both of us soaked in sweat and satisfaction.

We lie there, breathless, ruined in the best way as we stare up at the ceiling. I turn my head just enough to see his sparkling blue eyes.

He gives me a smile, and I feel like the luckiest woman on the planet. To be loved and understood is officially my kink, and Brody gets it.

I'M CURLED INTO BRODY'S SIDE ON THE COUCH, STILL DAMP FROM the shower, wearing nothing but a T-shirt and the kind of dazed glow that only comes from multiple orgasms from a man who knows how to use his mouth, hands, and cock. I like to call it the trifecta.

He has one arm slung around me, the other scrolling on his phone when he stills.

"Oh," he says.

I glance up at him. "Oh?"

He turns the screen toward me, and there it is—an article about me.

THE RING. THE MAN. THE SILENCE.
LET'S TALK ABOUT HARPER ALEXANDER.

"Oh *no*," I groan, grabbing the phone from his hand like I'm defusing a bomb.

FROM THE DESK OF LADYLUX

LuxBabies,

If you're new here, just know that this post is based on speculation about public figures, using information that's readily available online. My opinions are my own and purely for entertainment purposes. Now, since we have that out of the way, let's talk about the woman who just broke the internet without saying a single word.

Harper Alexander.

Yes, her. The Bellamore cofounder who's built an empire on quiet elegance, sharper-than-sin tailoring, and a PR strategy so tight that it could suffocate a scandal before it breathes. She's been missing from the front-row circuit, the headline carousel, and every red carpet worth photographing. Until now.

Because while you were sleeping, Harper Alexander stepped back into the spotlight—ring first.

That's right. No teaser post. No I said I DO *caption. Just a diamond that could make an heiress weep and a man who looked like he'd burn the city down before letting go of her.*

So, who is he? Brody Calloway.

Military background.
Zero social media presence.
Related to the Calloways—yes, those Calloways—by blood.

If Billie Calloway is a storm in stilettos, Brody's the hurricane that doesn't announce its landfall.

And if you've been paying attention—really paying attention—you've seen him. Behind her. Beside her. Quiet, steady, lethal if necessary.

Some of you are asking if this relationship is real or if it's another scandal. Let me clear that up for you.
It's more real than real.

And here's why: Micah Rhodes—yes, the very same Micah she was once engaged to—is currently serving the rest of his life in federal prison. The charges? Too many. The damage?

Measurable only by how long it took Harper to show her face again.

Except ... she didn't just show up. She arrived. And this time, she wasn't alone.

Word is, the engagement between her and Brody Calloway isn't new. It just wasn't ours to know about until now. Which, if you ask me, makes it even more iconic. Because while Micah made headlines, Harper made moves. She burned quietly. She rebuilt in silence. And now, she's wearing the kind of calm only survivors earn.

Let's also take a second to talk about that last name. Soon, she'll be Harper Calloway. And something about that just fits, doesn't it?

Maybe it's the fact that she and Billie have always moved like two sides of the same blade—opposite but equally dangerous. Maybe it's because Harper's always belonged to power, and now she gets to belong to a family that knows what to do with it. Or maybe it's just because she looks happy for the first time in her life. But it's right. It's meant to be. It's the real deal. And of course, that's just a LadyLux opinion.

But if you've been here a while, you know I tend to be ninety-nine percent accurate.

So, here's to the softest launch that ended with the loudest statement. Harper's story is encouragement to the other women out there who don't owe anyone their survival story. And now she has the kind of love that doesn't ask for applause—just permanence.

Harper Alexander, soon-to-be Calloway, didn't just walk away from the fire. She is the fire. Maybe I'll get an exclusive invite to the wedding.

Stay tuned, LuxBabies. I have a feeling this love story's just getting started.

xo,
LadyLux

I read it. Every damn word, every deliciously dramatic, perfectly penned word.

Harper Alexander, soon-to-be Calloway, didn't just walk away from the fire. She is the fire.

My mouth falls open, and my cheeks are somewhere between flushed and stunned.

"She's not wrong," Brody says, still holding me.

"She makes it sound like I conquered a country."

He leans in and kisses the edge of my jaw. "You did."

I scroll back to the top, skimming again, shaking my head. "Did she really say *burned quietly*?"

"*Iconic*," he tells me. "I might get it tattooed."

Laughter falls out of my chest and makes me feel lighter. Like someone else saw the worst version of me and still managed to write an ending where I won. Maybe that's proof that this is reality. *We won.*

Brody doesn't look away. "She protected you. That's all I care about."

I lean into him, my head on his shoulder, our fingers laced on his chest.

"Do you think people will believe that I'm okay now?" I ask.

He kisses my temple. "They don't have to believe it. Show them. The truth always sets you free."

For once, I don't feel like I'm surviving the narrative someone else wrote for me.

I finally feel like I'm the one holding the pen.

40

BRODY

The pasta's a little overdone, and the sauce is too thick, but Harper hasn't said a word about it. She just keeps smiling like I served her something five-star, twirling the noodles around her fork and leaning back in her chair like this is the best meal she's ever eaten.

We're sitting by candlelight—not because we planned it, but because she turned the dimmer too low and then decided it felt "romantic as hell" and refused to fix it. There's music playing softly from her phone, something slow and old-school, and every now and then, she hums along between bites.

This is our life.

She reaches for my plate and steals a bite of garlic bread.

I raise an eyebrow. "You have your own, you know."

"Yours is crispier," she says with a shrug as we finish eating. "Mine is just a little too soft."

"Forgot you like them *hard*," I say, and it's not lost on her.

"Sorry, I didn't want to hurt your fragile chef ego."

I smirk, sitting back in my chair. "Fine. Next time, I'll give you the burned toast and call it rustic garlic bread."

She grins, then tilts her head at me. "I was thinking, instead of getting married in Cozy Creek, what if we held an event at the cabin?"

The question lands softer than I expected. No fanfare. No dramatic pause. Just her, curious and open, asking as if she already knows what my answer will be.

"I'll marry you on the streets of New York, Harp. I want this to be the wedding of your dreams. I'm already marrying the woman of mine."

She grins widely, and I watch how she tucks her hair behind her ear. I love how her foot's resting against mine under the table, and she wiggles her toes to let me know she's there. This woman. This life. She's more than I ever could've imagined.

She leans forward, elbow on the table, chin resting in her palm. "I still want to get married when the leaves change. October."

"I can imagine it already. It'll be as beautiful as you." I reach across the table and take her hand, my thumb brushing over her mother's ring.

We finish eating and sit together for a while, chatting about her plans as the candle burns low.

I stand, placing our dishes in the sink, and lead her to the couch, where we curl up together. Her head is tucked beneath my chin, and a blanket is draped over us like a shield from the rest of the world.

I don't know how long we stay like this. An hour, maybe. Or longer. It doesn't matter. The clock doesn't run the same way when we're together.

When I glance down at her, I notice her long lashes are resting against her cheeks, and her breathing is even. Her hand rests on my chest, fingers twisted loosely into the fabric of my shirt. I just keep holding her because I can, because I want to.

Harper said she wants to get married in the fall, and now all I can see is changing leaves and her in white, laughing as she walks toward me while I wait. I let out a smooth breath as I smile. She shifts against me, and I press a kiss to the top of her head, breathing her in.

"Sleeping Beauty," I whisper as I run my fingers through her soft hair.

There was a time I didn't know how to rest without bracing for impact, without scanning rooms for exits. I didn't know how to live without replaying everything I should've done differently. Regret haunted me like ghosts, but now they no longer exist.

Now I'm lying with the woman I love pressed against my chest, and she's my peace. Harper will always be my purpose.

I smile at the stillness, the steadiness, and the softness I never thought I'd get. Harper shifts again, and I tighten my arm around her like a vow.

I used to think love was about standing in front of the fire for someone else. Now, I know it's about walking through it with them.

From the beginning, I thought I was saving her, but loving Harper is what saved me.

EPILOGUE
NICK

The flowers are already there when I arrive. Peonies and ranunculus this week. Last week, it was tulips. The week before that, wild roses. They're always fresh, always delivered on Friday, and are exactly what my sister would've picked. I didn't bring anything. I never do. Because I'm not the one who sends them.

Brody does.

He doesn't know I know, but I do. I've known for a while now. I knew it the second I saw the arrangement that matched the ones she used to buy herself every Friday, like it was her little holiday. My sister didn't need a reason to buy herself flowers, and she sure as hell didn't need a man to spoil her. They were a reminder that she deserved pretty things regardless of the situation she was in, regardless of her mood. She called it self-care.

I stand at her grave, with my hands in my pockets, as the silence presses in from all sides of Sleepy Hollow Cemetery. She requested to be buried there because she loved the story so damn much. When we were kids, she used to tell me that if she ever died before me, she'd haunt me for life. Right now, I wish she would because I'd love to talk to her just one last time.

Her headstone is simple and elegant, just like her.

EDEN GRACIE BANKS
Let light stay.

She used to sign her emails with that, even her professional business ones. *Let light stay.*

I never understood it and thought it was soft and sentimental, but now I think maybe it was brave. It means more now that she's gone than it ever did when she was alive.

I sit on the edge of the stone bench and stare at my sister's name, letting the quiet stretch on for minutes. No one else is here. Just me and my grief. I miss her every day. My sister was one of my best friends.

"You were always better at seeing people for exactly who they were," I whisper. "Even when the rest of us didn't."

I never told anyone what I knew about her and Brody. Not even Asher. Not because it was some great secret, but because Eden didn't need or want an audience. And Brody? He never tried to be anything but there for her.

When she died, I told myself I'd do one last thing for her—protect him. I refused to let him ruin his fucking life and made sure he had the space to become whatever version of himself she had seen when she looked at him. It was the version of him the rest of us hadn't seen yet.

That's why I helped him. That's why I've kept my mouth shut. That's why I'm here. Because my sister is still the only person who's ever made me want to be better.

Brody placed every goddamn petal on this grave and has for five long years.

I exhale and run a hand over my face, wiping away the emotions that creep in around the edges. I'm late for Weston's party, and I'm sure he'll call me dramatic and say I was begging for an entrance.

Billie will say I'm an attention-seeking man-whore while Carlee takes note.

Let them.

They can have a fancy party because, right now, I'm taking this moment. Right now, I'm not Nicolas Banks, ex-hockey player, golden boy, or notorious screwup. I'm just a big brother who cares about and loves my family deeply, even in death. And that's enough.

○

BY THE TIME I ARRIVE AT WESTON'S PENTHOUSE, EVERYONE'S already a drink ahead and half a scandal deep. Billie's at the far end of the room, arguing with a man in a linen suit about the ethics of themed weddings. Harper is tucked under Brody's arm like she's never known anything but peace, and Weston's making the rounds like he owns the floor—because he does. Easton and Lexi have their hands full, and I don't expect to see them out and about for a while.

I enter, just enough to be seen by everyone, then stop. I like grand entrances. They make people nervous, but not me. I'm immune.

Carlee glances up from her phone the second I cross the threshold, eyes narrowing like she's caught a headline forming in real time.

"Tardy," Carlee calls out with a simple shake of her head, but she's grinning.

"Tragic," I reply. "Did you miss me or just my ability to fix the vibe?"

She doesn't answer. Just smiles that quiet, terrifying smile that says *I know more than you think.* I'm not too quick to dismiss it.

Billie sees me and immediately narrows her eyes when I'm close to them.

"You're late," she says as I join the group.

"Was lighting a candle," I tell her. "For my sins."

Weston raises his glass. "That's rich, coming from a man who hasn't repented since … well, ever."

"Oh, come on. Don't ruin my growth arc," I reply.

Harper walks over and arches a brow. "You good, stepbro?"

"Yuck. No more stepbro." I shake my head. "But I'm better than good," I tell her.

It's not a lie because somewhere out there is a woman who knows exactly what I sound like when I stop pretending. A woman who, if she were here right now, would see straight through me and my bullshit.

I snatch a drink from a tray, and I excuse myself, making rounds with different groups because that's what I do. I'm a social butterfly, and I smile here, laugh there, dodge three loaded conversations and one not-so-subtle proposition involving a tech heiress and a rooftop in Ibiza.

Billie corners me near the bar, wineglass in hand. She gives me a look that could fillet someone if she focused. "Where have you been?"

I smirk. "Out of town. Needed a break."

"From what? Attention?"

I sip my drink. "From expectations."

She narrows her eyes. "You found someone, didn't you?"

I offer her my best poker face. "Define *found*."

She reads people like contracts. Every pause, every flicker, every deflection is something she studies. I give her nothing, and still, she looks like she's won.

"You're transparent," she tells me.

"Maybe I'm evolving."

She scoffs. "God help us all."

I leave her with that and move back into the flow of the party. There's chatter about the triplets, Harper's ring, Brody's "domesticated" era, and a newly launched resort collaboration that I may or may not be casually invested in.

My phone buzzes, and I slide it from my pocket. I glance at the text message.

UNKNOWN

Thinking about you.

I don't reply—I never do—not because I don't want to, but because I shouldn't. The smiley face at the end tells me exactly who it is. I lock the screen and slip the phone back into my pocket. This, whatever it is, started a while ago. I haven't figured out how to stop thinking about her, even though I have a strict policy of only hookups, but she doesn't play by the rules.

Across the room, Brody's watching me like he knows my secrets. Like he's waiting for me to confess things I don't want to admit to myself.

I raise my glass in his direction, giving him a head nod.

He raises an eyebrow and shakes his head.

Seconds later, my phone buzzes again, and it's a text message from Brody, but it comes with a link.

It takes me to the website where the blinds are posted.

Blind Item #237

The ex-hockey player and golden boy turned billionaire marketer baddie has been dodging the spotlight and the one woman he's trying to keep secret.

I READ IT A FEW TIMES, FEELING LIKE MY PHONE MIGHT BURN through my hand. My mind wanders back to a few months ago, and memories of her flood my mind. I push them away, not getting lost in my thoughts. Not here. Not now.

When I glance up, I realize I'm in the same room, with the same voices, and have the same damn spotlight on me that's always chasing me. No one knows I just got blasted by a blind item, except for Brody Calloway.

As he watches me, I plaster a cocky-as-fuck smirk on my face, trying to mentally prepare myself to be the talk of the gossip magazines again. *Fuck.*

Continue Nick's love story in
THE HOOKUP SITUATION
https://books2read.com/hookupsituation

Need more of Brody & Harper?
Download an exclusive bonus scene featuring them here:
https://bit.ly/thebodyguardsituation-bonus

WANT MORE OF LYRA?

The Billionaire Situation Series

The Wife Situation

The Friend Situation

The Boss Situation

The Bodyguard Situation

The Hookup Situation

The Hockey Situation

The Royal Situation

Fall I Want (connects with this world)

Valentine Texas Series

Bless Your Heart

Spill the Sweet Tea

Butter My Biscuit

Smooth as Whiskey

Fixing to be Mine

Hold Your Horses

Very Merry Series

A Very Merry Mistake

A Very Merry Nanny

A Very Merry Enemy

Every book can be read as a standalone, but for the full Lyra Parish experience, start with book 1 of the series, as they do interconnect.

KEEP IN TOUCH

Want to stay up to date with all things Lyra Parish? Join her newsletter! You'll get special access to cover reveals, teasers, and giveaways.

lyraparish.com/newsletter

Let's be friends on social media:
TikTok 🖤 Instagram 🖤 Facebook
@lyraparish everywhere

Searching for the Lyra Parish hangout?
Join Lyra Parish's Reader Lounge on Facebook:
https://bit.ly/lyrareadergroup

ACKNOWLEDGMENTS

I want to extend a big thank you to my readers. Your love for my words is one of the only reasons I continue to do this. It's not lost on me that there are millions of other books you could be reading, but you chose mine. I will always be grateful to you for giving me the chance and for helping make my literary dreams come true. Super HUGE thank you to my fabulous ARC team and my bookish influencers. Every single one of you continues to blow me away with your support and excitement, and I'm so super appreciative!

Big thank you to the best assistant on the planet, Erica Rogers! I don't know if I would've survived the first half of 2025 without your help. I am so thankful for you and how excited you always are for me and the magic that's happening! Also, a big thank you goes to Kate Kelly! Omg, you are the best! Seriously, thank you both for everything. I finally feel like I can breathe again after finishing this book. I say that now...

Another thank you goes to Bookinit! Designs (Talina & Anthony) for creating these covers for me and helping bring my vision for this series to life! Thank you to my editor, Jovana Shirley, for being so kind and helping me meet my deadlines. I'm very grateful for your hard work and your ability to bring my words to life. Thank you, Marla Esposito, for always having that kismet schedule and doing the final sweep. Super big thanks to beta bishes (Brittany, Mindy, Lakshmi, and Thorunn). I appreciate all of your help so very much! I don't remember who claimed Brody. Was it Mindy? LOL!

And as always, gigantic thank you to my hubby, Will

(Deepskydude). You kept telling me I'd make my deadline because I always make my deadlines, and guess what happened? I made my deadline. Woohoo! Thanks for always being that voice of reason when I need it the most! I love you always and forever! I'm officially ready for fall!

ABOUT LYRA PARISH

Lyra Parish is a hopeless romantic obsessed with writing spicy Hallmark-like romances. When she isn't immersed in fictional worlds, you can find her pretending to be a Vanlifer with her hubby and taking selfies with pumpkins. Lyra loves iced coffee, memes, authentic people, and living her best life. She is represented by Lesley Sabga at The Seymour Agency.

Made in the USA
Monee, IL
09 August 2025

22947712R00239